Unsettling

Unsettling

Lynda Sandoval

A NOVEL

rayo

An Imprint of HarperCollins*Publishers*

HarperCollins books may be purchased for educational, business, or sales promotional use. For information, please write: Special Markets Department, HarperCollins Publishers Inc., 10 East 53rd Street, New York, NY 10022.

FIRST EDITION

Designed by Gretchen Achilles

Printed on acid-free paper

Library of Congress Cataloging-in-Publication Data is available upon request.

ISBN 0-06-054687-5

04 05 06 07 08 DIX/QW 10 9 8 7 6 5 4 3 2 1

Good things happen in threes.
In light of that, this book is dedicated . . .

. . . to my beloved agent and friend, Jenny Bent,
for giving me the push to tackle this project,

. . . to my "fairy godmother," Robin Vidimos,
for giving me a showcase I never expected and will never forget,

. . . and finally, with great respect and affection, to my esteemed editor,
Rene Alegria, for giving me the chance.

Long live lucky number three.

ACKNOWLEDGMENTS

Writing a novel is like a solo drive down a dark, curvy road behind the wheel of a Yugo with one crappy headlight and a busted radio. Luckily, the circuitous route from idea to finished book is well-traveled by wonderful people who are willing to give you directions, or a tank of gas, or simply a honk of encouragement to keep you in your lane and puttering forward. I can't thank the following people enough for sharing this particular road trip with me: My agent, Jenny Bent (goddess); my editor, Rene Alegria (the fabulous), his assistant, Andrea Montejo, and everyone else at HarperCollins; Deborah Dix from the beautiful Brown Palace Hotel; G. Miki Hayden, for the NYC help and occasional sushi dates; Karen Templeton, for Albuquerque details and sanity e-mails; true friends, Nicole Burnham, Terri Farley, Karen Drogin, Patricia McLinn, Chris Fletcher, and Amy Sandrin, along with the rest of the Bad Girls, for simply being there; Terri Clark for reading and critiquing the manuscript (and frequently talking me down from the proverbial ledge!); my coworkers and friends at Littleton Fire/Rescue in Colorado, especially Cathy "CJ" Jones-Gooding and Barb Thomas, who were invaluable to me during this process. I can't tell either of you how much your support has meant to me . . . but, thank you; and last but definitely not least, my family—Mom, Elena, Frank, Loretta, Chris, Trent, Cal, Pat, Leah, Scott, Janice, Grandma B., and Grandma C.—I love you all and will forever, no matter what. I know (as you all surely know) that we writers are not the easiest breed to housebreak. This is my chance to offer heartfelt thanks for putting up with me and my crazy, introspective life, above and beyond the call.

Dreams that do come true can be as unsettling as those that don't.

—BRETT BUTLER

Part One

This month's issue is dedicated to the topic of unsettling. Not the adjective, but un-<u>settling</u>, the verb.

Too often in life, we settle for less than we deserve. We want a suicide by triple chocolate, but settle for the low-fat sorbet instead. We want quality time with our children but settle for working in the same room while they watch a video.

We want foreplay, but we settle for quickie sex.

And then, one day, we look back on our choices and realize we're in a place that doesn't feel like the life we've always dreamed for ourselves. Sound familiar? Don't despair. Eventually we all hit a fork in life's road that makes us stop short and realize we've settled one time too many, and it is time to make a change.

Unsettling is the only logical option.

When you reach that point, dear reader, never fear. The decisions you make could send you off on a completely new path, the path you were born to follow. Suddenly you'll realize that settling for less than you deserve is no longer an option. So, take a deep breath, call your closest friends for support, and go for it. The only thing you've got to lose is the rut you fell into when you weren't paying attention in the first place.

—MERCEDES FÉLAN,
Editor in Chief,
WHAT'S IMPORTANT magazine

From: OfficerO@CopWeb.com
To: MomOf5@MartinezFamily.com;
         ZachAragonFan@texasnet.org;
         Editor_in_Chief@WhatsImportantMagazine.com
Time: 04:11:11 AM Mountain Daylight Time
Subject: SAVE ME FROM MY FAMILY!!!!!!!

Annie, Mercy, Cristina:

I know you're all swamped, and I know you'll be here in a few days. But, HOLY MOTHER OF GOD, someone has to save me from the Oliveras. My friggin' family is going to drive me to drink, I swear. The bridal shower is Friday afternoon at 5:00 PM. Who the hell has a bridal shower on a Friday afternoon??? Aren't those reserved for wakes and funerals, memorials, FACs? Maybe that should serve as an omen?

Anyway, I'm leaving my cell phone on and I need you to call me at the party. I'm trying to coordinate time zones—Mercy, since you're in NYC (what is that, 2 hours diff.? I can never remember) why don't you call me at 5:45 PM my time. I'll only keep you guys for about 5-10 minutes, but I need this for my sanity. Cristina, can you take 6:30? If I'm correct, San Antonio's an hour diff. And Annie, if you'll call me at 7:15 since we're on the same time zone (aren't we?), that would be great.

I'll pretend you're calling me from work about a case until I can escape from the room.

Shit! I don't know if I can go through with this wedding!!!!! :-O

Somebody kill me!!!

Lucy

P.S. Write back and let me know if this works for you all.

P.P.S. Thanks for being such good friends.

P.P.P.S. If you get married while under the influence of tranquilizers, and/or handcuffed to the altar so you can't escape, does it count?

Just wondering.

From: Editor_in_Chief@WhatsImportantMagazine.com
To: OfficerO@CopWeb.com;
           MomOf5@MartinezFamily.com;
           ZachAragonFan@texasnet.org
Time: 05:35:58 AM Mountain Daylight Time
Subject: RE: SAVE ME FROM MY FAMILY!!!!!!!

<<<<My family is going to drive me to drink, I swear.>>>>

Lucky Girl,

Lying to your oldest friends already? No one's driving you anywhere, Miss Daisy. You already drink. And if you don't, I'll have to back out of your wedding, just on principle. (Kidding. Like you need another thing to Prozac out about.) Lighten up, dollface. It'll work out. We've seen pictures of Lieutenant Ruben del Fierro, and trust me, you ARE a lucky girl. If not, there are always martinis. (Extra dirty, like my thoughts.)

Talk to you Friday at 5:45 MST. My secretary has put it in my schedule and I've set alarms in my Palm Pilot and cell phone as well.

Cheers,

Mercy

P.S. Annette and Cristina—it's been a long time. See you next week.—Mercedes

From: MomOf5@MartinezFamily.com
To: OfficerO@CopWeb.com;
           ZachAragonFan@texasnet.org;
           Editor_in_Chief@WhatsImportantMagazine.com
Time: 07:40:32 AM Mountain Daylight Time
Subject: RE: SAVE ME FROM MY FAMILY!!!!!!!

<<<<But, HOLY MOTHER OF GOD, someone has to save me from the Oliveras.>>>>

Lucy, you better stop taking the Lord's name in vain like that!!!! And in writing! YOU, the godmother of my twin babies. Shame on you. :-) Need I remind you I have children who read e-mail over my shoulder at virtually all times of the night and day?

Of course I'll call you, girl, but stop worrying so much! Ruben is the perfect man for you and we all know it, don't we, Mercy and Cris? You know it, too, Luce! Forget your so-called family curse—I don't want to hear another word about it. It's ridiculous. Think happy thoughts! Have fun at your shower and I hope you haul tons-o-goods home. :-)

XOXOXOXO—Annie

P.S. Mercy, love, love, love the magazine! I'm a faithful subscriber. <g> You're my most famous friend, too, you big-whig editor. (Even though I haven't seen you in a hundred years.) Can't wait to see you, either. Cris, where are you, girl?

From: ZachAragonFan@texasnet.org
To: OfficerO@CopWeb.com;
MomOf5@MartinezFamily.com;
Editor_in_Chief@WhatsImportantMagazine.com
Time: 12:27:08 PM Mountain Daylight Time
Subject: RE: SAVE ME FROM MY FAMILY!!!!!!!

<<<<I'll pretend you're calling me from work about a case until I can escape from the room.>>>>

Make it a really juicy sounding case, Lucy. Spice up my boring life a little, I beg you. No problem on the time from my end. I have to be at some charity something-or-other with Zach that evening, but this will give me a good excuse to slip out for a break, too.

Stop that talk about not going through with the wedding. Need I remind you, you have 500 guests coming? Okay, okay, not a good enough reason? How about this, then: Ruben is a good man and he obviously adores you. Hang on to that one (AND YOU *WILL* HANG ON TO HIM—DON'T LISTEN TO YOUR FAMILY!).

Mercy, I echo Annie's sentiments about *What's Important.* Truly a wonderful and inspiring magazine. You've done amazing things with your life and should be proud. And, Annie, kiss those gorgeous girls of yours from their long-distance Tía Cristina, and thanks again for the pictures of them at Christmas.

It'll be interesting to get together after all these years, gals, no? Too many years between us, too much distance. Plus, we've got to get our girl, Lucy, to the altar, if for nothing else than the historical significance. I mean, who ever thought this day would come?? Lucy Olivera taking the plunge? I haven't read the papers yet today, but Hell must've dipped below freezing—for a few minutes at least. <wink>

Abrazos, Cristina

From: OfficerO@CopWeb.com
To: ILoveLucy@CopWeb.com
Time: 10:55:15 PM Mountain Daylight Time
Subject: Are you sure you want to marry me?

Ruben—

I'm freaking out. I'm sorry. It's not you, it's me, and this damned shower.

Listen, will you call me on the cell during the shower tomorrow at 7:40 PM? On the dot, please. I'll just need to hear your voice after being Olivera'd for two straight hours. I miss you. And I do love you so much. Too much.

Your Lucy

From: ILoveLucy@CopWeb.com
To: OfficerO@CopWeb.com
Time: 10:58:40 PM Mountain Daylight Time
Subject: RE: Are you sure you want to marry me?

Mellow, baby. Just chill. Everything will be fine. You and me against the world, I promise.

But, to answer your questions—

Yes, I want to marry you. I WILL marry you.

Yes, I'll call you at the shindig.

Miss you, too, babe. So much. Not so sure about this two-weeks-apart-before-the-wedding plan of yours. I go crazy at night without you . . . can't sleep.

The boys miss you, too. Rebel won't eat anything (I think it's half misery, half dog ploy for people food, though. You know him.) and Rookie ate one of the couch cushions (new one on order—don't worry). What a mess one little fifteen-pound mutt can make. I clogged the vacuum sucking that foam filling up. More about that later.

One note: you could never love me too much, so just bring it, baby. I'll match you beat for beat. You're meant for me. Can't wait to hold you, make love to you—my WIFE, Lucy del Fierro. (Get used to that, because I'm not going anywhere.)

Your husband (soon), Ruben

From: OfficerO@CopWeb.com
To: ILoveLucy@CopWeb.com
Time: 11:04:44 PM Mountain Daylight Time
Subject: RE: Are you sure you want to marry me?

<<<<I'll match you beat for beat. You're meant for me. Can't wait to hold you, make love to you.>>>>

<sigh> You're too good for me, Ruben. XO

From: ILoveLucy@CopWeb.com
To: OfficerO@CopWeb.com
Time: 11:06:00 PM Mountain Daylight Time
Subject: RE: Are you sure you want to marry me?

<<<<You're too good for me, Ruben.>>>>

Wrong. I'm perfect for you. And you for me. I dare you to let me prove it.

Me

Chapter One

The door squeaked open, and Betty unceremoniously clamped a clothespin on Lucy's shirt collar, then grabbed her wrist and yanked her over the threshold. "Finally! What took you so long? Your Tía Dulcinea can only wear her teeth for a couple hours at a time, you know."

"Sorry, Mama. I got caught up at work." Got caught up, dragged her feet about leaving—whatever. Truth was, Lucy had been dreading the shower for weeks. It might have been different if her family believed in her marriage, but they didn't. Sort of made the prospect of a shower ludicrous, if you asked her.

"Work. Always work." Betty bustled ahead, shaking her head but suddenly seemed to think better of her scolding and beamed over her shoulder. "Never mind. You can be fashionably late. It's your day."

From inside the house, a staccato burst of raucous laughter jolted Lucy's heart. She took a steadying breath, then fingered the wooden clothespin dangling from her collar. "What's this for, anyway?"

"Oh." Betty spun to face her and snapped her fingers. "I forgot you don't attend many Olivera wedding showers."

A barb. Lucy wanted to ignore it but rose to the bait. "Yeah, well, it's the hypocrisy that gets me."

Her mother brushed the comment away, lifting her chin toward Lucy's clothespin. "Each guest has one, and any time you hear someone using the words 'divorce' or 'breakup' or 'split,' you can take her pin." Betty grinned as though to imply that the game couldn't possibly be more fun. "Whoever has the most pins at the end of the shower wins a prize." She leaned in. "It's a five-pound box of Godiva."

"Yum." Lucy vaguely remembered the game from showers gone by, but something seemed off. She pulled the clip from her shoulder, pinching and unpinching it thoughtfully. "I thought the object of this game was to avoid saying 'bride' or 'wedding' or 'marriage'?"

"Well . . . that's how other families play. But we Oliveras—" Betty covered her conspiratorial *hee-hee-hee* with the side of one fist. "Marriage, divorce. What's the difference?"

"Mama!" Lucy's clothespin slipped, biting into the back of her ring finger. She yanked it off, then sucked the rapidly growing blood blister, scowling at her mother over the back of her hand. When the sting eased, she wiped her hand on the side of her jeans. "Isn't that attitude a little fatalistic?"

"It's just a silly family tradition, Lucy." Betty shrugged. "You take everything so serious."

"Yeah, like marriage? Vows?" Lucy muttered under her breath. "God forbid someone take *those* seriously." Just like her mother to gloss over the not-so-niceties of life.

"Well, no matter. Everyone's here, and now you, so we can get started."

Everyone *was* here—no overstatement there—and an outsider would've thought each guest had brought along a megaphone. Lucy had given a heads up to the District Two cops who patrolled West Highlands about possible noise complaints that might crop up that Friday evening. As history had proven, the volume level from thirty Olivera women all talking and laughing at once could reach law-breaking decibels without a helluva lot of effort. The last thing she needed was her brothers in blue dispatched to a noise disturbance at her first-ever-shower-for-a-marriage-that-won't-last-(mark-my-words)-thing.

Talk about embarrassing.

It had turned out to be good foresight. The festivities hadn't even really begun, and already Lucy's eardrums vibrated from the clatter. And, if the noise pollution weren't enough to lay someone out, Lucy realized, the visual overstimulation could give even the strongest person vertigo.

Indeed, the Pastel Gods of Festive Decorating had danced orgiastically upon Lucy's mother's brick Tudor.

Holy Mother of God.

Lucy stopped in the archway to the front room, her jaw slack with something akin to horror. It was like a car accident; she couldn't look away. Tiny foil cutouts shaped like champagne glasses and entwined rings glittered from every tabletop. Copious amounts of twisted crepe paper streamers and paper bells festooned the doors and archways, in shades of pink, baby blue, seafoam green, and pale yellow—all to match the little opaque mints which had been set about the room in her mother's collection of antique candy dishes. A canopy of multicolored, helium-filled balloons completely obscured the arched ceiling, their curly strings dangling and dancing in the air above the throng of women.

The room even smelled pastel.

"Mama"—*Jesus*—"you've outdone yourself."

"Isn't it lovely?" Betty clasped her hands together at her chest and studied the room with pride.

"It's—" Lucy gulped. "Something else. That's for sure."

"Thank you, sweetie." Missing the subtext altogether, Betty laid a palm against Lucy's back and raised her voice above the din. *"Mira,* everyone. Look. Our girl has arrived."

The room's volume level dipped momentarily, then spiked as guests shouted out greetings to Lucy and even applauded. Lucy fought very hard not to cover her ears and smiled stiffly as she was sucked into the smothering vortex that was her *familia.* Knowing she had to go through all of this before she could even begin to put it behind her, Lucy drew a deep breath and entered the room.

Here goes nothing.

Half an hour later, bloated with Chex mix, mints, spiked punch, and taquitos, Lucy felt dazed and desperate to escape. They'd played one evil game, in which selected guests were made to act out the parts of Lucy's former boyfriends, men she *could* have married but didn't, and the others had to guess who the men were. Lucy was horrified. Afterward, the horde thankfully decided to break for snacks. Lucy watched as festively dressed women swarmed the dining room table to eagerly load up their Chinet with yet another round of jalapeño-tinged pigs-in-a-blanket.

As her aunts, sisters-in-law, mother, grandmothers, and various once-or-twice removed relatives cavorted, shrieked, and guffawed, she sat shell-shocked among them and directed her attention to the soothing tableau outside the window.

She had always loved this quiet, historic neighborhood, even before it had become fashionable to live here. She and her brothers had grown up in the Highlands, back when Denver suburbanites considered the entire area a wasteland of drug dealers, gangbangers, and (gasp!) Hispanics—to be feared and avoided at all costs. Eventually some savvy urban renewal advocate had realized the value of the classic Denver-style brick homes, bungalows, and Tudors situated on large lots with mature trees, and, indeed, a renewal had ensued.

Once word got around that West Highlands was "in," a frenzied Yuppification had followed. Upscale restaurants, funky shopping districts, and the world's best coffee shop, Common Grounds, now thrived, drawing visitors to the area in droves. But Lucy knew who lived there because it was "cool," and who had lived there *before* it was cool. Yeah, it made a difference. She could appreciate the eclectic feel of the area now, thanks to the mixture of cultures, ages, and lifestyles of those who had moved in, but to her, it would always be her old haunt, homey and peaceful.

Well, usually.

She forced herself back into active participation in the feeding frenzy by refocusing on the riot of colors before her. Hideous. Lucy could, however, appreciate her mother's effort, if not the actual motif. Betty Baca Olivera Serna had gone all out—a surprise considering her attitude about the marriage in the first place.

That familiar acid churn burned Lucy's gut; she put a hand to her solar plexus as she thought about it. Make no mistake, they all adored Ruben. But he was to be her *first* marriage, you see, and they all knew a first marriage spelled Doom with a capital D among the broken branches of the Olivera family tree. The incessant reminders of divorce, as if it were a foregone conclusion and nothing to brood about, deepened the scowl on Lucy's face and kept her from fully enjoying the day.

It wasn't that she disliked her stepfather—or her stepmother. Or, for that matter, any of her stepgrandmothers or grandfathers, stepaunts or uncles, stepbrothers or sisters, or stepcousins. But, frankly, her family had more steps than the goddamned ruins of Machu Picchu and she was sick of climbing them. She had no desire nor any intention of joining the ranks of the happily divorced and remarried Oliveras. *Ever.*

She loved Ruben. Couldn't they respect her intention to stay married? Instead she'd spent the first half hour of the shower suffering well-meaning but galling comments passed to her by her aunts and cousins, like trays of hors d'oeuvres, without offering a word of defense.

Get your feet wet with this one, baby. Lots of other men out there to marry for good.

Enjoy that one while you can, m'ijita. *He's a looker.*

We're all so glad you're finally getting this one out of the way, Lucy.

For God's sake, she was thirty-eight years old. Give her a little credit for knowing her own heart and mind. But defending her impending marriage was an exercise in futility. They all thought they knew better—why waste the breath? God, since her thirtieth birthday, she'd been considered *una soltera*—the weird, unmarried one in the family. It should've bothered her. Instead she withdrew further behind her self-protective wall and wished fervently that her surname were anything other than Olivera.

And that her marriage to Ruben would last, damnit.

But she'd be a liar if she claimed she had no doubts. The evil seed had been planted and had begun to sprout. Each time she'd almost convinced herself she and Ruben would be together forever, the misgivings crept back in.

Just suppose the pathological Olivera marriage/divorce pattern *was* genetic? What if her family was right, and she was no more than a pawn in her future? What if, despite her best intentions, regardless of the depth of her love, her marriage to Ruben was destined to end?

Lucy stifled a groan of misery. A vivid image of her husband-to-be floated to the edge of her consciousness, gripping her with desire—and sadness. Ruben del Fierro, the undercover drug task force lieutenant she'd fallen in lust with the first time she'd worked a case with him, in *love* with the first time he'd cooked her a meal and spoke of the spices he used like they were exotic and cherished lovers. She pictured him straddling his beloved motorcycle, worn denim hugging those thighs. His wrist would twist, bulging the muscles of his arms, revving the engine of his bike into a deep growl. And that private look on his face just for her would say, "Later, baby. You and me, and it's gonna be go time."

How could she lose him?

Her mind hurtled back to the awful Men You Could Have Married game. Why, why, WHY had she stubbornly avoided tying the knot when she was younger? She could have averted all potential disaster by marrying and divorcing one of the many throwaway guys from her past so that this marriage to Ruben would be guaranteed forever. Instead, feeling superior to the rest of her relatives, she'd eschewed the prospect of marriage altogether, until her fool ass fell in love with Ruben, that is, and she'd said yes to his fateful question without a moment's hesitation.

Now she was, in a word, screwed.

If only devotion alone were strong enough to keep the marriage together, because she loved him with her whole heart and soul. He loved her as much if not more.

She wanted to prove them all wrong, to be the Olivera to break the trend, but that nagging sense of doubt swung like a poleaxe through her life and left her teetering on the brink of panic every time she thought about the wedding. Today's so-called festivities weren't helping. Why wouldn't her relatives get off the marriage-is-the-first-step-toward-divorce diatribe, already? Couldn't they see they were killing her?

"Why so long-faced, honey?"

Lucy glanced up at the whispered words to find her mother leaning in to hand her two identically wrapped large silver boxes, tied together with a cobalt velvet ribbon and topped with a matching bow. "It's time to open gifts, and you look like the marriage is already breaking up, not just starting, no?"

"It's just hard, Mama." She shrugged, wanting so much to be comforted by her mother and knowing it was unlikely, given her mother's stance on the whole wedding thing. "Everyone's so . . ."

"I know. They mean well."

Lucy nodded, the lump in her throat preventing words.

Mama squeezed her shoulder, prompting a sting of tears to form behind Lucy's eyes. "But don't worry. You'll have lots of good times before the breakup, baby. It's not all bad."

Lucy sat stunned by the comment she should've expected. A surprised snort escaped, choked emotion hardening instantly to loneliness. "Gee," she managed. "Thanks."

Why didn't they just beat her to death with their shoes and get it over with?

Oblivious to the hurt in Lucy's eyes, Mama nudged her with the boxes. "This is from your Tía Manda."

Lucy clamped her lips together to keep from spouting something she'd regret, then took the gifts and smiled tentatively at her eldest tía.

"I didn't buy a card, Lucita. Save a tree."

"No problem. Gets me to the present quicker." She winked, struggling to pull herself out of the melancholy, then carefully removed the ribbon and bow before opening the first box.

"Oh!" A four-slot bagel toaster. Excellent. And not just any old toaster, but the sleek, upscale model from Williams-Sonoma that she'd admired but would never, ever have bought for herself, not even during a PMS-fueled splurge. Did a person really need to toast bread in a contraption that cost more than a month's car payment? But as a gift, it rocked.

She grinned at her aunt, still sprightly in her mid-seventies. "Thank you, Tía. It's lovely. You really shouldn't have spent so much."

Tía Manda waved a gnarled hand toward the other box, ignoring Lucy's chiding. "Not yet, not yet. You're not done."

Lucy bit her bottom lip, then set about pulling the tape from the razor-sharp edges of the silver wrapping paper on the second box. Tía Manda perched across from her on a kitchen chair, leaning forward to watch every moment of the unveiling. Glancing up at the mischievous, pointy-chinned face of her aunt, then around to all her relatives, an unexpected gush of affection knocked Lucy off her high horse. All at once, her heart filled with love for this room full of annoying, meddling, loud-ass, know-it-all women. She didn't want to feel so angry and defensive with her family. She was a part of them, and they of her. Inexorably connected. At that moment, looking into their expectant faces, she wanted to be more charitable toward their collective point of view. Given the long and illustrious Olivera family history, how could she blame them for believing her similarly cursed?

Lucy straightened her spine and decided right then and there to adopt a more positive, forgiving attitude, no matter how difficult the task. She'd probably need muscle relaxants for her jaw after clenching her way through the evening—one moment feeling the love for her family, faults and all, the next moment wondering if Ann Rule would write the book after she picked them off one-by-one with a scope rifle—but anything was better than sitting here angry and defensive.

And this gift opening part was proving to be a spirit booster, material girl that she was under stress.

Feeling as benevolent as Mother Teresa, Lucy paused before pulling the last piece of tape free, letting her hands rest atop the box. "Tía, you know, the toaster was more than enough." She telegraphed a respectful reproach with her eyes. "You didn't have to buy us two gifts."

"Ah, *m'ija,* but of course I did," insisted Manda, smoothing the cotton of her skirt across her knees.

For as long as Lucy could remember, Tía Manda had sewn her own dresses, and Lucy would bet she had only the one pattern.

"It will simplify things. Just open it."

Simplify? Ignoring a jab of alarm, Lucy handed the velvet bow to her cousin, Nicole, who was weaving them through a paper plate, creating an elaborate bridal bouquet for the rehearsal. She took a breath, then rid the box of its remaining paper. Surprise riddled through her as she stared down at . . . another toaster? Yes, identical to the first.

Warning thudded in her chest, and she didn't know whether she should gently suggest her Tía Manda go get checked for early stage Alzheimer's, or just shut her pie hole and be grateful for the eight—count them—*eight* bagel-size slots her new home with Ruben and the dogs would feature.

Lucy swallowed, choosing her words. "Why, thank you, Tía—"

"For the split." Ten women leaned forward and shrieked for Manda's clothespin. Giggling at her gaffe, Tía Manda pulled it from the pocket of her shirtwaist and handed it to Lucy's cousin, Ginger, the current leader in the clothespin game. Her eyes never left Lucy's face.

Manda leaned forward and patted her knee, stage-whispering the appalling explanation for all to hear. "To make things easier on both of you when . . . you know." Around her, the other women nodded. "When it comes down to it."

Lucy sighed, her pleasure over the pricey appliances dimming, the altruistic they-all-mean-well bullshit she'd been spoon-feeding herself moments ago steaming in her gut.

A balloon chose that moment to burst, whipping around the room belching helium before landing limp and defeated at Lucy's feet. Boy, could she ever relate.

Listlessly, she handed the gift off on its roundabout path through the room. It volleyed guest to guest, so each woman could *ooh* and *aah* over it just as they had its identical twin moments earlier. She was surprised Tía Manda hadn't sprung for engraving—HERS and HIS.

No matter. She would play dumb and ignore all further divorce references, and later she'd drink a whole bottle of wine herself and sing out loud to the *Bridget Jones's Diary* soundtrack. She'd survive this.

"Thank you," she managed in a surprisingly light tone, despite the Ann Rule scenario swinging back into favor in her mind. "They're *both* . . . very nice."

"Pick whichever you like better, *m'ija,* and set the other aside for Ruben." Manda nodded knowingly. "It's best that way."

Lucy bestowed a grimace of a smile and stole a peek at the wall clock. Five minutes until her first sanity break. She'd never been so anxious to hear Mercy's whiskey-deep voice.

Chapter Two

Mercy stood in the center of the ascending marble-and-brass elevator, surrounded by a huddle of visibly intimidated underlings, and wondered what they'd do if she suddenly turned and bared her teeth at them.

Wasn't that what they expected of her?

Screw 'em. She tossed her hair, squared her shoulders, and brushed off the pervasive feeling of dislike emanating like a bad odor from the group. At least it was tempered with fear, and really, who the hell cared what they thought of her as long as they produced? She had more important issues to ponder than a bunch of petty, disgruntled employees, thanks to that cretin, Damian Duran, and his squishy little slut of a girlfriend.

She focused what she hoped was a bored-shitless expression on the numbers above the brass doors and tried to calculate just how many days she had before *World's Real News* published the character assassination of her in their tacky pages and, more than likely, destroyed her career. Two? Five? A week? Certainly the other tabloids wouldn't be far behind, gluttons that they were for people's misfortunes. She had no doubt they'd found more than enough people in her employ willing to sell her out for a few bucks. Traitors.

With any luck, she'd be in Denver when it all hit, and everyone would be too focused on the wedding to peruse the trash in the supermarket checkout lanes. But there would be fallout. That was the part she didn't want to think about.

Mercedes pulled her bottom lip between her teeth and angrily blinked away the needling pain of betrayal. God, she despised Damian, that rat-bastard. It was bad enough he dumped her for a nose-wiping day-care provider in an embroidered jumper, but running to the tabloids? Destroying her public image? The career she'd worked so hard to build? Didn't the man have a mirror? Christ, they were cut from the same soiled cloth, she and Damian. She had enough dirt on him to annihilate his world, but she also had the decency to keep it to herself. Up until now, she'd believed the same of him. She never thought he'd actually use what he knew against her.

With derision, she recalled the day Sunshine Sanderson—Christ, who named her? Mary Poppins?—the magazine's nursery manager, came to her office for a heart-to-heart. Sunshine, spine erect, blond hair curling softly around her rosy cheeks, had felt it her *moral duty* to speak to Mercy on behalf of the unhappy employees, who felt the mission of *What's Important* magazine wasn't being carried over into the workplace, thereby affecting morale. Yeah? Well, Mercy had felt it her *moral duty* to relieve Sunshine of her duties and boot her ass off the penthouse floor. If Little Miss Sunshine couldn't grasp the simple fact that her job was to stay in the nursery and focus on boogers and boo-boos, then Mercy had no use for her.

Despite what her ridiculously idealistic staff imagined, this magazine—indeed, all magazines—existed to turn a profit. No sense putting lipstick on the pig. *What's Important* had a bottom line, and as editor in chief, Mercy would damned sure do everything to meet it. She had created *What's Important,* built it from the ground up, and no glorified baby-sitter was going to come in to her office—uninvited—and tell her she was mucking things up.

Her reaction had been reasonable. Expected.

Sunshine should have known better.

Unfortunately Mercy hadn't had any idea Damian, her supposedly monogamous lover of the past four years, had been putting it to little it's-my-moral-duty Sunshine for six months. That's where things had gotten sticky.

Rage surged through Mercy until she thought her ears would explode from the sides of her head. More than the thought of Damian cheating, what really chapped her ass was the thought of him cheating with *Sunshine*. What in God's name did the little pudding-faced wench have that *she* didn't have? The very question had Mercy wrapping her palm around the comfort of the cylindrical Vicodin bottle through the soft leather of her purse.

She'd never liked Sunshine Sanderson, but how *dare* the woman come into Mercy's office spouting morals when she was regularly spreading her legs for another woman's man. If she hadn't fired the little bitch for adopting open-door-policy behavior when no such policy existed, she would have canned her immediately when she found out about her and Damian.

If she'd found out about her and Damian. Ugh.

Another aspect of this debacle she hated to think about.

How could she have been so blind? So stupid? Certainly the rest of the company knew about the tawdry little liaison between Damian Hell-Spawn and Sister Mary What's-Her-Face. The entire company had probably been laughing behind her back for months. She *despised* being laughed at, and Damian knew that. She could kill him for putting her in this position.

A couple days after the perfectly justified termination of the interloper, Damian'd had the nerve to show up at her Sutton Place condo and engage her in a knockdown, dragout over her mistreatment of his mistress. The gall of it still stole Mercy's breath. A neighbor, alarmed by the raised voices and commotion, had called the doorman, who in turn called the police. No, she wasn't kicking Damian's ass when New York City's finest stormed her flat, but after this despicable, underhanded tabloid move, she wished she'd gotten in at least one solid punch.

So embroiled in her fuming, Mercy failed to notice that the elevator had slid gently to a stop on the floor that housed production and marketing. The doors swished open, and behind her, a hesitant rustling ensued.

"Um, Ms. Félan?" came a small, hesitant voice just over her left shoulder.

"What?" Mercedes glanced around. No one quite had the nuts to meet her gaze, which didn't surprise her at all. But it did disgust her. "Oh. Excuse me."

She moved aside, and the elevator emptied in a solemn, single file train. She knew the employees were unhappy about being forced to work overtime on a Friday evening, but they had a deadline. Period. Hell, in these economic times they should be grateful to have jobs. And she didn't have time to worry about their unhappiness anyway, because she was too busy reveling in the feeling of being blissfully alone. At last.

Alone, she could be Mercy. Alone, she didn't have to show the world her I-mean-business face. Alone, she could explore the catastrophe of Damian without having to pretend it didn't hurt. Everyone believed ol' "Merciless" Félan was devoid of human emotion, and damned if she didn't *try* not to feel. But in the course of two weeks, Damian dumped her, betrayed her, shamed her, fought with her, and sold her ass out. Oh yeah, it hurt.

When the doors finally had the decency to shut, she sagged, leaning against the back wall. She rested her briefcase and purse between her favorite black suede stiletto Blahniks, the pair with ankle ties and four-inch fuck-me heels that always made her feel like she could take on Attila the Hun without breaking a sweat. Today they just made her feel like she was trying too hard. Seven hundred bucks' worth of false courage.

Massaging the pinpoint of pain between her brows with the knuckle of her middle finger, eyes closed, Mercy wished she were already in Denver, cloaked in the safety that was "home." At least in Denver she had people who gave her the benefit of the doubt, friends who didn't subscribe to the rumor that she bled antifreeze. Well, one friend, at least.

Checking her watch, she noticed it was almost time to telephone Lucy and give her a break from her whack-job family at the shower. As if on cue, the reminder alarms she'd set in her Palm Pilot and cell phone went off simultaneously. The thought of hearing Lucy's voice provided a small boost. The call might be for Lucy's sake, but it would serve double duty by giving Mercy a distraction from her own train wreck of a life, and damned if she didn't need it.

Her mind ping-ponged from the impending wedding, back to Damian and the tabloids, and then to the wedding again. Feeling suddenly ill, she reached into her purse, opened the Vicodin bottle with a shaky hand, and swallowed one dry.

She couldn't wait to see Lucy, was even looking forward to catching up with the prolifically reproducing Annette after all these years—talk about a blast from the past. But wasn't it just Murphy's Goddamned Law that this tabloid fiasco cropped up just before she was set to meet up with Ms. Perfect again, after two decades?

Cristina Trevino Aragon.

Prettiest Girl. Most Likely to Succeed. Most likely to make her ex-friend, Mercy, feel like more of a loser than she already felt, and probably without even trying.

Fuck. Life just wasn't fair.

By the time the elevator dinged again, Mercy just wanted to lock herself in a dark room and wait for the narcotic-induced euphoria to hit. Instead, she came to a difficult decision. She trusted no one at her office really, but of all of them, her secretary, Alba Montoya, was the closest thing she had to a nonenemy. They'd never been particularly friendly, of course, but right now Mercy needed some honesty. Alba was her only choice.

Her footfalls were silent on the plush carpet as she forged ahead. Alba, clearly not expecting her, jumped and emitted a little shriek when Mercy entered.

Mercy swept the woman with a less-than-focused glance and murmured, "I didn't mean to startle you," as she flipped through a stack of mail on the marble countertop.

Recovering, Alba lifted a shaky palm to her throat and sagged back in her chair. "No problem, Ms. Félan. It's just . . . always so silent up on this floor."

It was, Mercy realized suddenly. She dropped the mail in a messy stack and glanced around at the austere, minimalist decor that had cost her a fortune, and a month of suffering the presence of the prissy-ass designer, Jean-Luc. Marble, steel, glass. She saw it as though for the first time. Tasteful, no doubt. Intimidatingly so. But she felt like an ice princess in a stone tower. Who in hell would want to venture up?

Then again, hadn't that been the point?

"But, anyway, thank God you're here. I—"

"Not now, Alba. Please." Mercy flicked a hand. "I need a few minutes to myself." She paused, then made another decision. "Get some estimates on redecorating this hellhole. It feels like a goddamned jail cell."

Without waiting for acknowledgment, she skirted Alba's desk and shut the door to her palatial, window-walled office without a further word. Alba let her go without comment. To her credit, Alba put up with an inordinate amount of shit from Mercy without a single complaint. Always had. She kept the wheels spinning in the office, despite the emergencies that always cropped up around deadline time.

Mercy stopped, back against the door, and leaned her head against the wood, staring up at the ceiling. She ran through the exchange with Alba like a film in her head. Was that what Damian had meant when he'd accused her of rough, prima-donna treatment of her employees?

Well—she sniffed—too late now. She'd already cut the woman off in mid-sentence as though her comments didn't matter, and surely Alba was used to it enough to know it didn't mean anything. It probably hadn't even registered. Shrugging off the wall, Mercy headed wearily to the business side of her desk and took a seat, annoyed by the uncharacteristic twinge of guilt on her conscience. It wouldn't go away.

Okay, fine. She'd apologize to Alba. She'd atone for her damned sins. *Happy now, Conscience?* But the whole thing pissed her off. No one ever gave male CEOs this much trouble if they were tough, driven, preoccupied with the business of success. But a woman? Forget it. Women were held to different standards. And minority women? She felt a familiar flare of temper.

Don't even go there.

Men were another giant problem area. She thought back to the exact moment each of her three marriages had become divorce-bound—always at the precise second she realized her husband couldn't handle her career. God forbid they make her choose. Then she'd met Damian and thought her problems were over. He was the male version of her—a snake—and she meant that as a compliment. Single-minded and unwilling to let anything interfere with his quest for success. He both understood and respected her barracuda philosophy about work.

She'd thought.

Then again, she'd thought he understood and respected *her,* too. Ha, fucking ha. Sure, they'd never exchanged "I love yous," but she'd never needed that from Damian. He was around when she needed him, scarce when she required time alone. They were compatible enough in bed; she knew how to extract her own pleasure out of just about any situation, no matter how dismal. Most of all, though, was the knowledge that he couldn't accuse her of anything he hadn't done himself in the name of business, and the reciprocal dirt they had on each other had made her feel secure—falsely so, apparently. In a twisted way, that false security had been the whole basis of their relationship.

Until he dumped her for the baby-sitter.

She's sweet, he told her. *Nurturing. She cares about me.*

Mercy squeezed her eyes shut until she saw stars.

Alba knocked tentatively on the door, then poked her head in. "Coffee?"

"No, thanks."

"Then, if you have a moment . . . ?"

Opening her eyes reluctantly, Mercy beckoned with her arm. "Alba, yes. Come in. Close the door behind you."

Alba looked uncertain, as though Mercy had suggested she pop a window open and take a giant, splattering leap onto West 57th Street. But like the impeccable employee she was, the woman entered, closed the door soundlessly, and then stood, still and obedient, waiting to entertain Mercy's requests or needs.

Mercy studied her without speaking for several long moments, feeling uneasy. Why hadn't she ever noticed the vaguely "massah/slave" quality to their relationship? How perfectly horrid. The moment of revelation passed, and Mercy was taken aback by it. She wasn't accustomed to giving a shit, and frankly it interfered with her thinking. Clearly, Damian's ploy had cracked her carefully cultivated survivalist veneer, and the icky softness of her humanity was oozing out. She could hardly bear it.

Alba began to squirm beneath the pinpoint of her stare. Averting it, Mercy inclined her head toward a leather chair facing the desk. "Aren't you going to sit?"

Alba did so, smoothing her skirt primly before glancing up and meeting Mercy's gaze directly. "If you're going to fire me, I feel I must point out, I've never had a poor job performance review in the five years I've been with the magazine."

Inside, Mercy jolted. Fired? "What would give you the impression I was going to fire you?"

Looking mottled and mortified, Alba shrugged one shoulder, then lifted her chin. "Ms. Félan, I've never seen you bring an employee into your office for a closed-door meeting that didn't end with the employee fleeing in tears. I won't fool myself that you wanted a friendly *chat*."

Mercy's lip quivered at one side but she squelched it before it cracked into an actual smile. Well, well, well. Little Alba had a bit of the barracuda in her as well. A secretary after her own heart. "Alba?"

"Yes?"

"You're not fired."

The older woman blinked convulsively a few times, then sagged just enough that Mercy knew she'd been really, truly scared by the prospect. "Okay, then. I need to tell you—"

"Wait. I'm not finished."

Alba pressed her lips together but managed a stiff nod. Her eyes seemed to say, "It's your funeral," but Mercy ignored that. Whatever Alba had to tell her could wait. Mercy needed to say a few things . . . and hear a few, too, before she lost her nerve.

"I won't hesitate to fire you, Alba, if you don't answer—honestly— a few questions I have. That's all I'm asking from you. Brutal honesty." Mercy swiveled her leather throne to the side so she could cross her legs, watching Alba over one shoulder. "Can you do that for me?"

She watched Alba's throat tighten with a swallow, but her face didn't display any of the fear the motion had telegraphed.

"I'm always honest," she said finally.

Mercy nodded once, collected her thoughts, then asked, "Do you like working for me?"

Hot color rose to Alba's cheeks, and she remained perfectly still for several moments before moistening her lips with a small flick of her tongue. "Frankly?"

"Please."

"No. Not especially."

A beat passed. Some organically vulnerable part inside Mercy hated that answer and didn't want to hear the next one. She knew what it would be, but the prospect of hearing it out loud made her fists tighten in her lap. "Does anyone?"

"Not really."

Mercy schooled her voice to sound casual, even curious. She flipped one hand. "Why not? We pay well. Benefits are generous. We're successful—"

"Because you're mean," Alba blurted, reddening.

"*Mean?*" Mercy drew out, emphasizing the n.

"Yes. I'm sorry. And unpredictable." Having said the worst, Alba seemed to pick up speed, even risking a few sweeps of her arms for emphasis. "You never even try to bond with any of us. You're like a . . . a dictator."

Bonding. Interesting concept. Mercy sat back slowly, trying not to flinch from the blow of Alba's words. But she felt every punch, and each one stole a bit more of her air. She made a conscious effort to raise one brow, which had been expertly arched at the waxing salon just yesterday. "And that's why people refer to me as the Mercenary?"

Alba looked briefly stunned. "Yes."

"And Merciless?"

"God." Alba sat back, her expression softening with what looked like a swirl of embarrassment and pity. "Yes."

"And Shows No Mercy?"

The secretary had the decency to look chagrined and a bit horrified by the conversation. "Wow. I didn't know you were aware of the . . . names."

"Well aware. And you've used them yourself."

It wasn't a question, and Mercy could see Alba knew it. "A time or two, yes. I'm not proud of that."

Mercy uncrossed her legs and leaned forward, planting her elbows on the desk blotter and weaving her fingers together beneath her chin. "Let me ask you this. Would you be upset if I fired you?"

Alba's head tilted slightly to the side as she considered the question. "Yes. And no."

"Meaning what, exactly?"

"Would it bother me knowing I wouldn't have to work for you anymore? No." She hesitated, casting a sidelong glance at Mercy before hiking one shoulder in a gesture of apology. "I'm sorry, you told me to be honest."

"That I did. Please go on."

Alba cleared her throat. "Would it bother me knowing I wouldn't have to work under these stressful, eggshell-like conditions? No. But I would be upset if you fired me, because I need the job, I'm good at it, and I have three kids at home."

A sort of I'm-too-dignified-to-openly-plead tone had crept in to Alba's voice. Mercy registered it at the same time she made another split-second decision. She grabbed a notepad and snatched a Mont Blanc out of her desk drawer. "Alba? I told you I'm not firing you, and I meant it. In fact"—she scribbled a note to herself—"I'm giving you a raise."

"A raise? But—"

Mercy smacked her pen down decisively. "Do you have a problem accepting a raise from the Mercenary?"

"N-no. Of course not."

"Good. Because you're the first person who's had the guts to be un-flinchingly honest with me in a long time. And I respect that." Her heart started to pound, and something caused her throat to tighten. She took the risk and forged on with this difficult, indeed godawful, admission. "I don't want you to quit, either . . . because I need you. Hence, a raise."

Mercy picked up the pen and returned to her note-making, enjoying the fact that Alba appeared shell-shocked. Fact was, Mercy would be hard-pressed to find another competent secretary willing to work in Rapunzel's Tower, and she wanted Alba to know she was valued, if not always treated well.

She wanted *one* ally. If that made her weak, so be it.

Alba eventually found her voice. "I . . . I don't know what to say. Thank you. But, Ms. Félan, if you're done, I really must tell you that—"

"That's another thing—"

Alba's jaw snapped shut.

"From now on, call me Mercedes unless there is another employee around." She pointed a finger at Alba. "Just Mercedes. Not Merciless, not Mercenary, not Shows No Mercy. Not even behind my back. Okay?"

"Of course. But—"

Mercy waved her hand vaguely toward the outer lobby. "And I'm sorry for cutting you off when I first came in," she muttered. "It was rude and uncalled for."

"Apology accepted." Alba's tone became more strident. "But I really *must* insist that you listen to what I have to tell you. What I've been trying to tell you since you walked in."

Mercy felt a prick of malevolent premonition and sat back, as though distance from the words themselves would protect her. "Yes?"

If Alba had looked apologetic before, she seemed almost prostrate with it now. "*Hard Copy* picked up on the tabloid stories . . . Mercedes. They're on their way here as we speak."

Chapter Three

The camera flashed, and Cristina blinked convulsively, wishing to God she had worn her red Chanel that day. Her world, as she knew it, would be destroyed by this goddamned mug shot, and it sure would have been nice to go down looking her best.

Not that the Donna Karan she'd thrown on this morning was a rag. But still.

"Turn to the side, Mrs. Aragon."

Lost in her own thoughts, the ruddy-necked young police officer's instruction confused her. She glanced up questioningly at him, shivering in the cool austerity of the over-air-conditioned cinder block and metal booking room. The back of the patrol car had been stifling in the San Antonio heat, and the sweat now cooling on her skin chilled her.

Or maybe it was shame that made her shiver.

"To the left." He pointed toward her Bruno Maglis. "Feet on the yellow markers there, if you wouldn't mind. Thanks."

If she wouldn't mind? Cristina gulped back the sudden urge to laugh. Or weep. Or scream. So that's what being married to a local

celebrity earned a woman—extra-polite treatment while you were pro-
cessed through the system. Splendid.

Cristina glanced down at the worn yellow sole-shaped spots the
officer had indicated, then turned and positioned her turquoise and
white woven leather mules directly over them. Sucking in her stomach
was something she did automatically, even though her rational mind
knew the photo would only show her profile from the shoulders up.

Her left hand tightened. Glancing down, she noticed she still
clutched the soiled paper towel she'd used to remove the ink the officer
had used to fingerprint her. She spread her palm and realized she'd worried that unsuspecting sheet of Bounty into a sad, twisted mess—much
like she'd done to her life.

"One moment." With an apologetic glance at the officer, she leaned
forward and pitched the dirtied wad of paper in the trash can, then
smoothed her palms together and repositioned herself for the mug shot.
"Sorry. I'm ready now."

Mug shot. Holy mother, what in the hell had she done?

What would she tell her children? What would they think?

They don't have to know.

Another flash. Another convulsive blink.

"Okay, you can have a seat."

She glanced around until she located a scratched metal bench
bolted to the wall. Not exactly comfortable accommodations, but beg-
gars couldn't be choosers, and thieves had even less room to talk.

"Can I get you something to drink while we finish up?"

Cristina sat wearily and furrowed her hands through her hair. Her
wrist bones ached from the handcuffs, which had gouged into her
skin during the drive. "Do you offer refreshments to everyone you
arrest?"

The officer laughed a bit self-consciously. "Well, no. Just trying to
make this easier for you."

"I appreciate that. But I don't expect special treatment."

"You're not exactly a hardened felon, Mrs. Aragon. Although"—he
glanced at his paperwork—"another couple hundred bucks' worth of

them fancy drawers and this would have been a felony. Your lucky day, I guess."

Cristina gulped, and her stomach plunged down to press uncomfortably on her rather full bladder. She really needed a restroom, but hesitated to ask. "Can you just call me Cristina?" His persistent use of her last name made her all too aware of what she'd soon have to face. Avoidance was preferable.

"Whatever you like. Cristina." He rested one booted foot atop the other as he made a notation on a clipboard, then returned it to its designated hook on the wall. Slipping the pen into his shirt pocket, he dipped his chin. "I just hope you realize you're playing a dangerous game."

"Yes, I . . . I'm . . ." What could she say? Sorry?

Glancing at the black and white clock, its glass face protected by metal mesh, Cristina realized two things with a jolt. One, she wouldn't make it to that evening's scheduled appearance at the Take Back the Streets crime prevention fund-raiser, which would take some fancy explaining when she next saw Zach. And two, she had less than half an hour before she was supposed to call Lucy.

A pang of regret stabbed her.

Having an excuse to miss this event in particular—even one so tawdry as having been arrested for stealing lingerie—was a relief, she realized. But she hated to let a friend down. Especially Lucy, *especially* now. The poor thing was practically psychotic over this whole Olivera Curse thing. It was baffling. In every other way, Lucy was an intelligent, savvy, practical woman. But when it came to the wedding, she was one short step above a 1-900-Psychic line regular.

Glancing up, Cristina found the officer had gone back to his paperwork. He stood at a counter opposite her, scribbling away. Feeling dizzy, she cleared her throat. "Do you know how much longer this might take?"

He looked up sharply.

"I don't mean to rush, but—"

"Not long." He held up the small rectangular metal clipboard on which he'd been writing. "You have somewhere you need to be?"

"J-just . . . a phone call to make in a few minutes."

"Well, you still have a phone call coming." He lifted his chin toward a phone on the wall. "Be my guest."

"Not yet."

He shrugged. "Suit yourself. I'll scratch you out this summons and then you'll be free to leave. If you need to make the call before then, just holler."

A knot rose in her throat.

Free to leave.

A couple hundred bucks more and this would've been a felony.

All of a sudden, she realized she'd traveled here in the back of a police car. Handcuffed. Her own vehicle was still parked at the mall. The gravity of the situation slammed down on her. "Will you . . . take me back to . . . the mall after. My car—"

"Sure," he interrupted, and the gentleness in his voice undid her. "I'll drive you back."

"I'm sorry," she whispered, choking on the ache of mortification still lodged in her throat. It took every bit of strength for her to hold her head up and look him in the eye. "Maybe . . . maybe I should actually call a cab instead. I'm sorry."

The officer set down his pen and dragged a chair over to sit directly in front of her. She cringed at the sound of its metal legs scraping the linoleum. He planted his elbows on his knees and steepled his fingers beneath his chin, then exhaled and studied her without speaking for several excruciating moments. Tapping the pads of his index fingers together at regular intervals, he said, "Look. Don't sit there beating yourself up about this. I know you're sorry."

"How?" The word sobbed out of her.

His weary half smile tooled lines around his blue eyes. "Because I'm older than I look, and I've been at this longer than you might imagine."

For a moment, they just sat there. Cristina squeezed her hands between her knees to quell the shaking. She held her breath and thought she saw a shadow of worry cross his expression before he spoke again.

"I don't mean to be presumptuous," he ventured finally, "but I do sense your remorse. And that's a good thing."

"Yes. I . . . I am sorry. I never meant—"

"To get caught?"

Guilt washed through her. Sympathetic, this officer. Yes. But savvy, too.

"You can do something about this, Cristina. There are support groups for . . . women like you."

She smacked away a single tear that had escaped from her eye and pulled her shoulders back, trying vehemently to maintain even one tiny modicum of pride. "Women like me?"

He rubbed at his square jawline with the back of his hand, staring off into the distance and seeming to weigh his words. "Wealthy women who—"

"Steal?" The word shot out into the bright white room like an arrow.

His ruddy neck blotched up even more. "Well . . . yeah. It's not just you. I mean, look at Winona Ryder."

All at once, Cristina felt small and dirty and desperate. She wanted to tell him she wasn't one of those women, that she didn't *steal.* But the truth was, she did. Not once. Not twice. All the goddamned time. She knew what it meant to experience that exhilarated thrill when you knew you'd succeeded. Craved the high, even. She *was* one of the statistics she'd read about in *Good Housekeeping* and *Redbook* and . . . oh, God . . . even in Mercy's magazine, she supposed, feeling sicker.

It didn't matter that she always found ways to repay the shopkeepers from whom she'd stolen. It didn't matter that her guilt prompted her to skulk through the most dangerous parts of San Antonio handing out hundred dollar bills to homeless people. Atonement didn't matter one bit. She was a thief.

Her breaths came rapidly. Shallow. Jesus, Mary, and Joseph, how had she sunk so low?

Tears sprung to her eyes, and Cristina covered her face with hands that still bore the black evidence of her guilt in the lines and whorls of her fingerprints. "Oh, God."

She knew what the officer was seeing when he looked at her with those blue X-ray eyes. Not the wife of former Houston Astros star Zach Aragon, a woman to be envied. Not a society woman, born to grace the arm of one of San Antonio's first sons. No. This officer, who had gone out of his way to treat her kindly, could see through her facade to the poseur beneath. A cheap little *chica* from the wrong side of the tracks who'd wormed her way into a world where she didn't belong just because she happened to be pretty. Wasn't her mother-in-law always insinuating as much?

That's it. That's all she was. A pretty package. Not smart like Mercy. Or tough like Lucy. Or even bighearted and genuine like sweet Annette. She didn't have anything going for her except looks, and unfortunately, pretty at twenty didn't equal pretty at almost forty. Despite the Botox, the expensive skin care regimes, regular facials, frantic workouts—despite all her advantages, she couldn't keep Father Time at bay. Her North Side roots were beginning to break through the manicured lawn of her perfectly imperfect life, and soon the world would see exactly how weed-choked everything had become.

She didn't belong in Zach's world. She had never belonged, and maintaining the pretense for the past eighteen years had taken its toll. Her whole body shook with her futile efforts to restrain her tears. She needed to get out of here, to go home.

"Hey." The officer reached out and touched her forearm lightly.

Cristina dragged her hands away from her tear-stained face, staring at the blotches of eye makeup smeared on her palms. Funny—shame even made fifty-dollar mascara run.

"Look, don't cry. What's done is done."

"How can you say that?"

He hiked one shoulder in a confident shrug. "Because it's true. The past is over. You committed a crime; you were caught. That part is over and done with, and there's not a whole helluva lot you can do to change it. How you choose to deal with it from here on out is the key."

She nodded. He was right. She couldn't change what had happened. She needed to move on, to *deal*.

And, deal with it, she would.

Arrests were public record, after all, and Cristina knew with blood-chilling certainty that the moment local media realized Zach Aragon's wife had been arrested, the shit would officially hit the fan.

Chapter Four

It had been thirty-three days since anyone in Annette's family had asked her how she was. Not—What did you do today, Mama? What are you thinking, *querida?* Do you need anything?

Nada.

Thirty-three days closer to invisible.

It wasn't that she blamed her family for going about their own lives, oblivious to her own. On the contrary, the fact that her daughters were growing into such well-rounded young adults with friends and interests and activities couldn't have pleased her more. And Randy—well, supporting a family of seven took a lot of work and a lot of time. She'd always understood that, had always felt blessed to have married such a caring and honorable man. No, she didn't begrudge them. On the contrary. She envied them their lives so much that it made her chest feel hollow. Deep inside, she yearned for a life of her own. Just hers.

With a sigh, she pulled to a stop at the intersection, lost in her thoughts as she waited for the signal to change. She glanced unseeing down the street in one direction, then the next, rubbing a knuckle against her breastbone to push away the acidy pain that seemed to have set up camp there.

What would happen when the light turned green if she simply turned left here instead of right? A right turn would take her to the karate school, where, according to the omnipresent and ever-changing schedule in her head, she was due to pick up the twins from sparring class in ten minutes.

But what if she didn't turn right?

What if she turned left?

What if she turned left and just kept on driving, shedding layers of expectations as each mile passed beneath her tires? What if she drove so far she reached a place where she was no longer Randy's wife, or the girls' mama? Where she was just Annette and people would ask her, "How was *your* day? What are *you* thinking? Do *you* need anything?"

What would her family do then? Fall apart? Go on without a hitch? Would they eventually sit back and wonder, where did that invisible woman who used to do everything for us go? The one who kept the world spinning? What was her name again?

A zing of resentment shot through her, followed quickly by a dousing wash of guilt. She reached out to close her hand around the amethyst rosary that hung around her rearview mirror and whispered a short prayer, letting her eyes flutter shut. She shouldn't be having these thoughts. She'd been waking up at four o'clock every morning, just to have time to pray at the church down the street before the family came to life. She'd prayed so fervently for help in finding some peace in her world, and yet each day she felt more tightly wound, and she didn't know what else to do.

She'd always been happy, or . . . fine, at least. But lately there'd been an itch in her soul that made her mind drift during the day and caused her to toss and turn in her bed at night.

Lord, she didn't have time for this.

Bottom line—she *was* Randy's wife and the mother of five children. That was God's plan, and she knew it. Embraced it. Things could be so much worse. There were duties and responsibilities to fulfill to make her family run smoothly, and if those duties fell to her, well . . . that was her job. There was absolutely no shame in the life she lived or the tasks, neverending as they might be, that comprised her lot. Who was she to question God's plan?

But that wasn't even it. She didn't resent where life had brought her. All she'd ever wanted was to be Randy's wife and to raise a family. She would gladly complete the gajillion daily chores and meet every obligation that would make life easy for her husband and children if they—just once—let her know they were grateful. If they let her know they recognized how bleeping hard she worked, and if they respected her for it. If, every now and then, they simply allowed her to wander beyond the realm of marriage and motherhood, so she could explore the inner core of herself.

She had felt on the verge of tears for days now, and as she sat behind the wheel of her Odyssey minivan, she bit her bottom lip to stave off a fresh torrent. PMS sucked. Single women with PMS could lounge in a bathtub, eat chocolate, wear pajamas all day. Not her. She had to tuck it away and go on with the business of living because there was a pecking order in life, baby, and she wasn't first in line.

Darn it all. Her emotions were out of whack, and this thing with Deborah wasn't helping matters. Her hand tightened on the rosary until she thought she might snap it off.

A short horn tap sounded behind her, and Annette jumped, releasing the beads so fast they swung wildly, clacking against the windshield a couple of times before settling into a gentler sway. The light had turned green; she flicked a quick glance into her rearview mirror, then waved an apology at the driver behind her. She had a passing acquaintance with the woman, she realized belatedly. Her little *gordito* son, Antonio, was in sparring class with the twins. Annette had been worried he might fall on one of her petite girls and accidentally squash them, but so far, no trouble. She shouldn't be having such uncharitable thoughts about the little guy anyway. Such a sweet boy, really.

Annette might have imagined it, but the short, polite honk and the understanding smile the woman had given when she'd looked back seemed to say, "Yoohoo. I know you're daydreaming about turning left instead of right, about driving down that gray ribbon of road until the horizon is behind you instead of in front of you. We all do it sometimes, and I sympathize. But could you move out of my way before getting too mired in your midlife crisis so I can pick up my child on time?"

Feeling shaky, Annette turned.

Right.

Of course she turned right, because she had been married for two decades and had brought five girls into the world. Wife, mother—these were her roles, and each came with an extensive set of responsibilities—part and parcel. The option to turn left no longer existed for her.

She tried to resent that, but what the heck? She wouldn't have turned left anyway, no matter what she fantasized about nor how deeply her soul ached for recognition. The truth of the matter was, Annette Martinez might entertain the occasional subversive thought, but when push came to shove, she always did what was *right*.

Just ask her family.

By the time she pulled into the lot at the karate school and parked her minivan in the same slot she always chose—three spots north of the doors, facing the building so she could watch the end of class—Annette had mostly stopped shaking. But a sticky residue of guilt for her thoughts remained, and her mind felt frantic with the need for release. For confession. She needed to talk to someone, to exorcise all her pent up . . . whatever you'd call them. Fantasies? Didn't seem quite right. She would be talking to Lucy in less than an hour, but she didn't want to lay all her stuff on poor Lucy when the *muchacha* clearly had enough of her own problems.

Really, what did Annette have to complain about? Her family was healthy, they had a roof over their heads and food on the table. They were blessed. Truly they were. Annette tried for a light laugh, but her monosyllabic exhalation sounded more like a moan. She'd read something once about the primal scream, and right then she could feel one building in her chest.

The knock on her window startled her, and Annette jumped, holding a hand to her throat. Her heart beat wildly in her chest. Lord, she needed to stop zoning out.

Turning to the closed window, Annette saw the woman—Antonio's mom, from the stoplight—wave and make the universal roll-down-your-window motion with one hand. Her fleshy face was spread into a smile that made her sparkly brown eyes almost disappear.

Annette bestowed a weak smile in return and pressed the automatic window button, hoping the woman couldn't read minds. Wouldn't Annette be the scandal of Las Vegas, New Mexico, if everyone knew she entertained notions of running away? The window glided almost soundlessly open, inviting the summery smells of dry dirt and sage into the car. She inhaled slowly, taking in the familiar scents as she tried to recall the woman's name. Barb? Betty? Berta—that was it. "Hello, Berta. You scared me. Phew!" She pantomimed wiping sweat from her brow.

Berta's grin widened, if that were possible, and she crossed her arms beneath her ample bosom. "You do seem lost in your own thoughts today, Annette."

Heat rushed to Annette's face. Chagrined, she hiked one thumb in the direction of the fateful intersection. "Goodness, sorry about that. My mind was spinning with everything I have to do. You know how it is."

Berta rolled her eyes and gave a little snort. "Tell me about it. It never ends, no?"

"Mmmm." Annette wrapped her hands around the top of the steering wheel and then slid them down either side until they stopped at the midway point. Her gaze sought and found her nine-year-old twins among the throng of identically dressed children through the plate glass studio front. "Looks like they're just about done. How's Antonio liking the class?"

"Oh, gosh. It's a struggle to get him here but, *pobrecito,* he takes after his mama with his fondness for eating." She patted her round belly. "Needs the exercise."

"Don't we all?"

Berta gave the studio one more passing glance, then leaned a hip against Annette's door and tilted her head to the side. "Enough about exercise. Like I need another thing to feel guilty about, no?" She glanced heavenward. "What's new with you, Annette? Anything going on this summer?"

A question.

About her.

Blinking with surprise, Annette turned back toward Berta with her lips pressed together to keep back the emotional torrent that was bubbling inside like lava. It was a simple question, not an invitation to vent. Still, she ached to say:

"New? Well, my oldest daughter, Deborah, came home from college last weekend and told her father and me that she's fallen in love. With another woman. Yes, that's right. My twenty-year-old daughter just announced that she's a lesbian. I was startled, of course, but she's a wonderful girl. And so is her girlfriend, this Alex? I adored her before—why would things change now?

"But Randy, well, the shock of it made him react . . . wrong. Poor man. He didn't berate Deborah, but he didn't accept her, either. Deborah fled in tears and Randy has been morose ever since, and of course both of them are expecting me to play mediator. I just don't know how to fix this one, and I wish one or the other of them would take the initiative.

"Not only that, but my eighteen-year-old daughter, Sarah, who has been researching colleges for a year, is suddenly unsure if she even wants to attend or if she'd rather hike through South America and 'find herself.' I told her she's never been to South America, so clearly she couldn't have lost herself there, and now she's angry at me. We're not talking. All I see of her is flashing eyes and her straight, proud back as she flounces out of any room I enter.

"My sixteen-year-old, Priscilla, is a giant bundle of hormones, and I swear if I hear her bedroom door slam one more time, I may seriously go over the edge. You might see me on *America's Most Wanted,* Berta. No lie.

"The twins are still sweet at age nine but they're also needy, and

I'm about up to here with fulfilling everyone's needs except my own. Do you know I realized recently I haven't bought a new pair of shoes for myself since Clinton's first presidential election? How can that be possible?"

But, of course, she didn't say all that. She didn't say any of it. Instead, she shook her head, laughed softly, and said, "You know, Berta. Same old thing. I just never get caught up."

What a coward.

The truth was, she didn't think she was ready to let it all hang out with Berta, who was really no more than an acquaintance. But she couldn't wait until Lucy was married and happy, back to her old self and over the hump. God knew, she really needed to talk to her best friend. But not until *after* the wedding.

Her mind wasn't in the rest of the conversation, which ended quickly when sixteen little chatterboxes, in their black cotton gis and belts of various colors ranging from white to blue to black, erupted from the karate studio. All too soon Antonio was tugging on his mother's arm and Berta had bid her a hasty good-bye. Mary and Ruthie, smelling of the healthy, active sweat of children, had tumbled into the minivan and slammed the door loud enough to make Annette's teeth vibrate. Moments later, she was backing out of her parking spot, her mind occupied with the list of umpteen other things she needed to get done before she could sink into unconsciousness that night. But then—

"Mom?"

"Yes, honey?" She smiled at Ruthie in the rearview mirror.

"I forgot to tell you that I'm supposed to bring six dozen cookies to school for the play thingy."

Annette's stomach plunged, and she felt her entire body going cold and still. Was this the physical manifestation of denial? Was her mind going to grind its gears and then spring apart into a million broken pieces at any moment? "Ruth Ann!"

Ruthie shrugged and tried to yank the Game Boy out of her twin's hand, but Mary leaned out of her reach. "I forgot."

Annette squeezed her eyes shut and counted to ten before slowly reopening them and exiting the parking lot. "When?" she finally asked, once she was able to keep her voice calm and even.

"Tomorrow," Ruthie said, distractedly, her focus on the Game Boy. "Come on, Mare. Let me play."

"Just a second. I'm almost done." Mary's attention flicked up to the reflection of her mother's eyes in the mirror for the briefest of moments. "What's for dinner, Mom?"

Annette released a soul-deep sigh and felt an invisible weight settle on her shoulders. Unshed tears stung her eyes. Shoot. Okay, regroup.

To the store, first, and then straight home into the kitchen. Six dozen cookies? No problem. She could handle it. Heck, she was Super-woman, wasn't she?

"Mamaaaaaa," Mary whined, clearly finding her mother's silence unacceptable. "I'm starving. What are we going to eat?"

Eat? What are we going to eat?

"Reality," Annette told them. "Big steaming chunks of it."

Two identical sets of eyes looked up, registering confusion. For a moment, the only sound in the vehicle was the electronic bleeping from the Game Boy.

"Huh?" the twins said in unison.

Annette shook her head. "I meant meat loaf. Sorry."

And just like that, life returned to normal.

God help her, she couldn't wait to leave for Denver.

Chapter Five

Lucy snapped open her cell phone face before the first ring had finished. "You're late," she rasped into the phone. And then to her mother and the other shower guests, "I'm sorry. I have to take this." She shrugged as if to say, what can you do? "It's about work. I won't be long."

On the other end of the line she heard Mercy singsong, "Lucy's going to He-ell."

"Shut up," Lucy muttered.

Betty clasped her hands together. "Ah, my Lucy. Always with the work." The older women in the room tsk-tsked their agreement.

Lucy smiled her apology with one side of her mouth as she eagerly lunged over wadded piles of discarded wrapping paper.

Once in the downstairs powder room, behind a locked door, Lucy sank to the toilet seat and hung her head, one palm pressed to her forehead. "Jesus H. Christ, Mercy, what's wrong with my family?"

Mercy chuckled. "Do you want me to read off the list?"

Through the phone line, Lucy heard an odd sound, like feet pounding on metal bleachers. "No thanks. It's nightmare enough without hearing it verbalized. Where are you? What's that weird clanging sound?"

"Oh." A short pause. "I'm, ahhhhh, taking the back stairwell down from my office. You know, exercise."

Lucy frowned. "The stairs? From the penthouse level? That's a long-ass way."

"Tell me about it."

"Mercy, are the stairs safe to take alone this time of night? You are in New York City, need I remind you."

"Believe me, they're probably the safest way out right now," Mercy said in a wry tone.

"What does *that* mean?"

"Nothing. Forget it." Lucy could hear Mercy shuffling the phone from one ear to the other. "My secretary is with me, anyway. Stop worrying. Can't a girl get a little exercise?"

A red flag lifted inside Lucy, and she leaned forward, alert and concerned. "Is everything okay there, Mercy?"

"Of course! What could possibly be wrong?" She didn't give Lucy a chance to come up with anything before asking, "So, you surviving the hoopla, lucky girl?"

Maybe she was imagining things, creating drama to shift focus from her own. Lucy shrugged off the instinct that said something was up in Mercyville. If something was wrong, Mercy would tell her. "Surviving?" She tried to snort; it came out a whimper. "Let me sum it up. Puff the Magic Dragon consumed Sherwin-Williams's pastel division and then vomited on the house, my eardrums are blown from the noise, and my Tía Manda bestowed not one, but *two* top-of-the-line Williams-Sonoma toasters on me so we don't have to fight over it when we divorce."

"Holy shit!"

"Didn't I tell you?" Lucy moved to the sink and washed her hands. "They're all nuts."

"Yes, but you have to admit, they're entertaining."

Lucy groaned. "Hurry up and get here, Mercy. I need to be around normal people for a while. I can't wait until next week when you're all here."

"I'd come today if I could. In fact"—she seemed to be pondering—"I might come tomorrow if the hotel can get me in."

"Are you serious? That's fabulous."

"Serious. And don't worry about picking me up. I'll take a limo to the hotel and call you when I get there. Maybe you can come meet me for a drink."

"You know it."

"Good. Now go back to your party. Try to enjoy. You can return all the duplicate appliances after the wedding."

"I'll be rich!"

Mercy laughed. "And . . . do me a favor, will you?"

"Anything."

"Don't tell anyone I'm coming early."

"You hiding out?" Lucy teased.

"Ha!" Mercy said, sounding nervous. "I could really use a few days of peace and quiet, that's all."

6:40 P.M. MOUNTAIN STANDARD TIME

"You're late, too," Lucy marveled into the phone. "Can't any of you wome—uh"—she glanced around at her relatives—"officers make a call on time?"

"I got . . . tied up," Cristina said. "Sorry. And obviously you've forgotten the concept of Latina Standard Time. Looking at it from that perspective, I'm early."

Lucy snickered once she'd escaped from the room. "Cris, you know 'Latina Standard Time' is a politically incorrect concept, don't you?"

"I'm Latina, Luce. I can use it if I want. Now, if someone else used it to describe my tardiness—"

"The fight would be on."

"Uh-huh. It's the whole, you can bad-mouth your own family, but God forbid anyone else do the same, concept. Hang on."

Lucy listened to muffled sounds on the other end but couldn't make anything out. Cristina must have covered the phone receiver. She quickly returned.

"Lucy, you still there?" Cristina's tone had turned serious again, slightly distracted. Almost as if she was trying not to be overheard.

"Of course."

"Listen, I'm sorry, but I only have a minute to talk, so let's not waste any of it."

Lucy frowned. "Cristina? Is everything okay there?"

"Of course!" she said, a little too brightly. "What could possibly be wrong?"

"Well—"

"Speaking of families, how are things going at the party?"

Lucy shook off her worry. If Cristina had something on her mind, surely she'd say so. "It's miserable. I don't want to talk about it. But I will tell you one bit of gossip you might enjoy. You know the purse game? Who has what in her purse?"

"All too well."

"Well, for a twist, we each passed our purses to the right so someone else would rummage through it. My stepcousin Renée had Tía Belinda's big-ass leather thug-pounder handbag, and you'll never guess what she pulled out of it."

"A gun?"

"No, that was in my purse, but I'm allowed. Aunt Belinda? She had a bottle of Viagra." She'd lowered her voice to a raspy whisper on the last word.

"Oh, my God! TMI, babe—too much information. That's a piece of knowledge I could've lived without. Was she mortified?"

Lucy snorted. "Proud. You know my family." Feeling better, Lucy splayed a palm on her abdomen and leaned back against the wall. "Enough about me and my nightmare. How's the crime prevention charity gig going?"

"Oh." Again, Cristina's pause seemed wrought with tension. "I . . . uh . . . didn't make it, actually."

"Where are you? At home? Are you and Zach fighting?"

"No." A sigh. "It's a long story."

"I've got time."

"No, you don't. And, anyway, I don't. Besides, it's nothing. Lucy, go back to your party and try to have fun. Okay? I'll be there soon with the others, and we can laugh about it."

Something in her tone or words, or just because she knew her so well, piqued Lucy's instincts. "Cris, are you okay? Really. This is me, Lucy."

The laugh Cristina blurted in response seemed tinged with hysteria, or maybe Lucy was reading into it—who knew? "Me?" Cristina asked. "Don't worry about me. I always land on my feet. You're getting *married* in a week—focus on that. Besides, I have a surprise for you."

"Yeah?"

"I've decided to come early. I'll be there tomorrow as long as the hotel can get me in."

"Oh, God. That's wonderful! Mercy's coming early, too."

"That's . . . that's great," Cristina said, without enthusiasm.

"Come on, Cris. You and Mercy used to be so tight."

"Yeah, that was twenty years ago before she decided to hate my guts." Cristina's words had a shadow of hurt on them.

"She doesn't *hate* you."

Lucy heard her friend's dry, mirthless chuckle. "Oh, Lucy. You and your rose-colored glasses. But, don't worry. Mercy and I are grown women now. We'll get along just fine. It's your *wedding*. It's all about you, babe."

7:15 P.M. MOUNTAIN STANDARD TIME

"For once, someone who is actually punctual."

"I have five children. I have a schedule." As usual, Annette sounded harried. "I don't have leeway to be fashionable. What kind of cake did they make?"

Lucy stood off in the corner, out of the party limelight for once. Not bothering to hide away, she tipped her small paper plate to the side to examine the interior of the slice she'd just been handed. "Sort of a hazelnut cream deal."

"Yum. Okay, so how's the party going? Ruthie! Don't touch that, it's still hot."

"What are you doing?"

"Me?" Annette sounded vaguely angry. She spoke each word sharply and didn't sound Annette-like at all. Lucy heard something slam in the background. "Oh, I'm just spending my evening baking cookies with the girls."

"You're such a good mama."

Annette scoffed. "Yeah. Keep telling yourself that."

Come to think of it, though Annette always sounded harried, she didn't usually sound harried and pissed off. Annette never sounded pissed off. "Is everything okay, Annie?"

"Of course! What could possibly be wrong?" Annette barked a few cookie-related orders to her daughters, but unlike Cristina, she kept the phone uncovered. "Sorry. Now, back to you. What's going on at the party?"

Lucy decided to set aside her worry. If something was wrong in Annette's world, Lucy knew she'd be the first to know. "They're getting ready to wrap me in toilet paper and stuff. You know, that bridal dress-up game, whatever it's called?"

"Pin the veil on the donkey?"

Lucy laughed. "Yeah, ha ha, pin the veil, comedienne. But I can survive that. It's not even close to the worst part."

"What's the worst part?"

"My sisters-in-law all pooled their money and bought a gift certificate for us."

"So? What's bad about that?"

"It's to a divorce lawyer."

"Lord have mercy. When God was divvying up the crazies, he assigned more than average to your family, Luce. I'm so sorry." Annette laughed, sounding genuinely amused for the first time in the conversation. "How'd you manage to turn out normal?"

"Normal? Hon, I almost go into convulsions whenever I think about marrying the man I love and adore. My soulmate. What's normal about that?"

"You're right. Nothing. But that's why I love you. You keep my otherwise drab life interesting."

Lucy warmed. "So, everything's all set with the kids so you can come out here worry free, right? It wouldn't be the same without you here."

"Yeah, so long as no bleeping emergencies crop up."

"Randy can handle *bleeping* emergencies, Annette."

A short pause ensued. "You know what? You're right. Speaking of Randy, he's sorry he'll miss the wedding and sends his love, but this way I have ten blessed days away." Her voice lowered to a whisper. "I can't wait. You have no idea."

"I'm glad for you. You work too hard. Mercy and Cris are coming out early. Tomorrow. I wish you could, too."

"Me, too. But no way in heck could I pull off tomorrow. Mercy and Cris are women of the world. I'm resident cookie baker, chauffeur, nurse, teacher, priest, judge, jury, and executioner. And trash collector." Annette sniffed. "Hey, on that note, I gotta go. Ruthie and Mary are about to kill each other and I'm on the verge of killing them both just to expedite things. Guess I'm the resident cop and serial killer, too. Lucky me. But, Lucy?"

"Yeah?"

"Hang in there, girl. We're going to help you through this. Oh, and keep all that toilet paper after they dress you up."

"What for?"

"To use! It's the environmentally sound thing to do. Sheesh, do I have to spoon-feed you and everybody else common sense?"

7:30 P.M. MOUNTAIN STANDARD TIME

"Not again!" Betty said, when Lucy's cell phone rang for the fourth time.

"Mama, I'm sorry. I won't be long." She flipped open the phone, but didn't speak until she was out of earshot of the party guests. She could pull off the work-related act with her friends, but she knew her voice's tendency to go soft and breathy whenever she spoke to Ruben. Her heart constricted just thinking his name. Damn, she was really far gone.

"You there, babe?" That rough voice, with just a tinge of an accent, could take her from tough to shaky in two seconds flat.

"I'm here," she said, soft and breathy as predicted.

"You tied to that two weeks apart thing?"

Lucy stopped short and felt a burst within her—a combination of hope and lust. "Why do you ask?"

"Because I'm outside. In the alley. Waiting."

"Don't move." Lucy heard Ruben's low, lusty chuckle as she switched off the cell phone and set it on the kitchen table. Heart lodged firmly in her throat, she ran out the back door. The prospect of seeing Ruben, of smelling his skin and touching him, made the agony of the shower disappear just like that. She stopped on the porch and shaded her eyes from the bright setting sun.

There he stood, beautiful and dangerous, looking at her with such love her skin seemed to vibrate from its intensity. He stood next to his muscle-and-chrome motorcycle wearing faded blue jeans that cupped him perfectly, and a crisp white T-shirt that fairly screamed "Tear me off." A slow smile lifted his lips and he removed his mirrored sunglasses with one hand, his deep blue eyes boring into hers. Then he opened his arms.

She felt his welcome like a punch to the solar plexus and did the only thing she could—she ran to him. Across the backyard and the circular gravel driveway until they stood face-to-face, locked in each other's gazes.

"Babe?"

Her lips trembled. "Yeah?"

"You're covered in toilet paper."

Lucy erupted in laughter, then threw her arms around his neck and her legs around his waist. And she kissed him. He held her tightly and kissed her, the familiar roughness of his whiskers scraping her face.

This was what had made her say yes to his proposal, despite her notorious family history. When he held her, when they were together, everything else seemed to wash away. She adored this man, couldn't get enough of him. Hiking her higher with his big hands on the backs of her thighs, Ruben walked slowly forward until her back met the warm, wooden slats of the six-foot privacy fence, and he pressed against her.

Lucy threaded her fingers up into his long black hair and gripped tightly. She wanted him forever. And right now, she wanted them to climb onto his Harley and run away and get married, away from the prying eyes and knowing looks of the Oliveras.

An idea struck. She pulled back from the mind-numbing kiss, licking the taste of him off her lips. "Let's go away."

"I'm trying to take you away right now, *querida,* but you're talking," he teased. More kissing, deep breathing. Finally, he pulled back. "And, incidentally, we are going away, babe. This fall. I wish we could take the honeymoon sooner, but—"

"No. I mean let's go away now. For the wedding." The unexpected sting of tears blurred her eyes. "Let's just elope . . . and never come back."

He dipped his chin and studied her with sympathy. "Come on, Luce. We have five hundred guests."

"Yeah. How exactly did that happen?"

Ruben laughed, then growled, then captured her mouth again. In between sense-draining kisses, Ruben told her, "Here's the deal, yeah? We . . . you and me . . . are going to get married . . . and live happily . . . ever . . . after." He sucked her tongue into his mouth and then pulled back and planted small kisses on each cheek, her chin, her forehead, and her eyelids. Finally, he just held her, and his voice softened. "Didn't you ever read any fairy tales, Lucy Olivera?"

She rolled her eyes. "Life isn't a fairy tale."

"Nor is it a family curse." He took her mouth again to keep her from voicing a protest. When they finally stopped kissing, Lucy concentrated on slowing her heart rate as he slid her slowly down his body until her feet rested on the ground. His hands remained firmly around her waist, though, and his body pressed against hers from chest to knee. Streamers of toilet paper flapped around them in the breeze. She implored him with her eyes. "I need to get married."

He looked around, as if for the hidden camera. "Ahhhh . . . we are getting married, babe. In seven short days. Remember? Five hundred guests, you freaking out, the cake that took us three weeks to decide on." He shook his head and glanced at the house. "You smoking something funny in there? Because I probably should remind you we're narcotics officers, and unless you want to give all that up to go flip burgers—"

"Stop." Lucy shook her head at his joking, and the tears came. They were unwelcome, and she brushed them away with the back of her hand. "Just listen. I've figured this out. I need to marry someone else. Soon. So I can divorce him before our wedding, and then the curse won't affect us. I-I love you so much. I should've thought of this before now, Ruben, but I was trying to block the whole thing from my mind—"

"Lucy Olivera, my angel." He tucked her head beneath his chin, and she could feel the steady beat of his heart against her cheek. "My crazy mixed-up angel. You are not marrying anyone but me. And that, *querida,* is a promise."

"But—"

"You're not leaving me, either. You're stuck with me."

"Another promise?"

"If you'll promise, I'll make damn sure you keep it. And I promise you, right here, right now, that I will do whatever it takes to have you with me, as my wife, forever. Do you promise?"

They stared into each other's eyes for several long moments. Lucy finally nodded, then rested her head back on his shoulder. She didn't want to talk, couldn't look at him, because, as much as she wanted it to, the promise he wanted just wouldn't come out of her throat. It was locked somewhere in the vicinity of her heart, which felt scared and strangely hollow. Almost like it was about to break.

Chapter Six

Mercedes gaped at the impeccably garbed and clean-cut young man behind the Brown Palace front counter. Outside, the summer air in downtown Denver had felt balmy and dry, but inside, the hotel air was cool. Cooler still when ice stuttered through her veins as she replayed the front desk clerk's last statement. Surely she'd misunderstood. *Please, God, let me have misunderstood.* She blinked at the man convulsively, but managed an even tone. "Excuse me. What did you just say?"

He beamed, leaning in conspiratorially. "I said another member of the wedding party is staying in the Roosevelt suite, one floor above your Reagan suite." He winked. "I assumed you'd all know each other?"

"Yes, of course. We're all old friends. Who is it?"

"A Mrs."—he consulted the computer screen—"Aragon?"

Mercedes's gut clenched as though someone had kicked it. Okay, so she was a grudge holder, but despite that admitted fault, she *so* didn't need this shit right now. "Cristina Trevino Aragon got the Roosevelt suite?" Sticking her with the dreaded Reagan suite, of course. She should've known.

"That she did." He bestowed his practiced customer-service grin. "How lucky you'll be so close, isn't it?"

Fuck. Cristina had probably done it on purpose, fully aware of Mercy's bad memories of the Reagan suite on their awful prom night. Cristina damn well knew Mercy had been forced to escape to the Reagan suite alone, hurt and miserable. She had to know. Then again, Cristina had always been more oblivious than malicious, not that that made the situation any less galling.

Mercedes gripped the slick countertop with both hands. "Yeah, that's just grand. Listen, it's been a long travel day. I could really use a drink, and I'm supposed to meet a friend." She indicated her luggage vaguely, her eyes scanning the various doors beyond the central lobby. She knew the name of the bar Lucy had suggested for their meeting, of course, but not where it was. "If we're done here, can you just . . . ?"

"Of course, Ms. Félan. We'll have your bags taken up. Is there anything else we can deliver to your room in the meantime?"

Arsenic? A pack of razor blades? Anything to take me out of my misery? "No, thanks. Which direction is the Ship Tavern?"

He pointed with his chin to the left, fingers clicking rapidly over the keyboard in front of him. "Just over there. At the end of the hall. Enjoy your stay."

Mercedes tossed the bellman a ten-spot and half smiled as she wobbled away. Enjoy her stay? Not bloody likely. Realistically, when had she ever had a truly good time here? She struggled to block the memory of their ill-fated prom night, but the goddamned Technicolor replay kept flashing in her mind to spite her. Under normal circumstances, she never thought of this stuff. She didn't care. Well . . . not really. She'd moved on. Okay . . . sort of. But maybe it was being back in Denver, the prospect of seeing old friends . . . facing old enemies.

Old insecurities.

Cristina.

Compounded by the fact that, of the three presidential suites available to reserve for this wedding—Eisenhower, Roosevelt, and Reagan—she'd gotten jammed yet again. Just like always when Cristina was in the picture. A pout threatened to emerge, but she shoved it away. Self-pity was a weak woman's trait in which she refused to indulge . . . at least openly. All she wanted to indulge in at the moment was a martini. Or five.

She entered the Ship Tavern, glanced around at the charming waterfront tavern decor, then chose a table where Lucy was sure to see her when she entered. Model clipper ships were displayed behind the back-lit bar, a fitting enhancement to the warm, gleaming wood expanse of the bar itself. She glanced up at the ceiling beams, heard the clinking of glasses being filled at the bar, along with pockets of conversation and laughter. The pianist, John Kite, was knocking out a great rendition of Looking Glass's famous one-hit wonder, "Brandy," and a lot of would-be singers were lifting their glasses and singing along.

She ordered her first martini by rote, then propped her elbows on the blue-and-white checkered tablecloth and rested her forehead against her palms, stewing while she waited for the drink to be delivered.

Maybe it was just Cristina.

Maybe it's just you, dumbass. She had a chip on her shoulder where Cristina was concerned. Why deny it? Mercedes knew she needed to get over these issues. It had been decades. Why did the injuries of youth seem to stick around longer and hurt more than the injustices of adulthood?

The specter of Cristina seemed to have been fuel-injected into her brain, those antiquated and seemingly inconsequential memories flooding back with a vengeance. It always happened this way. That was the thing. The suite debacle, prom, all that tamped-down bitterness had intertwined itself into one huge hideous ball of *pissed-off* and Mercedes just couldn't shake it.

The Brown Palace was unarguably beautiful and palatial, the very finest in Denver accommodations, and the Grand Ballroom would make a stunning wedding and reception backdrop for Lucy and Ruben. Mercedes loved the old gal for its inherent beauty and historical importance to the community, blah blah blah, but bad memories tainted that affection with something uglier. And yet she hadn't begged Lucy to choose a different venue because (a) she wasn't that much of a self-absorbed bitch, contrary to popular opinion, and (b) her subconscious apparently wanted to press on that old bruise to see if it still hurt.

It did.

The thing was, Mercedes had been flat-out in love with Johnny Romero their senior year, but as luck would have it, he only had eyes for Ms. Perfect. The irony? Cristina didn't love the guy. Mercedes doubted Cristina even really liked him, but he gave her attention—poured that shit on like syrup—and if there was one thing Cristina loved, it was attention.

Still, Cristina had accepted a date to the prom with another guy whom she'd deemed higher on the food chain and turned Johnny down when he asked. He was devastated; Mercedes had been thrilled. She'd seen her chance, and she'd nonchalantly suggested to Johnny that the two of them go to prom together. Inside, she just knew once he got to know her, he'd forget all about Cristina. Johnny had agreed to the date, and Mercedes was jubilant. It had been . . . a moment. She hadn't even told any of her friends.

Then Cristina's date fell through.

Hence, so had Mercedes's.

Johnny, using his eighteen-year-old logic, had asked Cristina first and figured Mercedes was only trying to be nice when she'd made her suggestion anyway. Surely she didn't mind if he went with Cristina instead, right? Wrong. But who had time to consider the also-ran? Unwittingly stomping Mercy's heart, Cristina had dated and discarded Johnny without a second thought. Mercedes, on the other hand, attended the abysmal prom night fiasco at the Palace Arms restaurant with her supremely annoying cousin, Tito, who picked his teeth at the table and left the toothpick dangling from his insolent mouth throughout the dance. And Tito, to add insult to injury, also had the hots for Cristina. *Fuck me, who doesn't?* If Damian were here, that rat bastard, he'd probably dump the baby-sitter and set his sights on Cristina, too.

Mercedes shuddered. Okay, not going there. She'd come to Denver in the hope of escaping the looming cloud of Damian and her impending demise at his hand, so she firmly booted thoughts of him and his little puffy whore out of her mind.

Bottom line, Johnny Romero had *mattered* to Mercedes. The suites mattered, too. When Cristina entered the picture—any picture—what mattered to Mercedes simply didn't count.

The old fury licked up inside Mercedes's gut, causing her to clench her jaw and fumble in her purse for the blessed bottle of vitamin V. She ignored a stab of guilt. She really needed to kick her craving for this shit, but it smoothed out the sharp edges of her life, and right now her entire world was like a field of splintered glass.

God, how she dreaded seeing Cristina again.

She'd known this, but she hadn't realized the extent of the dread until right then. If only Cristina had noticed she'd been crushing Mercedes all those years ago. If only she'd cared, perhaps apologized, their friendship—competitive as it had always been—might have survived. Instead, it was just another loss in a long line of them. The worst part of all was Cristina's utter, inconceivable cluelessness.

She fucking hated the woman.

Mercedes groaned and squeezed her eyes shut. She might be successful, attractive, fit enough to turn the head of her twenty-two-year-old personal trainer . . . but here in the old neighborhood, Cristina still had the goddamn power to make her feel not quite up to par. Especially now, with this tabloid thing about to explode and no way to shield herself from the media shrapnel.

She supposed, if she were honest, she'd have to give Cristina props for one thing. Had she *not* made Mercedes feel so inadequate in high school, Mercy might never have had the I'll-show-you drive to make it to the top. Sure, she'd always yearned for success—who doesn't? But that natural drive had been fueled by a need to show Cristina she wasn't second-rate.

Not that it worked.

She felt like an imposter of the worst kind. How successful could a thrice-divorced, recently dumped, universally loathed CEO of a magazine really be, after all?

Mercedes drained the extra dirty triple olive martini the waiter had set down while she hadn't been paying attention, washing down a Vicodin with the last of it. Catching the waiter's eye, she signaled for another, ignoring the shocked look on his face at how quickly she'd downed the first. What was he, the alcohol police?

A glimpse at her black-faced Movado watch told her it was past time for Lucy to show, but when she looked up, she caught sight of her beloved friend weaving her way through the tables of the bar. Mercedes felt a glimmer of hope . . . and vulnerable lump in her throat. What was it about Lucy that always brought that out in her? Lucy was a buff, kick-ass drug cop—not exactly the quintessential Earth Mother type. And yet she was the most nurturing person Mercedes had ever known.

God, how she needed that nurturing.

Unfortunately, now was not the time to discuss her own problems, when the whacked-out bride-to-be had her own troubles, psychotic and irrational though they may be.

She waved just as the waiter set down her fresh drink, and Lucy waved back, grinning. Even horrendously underdressed in low-slung jeans, scuffed Doc Martens, a cropped Marilyn Manson T-shirt that displayed her pierced belly button, and black leather motorcycle jacket, Lucy drew the smiles and admiration of those she passed. No doubt about it, the woman was rock-solid special.

Mercedes would've stood, but her self-medication program was kicking in, and she didn't relish the thought of a mishap. She did, after all, have some sort of pulled-together image to maintain, even though it was utter bullshit.

"Well, if it isn't Lucy Olivera in the flesh."

"Hey, girl," Lucy said, bending down to pull Mercedes into a hug. She laid a big, fat smack on her cheek. "God, it's good to see someone sane."

"Ha. If you only knew."

Lucy studied her. "You look fantastic. So New York. A little tense, but . . ."

Mercedes hiked a shoulder. "Well, I do live in the city. Tension is an accessory. You look amazing, too, Lucky girl."

"Yeah, right." Lucy scoffed. "Glamour girl—that's me. I just got off work." She held out the front edges of her jacket and struck a sexy pose. "Modern drug subculture chic. What do you think?"

"I think you still turn heads, no matter what."

"Whatever. You're biased as all hell, but I love you for it." Lucy sat, lifting her chin toward Mercy's glass. "What's your poison? Looks like used bathwater."

"Bathwater?" Mercedes frowned at the swirling greenish gray olive dregs in her glass, then gaped at Lucy. "Jesus, how often do you bathe, girl? It's a martini. Extra dirty."

"Ah, yes, I should've known." Lucy folded her hands on the table. "Looks horrid. I'll have one, too."

Mercedes raised her hand to get the attention of the waiter, then pointed to her glass and held up a finger. Her practiced, hard-ass expression dared him to pass judgment on her ordering a third. He didn't. "So, what's with you working? I thought you were taking time off to prepare for the wedding?"

Lucy sighed. "I go crazy whenever I think about it, so being at work helps. I didn't have to be there, I chose to. It was nothing major. Caught up on some paperwork, did a few simple buy-busts, and assisted on a no-knock warrant."

Mercedes blinked. "You say that like it's normal."

"It is when you're in my line of work. Another day, another drug bust." She winked. "Hey, didn't you get my phone messages? I've left two. Your battery dead, or what?" Lucy shrugged out of her beat-down motorcycle jacket. The multiple chrome buckles clanked against the wood as she hung it over the back of her chair, watching Mercedes intently as she did so.

Mercedes tried her best not to avert her gaze. "I'm sort of . . . not answering my cell."

Lucy cocked her head to the side. "Why not?"

Trapped. But she was the queen of evasive conversation so this was not a problem. "It's a long story." Mercedes sighed, running her fingers through her hair. She ached with the desire to unload her worries, to share the burden. But she just couldn't do it if she wanted to live with herself. "Let's just say everyone wants a piece of me and I'm in desperate need of time alone. Damian and I are on the outs, too. Nothing major."

"Makes perfect sense. Okay, no more badgering." Lucy held up her hands. "But I'm here if you need to spill your guts."

"Nothing to spill," Mercedes fudged. "I'm just overworked and men are a pain in my ass." Mercy reached across the table and squeezed Lucy's hand. "But, I know you're here for me, Lucky girl. You always have been. And I'm here for you, because this is your wedding week and it's all about *you.*"

"No wedding talk!"

"Okay, okay. Jesus. Most brides talk incessantly about their weddings. How was I supposed to know?" She wondered about the wisdom of letting Lucy deny and avoid her upcoming nuptials, but whatever. What was one night? Feeling infinitely calmer—better living through pharmaceuticals was her motto—Mercedes lifted her martini glass. "So, what was the all-important message about?"

"Cristina."

Mercedes set the glass back down, a bit unsteadily. "Oh?" She fought for a pleasant expression and bit back the reflux of annoyance that burned unbidden in her chest.

"Yeah. She's staying here, too, you know. In one of the presidential sui—"

"Yeah, the fucking Roosevelt," Mercedes blurted, before she could stop herself. "While my sad-sack ass is stuck in Reagan." Damnit, she hadn't planned on broaching the topic, but the alcohol-and-pill combo will do that to a person. "That didn't come out right, but never mind. It's no big deal," she amended.

"Come on, Mercy, I've seen the Reagan suite. You know it's fantastic."

"To reiterate, it's not an issue. It's just a hotel room, okay? No biggie."

The expression on Lucy's face clearly telegraphed her skepticism. Mercedes ignored the pull of guilt in her gut for lying and went on. "So when's the big moment?"

"Excuse me?"

"When do Cristina and I get to reunite after all these long pining years apart?" she asked wryly.

Lucy smiled up as the waiter set down her martini, then bestowed a chastising look on Mercedes. "She's going to meet us down here for a drink in a few minutes."

For a moment, Mercedes simply stared at her longtime friend, then she picked up her martini and drained the glass. She'd need the additional anesthesia to get her through this unwelcome and undoubtedly awkward moment. With her luck, Cristina had probably picked up a tabloid to peruse on the plane and knew all about her little scandal. "Swell. Can't wait."

"Mercy, be nice. Please?"

"When am I not nice? That was nice. I said I can't wait."

"You didn't say 'I can't wait,' you said 'Can't wait.' "

"Same thing."

"Not even close, sister. Don't think I can't read through your bullshit because I deal with the stuff all day long."

Mercedes sniffed, nonplussed. She flicked a hand. "So you busted me. What next, reservations in hell? Trust me, they've got a name plaque on my door already. Don't bother."

Lucy leaned in and lowered her voice to a stage whisper. "You're intimidating and you know it. Cristina has never been as strong as you are. You scare the shit out of her."

A little curl of pleasure moved through her, but it was quickly usurped by indignance. Mercedes spread her arms. "Why am I the bad guy in all this? If she's scared, it's her issue. But I can guarantee you—not that anyone listens to me—fear isn't in her repertoire. Manipulation, maybe. Flirtation, definitely. I've never done a goddamned thing—"

"Mercy, for Christ's sake."

"Okay, okay." She sat back in her chair and held up her palms in surrender. "You're right. I'm sorry. Nice you want, nice you get. Besides, I meant it when I said I can't wait. Might as well get the damned reunion debacle over with." She proffered a saccharine-sweet slash of a smile. "Who knows, maybe Cristina and I will become fast friends again."

Lucy's expression remained droll.

Mercedes arms shot out to the sides. "Look, I'm not going to bitch-slap her, if that's what you're worried about. Give me a little credit for being an adult."

Lucy pushed her artfully tangled drug-chic mane out of her face. "I just wish the two of you would make up. You used to be tight. No one even knows what happened."

And no one would know, if Mercedes had anything to do with it. She held up a finger. "First of all, we were never exactly tight—"

"Right."

"—and there's nothing to 'make up' for." She sniffed and tried for nonchalance. "Don't sweat it, Lucky girl. Everything will be fine, promise. We're here for *you,* not to kick some decades-old drama into high gear again. Cristina and I are adults. You don't have to fix it. It's not your problem."

"But it is," Lucy pleaded, "because I love you both."

"And *we* both love *you.* That's what matters."

Lucy studied her for several moments, then released a surrendering sigh. "Speaking as the bigwig editor in chief of *What's Important* magazine, Mercy, I guess you'd know." Lucy raised her glass in a sincere salute, clearly wanting to move on to more lighthearted conversation.

Mercy's gaze slid away. She felt sick and phony, stuffed to bursting with lies and secrets and old, festering anger. How was she going to survive this trip? More to the point, how was she ever going to return to the reality of her life after everything she'd built had been destroyed?

Cristina backed away from the front door of the Ship Tavern once again, her heart pounding so hard she couldn't force herself to walk in. Instead, she sank into one of the plush Victorian couches in the atrium lobby beneath the spectacular stained-glass canopy, and fought to catch her breath. She pressed her palms to her torso, breathing deeply. In, out. In, out. Deep. Slow.

She'd seen them, Mercedes and Lucy, cozied up at a table sipping martinis, but she just didn't feel ready to join them. Fear—she could taste it. Hell, she could choke on it, there was so much. She had never felt more like a phony, like such a useless waste of womanhood, and to walk in on two incredibly successful women, only one of whom actually liked her . . . it was too much. She could pull off the regal act with all the society people back home, because none of them really knew her. She made damn sure of that. But here, with women who'd known her before she was Zach Aragon's wife, Cristina knew the image was just a transparent, self-protective shell.

She'd come from a middle-class family that was, yes, very supportive. She'd never lacked the essentials. But she didn't have breeding and she didn't have poise—not really. And the only one who could see through her superficialities was her Dior-clad, sharp-tongued monster-in-law. The woman knew Cristina was second-rate, out of her league with the Aragon aristocracy, and she never failed to let her know it. Cristina had done her best to carve out a persona to placate Zach's mother over the years, and most of her acquaintances bought it. Hell, she almost bought it herself. But wouldn't Mercedes and Lucy see through it to the real, worthless Cristina? Lucy wouldn't care. But Mercy?

Certainly neither of them had ever shoplifted.

Or been arrested.

They were too busy living worthwhile *lives,* for God's sake.

She pressed the pads of her shaky fingers to her temples and closed her eyes, mired in agony. She wanted to be there for Lucy, but God, she had so much to hide right now. So much to face when she finally returned to the real world, a world that might not even be there for her when Lucy's wedding was over. And then what would she have to show for her life? A police record and a shitload of pricey skin care products? Whoopee.

"Can I help you with something, miss?"

Cristina's gaze flew up to the concierge standing before her, and she managed a weak smile. At least he'd called her miss and not ma'am. There was a plus to being caught in the middle of a breakdown just a week after Botox had erased a few years from her face. "No, really. Just a headache. I'm meeting friends in the Ship Tavern, but I'm . . . waiting for my Excedrin to kick in." She hadn't actually taken any, but it sounded good.

"May I bring you a cocktail while you wait for your friends to arrive, then?"

No sense clearing up the fact that her friends already *had* arrived, and she was simply too chickenshit to go join them. She sat up straighter and fought for regal bearing. Act the way you want the world to see you. Wasn't that what her mother had always told her? Wasn't that her entire defense mechanism repertoire? "That would be lovely. Something quick." She paused. "How about a shot of tequila. Your best."

To his credit, his mouth quivered only slightly at the request. He probably thought she'd order an expensive wine or the Brown Palace's signature Cascade Cocktail. Something *fitting,* as her monster-in-law always snidely encouraged. Tequila shots were a cheap *pocha's* choice.

"Salt and lime with that?"

"Please." She smiled again as he turned to walk away, then slumped again and formulated a plan. She'd throw back her shot, and as soon as she felt a bit mellower, she'd suck it up and forge ahead into the bar. Surely she could face Mercy after stout fortification from top-shelf tequila. And, really, the shoplifting thing? They wouldn't know she'd been arrested unless she told them, so her secret was safe. Nobody in Denver cared about misdemeanor theft charges in San Antonio. She could pull this off. God knew, she'd been playacting through most of her life anyway. Why should this be any different? Except for the niggling fact that Lucy was her only true friend and she hated lying to her. But it had to be done.

The reality of her arrest slammed into her again.

God, she really needed to get hold of a San Antonio paper, see what, if anything, had hit the social circles. She'd built herself a carefully orchestrated life far away from home, where she could pretend to be somebody, and now she'd screwed all that up. Stress over the constant role-playing, the omnipresent need for approval from Zach's mom—which she'd never earn—had prompted her to shoplift. Blind bravado had caused her to get caught, and now the whole thing was about to blow up in her face. Sooner or later, she'd have to talk to Zach. Later, she decided. Much, much later.

Just then, a waiter arrived with a tray perched on his fingertips, and he set out her shot of ta-kill-ya with flourish. "Here you go. Can I bring you anything else?"

"Why don't you . . . bring me one more of these when you have a chance." She bestowed a dazzling smile, hoping to offset the drunkard's request. "I like even numbers."

Thirty minutes later, not one but two shots sluicing through her bloodstream like liquid courage, Cristina lurched her way through the doors of the Ship Tavern. Her limbs felt loose, her brain carbonated, but her throat squeezed with anxiety nonetheless. As luck would have it, Lucy had moved to the chair adjacent to Mercy, leaving the one across the table open for her. Lucy saw her, face brightening, then jumped to her feet and crossed the bar to meet her halfway and wrap her in a hug.

"God, Cris, you're more beautiful every time I see you."

Cristina hugged back even more tightly—clinging on for dear life was more like it. "That's a damn lie and you know it. A cruel lie to a woman who's almost forty, as a matter of fact. But thank you anyway.

You, on the other hand, look like a hot eighteen-year-old bad girl who fell in with a rough crowd."

"Yeah, and who rocks the ganga daily. It's the job."

"I meant it as a compliment, believe me. But why are you working this week?"

"Long story."

Cris whispered, "Avoiding wedding thoughts?"

"Why yes, Miss Cleo, and now let's not talk about it."

They pulled apart, laughing, but the insecurities rushed back in. Cristina didn't dare look over Lucy's shoulder toward Mercedes, but her stomach convulsed and her smile went brittle. "So . . . should I be scared?" Her voice had wobbled and her eyes stung. She hated herself for the weakness.

"Not at all, honey." Lucy said, her voice like a balm. She wrapped an arm around Cristina's waist and began guiding her to the table, leaning in to speak confidentially. "Mercy said she's looking forward to seeing you."

"Were the words 'in a shallow grave' at the end of that statement?" Cristina scoffed, but a dart of hopefulness pierced her heart. Could it be?

"Don't be absurd."

Cristina took a deep, calming breath then blew it out. "Well, let's get it over with then."

Lucy snorted. "You two are more alike than different."

"Whatever."

As they approached the table, Cristina studied Mercy, all the while trying to feign nonchalance. God, she'd grown into a beautiful, polished, professional woman. She'd always been a notch above all the other girls, but now that natural Alpha dominance had been honed into hard-edged, feminine perfection. Next to her, Cristina felt like exactly what she was—an aging piece of arm candy whose wrapper was getting tattered.

Mercy regarded her with a level, chocolate brown gaze, her expression unreadable and intimidating. Just as they got to the table, she bestowed a controlled smile. "At last. The notorious Cristina Trevino Aragon."

Something about the cryptic statement made Cristina's heart leap up to lodge in her throat. Notorious? Had Mercedes somehow found out about her—no. No, of course not. She was being paranoid. It was just Mercy's way of saying something while saying nothing, all while avoiding what should've been said in the first place. Typical Mercy. Cristina swallowed thickly. "Mercedes, it's so good to see you," she lied. "I read your magazine faithfully. You must be so proud."

Mercy shrugged like it was nothing, but Cristina could see the satisfaction beneath her carefully controlled nonchalance. "Pays the bills. Thank you."

Knowing a hug would be awkward at best and disastrous at worst, Cristina stuck out her hand for a shake.

Mercy's almond-eyed gaze dropped to the extended hand and her expression changed to one of alarm. She grabbed Cristina's fingers rather roughly and examined the dark, angry bruises left on her wrist from the biting metal handcuffs. "Good God, Cris. What in the hell happened to your arm?"

Cris snatched her hand back, wrapping her opposite palm around the tender, telling marks. Of course, doing so exposed the identical bruises on the other wrist. The officer hadn't been rough with her, but sitting seat-belted against the hard plastic backseat of the patrol car with her hands cuffed behind her hadn't been exactly ergonomic. Plus she bruised so easily. Damnit, why hadn't she remembered to cover the evidence? She gulped back her panic, her mind racing for an explanation. "I, um, slammed my wrist in the car door."

Mercy's gaze shifted, and one eyebrow arched. Lucy had leaned in for a look, too, her face lined with concern.

"Both wrists? How does one slam both hands in her car door?" Mercedes asked.

Shit. She hadn't had time to think before she'd blurted that impromptu lie. "I w-was loading groceries into the car and the wind caught it. Slammed before I knew it. But, really, I don't want to talk about my klutziness."

"So you're still a klutz?" Lucy joked, taking her seat again. "It's nice to know some things haven't changed, but I'm sorry about the wrists." She crinkled her nose with sympathy, lightening the mood, but Cristina could see the perceptive worry in her expression.

Still, Cristina felt a wash of shaky gratitude. Lucy always did know how to restore order to a tense situation. "Some traits you just don't lose."

"Isn't that the truth?" Mercedes said wryly.

Cristina ignored the pointed comment. She sat, tucking her purse in the chair behind her and straightening her skirt. When she looked back, Mercedes was still studying her with that piercing, all-knowing stare. It creeped her out, almost as if Mercy could see right through her to the emptiness inside.

"Joining us in a martini?" Mercy asked, her voice as smoky-smooth and intimidating as always.

"Actually, I had two shots of tequila in the lobby. I'd better stick with that."

Some subtle shift in Mercy's expression told Cristina her astute former friend was digesting the idea of solitary tequila shots and drawing her own conclusions, whatever those may be. Frankly, Cristina didn't want to contemplate it.

"And, how's *Zach*?" Mercy asked, almost like an accusation. It confused Cristina, until she remembered the bruises. Oh, God. Mercedes couldn't possibly think—

"Mercy, I assure you, Zach did not give me these bruises."

"I never said that."

"You didn't have to," scolded Lucy, holding her hands in the shape of a T for time-out. "Cris, if you say you slammed your wrists in a car door, we believe you. Don't we, Mercy?" Lucy added in a tone that said Mercy had better damn well agree.

"Well, gosh, of course we do," Mercy said, her words laced tightly with skepticism. She leaned back slowly in her chair and schooled her features into a sardonic, knowing stare.

"I mean, stranger things have happened." Lucy flipped her hand, sounding way too much like someone trying too hard to rationalize. "I read an article in the *Rocky Mountain News* about a Japanese tourist on a deep-sea fishing expedition who died when a fish jumped out of the water into his mouth and choked him to death." She shrugged. "Weird stuff happens."

Okay, so neither of them believed her. Just great. It almost made Cristina want to confess the ugly truth. Zach? Beating her? As if. But what would she say? *If you must know, the bruises are from handcuffs. No, Zach's not into the kinky stuff. I came by them legitimately. I've got the arrest record and mug shot to back me up.*

Yeah, right. Better to let Mercy think Zach was an animal.

"How are the kids, Cris? I bet you miss them."

Cristina flicked a glance at Mercedes. "They're trekking in Europe for the summer," she explained quickly. She didn't know how much Mercedes knew about her life, but if she had to venture a guess, not much. A waiter interrupted their conversation and Cristina ordered another shot. Last one, she promised herself, as she turned back toward Lucy. "They're both having a great time, judging from their e-mails and phone calls. And, confidentially, it's nice to have some 'me' time. Though I do miss them."

"Speaking of kids, when does Annette arrive?" Mercy asked.

"Tomorrow night. Randy actually encouraged her to come early. She wasn't supposed to be here for a few more days but when she heard the two of you were coming early, she worked it."

"Randy's a good guy," Cristina said. "It doesn't surprise me that he looks out for Annette that way."

Lucy crossed her arms and frowned. "You know, I talked to her yesterday and she sounded so rushed and . . . snappish. I was worried about her."

"Of course she's snappish. She has five children. Christ, if I had five children, I'd be a homicidal alcoholic."

Lucy gave Mercedes a rueful smile. "True. She did say she was dying to get here, so that's a plus."

"She probably just needs a break, Lucy," Cristina said softly. "Parenting can really take it out of you."

"Speaking from experience?"

"You know it."

Lucy took in a deep breath and blew out a long, contented sigh. "You know, I'm not going to worry about Annette. Or either of you. Or me. Let's just take advantage of our time together while we can. I'm sure we all have little problems in our lives, but they can wait, right?"

Cristina's gaze clashed with Mercy's, then they both looked away quickly. *If they only knew.* The waiter set down Cristina's shot glass, a salt shaker, and a wedge of lime. She licked the edge of her hand, salted it, then picked up her small glass.

Lucy held her martini glass aloft. "To us," she said, her tone overly hopeful. Neither Mercedes nor Cristina echoed the toast, but glasses did clink. Somehow that seemed to signal progress . . . however slight.

Chapter Seven

"So, have they killed each other yet?" Annette asked as she and Lucy embraced on the front porch of her brick bungalow just after she'd arrived.

Lucy laughed, a full-out, unrestrained sound that made Annette's heart feel like singing. She missed being near Lucy so much, sometimes she simply had to put their friendship out of her mind to survive the distance. Annette had never been as close to another friend, and she spent a lot of time feeling cut off. Sure, she loved New Mexico. She had her family and loved them, too. That was a given. But no one understood the depth of friendship between women like . . . other women. And a soul-friend like Lucy, if you were lucky, came but once in a lifetime.

"Not yet," Lucy said, her tone wry.

"Thank goodness." The golden sun blazed low and rich in the sky over the Front Range, but it was still daylight, and that was something. She'd made good time, better than she'd expected. She'd never been much for vacations, but traveling without children was a whole different experience, one she found she thoroughly enjoyed. She stopped when she wanted, listened to the music she wanted. Listened to nothing but silence and the whir of the engine if she wanted. It was all about her, for once, and she'd loved every moment. The drive had been long, but relaxing. So tearfully grateful to be alone, she hadn't even turned on the stereo for the first three hours, and the silence had been a balm to the wounds inflicted by the last several years of stress and schedules and spaghetti on Tuesdays. Now here she stood. In Denver. With Lucy. No kids for ten blissful days.

She couldn't believe how elated that made her feel, and at the same time, the elation prompted a needle of guilt. Surely other mothers weren't giddy at the prospect of being without their children, were they?

She shoved away the disturbing question. She hadn't had private time with her friends in years, and she was going to indulge, guilt free. She deserved this time, darn it. For the first time in years, she felt not like a wife or a mother, but like a woman. Whole and rich and ripe. They pulled apart, and Annette smiled up at her best friend. "Goodness, it's great to see the real you and not just your screen name."

"You, too, hon. I thought you'd never get here."

"Colorado Springs to Denver was the worst stretch. The traffic, man-oh-man." Annette eased her neck side-to-side, grateful to be out of the van. She took a deep breath of the Denver summer air, which had always smelled like fruit to her, and noted the birds chirping in the Russian olive tree at the side of Lucy's house. The whole experience made her want to spin around in a circle, soaking it in. No time for that, though. Mercy and Cris had arrived yesterday, and she wanted all the dirty details. She leaned against the porch railing. "Okay, enough small talk. Elaborate on the not-killing-each-other story. I worried about those two the whole trip."

Lucy shook her head, her messy wad of a ponytail swinging side-to-side. She wore cut-off DPD sweatpants and a tank top that accentuated her strong shoulders and toned arms. She looked like a perfect caricature of herself. And she looked about twenty-five years old, too. "Well, let me put it this way. No one's drawn first blood, but it was deadly tense from the moment Cris walked into the bar last night." Lucy pressed her palms to her temples. "And both of them were drinking like fish."

"Eh, don't worry about that. They're women of the world, you know." Annette shrugged matter-of-factly. "Women of the world have cocktails."

"Cris was doing tequila shots, not sipping mint juleps."

"Oh. Uh-oh." Annette pulled a face. "Then this is probably an inappropriate time to bring up the fact that I could sure use a glass or two of wine myself."

"I'll definitely join you in that. A nice *relaxing* time with a friend. What a novelty." Lucy rolled her eyes, then twisted her mouth to the side. "The way these two are acting, you're probably going to be running interference between them all week long."

"Like hell I am." A rush of stubborn rebellion and simultaneous shame over her outburst suffused Annette's skin with heat. Her mother had always taught her that swearing was the language of the ignorant, and she agreed. She never swore, not even when she jammed a toe or bent back a fingernail.

Lucy looked startled by the outburst, too. "When did you start cussing like a sailor?"

"I don't cuss."

"Just did."

"That was a fluke, and I only said the H-word anyway." Annette picked up her suitcase and set her jaw, leveling a resolute gaze at her friend. "But the point is, I run interference between five girls and a husband every day of my life. I'm here for you and a much needed break from reality. Mercy and Cris are grown women—"

"One would think."

"They *are.* And life is hard, but you know what?" Annette squared her shoulders. "It's hard for all of us. Suck it up."

"Damn, girl." Lucy pulled back her chin, but Annette could see the approval sparkling in her eyes. It strengthened her. "And they say I'm a hard-ass. You make me proud."

Annette flushed with pleasure. "I say we let them have at it, Luce. God knows, I love them both and I love you, but they're not my responsibility. I'm sick to death of being the sane, dependable one. The one who makes everything better."

Grinning, Lucy took the suitcase from Annette, then hooked arms with her and steered her over the threshold. "Know what? You're absolutely right. You've earned a little insanity. Maybe this way, Mercy and Cris will finally be forced to work out their differences."

"What *are* their differences, anyway?"

Lucy shrugged. "No one really knows."

"Mercy knows," Annette said sagely. "Poor thing."

Lucy shot her a sharp glance. "You know something I don't?"

"Of course not. Mercy and I don't talk privately. Be real." She looked at Lucy like the woman was nuts. "The two of us couldn't be more different if we tried. We're almost a different species. But it's obvious. Cris is bewildered by the whole thing—"

"Cris is bewildered by life."

"Perhaps, but that's a whole 'nuther Oprah show." Annette shook her head. "As far as the two of them go, Mercy is the one with all that simmering anger beneath the surface."

Lucy angled her head, seeming to consider this. "Good point. You're pretty astute."

"Of course I am. I have five girls."

"Well then, if you're right, I guess it's up to Mercy to come out with it or get over it. And if I know Mercedes, she won't do it till she's damn good and ready." She sighed with weary amusement.

"Poor Mercy." A cloak of sadness settled over Annette's shoulders. She hated to see anyone hurting, and Mercy had been hurting longer than anyone she knew. But Annette couldn't fix this. Wouldn't even try. Heck, she couldn't find a remedy for her own crazy life. She certainly didn't have the energy to worry about anyone else's. "If only she'd realize what an amazing, inspiring woman she is to all of us."

"Yeah, well. You'd think that would be a foregone conclusion."

Lucy headed toward the hardwood staircase that led to her second floor. "She's beautiful and successful—"

"Sometimes knowing your own worth isn't that easy."

"Spoken from experience?" Lucy cast Annette a sidelong glance. "I meant to mention, you sounded a little stressed out the other night on the phone."

"Just making an observation," Annette lied. No way would she lay her problems on Lucy before the wedding. "And I'm always stressed out, FYI. It's part of my mama job description—the part no one tells you before you get pregnant."

"Well then, let me show you to the guest room. I want you all to myself for a while, but you're probably tired from the drive and everything else, yeah?"

"Exhausted. And I smell like an inmate. I need a shower. No, a bubble bath." God, that sounded like heaven. The surge of pleasure at the mere thought of a long, uninterrupted soak felt vaguely sexual. "But after that, you and me, on the porch with a bottle of wine."

"Deal. The wine's already breathing."

"God bless you."

They headed up the stairs toward the second level, Lucy first, carrying the suitcase, and Annette behind her stretching her stiff lower back. She glanced around, trying to absorb the moment, to store it away like a private elixir she could sip when things got crazy in the real world. The distinctive spicy wood-polish and clean dog smell of Lucy's house imbued her with calm. The creak of the stairs. Everything. If only she could hide out here forever. Gosh, what she wished for. She should be ashamed. Frankly, she was lucky to be here now.

She blinked up at Lucy's back. "Listen, I really appreciate you letting me stay here for a few days." She suffered a little bite of shame for having to take charity, so to speak. "We couldn't swing the hotel for more than a couple nights, especially with me coming early, though I'm glad I could."

"Me, too."

"But, gosh, kids are expensive. You have no idea. I just wish I didn't have to burden you, especially now."

"Stop apologizing. It's no burden; are you kidding? You're always welcome here, Annette, and you don't have to explain."

"I know." She hesitated and bit her lip. "But . . . well, did the other two feel slighted having to pay for their rooms?"

Lucy barked out a laugh. "Need I remind you, Mercy and Cris are both loaded? They thrive on luxury and twenty-four-hour room service. They didn't blink an eye."

"Okay, well, good. No room service here?"

"Nope. But unlimited access to the fridge."

"Excellent," Annette joked. "My kind of pre-wedding joint."

Lucy shuddered involuntarily, set the luggage down, then turned to face Annette. "Oh yeah. One more thing. I don't want to talk about the wedding."

"Lucy, that's what we're here for!"

"Just for a while. Okay?"

Annette studied her for one long moment, then held up a scolding finger. "Only for this evening, and only because I love you." She grabbed Lucy's elbow and held her there so she couldn't turn away. "But Ruben and this marriage are the best thing to ever happen to you, and I'm not going to let you deny or forget it no matter what your neuroses are."

Lucy embraced her friend tightly again. "I do need you here to get me through this. And I do want to get through it. I do. I love him so much. It's just this goddamned curse—" Her voice caught.

"I know, Luce. Forget the curse. The curse doesn't exist."

"I'm trying, but if history is any indication . . ." Lucy sighed and shook it off. "Never mind. I don't want to get into it. You're the best. You know that?"

"Duh," Annette said. With a grin on her face, she pulled away and made shooing motions with her hands. "Now, be gone, and let me lounge in the bathtub like the lady of leisure I'm not. I swear I haven't lounged in a tub since 1989."

"If you think a mere bath is luxurious, wait until you see what Mercedes planned in lieu of the bachelorette shower."

"What?"

"A full-treatment spa day for all of us."

Annette gasped. "Shut up. My heart can't take it."

Lucy laughed. "I know. Can you imagine?"

"I can't. One step at a time, starting with this bath. I have a wine date with my best friend in exactly one hour."

"Dress is casual," Lucy quipped, indicating her own ensemble with a flick of her hand.

"Like I'd have it any other way. Although I'm dying to strut around in that Serafina sheath you chose for us for the event-which-will-remain-unmentioned."

"You just mentioned it!" Lucy cringed.

"No, I didn't. But have you seen those gowns?" She fluttered her eyes and inhaled dramatically. "They're gorgeous!"

"Ah! No wedding talk."

Annette clicked her tongue. "You're impossible. Get out. Go make yourself useful and slice some cheese or something to go with our wine."

Lucy lifted her fingers to her lips and blew Annette a kiss. As Annette closed the guest room door, a smile lifting her lips, she felt like she'd finally arrived in a safe, loving place. A best friend's embrace was infinitely different than the love of family or the commitment of marriage. Not better, just different. She adored Randy with all her heart, and nothing would ever change that. But being here with Lucy made her more easily comprehend Deborah's love for Alex. She'd never even contemplated such thoughts in relation to her friends, but this thing with Deborah was opening her eyes. And it didn't bewilder or disappoint her, Deborah's love for another woman. Right now, it made a philosophical kind of sense to her. Woman power. Gotta love it.

Chapter Eight

Annette marveled at Mercedes's generous spa day gift to all of them. After all these years apart, the forced, intimate proximity had been a brilliant icebreaker. They'd indulged in mud baths, facials, manicures, pedicures, massages, waxing, and she found it gratifying that they seemed to be warming up to one another. Now everyone wanted to head into the hot spring caves for some mineral soaking—everyone except Annette herself, that is. She had never been so pampered in her life, and she'd loved every last minute of it, but she was feeling a little iffy about the nude only, gender-divided hot springs. Her heart pounded, leaving her shaky and off-kilter.

Mercedes and Lucy had killer bodies, untouched by the torments of childbirth and honed into perfection by regular workouts. Cristina had birthed two children, but so what? She had a personal trainer and unlimited funds. Annette would bet money the former beauty queen's frame wouldn't show a mark. She, on the other hand, had given birth to five children, with above average weight gain during the first two pregnancies and twins for the final hurrah. Sure, she'd slimmed down to a curvy shape that looked fine enough in clothing, but naked her body was a stretched out, tired version of its former glory. She felt self-conscious, bottom line. No one except Randy had seen her in the buff for years and she wanted to keep it that way.

"Come on, Annette," said Lucy. As she twisted her long hair into a messy spray and secured it with a claw clip, she met Annette's eyes in the mirror. "Get a move on, girl."

Annette curled her hands around the edges of the bench and squeezed. She pasted on what she hoped wasn't too fake a smile and glanced up at her three friends wrapped in the plush beige towels provided by the spa. In the breeziest tone she could manage, she said, "You know, I think I'm going to skip the mineral caves."

"What?" Cristina looked incredulous. "Oh, you can't! It's the best part."

"Very Zen," Mercedes added.

Annette glanced over toward Lucy's reflection in the mirror, above a makeup counter that ran the length of the room, only to find her friend's intent gaze narrowed. Their eyes locked for several tense moments before Annette let hers slide away. She swallowed tightly, knowing Lucy could read right through her. She'd always been able to do so.

Lucy exhaled and turned from the mirror to face her, arms crossed beneath the knot in her towel wrap. "Okay, what's up, Annette? Spill it."

Annette's shoulders slumped. She ran shaky fingers through her hair, lank from the steam and facial. Finally she lifted her chin and sniffed. "If you must know, I'm intimidated to be naked in front of you three temples of bodily perfection."

"Are you nuts?" She and Lucy stared at each other for a moment before Lucy dropped her towel and turned around. She pointed at her ass, addressing Annette over her shoulder. "Look at the hail damage in these cheeks, sister. There is no perfection. We're women. Women have imperfections, and that's what makes us all unique and beautiful. Real-life women don't have the luxury of being airbrushed like magazine models."

Annette laughed. True enough, Lucy's body was perfectly shaped and sleekly muscular, but her skin wasn't the model-smooth expanse Annette had feared. Still, her flaws were so minimal. She didn't have stretch marks or sags or—ugh. "I don't know."

Cristina dropped her towel and pointed at her boobs, high and round and perfect. "Perfection?"

"Uh, yeah. Complete perfection," Annette said, wanting to stare and not wanting to stare at the same time. What exactly was the protocol when someone was showing you her breasts?

"Yeah, well, not really, because they're fake. I like them in clothes, but they don't even move when I lie on my back." She crinkled her nose. "It's sort of . . . distressing. If you want the truth, I wish I had kept the ones God gave me."

"At least they don't point at your feet."

"At least yours point somewhere," Mercy said, dropping her own towel. "I'm flat. See?" She looked at Annette. "But who cares? You have to love the body you're given."

Annette took note. Mercedes wasn't exactly flat, but she was quite small. Still, the rest of her body was exquisite, and even her breasts were lovely, in a proud Kate Hudson I-don't-need-huge-knockers-to-be-gorgeous kind of way.

They really were all so close to perfect, and she was so, so very far on the opposite end of the spectrum. But, she appreciated what they were trying to do for her. "You women are stone crazy," she said, her eyes misting. She looked from one naked, smiling friend to the other. When she got to Mercy, her startled gaze dropped to the trim, narrow patch of black pubic hair about an inch wide, running straight up the center.

"Wow," Annette exclaimed, unable to keep it in. She looked sheepishly up at Mercedes's face, then pointed. "I'm sorry. Do you grow that way?" She'd never seen anything like it.

Mercedes laughed, an unfamiliar sound to all of them. "God no, girl. It's called a Brazilian. It's a wax job. You could've gotten one today if you wanted."

Annette balked. "There are no drugs strong enough for me to put myself in the position of getting that part of my body waxed, thank you very much." The eyebrow wax had been painful enough. "But I'm impressed. I mean . . . it looks good." She flipped her hand, realizing the absurdity of their conversation. "Not that a person should really compliment another person on her pubes, I guess, friends or not."

"I don't mind." Mercedes turned and scrutinized her body in the full-length mirror, then squared her shoulders. Her expression turned sour. "You know, I used to go natural until one night during a so-called romantic interlude, Damian told me it looked like I had Buckwheat in a scissorlock."

"That's horrid!" Lucy exclaimed, before busting into laughter. "But kind of funny."

The other three women joined her.

Mercy smirked. "His bluntness was one of his charms, actually. *Was* being the key word in that statement." She sighed. "I hate to admit I caved, but I decided, after his lovely comment, perhaps some shaping up was in order."

"I probably would've done the same," Cristina said softly.

Mercedes peered over at her sharply, clearly surprised that Cristina would agree with her about anything. She didn't comment, though. Instead, she turned to Annette. "I'm thinking of going back to natural. Screw Damian. It never bothered me until the Buckwheat crack, and it's much less work."

"I'm so out of the loop, I didn't know there was anything *but* natural," said Annette, still marveling at the tidy little strip. She turned her attention to Lucy who had rewrapped her towel around her waist. "Are you Brazilian, too?"

"I'm Chicana, baby." Lucy winked.

"You know what I mean, smart alek."

"I do. And nope. Natural. I did shave once completely as a treat for Ruben. He likes it better this way, though. And, damn, the growing out process was a bitch. There are just some places on the human body that shouldn't have stubble."

Annette blinked twice, then looked at Cristina. She'd covered up again, too. Only Mercedes remained boldly uncovered. "What about you?"

"I've had both. Hell, I've had it waxed into a heart shape and dyed Elmo red, but that was a special treat for Valentine's Day." She smiled. "Right now, I'm natural but bikini waxed and trimmed short. It's just my preference, but they all look fine. Face it, the female bod is a beautiful thing."

Mercedes spread her arms in disbelief. "We're standing here discussing pubic hair grooming at length, for God's sake, and we're not even drinking. Let's go to the hot springs. All of us." She pointed a finger at Annette. "You have brought five beautiful girls into the world and you look fantastic. Be proud of your body. You've earned whatever marks you might have and none of us care. Shame on you for thinking otherwise."

Lucy reached out and squeezed Mercy's hand. Lucy, always the mediator, always the one to provide kudos. "She's right," Lucy said to Annette. "You look wonderful. If I'd birthed five kids, I'm sure I'd be big as a house."

"Yeah, right, six-pack ab queen," Cristina muttered.

Lucy flicked her a quick grin before refocusing on Annette. "Look, bottom line is, we're friends. We aren't here to judge each other's bodies."

Annette tightened her towel above her chest and quirked her mouth to the right. "I have pretty bad stretch marks."

"Didn't you hear what Mercy said? You've earned them. *We've* earned them," Cristina added, opening her towel once again. Annette glanced at Cristina's flat stomach and noticed, for the first time, the telltale silvery striations. Seeing them eased her tension. "You're a mommy," Cristina continued. "Be proud. I admit, sometimes when I look down I am less than pleased with the marks, but then I remember Cassandra and Manuel, and it's all okay. The marks were worth it."

Annette hesitated, chewing on her bottom lip before standing up. She was nervous, but what the heck? They loved her. She knew now she could look like Jabba the Hut and they'd still love her, but the bright side was, she didn't resemble Jabba in the least. In fact, for an almost-forty mother of five, she looked better than average. She had nothing to hide. "Know what?" She ripped the towel off with flourish, dropping it to the floor. "You're right. I won't be ashamed of being a woman or a mother, no matter what that's done to my body."

Mercedes, Cristina, and Lucy clapped and cheered as Annette strutted around the small locker room. It was the first time since they'd all been together that Annette felt the strength of connection among them, and it imbued her with hope. Perhaps physical nakedness was the first step. Eventually, if they worked hard enough at rebuilding their trust in one another, they might be able to be emotionally naked, too. It was only natural that it would take a little time. For goodness sake, except for each of them seeing Lucy separately on various occasions, the four of them, as a group, had been apart for two decades.

A lot of time. A lot of changes.

But every moment they spent together, Annette had more hope that things would work out just as they were meant to. The *girls* together again. All for one and one for all—*even* Mercedes and Cristina.

Chapter Nine

A few hours later, limp and relaxed from their day of pampering, the four women filed into a high-backed wooden booth on the grill side of the Elk Bugle Bar & Grill and ordered a round of local microbrew on tap.

Cristina looked around. The place was a dive, but it had a certain mountain charm, and she was glad Lucy had suggested it. She felt infinitely calmer after their day of bonding—especially after the thing with Annette. It didn't hurt that she and Mercy were conforming to an unspoken pact to avoid each other. Whatever. It worked for her. In any case, she hadn't heard a peep from San Antonio, Lucy had begun to talk about the wedding, which was a fantastic sign, and—Cristina spread her hands out on the slightly sticky table and studied them—the bruises on her wrists had faded to a lighter plumish red color. She would still have to use the Dermablend makeup she'd purchased for the wedding, thanks to the strapless gowns Lucy had chosen for them, but that wasn't a problem. She sat back and, for the first time in days, truly relaxed. Well . . . truly relaxed considering she'd most likely decimated whatever credibility she'd had back home.

The really interesting thing was that she hadn't felt that urge to go for a little five-finger discount since she'd been here. Sure, some of it was probably due to the reality smackdown from the arrest. Just being around her friends, even Mercedes, made her aware of the blood coursing through her veins, her heart pumping. It made her aware of herself in a way she hadn't been for a very long time. She felt real—finally. Real and valid and accepted.

But . . . Zach would find out about her arrest, probably sooner than later. She couldn't just smile through this incident, like she'd done through every bad spell in their entire marriage. This particular fuckup would have to be faced head-on, and she simply wasn't ready. She just wanted to spend time with her oblivious friends, pretend her life was as perfect as they all thought it was, and focus on Lucy.

Was that so wrong?

The restaurant smelled of grilling meat and hops, and eighties hairband rock filtered over from the bar. "This place is cozy and down to earth," she offered, pushing the thought of her arrest and the ugliness that was sure to result out of her mind. "I like it."

"Oh, good." Lucy grinned first at her, then at Mercy. "I was afraid it would be too low down for you fast-track babes."

Cristina scoffed. "Believe me, fast track gets old."

"I'll bet, not that I'd know. Not that I want to know." Lucy peered around fondly. "Frankly, this is one of my favorite hideouts. I always thought this would be a great place to come if you wanted to be totally alone. I mean, these booths are so high, no one can even see you. Very intimate. Not to mention"—she pointed across the expansive passthrough bar that separated the restaurant from the bar half of the establishment. The bar held a slapdash array of flooring and ceiling finishes, mismatched tables, battered chairs, dusty neon beer lights, and an eclectic jukebox mix—"you can't beat that side for well-priced drinks," Lucy finished. "And they don't skimp on alcohol. How often can you say that about a bar?"

"My kind of joint," Mercedes said.

Without makeup, and with her hair softly waving from the hot springs, Cristina thought Mercedes looked far less intimidating. More like the girl she'd been in high school, when they used to spend hours on the telephone just chatting and giggling. A wave of painful regret seized her, and she looked away. Why did Mercedes hate her so much? What had she done? And why hadn't their friendship meant enough to Mercy for her to talk about it? Painful bitterness crested inside her. How could she have just thrown it away like it meant nothing?

"How'd you find it?" Mercy asked Lucy.

"Ruben and I spend a lot of time at Little Bear down the street. It's a combination biker/local hangout with great live music, and you know Ruben and his Harley."

"Lucky girl," Mercy said in a droll tone. "We've all heard of Little Bear. Hello, we used to live here."

"Oh yeah. Sorry." Lucy looked chagrined. Little Bear *was* renowned in Colorado, after all. "Anyway, both Little Bear and this place have fun, weird crowds. We dig that."

"Speaking of fun, weird crowds," Mercy said, "how have we managed to avoid your mother and the rest of the Olivera family tree so far? Did you whack them all after that shower? I'm sure you cops know all the great locales to dump bodies."

"I thought about it, but the prospect of forty years in the Florissant women's prison gave me pause." Lucy tapped her beer glass with both sets of fingers. "Truthfully, I told my mom I'd call off the wedding if they didn't give me a few days alone with my friends. I think she got the hint. After the assault of that shower, she knew I was at my wit's end."

"But she'll be there for the getting ready part, right?" Annette asked, looking worried. "I'd be crushed if any of my daughters excluded me from that."

"Mama will be there, but not all the stepmoms, aunts, etcetera. I can't deal. That's what I have you three for. Sanity."

"Boy, you have an odd sense of who's sane and who's not," Cristina said. "And, forgive me for saying this, but I'm looking forward to partying with the Oliveras." She tossed a look of apology at Lucy. "Your family might have their quirks, but they're so colorful. Anything is better than one staid charity function after another with uptight society types who are more interested in the designer who created your gown than who you are inside, believe me. I'm ready for some excitement."

"Or a PTA function," added Annette. "Those get old. I'm looking forward to seeing the family, too. Sorry, Luce."

"Or a publishing party." A secretive smile touched Mercy's lips. "Although . . . those can get a tad wild and crazy if you hang with the right group." She raised her glass in a private little salute before sipping the brew. "But I'm with these two one hundred percent. Bring on the Oliveras."

Lucy shook her head, looking rueful. "Well, I'm glad you're all such fans of my family—traitors. But that's fine. You can run a screen for me at the wedding." She opened the large plastic-covered menu decisively. "However, this is supposed to be a relaxing day, and talking about my family does not relax me. What do you say we order some food and cut the Olivera talk for a bit, yeah?"

Just then a cell phone pealed. All four women dug in their bags. Cristina stared at the front of hers and felt the blood drain from her face. Everything around her went black, her vision pinpointed on the LCD caller ID display. She squeezed the phone tighter. Zach. From the television station. He rarely called her from work unless it was an emergency. Oh, God. Against her will, she started to shake.

It could be nothing.

It could be the beginning of the end.

Either way, she just wasn't ready to confront him.

She switched the phone off in mid-ring, stuffed it back into her bag, then looked up to find all three friends staring at her with curiosity written all over their faces. *Shit.*

She flipped her hand, trying for casual, but damnit if her voice didn't shake, too. "It was me."

"Yeah, we know," Lucy said gently. "You turned the phone off. After losing all color in your face, I might add."

Cristina could feel the blood pounding hot and hard through her veins. "I-it was just Zach. I'll talk to him later."

"Go ahead and call him back," Lucy suggested, a small line of worry bisecting her brows. "We seriously don't mind, Cris."

"No." The single word rang out, sharp and cutting, like a bullet fired into the room. She attempted to soften the reaction with a tremulous smile. "We talked earlier," she lied, feeling terrible for doing so. "I'm sure it's nothing. Besides, I don't take cell phone calls during meals." God, she was the queen of avoidance. And weak. She knew Zach deserved to hear about her run-in with the law directly, but she simply couldn't face it yet. Zach had never openly agreed with his mother's low opinion of her, but he'd never stood up for her to the woman, either. God, she didn't want to prove that shrew right.

The friends exchanged surreptitious glances before turning back to their menus. A thick, tense silence ensued, and Cristina knew they'd filed away her reaction as further evidence that Zach was some sort of abusive monster. She could see she'd eventually have to set them straight, but not until Lucy was safely past the "I dos." Not until she found her nerve.

If she ever found her nerve . . .

Exposing her ugly underbelly to Mercedes, of all people, held very little appeal. No doubt Mercy would be thrilled to learn her life wasn't so picture-perfect after all. "So," she said, falsely bright, desperate to get past this close call with reality and hide in the cocoon of denial, at least for a few more days. "What's everyone having?"

About fifteen minutes into their meal, Lucy's phone rang. A quick smile touched her lips. "Ooh, I bet it's my honey."

Lucy absolutely radiated love as she answered the phone. Mercedes wondered, with a pang of wistful envy, if she would ever feel that way about a man.

"Hello?" Lucy paused, listening. Her sunny, expectant expression changed completely, then her brow furrowed. "Uh-huh. Really? Okay, Mama. Listen, I have another call coming through, yeah? I'll tell her. Bye-bye."

Lucy disconnected and answered the second call immediately. "Hello?" This time, her smile reached two-hundred-watt levels. "Hey, baby," she practically purred. Again a pause. Again her forehead creased with worry. "You're kidding? Okay, I'll pass it on. Yeah. Yeah. I'll talk to you later. Hey, quickly, how are my dogs?" Lucy and Ruben went on talking.

Just then, Annette's cell phone rang. "Wow, I feel like we're working the Channel Six auction." She flipped open the front. "Hello?" A pause. "Hi, honey. How are the . . . what?" She listened for a few moments, her face growing solemn. Her eyes darted to Cristina's face, then away, and she reached up to tuck a lock of hair behind her ear. "Okay, I hear you. Listen, I'll call you back tonight, okay? *Bueno,* bye."

Annette and Lucy ended their calls simultaneously, both of them staring gravely at Cristina, whose face had gone pinched and pale. Mercedes looked on with morbid curiosity.

Lucy spoke first, her tone soft but almost reproachful. "Cristina, I don't know what's going on and I'm not going to press you about it. But Zach called both Ruben and my mother looking for you. He wants you to call. Now."

"And Randy," added Annette, her voice sympathetic. "Zach called Randy, too. He assured him it wasn't about the kids, though. Nothing has happened to the kids. And he's at the station, so call him there."

Mercedes sat back and soaked this all in, unsure what to make of it. Cristina was far from her favorite person in the world—no big news flash there—but if Zach was mistreating her, Mercedes would have his rich ass. She'd helplessly watched one of her stepfathers smack her mother around years ago, and that had fueled her absolute intolerance of domestic abuse.

She hated abusers.

She couldn't be a hundred percent sure, but Cristina bore a lot of the classic characteristics of a battered woman. She was jumpy, quiet, pensive. She made excuses for her bruises and shied away from anything but the most surfacy conversations about her life. Some of the signs didn't fit, but what other explanation could there be?

Cristina sighed, then scooted out of the booth. She held up her cell phone, waggling it. "I'll just go call him then, okay? Stop looking worried, all of you. My goodness, I can't imagine what's so important." Her laugh was tinged with mania, Mercy thought, her instincts on full alert. She was faking this. "You guys enjoy your dinners."

Mercedes, seated at the outside edge of the booth, surreptitiously watched Cristina head toward the nook that housed the bathrooms and a pay telephone. Curiouser still, Cristina glanced around guiltily, stuffed her cell phone into her purse, pulled a card out of her wallet, then picked up the pay phone.

Why would she use a pay phone when she had a cell?

Mercedes had to know.

Pressing her hand to her stomach, she took in a deep breath and blew it out. "Phew, this beer is going right through me. I'm going to run to the bathroom. Be right back." She slid out of the booth and split before Lucy or Annette did the woman thing and offered to accompany her for a communal pee.

Careful to stay out of Cristina's line of vision, Mercedes skulked toward the rear of the restaurant, then stood with her back against the wall, just around the corner outside the phone nook. Cristina was still punching in the zillion calling card digits. Finally she finished, clearing her throat twice as she waited for the call to go through.

It seemed like a long wait to Mercedes, but probably twenty seconds or less had elapsed. Suddenly Cristina began talking, in a falsely cheery voice that didn't sound anything like her own. "Zach, hi. Sorry I missed you, honey. The girls told me to call you at home. Guess that was wrong and you're still at the station, but you'll get this soon."

A lie, Mercy realized. Her tension heightened.

"I'm sorry I haven't called before now. Things have been really crazy with the wedding preparations."

Another lie. Hadn't Cristina told them all that she and Zach had recently talked? What the hell?

"Anyway, my cell phone is dead, but I'll charge it when we get to the hotel and give you a jingle back."

Okay, lie number three. Mercedes had watched Cristina switch her cell phone off. They all had. Damn, the woman *really* didn't want to talk to her husband. She'd sounded friendly enough, but maybe she was trying to keep the peace.

"Kiss Bruja for me, okay?" Cristina continued, in that canned happy-wife voice. "I'll talk to you later, Zach. Everything's fine, and I love you."

Mercedes heard the phone hang up, listened to Cristina's long, tense exhalation of breath, and then turned the corner, arms crossed. Enough. This confrontation would take place *now*. If Cristina was in a dangerous situation, she needed someone to shake some sense into her, and since the other two seemed all about sympathy and space, it was up to her to be the bad guy.

Cristina swiveled from the phone and gasped, faltering in her steps. She reached out and grabbed the edge of the wall, for a moment looking truly trapped. "Mercedes, what are you doing?"

"I think that's my line." Her eyes traced the look of panic on Cristina's perfect face, and a well of age-old hostility bubbled up inside her. It was tempered, however, by sincere worry about this woman. Her nemesis, sure, but a person, nonetheless, who didn't deserve to get pounded on. No one did. "I heard your conversation. You lied to your husband three times. Either that, or you're lying to all of us. Maybe both?"

They stood in tense silence, staring at each other.

Cristina's lips shook slightly as her eyes widened with incredulity. "How dare you?" she rasped finally. Her chest flamed a mottled red, and her hands trembled like an addict in need of a fix. "You had no right to eavesdrop on my call."

"I suppose you wouldn't believe me if I told you I care?"

Cristina barked a humorless laugh. "Spare me."

Mercedes implored her, "Cris, what the hell is going on?"

In a move that surprised Mercedes, Cristina stepped forward, confronting her straight on. She stood inches from Mercedes's face, eyes narrowed, fists rigid at her sides. "Look, I know what you think—"

"*What* do I think?" Mercedes demanded.

"That Zach is beating me."

"Is he?"

"No, goddamnit. *No.*" She clenched her jaw and shook her head as if to clear it. "Mercy, let me make this very simple and succinct. Zach has never and would never raise a hand to me or the kids. That is not what this is about."

"Then what? What is it about? What about the bruises?"

"I told you—"

"You told us a lie."

"Jesus!" Cristina released a little angry laugh as she spun away and then back again. "It's none of your goddamned business. Okay? We are here to help Lucy make it through the wedding. Period. Believe me, even if I wanted to talk about my life, which I *don't,* I sure as hell wouldn't bare my soul to you."

It made perfect sense; they weren't friends, after all. Not anymore. And yet hearing the words was like a boot to Mercedes's gut. Deep down, she'd always wondered if she had ever mattered to Cristina at all. Inside, she staggered from the blow, but she recovered quickly enough. It didn't matter what Cristina thought of her. It only mattered that she got help. "Your friends are worried, you know?"

"Oh, yeah? Does that include you?" Cristina snapped. Her eyes blazed with a mixture of rage and vulnerability that made Mercedes unexpectedly feel like shit.

She stared into them for a moment, then looked away.

Cristina huffed in disgust. "I'm going to say it one more time, Mercedes, and never again. My life is *my life.* You don't care. You never have. Hell, you'd probably throw a little party in your room if Zach was kicking my ass—"

"That's not true!"

Cristina raised a finger. "I want you off my back. Got it? We were doing fine ignoring each other, so just ignore me. You've had twenty years of practice at that, *friend.*" She spat the last word. "It shouldn't be too much of a stretch."

Mercedes held up both hands. "Okay, you know what? I give. You win." She'd imagined, perhaps, that their group bonding at the spa might launch some sort of benevolent truce between her and Cristina, at least long enough to get through the wedding. Fat chance, and what the hell did she want a truce for anyway? Lowering her tone, she couldn't help herself from adding, "But, you saw how my stepfather treated my mother, Cris. You were there. You were the *only* one who was there. You know how I feel about men who—"

"I don't need your hollow concern, and I don't appreciate your assumptions or your spying." Cris flicked her hand out angrily. "Zach and I are not your mother and stepfather. Just focus on Lucy, okay? She's the only one you ever really cared about anyway. Other than yourself, that is. So, do us both a favor and back the fuck off." Cristina brushed past her, knocking shoulders, and headed to the table with sharp, angry strides.

Mercedes released a long breath and closed her eyes. She could feel her pulse hard and fast in her temples, the adrenaline leaving her shaky and off-kilter. So. That had gone well. Granted, she would've ripped Cristina a new asshole had she busted her eavesdropping on one of *her* conversations. She supposed she deserved Cristina's wrath. Still, though she'd be hard-pressed to convince anyone, she really, truly had been trying to help, despite believing that most altruistic bullshit was for the birds. No one appreciated it.

Inside, she fought to harden her emotions into a cold stone. If the woman wanted Mercy out of her face, she was officially the hell out. What did she care about the mysteries in Cristina Trevino Aragon's undoubtedly fucked-up life? Didn't she have enough to worry about with her own fucked-up life?

Oh, God.

All of a sudden, she felt seized by emptiness and completely, horribly alone. *Focus on Lucy,* Cristina had said. *She's the only one you ever cared about, other than yourself, that is.*

A wholeheartedly unexpected burn of unshed tears made Mercedes clamp her lips together to stop her chin from wobbling. It was true.

She'd pushed everyone away for twenty years. Hurt them before they had the chance to hurt her had been her motto. Now, facing the most frightening career crisis of her life, Mercedes had no one. She couldn't burden Lucy, she was too ashamed to confide in Annette. And Cristina? Well, she supposed the hate was mutual. It's not like any of this was a surprise, so why did it have her so rattled?

Okay. She knew. She was scared.

Scared to lose her career. Scared to face the fact that the tabloid stories would be mostly true. Scared to look at herself in the mirror every morning and admit that she'd done her goddamn best to erect an unbreachable stone fortress around her heart. And it had worked. No one breached it.

No one wanted to.

Because the only resident was an emotionally void ice princess who was damn near impossible to trust or love.

God, she'd made a mess of things.

She hadn't imagined the trip to Denver would be like this, that she'd feel a pull to rekindle a few friendships, mend a few fences, hold on to something, for once, that was real. But now, here she was. Alone. And it felt like shit. You could only push people away so far before they simply . . . left forever.

Mercedes straightened her back and rolled the tension out of her shoulders. Deep breath in . . . and centered. She needed to control this unwanted watershed of emotion. She turned toward the dining area and worked on getting her head straight and her mind clear before rejoining the others. Cristina hated her.

Good. Fine. Fuck it.

Didn't she also claim to hate Cristina? She no longer had to worry one whit about the pampered little princess, which was just fine. Never should've bothered in the first place. *Live and learn, eh, Mercedes?* Too bad she never seemed to.

With that problem solved by way of expulsion from the game, her sole purpose for being in Denver became ultra clear and unfettered at last. Lucy.

From here on out, her goal was to get Lucy married off and then get the hell out of Dodge. Where she'd end up was anyone's guess. She supposed it didn't matter anyway as long as it was far, far away from the ugly reminders of her shortcomings.

Anywhere but here or home. She'd hidden before. She could do it again.

Chapter Ten

The day before the wedding, Annette moved from Lucy's house into her room on the fourth floor of the Brown Palace, overlooking the palatial lobby. Lucy could've checked into the Eisenhower suite that day, too, but she wanted to spend one final night at home alone, sleeping in the bed she shared with Ruben, hugging the pillow that held his spicy scent. As afternoon sun slanted in the windows and her mind raced with what-ifs and imagined worst-case scenarios, she was beginning to think staying in the house had been a mistake.

Except for a few forays into panic during the obligatory wedding preparations, Lucy had been able to keep most of the doubt demons at bay, thanks to the emotional insulation of her oldest and dearest friends. But now her house was empty . . . as empty as it would be if Ruben and the dogs were no longer in her life, as a matter of fact. She didn't have Cris, Mercy, or Annette to distract her from the sobering truth: she was getting married tomorrow, for better or, most likely, for worse. What in the hell made her think she'd be the Olivera to break the curse? Bottom line, this was her first marriage, and as much as she tried to pretend otherwise, she *was* an Olivera. She needed to be realistic and face the hard, cold facts.

Olivera first marriages did not last.

Lucy squeezed a pillow over her face and yelled into it. She didn't want to think that way, but couldn't help it. She was due to meet everyone in the Grand Ballroom of the hotel for rehearsal in a few hours, and all she could do was lie on her bed, curled up and shaking, on the verge of terror. Some badass she was. Ha.

The scary truth that nobody knew, was that it wasn't just the curse that had her frightened. She'd never been able to maintain a long-term relationship with a guy, not since . . . well, ever. In high school and college, she'd bolt every time she started to feel tied down. Girls just wanna have fun and all that. After she'd become a cop, the men turned tail and fled once they realized what exactly she did for a living. Why would a woman want to do that? That doesn't seem like a sensible job for a woman.

Yeah. Whatever. Buh-bye.

She'd never found a man secure enough in himself to accept her life choices, indeed to celebrate them.

Until Ruben.

He was the first man ever to take her job in stride. But what if that changed once they were married? Or what if, God forbid, she started to feel tied down and got the itch to leave? What if, love or no love, Lucy Olivera was simply meant to be alone in this life? She was thirty-eight years old and set in her ways. She knew that. Sure, she and Ruben had been successfully cohabitating for the past year, but they weren't *married*. The ugly reality was, they could still be in that goofy, romantic "honeymoon" period that inevitably faded with time. Somehow the M-word seemed to change everything. It even felt different just thinking about it.

God, she didn't want to lose Ruben, but she was buckled with doubts. Coupled with her illustrious family history and the astounding rate of divorce for female cops, which hovered somewhere around ninety percent, it felt like this marriage was all but doomed before it even happened.

Granted, as far as the cop thing went, she worked directly with Ruben. He'd seen her in hair-raising undercover situations and had never balked, had never insulted her by trying to "save" her, never questioned her skills or her professionalism. On the contrary, he seemed to respect the work she did, to know that she was damned capable of handling herself and thinking on her feet. She appreciated that so much. So maybe there wouldn't be an issue surrounding her career. But two facts remained: (1) she bolted whenever she felt penned in, and (2) no Olivera first marriage had ever lasted. Not a single one. Even if she got past all the rest, those issues clung, nagging her, mocking her, making her want to flee while she still had at least a little of her sanity intact.

She groaned, throwing an arm across her eyes. Jesus, why couldn't she have her shit together like her friends all had? She was acting like a total nut job, and she knew it, but she just couldn't shake the fear.

Her phone rang. She rolled over, cringing with trepidation, and looked at the caller ID display. Ruben. Overwhelming desire warred with dread inside her at just seeing his name. With a sigh, she picked up the phone but didn't say anything. She couldn't. She didn't want to disappoint this man whom she loved so much. She kept wondering when he was going to realize that her neuroses made the whole thing so completely not worth it.

For a moment they were both silent. She could hear him breathing, knew the sound so well. She could almost feel *his* breaths being pulled into *her* lungs. Her bottom lip began to tremble, and she clamped it between her teeth to stop it.

"You're gonna show at the rehearsal, right *querida*?" His voice was soft, gentle, understanding. But also worried and ever so slightly vulnerable. Big, tough Ruben, feeling unsure.

She warmed to him immediately because of his small show of defenselessness, despite herself, but it only heightened her anguish. "Of course I'm going to show, silly."

"You okay?"

How to answer that one? Hadn't she bared her soul to him enough? Exposed her faults and issues to a frightening degree? It was his turn to be placated. "I'm a little nervous. It's nothing to get worked up about." Lies, lies, lies.

"One promise I can make, baby girl, is that I will always get worked up over you."

"Stop it. I'm jittery enough already."

"I will never stop it. I'll never stop telling you."

He sounded so earnest, so compassionate and passionate, it choked her up. "Or showing me?"

"That either."

Lucy squeezed her eyes shut until tears pushed out the corners and trickled down her temples into her ears. Jesus Christ, how could she go through with marrying this wonderful man? How could she risk it? She loved him way too much to take the chance of losing him.

Why couldn't anyone else—not even her best, oldest friends—see the clarity of that point?

The rehearsal need only include the wedding party, but the entire Olivera clan had showed up to sit in the "audience" like it was some sort of monster truck rally that couldn't be missed. Mercedes could swear she smelled popcorn, and she'd witnessed the passing of Red Vines in several of the rows. She smirked as she looked out into the sea of faces, loving the spectacle of it. Deep down, she had always wanted to belong to the Olivera family for exactly this reason. They might be complete and total whack jobs, but they were rabid in their love for and support of each other. If she could bottle that, she'd be a billionaire. Her own family consisted of her mother, a weak woman who had subjugated herself to various men over the years in the hope of finding true love, someone to care for her.

Mercy had always wished her mother was strong enough to care for herself, to be an admirable female role model. She loved her mother— no question there. But she'd never wanted to end up like her, letting a man push her around, control her, destroy her. She'd never wanted to expose that vulnerability.

The rehearsal carried on, but Mercedes didn't pay much attention. She knew her part. Walk up the aisle next to some extremely doable cop buddy of Ruben's, smile, stand to the side, and fix Lucy's veil after her father undoubtedly fucked it all up in his attempt to flip it over. What was that about, anyway? Fathers were assigned exactly *one* job in a wedding. Walk the bride up the aisle and lift her veil, and yet they always left the damn thing looking like a wad of used toilet paper on top of the bride's head, and *they didn't seem to notice at all.* Thank God for attendants.

As the pastor provided some cadence and pacing instructions to Lucy during her hike up the aisle, Annette leaned toward Mercedes, pulling Cristina along as she did. Their three heads together, powwow style, Annette lowered her voice to a rasp and spoke out of the corner of her mouth. "Don't know about you guys, but I'm not liking the way Lucy looks right now."

Mercedes studied her friend, halfway down the aisle with her biological father and her stepfather flanking her. Indeed, Lucy looked like Dead Woman Walking. Her skin tone bore a greenish tinge, her lips were pressed together in a harsh line. She didn't glow, unless you counted her eyes, which had that distinctive fight-or-flight gleam to them.

A needle of apprehension pricked Mercedes, and she frowned. She'd thought they had done a good job talking Lucy down during the week, but apparently they still had some work ahead of them. She leaned closer to Annette and Cristina. "Listen, I know she didn't want a bachelorette party, but I think that's because she didn't want to combine alcohol and Oliveras."

"And who can blame her?" Cristina said.

"We are going to have to get that girl tipsy tonight," Mercedes said, grimly. "No two ways about it."

"I agree," said Cristina.

"She is way overthinking this thing, and as long as we can get her mind off the unknowns and onto the fact that Ruben is unbelievably perfect for her"—they all turned in unison and looked at the shockingly hot man standing at the front of the aisle—"we can get her through this."

"You think?" Annette said, biting her bottom lip and looking uncertainly up at Mercedes.

"I know. Believe me, I know."

"I think she's right, Annie," Cristina said. "And tomorrow morning, she'll take two aspirin, put tea bags on her eyes to eliminate the puffiness, don that phenomenal gown of hers, and she'll just know she did the right thing. All her doubts will fade. Ruben is . . ." Cristina sighed, gazing at him.

"Isn't he?" Mercedes added. "I wish there were men that hot in New York City. I mean, there are, but they're all gay."

Annette squeezed her hand. "Okay, operation get-Lucy-plowed is officially underway. I wouldn't advocate it in general—"

"We know."

"—but if she misses out on marrying that man—"

"I couldn't deal," said Mercedes.

"No kidding," added Cris.

"He is perfect. I mean, as perfect as any man can be." Annette sighed. "They're perfect for each other, and that's what matters most. Forget the Olivera curse. I know it can work."

"Yes. As long as we get her to and then through the ceremony," Mercedes whispered. "And, mark my words, that's not going to be a walk in the park."

The morning of the momentous event spun upon them like an F5 tornado, obliterating everything in its path except the seemingly unreachable goal of getting Lucy's psycho, slightly hungover ass to the "I do" part. The drinking idea had worked wonders the night before, but now she was stone-cold sober and bordering on insane. T-minus thirty minutes until go-time, and Lucy wasn't ready to go anywhere . . .

except maybe into a locked, padded room wearing a starched white straitjacket and the hand-knotted string of pearls she'd inherited from her great-great-(step?)-grandmother.

They were preparing for the big ceremony in Mercy's suite. The three of them were already poured into their strapless, midnight blue Serafina sheaths, coifed and made up, but getting Lucy into that gorgeous Badgley Mischka gown was proving to be more difficult than stuffing a fussy, wiggly infant into a pair of tights.

Mercedes checked the clock on the nightstand. They really needed to get this show on the road, but she didn't want to mention that fact and catapult Lucy over the edge. Through the fittings, the rehearsal, the last-minute checks, she had grown exponentially more panicked. Last night at the rehearsal, her doubts had been crystal clear on her face, evident to everyone in the room. But now that she was a certifiable basket case and the wedding was scheduled to commence in mere minutes, none of them was quite sure what to do. Mercedes had to admit, she had some serious doubts whether or not they'd pull this off.

"I can't do it," Lucy said, her voice muffled because Cristina had shoved her head between her knees when she'd started to hyperventilate during attempt number five to slip that gown over her head. The beaded satin lay in a limp pile over one of the leather chairs. "I don't want a divorce. I can't do it."

"You can and you will. And there will be no divorce," Cristina said, in a matter-of-fact tone that would brook no argument. Cris kept a hand pressed gently against Lucy's head to prevent her from sitting back up. Mercedes noticed that Cristina's wrist bruises were virtually undetectable beneath the expertly applied makeup she had used. Obviously she'd had plenty of practice covering the ugliness of her life. "Besides, it's not a divorce, it's a wedding. Now, take slow, deep breaths."

Mercedes rolled her eyes. *Oh, give me a break.* She'd given up on the placating and was sitting at the top of the bed, legs and arms crossed. Screw her dress. This day was about Lucy looking perfect, not her, and a little tough love was in order.

"Maybe a slow, deep shot of bourbon would be more effective at this point," she suggested, in a sarcastic tone. She toyed with the ethical dilemma of strong-arming a woman into marriage, but decided, in this case, it was more than warranted. Ruben was the grand slam, not a booby prize. "How about it, Lucky girl? Want a quick hair of the dog that bit ya?"

Annette, standing near the end of the huge bed, planted her fists on her hips and glared. "Don't be insane. Last night was one thing, but she can't be drunk at her wedding!"

Mercedes pointed at Lucy, raising her brows, as if that said everything. "You have any better ideas? Besides, one shot isn't going to intoxicate the woman. If we don't do something, there isn't going to *be* a wedding."

"No shots. Just . . . give . . . me a minute," Lucy muttered from between her knees. In her strapless bustier, lacy white thong, and thigh-highs, she looked quite ridiculous. The scene would be funny, except that it simply . . . wasn't. She was going to miss her own wedding, thanks to a stupid curse that didn't even exist. "I'm fine. Really. There *will* be a wedding. I'm going to get married. I love him. Oh, God." Lucy shrugged off Cristina's hand, jolted to her feet, and lurched toward the bathroom to toss her cookies—again.

They all listened, cringing.

"I swear, if she pukes on that gown of hers," Cristina said, crossing her arms.

"She won't," Annette said. "She'll be fine."

Mercedes snorted. If that was what fine looked like, she'd hate to witness a full-on mental break. Lucy's fretful mother had finally given up and gone to the Eisenhower suite to assure Ruben that Lucy was almost ready, not to panic. Mercedes was surprised Ruben hadn't said, "To hell with tradition," and stormed the room himself. Come to think of it, didn't they used to tie up reluctant brides in the Old West and marry them off at gunpoint? Ruben had a gun. It was a thought.

They all waited in thick, dubious silence until Lucy returned, pale-faced and shaky. Black mascara was smeared down below her eyes and her lipstick was half off. Plus, her hair had gone askew, as if she were standing against a hurricane-force side wind. She sank onto the end of bed and waited for her breathing to slow, but soon she flopped back and stared glazed-eyed at the ceiling, her chest rising and falling rapidly.

"You're squashing your veil," said Cris gently.

"I don't care. I'm an idiot."

"We know," the three chimed.

"I love him."

"Of course you do," Annette said soothingly as she patted Lucy's knee. "That's why you're going to go through with this wedding and you'll see, everything will turn out perfectly. Look at Cris and me. We're both happily married."

Mercedes couldn't help it. Her gaze immediately cut to Cristina's face to check for a reaction, but she saw none. Well, other than a small, corner-of-the-eye glance in *her* direction and a slight tightening of Cristina's jaw. They hadn't exchanged so much as a single direct word since their blow up at the Elk Bugle, which was fine with Mercedes. Annette and Lucy didn't have an inkling about what had occurred, and they wouldn't, if Mercedes had anything to say about it. But she knew in her gut Cristina had something to hide.

Then again, she thought, so do I.

Hmmm. Sobering concept. Maybe the smartest choice would be to lay off Operation Expose Cristina for a while. If they kept up their current tug-of-war in the dirty laundry basket, her tattered drawers were just as likely as Cristina's to end up splayed out on the floor, crotch up, for everyone to see.

Annette went on, trying to soothe Lucy. With five girls of her own, she really was the expert. Although this speech left a little to be desired—"I mean, sure, you have to face the fact that you're marrying a *man.* He's going to be annoying a lot of the time, but it's in his DNA. He won't mean to be. You and Ruben will be very happy."

Whoo-boy. Mercedes clonked the back of her head against the headboard. Enough of this touchy-feely shit. Her brain was ready to explode from sugarcoat overdose. If she had to kick Lucy's ass all the way across the hotel atrium above Tremont Street to the Grand Ball-room on the other side, she would. This wedding *would* happen, god-damnit. Someone in this miserable hellhole called life deserved to be happy.

Before she resorted to ass-kicking, however, she had another plan, but she needed to get rid of the other two for a few minutes to pull it off. Mercedes stretched her leg down and tapped Lucy's forehead with her toes. "Sit up, Lucky girl. Let's talk about this." Mercy leaned to the side and filled a glass with water from the bedside pitcher. Handing the water to Lucy, she glanced up at Annette. "Annette, do you mind run-ning for some more ice?"

"Not at all." Annette, seeming relieved to have a break, grabbed the ice bucket, and headed out the door.

Without looking at her directly, Mercedes said, "Cristina, why don't you run over to the Grand Ballroom and let them know . . . something. Anything. Maybe tell them the bride is experiencing some last minute jitters and not feeling well. But she'll be there. Let them know where we stand."

Cristina stared at Lucy for a moment, chewing her lip, then looked toward Mercedes. "But she's—"

"Just give me a minute with her," Mercedes said, her tone soft and firm at the same time. "Please."

Cristina shot Mercedes a narrowed gaze, then nodded. She picked up her small beaded bag, spun on her heels, and left.

Alone with Lucy at last, Mercedes breathed a sigh of relief. She could work this out the quick and easy way. She leaned over the side of the bed for her own bag and fished out the small vial of white pills. She didn't want to get Lucy stoned out of her gourd, but the woman needed something to take the edge off, and Mercedes was an expert at that. She knocked two Vicodin tablets into her palm and then sat up. "Come on, Lucky girl. Buck up." Leaning forward, she placed the pills into Lucy's palm. Lucy stared vacantly down at them.

"What's this?"

"Just take them," Mercy said. "Trust me on this one."

"Vicodin?" Lucy asked, studying the pills.

"Yes."

"Why do you have these?"

"I . . . pulled a hamstring in spinning class," Mercedes lied easily. "They're left over from that. Sometimes the leg still gives me pain."

Lucy stared down at the innocent-looking pills a moment longer, then tipped her head back and threw them in her mouth.

"If you can stand it, chew them."

"Are you trying to get me high?" Lucy asked, around a mouthful of pills. She lifted the glass Mercedes had handed her earlier, made a face while she chewed, then washed them down with water.

"I'm trying to get you married, hon. To a man who loves you so much . . . it's actually painful for me to even see you guys together." Her stomach clenched. Nice. Way to barf out her own emotional dreck at precisely the wrong moment. Lucy didn't need to hear a bunch of thinly veiled woe-is-me crap.

But, to her surprise, Lucy reached back and laid a hand on Mercedes's leg. She looked more alert and in control than she had all morning, probably because the focus was momentarily off her. "Do you really mean that?"

Mercedes rolled her eyes, really trying to sound nonchalant. "Yes, you dolt. I see the two of you together, or your face when you talk to him on the phone, and I wonder if I'll ever feel that way about a man." Sadness plagued her, and she found she couldn't keep her traitorous emotions reined in, no matter how much she wanted to. Lucy did that to her; scratched through her hardened veneer to the soft vulnerability beneath it. "Or if one will ever feel that way about me—pure love, without strings. It seems like the impossible dream." She sighed, then tossed her hair, trying to refocus on the matter at hand. "But it isn't impossible for you. He's waiting downstairs. You really are a lucky girl, you know."

"I am. I really am."

"You need to marry that man, Lucy, for those of us who'll never be so fortunate."

Lucy's face registered recognition, then crumpled into a mask of regret. "Oh, Mercy, I'm so sorry. Jesus, I'm such a self-centered asshole. And a horrible friend. Do you want to talk about Damian?"

Mercedes laughed. "For God's sake, it's your wedding day, you twit. No, I do not want to talk about Damian." *That piece of shit.* "Can you please stay focused for a few minutes? What I want is to get you into that gown and across the breezeway to the Grand Ballroom to marry Ruben."

"I know, I know. Okay fine." Lucy stood.

"And don't tell the others about our little pharmaceutical exchange. I don't think they'd understand."

Lucy nodded, and then plopped back down on the edge of the bed. Her eyes searched Mercy's face. "Wait. I have to ask you something, okay?"

"Go for it."

"Am I doing the right thing? I mean, really."

"Absolutely."

"But what about the curse?"

"There is no curse. It's all in your head."

"Okay, but I'm thirty-eight years old, Mercy. Set in my ways."

"And Ruben loves you anyway."

Lucy lowered her chin, pinning Mercy with a stare. "I know you'd tell me if you thought I was making a mistake. Right?"

"Of course I would. I'll always be honest with you." As long as it didn't have to do with her *own* life. She flipped her hand. "Like, for example, your eyes are bloodshot and your makeup looks like ass, thanks to all your repeated puking. In fact, at the moment, you look a whole lot like a bulimic dime-bag whore, and unless you want your wedding photos to record that lovely image, we're going to have to work on some serious reparations, and quickly."

Lucy's eyes widened with surprise, then she leaned her head back and laughed, long and hard. They sat in companionable silence for several minutes. Finally Lucy smiled at her, all soft and . . . unfocused?

Mercedes's gut jumped. Yikes. Did Lucy's eyes already have that dopey narcotic glaze? "Are you okay, Lucy?"

"Fan-fucking-tastic, I think. I love you, Mercy. But"—she gave a cartoon gasp and covered her mouth for a moment, before giggling—"I just broke the law taking someone else's prescription meds, and I'm a cop. Not just a cop, I'm a freakin' narc, in case you forgot."

Gulp. "I love you, too, babe, and you'll live through two little pills." Hopefully. "Now how about that gown?" she asked, in a jovial, completely un-Mercedes tone. Lucy's slurring had her alarmed. At this rate, the woman wouldn't have to tell Annette and Cristina about the Vicodin. Anyone who wasn't catatonic would notice the sudden and drastic change in Lucy's demeanor. Mercedes was going to be up shit creek. The least she could do was get Lucy dressed before she paddled off. "Won't the others be impressed if you're all dolled up and ready to go by the time they return?"

Lucy wobbled to her feet. "You know what? Bring it on."

Mercy retrieved the gown, saying a silent prayer that this might actually work. "You got it."

"I'm going to marry my soul mate."

"Damn straight, babe. Lift your arms."

"Screw the Olivera curse."

"Twice, for good measure. Lift."

"Oooh." She raised the pads of her fingers to her face and tappity-tapped the skin lightly. "I feel fuzzy. Or something." She cut a glance at Mercedes. "Do I look fuzzy? Come to think of it, you look fuzzy, too."

Shit, shit, shit. That vitamin V had hit her harder and faster than expected, Mercy thought with a twinge of guilt, as Lucy obligingly raised her arms and Mercy slipped the gown over her head. As she did up the back, catching Lucy each time she started to sway, she wondered if perhaps she should've given Lucy only one pill. Ah, well. Lucy was a lightweight. Who knew? At least they'd get her to the altar. Mercedes simply didn't have time to feel guilty about drugging her best friend right now. Sometimes the end *did* justify the means.

Chapter Eleven

By the time Mercedes, Cristina, and Annette were standing in a tapered row at the front of the palatial, cherrywood-paneled Grand Ballroom and the pianist was playing the same refrain for the twentieth time, all they could do was smile stiffly and pray that Lucy's father and stepfather could successfully drag her across the atrium, into the rear doors of the massive room, and up the aisle. She'd been pretty happy-go-lucky when they'd left her, but who knew when the mood pendulum would swing again.

Annette was still annoyed with Mercedes for giving Lucy alcohol, a fact Mercedes had denied until she was hoarse, but they didn't believe her. And it was true! But Lucy was more than half crocked—anyone with basic critical-thinking skills and two eyes could see that. Still, it had been such a relief for all of them to finally have the wedding underway, the other two hadn't berated Mercedes too much until now, when they were all waiting anxiously for Lucy to show. The whole room was waiting, tension radiating like electric static through the crowd.

Mercy pouted; she couldn't help herself. It wasn't as if she had "gotten Lucy drunk" to marry her off to a guy she *didn't* love. They belonged together; Lucy was just being a dumbass. And if she didn't actually remember her wedding, thanks to the unexpected and unintended intoxication level, at least she'd have the video. Come to think of it, Mercedes wasn't sure if that was a good thing or a bad thing.

Cristina, also angry with Mercedes (but what the hell else was new?), had done a remarkable quick fix on Lucy's hair and makeup after she and Annette had arrived back in the suite, amazed to find that Mercedes had accomplished in just a few minutes what the three of them—and Lucy's mother—hadn't been able to pull off in hours. Lucy was in her gown, much more chilled out, and singing really heinous renditions of heavy metal songs from the eighties. The Scorpions, in particular. "No One Like You" had been her song of choice, which she sang repeatedly, doing true damage to the lyrics and melody.

What a sight it had been, Lucy "singing" at the top of her lungs. And what a sound—ugh. But it was better than listening to her puke, and Annette and Cristina had simply been thrilled to find her dressed . . . until they realized Lucy was *high*.

"I swear," Annette mouthed to Mercedes, "if she doesn't come through those doors soon, I'm going to lose my mind. And I'm going to blame you, too."

"She's coming."

"If she hasn't passed out," Cristina said, her tone snitty.

Both Annette and Cristina scowled slightly in her direction, but Mercedes just blew them off. She'd done the right thing, no matter what they thought.

Just then the first bars of the wedding march rang out, and the rear doors swung open to reveal the bride and her escorts. The whole room seemed to share a long sigh. Mercedes whipped Cris and Annette a told-you-so smile.

Unfortunately it wasn't a perfect scenario, this entrance. Lucy's father and stepfather weren't so much escorting her as supporting her in a half-assed stagger toward Ruben. She'd removed her shoes, which hung from her stepfather's finger, and she appeared ready to happily bust loose and do cartwheels down the aisle if they didn't keep a death grip on her. Both men looked shaken, but both held on for dear life.

Thank God for small favors.

Lucy had a wide loopy grin on her face, and when the guests stood to acknowledge her entrance, per tradition, Lucy bounced up and down and said, "Ooh, look! A standing ovation. We rock!"

Annette and Cristina both smacked Mercedes in the torso with their bouquets. "What have you done? Look at her!" Annette rasped. "Thank God we're not in church. There aren't enough Hail Marys in the world to do penance for this spectacle."

"Hey, stop complaining. She's here, isn't she?" Mercedes stage-whispered in a snarky tone, brushing broken petals, leaves, and baby's breath off her gown. "What's the alternative?"

"She's drunk!" Annette exclaimed quietly, whacking Mercy with the bouquet again. "At her wedding! I can't believe it."

"She's not drunk," Mercedes insisted, rolling her eyes up toward one of the huge, round, crystal chandeliers. "I swear to you on my own life, she is not drunk. I did *not* give her alcohol." She softened her whisper. "And if she wasn't feeling a little . . . mellow, there wouldn't be a goddamned wedding, so get off me. I don't recall you two coming up with any bright ideas."

Cristina peered at Mercedes curiously for a few moments, then asked with trepidation, "Mercedes?"

"What?" she snapped.

"What exactly *did* you give her?"

Mercedes sighed, pressing her lips together while she toyed with the lie versus don't lie dilemma. Hell, they'd find out eventually. After a deep inhale and slow exhale, she whispered regretfully, "Vicodin."

"Holy shit," Cris gasped, closing her eyes. She actually swayed in her heels. "I can't believe you slipped Lucy narcotics."

"Narcotics?" Annette passed her bouquet into her left hand and crossed herself with her right.

"Oh, don't act like I shot her up with heroin, for Christ's sake. What

116 / Lynda Sandoval

else was I supposed to do? And I didn't know she was such a light-weight or I wouldn't have given her two."

"Two!" Annette exclaimed.

Simultaneous bouquet thwacks were followed by stony silence from Annette and Cristina, but Mercedes didn't give a rat's ass at this point. Lucy was halfway up the aisle. As long as she didn't bust into a Metallica air-guitar-riff during the vows or start singing in that cow-bellowing-in-pain voice again, then the Vicodin would have served its purpose. She didn't feel guilty at all. Her best friend was getting married, as she should, and if Mercedes'd had to assist the process along with a little illegal chemical boost, so be it.

She was well-known for being all about results. Results were the point. What the hell else mattered in this world?

Ruben watched Lucy jolt toward him up the aisle and his chest clenched hard enough to weaken his knees. She was, without a doubt, the most beautiful, talented, amazing, endearingly wacky woman he'd ever met. As she got closer, it became clear that she was also quite high. Startled, he blinked twice, then flicked a glance over at Lucy's friends. Mercedes made reluctant eye contact, lifted one shoulder, and mouthed, "Sorry."

He shook his head, offering a wry smile and a wink, then refocused on his bride. Okay, so they'd had to resort to extreme measures to get her there. She'd live. And he would, too. He knew Lucy's fear of this wedding didn't have anything to do with her not loving him. On the contrary, she loved him too much, and what with the whole Olivera thing, her brain just didn't work right. He could deal with that problem. All he had to do was get her through this day, and he'd have a lifetime to show her everything would be fine—better than fine—with them.

Finally she stood at his side. And laughed.

The pastor cleared his throat. His voice rang out loud and clear via the sound system over the crowd of nearly five hundred. "Who gives this woman to be married to this man?"

Ramon Olivera straightened, looking tightly trussed in his black tuxedo and all too relieved to pass off his toasted daughter to her intended. "Her mother and I . . . that is, her real mother"—he flicked an uncertain glance at the man on the other side of Lucy—"and well, also her stepmother, and then her stepfather there, who's married to her mother now. Her real mother, that is, whereas the stepmother is my—"

"Dad," Lucy whispered, stifling a chuckle.

He flicked her an apologetic glance and cleared his throat. "Sorry. *Sí, sí.*" He gave the pastor a sheepish shrug. "I guess we all sort of give her."

A soft wave of half-uncomfortable, half-amused laughter rippled through the crowd. Only at an Olivera wedding.

Lucy might have been a little high, but if anything it lowered her inhibitions, freeing her up to express emotions she might have otherwise kept reined in. The depth of her love for Ruben showed through her passionate reading of the vows they'd written, through the love in her eyes, through her attuned and open body language. By the time I-dos had been exchanged, sniffles abounded in the Grand Ballroom. Annette unabashedly allowed the tears to flow down her smiling face. Cristina dabbed at her eyes with increasing frequency, all the while maintaining her decorum. Mercedes had vowed not to cry—icky, stupid emotional release—but the whole thing had lodged a huge lump in her throat as well, and pretty soon Annette was handing her a tissue. Soon she was using it just like all the rest.

The pastor pronounced them husband and wife.

Ruben kissed Lucy.

The entire congregation broke into deafening applause and cheers. Just like that, after all the trauma they'd endured to get her there, Lucy was legally married to Ruben.

Lucy jolted, blinking around the packed ballroom that was lively with movement, music, and laughter. Her mouth felt cotton-stuffed and her head pounded like a gong, almost as if she'd just woken up after a particularly bad drunk. But how could that be? Wasn't this her wedding day? Disoriented, she glanced around for confirmation. The dance floor had been set up in place of the altar and the band was in full swing. That had to mean . . .

She took a slow, heart-pounding glance down at her left hand and the room blurred before her eyes when she spied the shiny gold band wrapped around the third finger. She was married. She'd somehow made it through the ceremony, and she didn't remember any of it. Oh. My. God.

Letting her eyes flutter shut, Lucy grasped her great-great-grandmother's pearls in her fist and struggled to think back to how it had all happened. They'd been getting ready in Mercy's suite . . . she'd been freaking out . . . and then there was all the hurling. She shuddered.

But then Annette and Cristina had left the room and—oh, God. It came down on her like a tumble of bricks. Mercedes had slipped her Vicodin, and she'd taken it. She remembered now. The pills had hit her unbelievably hard, probably because her stomach had been hollow-empty after blowing chunks so many times. She glanced frantically around the room for Ruben. Jesus, she'd gotten married while whacked on narcotics. Did that even count? Did Ruben know? He must be horrified.

How could she have lost several hours of her life?

And on the most important day of her life to boot?

She caught sight of Ruben dancing with her mother and realized (1) she had, indeed, married the man. Ruben del Fierro was destined to be her first husband, no matter how she tried to reframe it. And (2) he looked happy, his eyes creased with mirth, head thrown back laughing at something her mother had said. A surge of panic seized her, and she gasped for air.

Lucy lurched to her feet, desperate for escape. The last thing she wanted was to lose it in front of five hundred people. At the moment, she didn't even want to see her friends. She just needed to flee, to get her head together, to reflect on the gravity of what she'd gone and done *under the influence of narcotics*. She knew it wasn't logical behavior to feel so insane over this, but the fact was, she hadn't felt logical in months. Not since accepting Ruben's proposal.

Just then Ruben glanced over and their eyes met and locked. He leaned down to whisper something to her mother, his heated attention never leaving Lucy's face. And then he started toward her.

No!

Her blood pounded so hard in her ears, she couldn't even hear the music. Everything was happening in slow motion. Ruben approaching. Her backing away. In the midst of everything, a chair went hurtling through the air, and several women screamed. Suddenly a surge of people gathered at one corner of the room as though sucked into a cyclone, and Ruben's attention was diverted. Lucy glanced over at the melee—a couple of her uncles fighting again. Always the same, Olivera weddings. Lots of raucous laughter and camaraderie morphed into heated debates over God knows what. Eventually a chair was thrown and the fight was officially on. Like clockwork.

Ruben glanced back at her, held up a finger indicating she should wait, then turned and shouldered his way into the fray. She saw her chance and took it. With Ruben breaking up the warring uncles and the rest of the room's attention focused on the obligatory Olivera wedding brawl, Lucy lifted the long straight skirt of her gown in her fists and busted her way out of the ballroom. She dashed across the breezeway over Tremont Street, hung a quick left, then jumped on the Art Deco escalators and headed down to the lobby level. She nervously checked behind her a couple of times, but no one seemed to have followed. Thank God Mercy, Cris, and Annette hadn't been hovering.

Cutting a quick right around to the front of the hotel, she shoved her way through the revolving door, and didn't even give the doorman a chance to hail a cab for her. She spied a yellow cab coming down the street and practically threw herself in front of it. The cab squealed, fishtailed to a stop, and the red-faced cabbie jumped out. "Jesus, lady! Are you out of your mind?"

"Actually, yes. Funny you should ask." With one quick glance behind her, she yanked open a door, wedged herself into the backseat of the cab, and hunkered down. The cabbie slid into the driver's seat and blinked at her in the rearview mirror.

"You late for the wedding or already married," he asked warily.

"Just married."

"Ah. Running away then, I guess?" he asked, taking a moment to fill out his log sheet.

She sighed, rubbing her temples with the pads of her fingers. "Something like that. Not completely. I just . . . long story, but I need to get my head straight."

"I thought that was something the brides did before they said 'I do.'" He tossed his log sheet onto the passenger seat, then pulled into traffic, flicking his blinker in preparation for a turn onto 18th Avenue. "But it's none of my business. You do what you gotta do. I'm just here to transport you there. Where to, lady?"

Lucy realized, dismayed, that she didn't have a credit card, much less cash. "Shit." Her eyes brimmed with tears, and she didn't even bother to flick them away.

His gulping swallow was audible. "You wanna talk about it?"

"I don't have a purse. I can't pay you." God, she'd destroyed her entire wedding, and now she couldn't even run away correctly. "I . . . I guess you'll have to take me back."

She met his eyes in the rearview mirror and watched his expression grow worried, then soften. "Look, consider it my wedding present. I'll take you wherever you wanna go. Just don't cry, okay? I'm no good with crying women." He scratched his neck, then pointed to the red blotchiness. "I think I'm literally allergic. Hives. Instant hives."

"I'm sorry." She hastily smeared away her tears with the heels of her hands. "I can give you"—she glanced down at herself, clad in the gown she loved that had cost her so much damn money—"my jewelry or veil or something."

The cabbie sighed. "Just tell me where to. I'm not taking your jewelry or anything else. But I will take you where you want to go."

"I'm just . . . I'm not sure." Lucy chewed thoughtfully on the inside of her cheek. She needed to think. But where could she be absolutely alone, somewhere no one would find her? "Can you drive me to Evergreen?"

He winked. "Always did love a nice drive in the foothills on a Saturday." He headed toward Speer, undoubtedly planning on hitting I-25 first and then taking I-70 straight up.

"I can take your address and mail you the fare, too. I'm good for it."

"Whatever floats your boat, hon."

Lucy settled into the seat and breathed deeply for the first time since she'd blown out of the ballroom. As an afterthought, she buckled the seat belt over her gown, then settled back for the forty-five-minute ride. She wasn't actually *leaving* Ruben, technically speaking. But she *had* ditched him at the reception, a fact that didn't bode well for their future in general. She glanced down. No one had pinned money to her dress . . . then again, she'd requested that little tradition be excised from their reception. She couldn't even remember if they'd had toasts, cut their cake, or danced. And yet, right now she just wanted to run fast and far. Could the Olivera self-fulfilling prophecy be in motion already?

Annette was seated on the dais behind the head table, searching the crowd for Lucy, when her cell phone rang from inside her small handbag. She hadn't had it on during the wedding, of course, but she switched it on at the reception. With five kids, accessibility was a necessity, not an option.

Fishing it out of the bag, she held it to her ear. "Hello?"

"Annette, it's Ruben."

Something in his tone put her immediately on edge, and she leaned forward in her seat, back rigid. "What's wrong? Where are you?"

"Can you and the others come up to the Eisenhower?"

"The others? Mercy and Cris?"

"Yeah. Just you three."

"Of course, but—"

"Hurry. And don't tell anyone where you're going, okay? This is very important."

Annette's heart started pounding with dread. "Is something wrong with Lucy?"

"I don't know."

"What do you mean, you don't know?"

"I mean, she's gone." He sighed. "Must've been right around when the fight broke out. That's the last I saw of her. But . . . she left. I've searched everywhere. Finally the doorman told me he'd seen a bride hauling ass out the front doors."

Annette squeezed her temples with the thumb and forefinger of her free hand, her heart heavy. She had been so sure Lucy would be fine once they got her over the hump of the wedding itself. "Oh, Lord. Left for where?"

"That's what I'm hoping the three of you will help me find out because I have no clue. Hurry, okay?"

"We'll be right up. And you listen to me," she said, as she glanced around the ballroom for Cris and Mercy. "Don't worry. Lucy may have flipped out, but she loves you."

"I know."

"And you're married now. That's not something Lucy takes lightly, believe me."

He uttered a monosyllabic laugh, but there was no mirth to it. "That's the whole problem."

"Oh, Ruben."

"We're going to stay married, Annette, I promise you that. I'm not scared off by her Olivera issues. But first," he said, in a grave tone, "we have to find her."

They'd been driving aimlessly around downtown Denver for an hour, hunting for a bedraggled bride on the run. Although they had questioned mall shuttle drivers, as well as some of the multi-pierced homeless kids who hung out on the 16th Street mall, no one had seen any brides.

"This wouldn't have happened if she'd gotten married in a proper state of mind," Cris muttered, from the backseat of Annette's minivan.

"Probably not," Annette agreed, softly.

"She came down from the Vicodin and it was over and done with. That would scare anyone, but especially someone who already had more than her share of reservations."

Mercedes, in the front passenger seat, tightened her hand around the shoulder strap of her seatbelt, sick of feeling like the bad guy. "Look, both of you get off me, okay? I'm sorry about the Vicodin." She paused, letting that sink in. "But we need to band together if we're going to find Lucy and get her back to Ruben where she belongs." Her voice raised slightly. "Can we please keep the focus on what's important rather than lambasting my ass for the rest of the night?"

After a moment, Annette said, "She's right, Cris. God knows, I've made mistakes in my day. I forgive you, Mercy."

"Well . . . thanks."

Cristina sighed. "Where could she be?"

They drove in silence for a few minutes, scanning the crowds along Larimer Street heading toward Speer. It's not as if a bride in full regalia would be hard to miss, but they still scoured the crowds as if they might somehow scan right past her.

Suddenly Cris snapped her fingers. "Wait, wait, wait. We're scouting out the wrong place. I've got it."

"What?" Annette peered back at her in the rearview mirror.

"When we were eating at the Elk Bugle in Evergreen, Lucy said it would be a great place to hide out. Remember?"

"Oh, my gosh!"

Even Mercedes smiled at the little brainstorm. "You're absolutely right. It's logical. Worth a try, at least. Do you know the way, Annette?"

"Sort of," she said, sounding completely unsure.

Mercedes pointed. "Turn here. We'll take Sixth Avenue out to I-70 and head up to Evergreen from there." She paused, seeming to consider her words. Finally she cleared her throat and grudgingly offered, "Good sleuthing, Cristina."

A beat passed. "Thank you," Cris said, tightly. "And about the

Vicodin thing? Well"—the pause hung thick—"I'm not so perfect, either, I guess. Let's all just forget it."

"Ms. Perfect, admitting she's *not* actually perfect?" Mercedes said in a wry tone. "Mark this day on the calendar."

"Oh, shut the hell up," Cristina snapped. "Can't you ever leave well enough alone?"

Annette bit her bottom lip to keep from smiling. They worked so hard at hating each other, these two. It would be amusing if it weren't such a darn waste.

They found Lucy in her big, conspicuous wedding dress, stuffed into a sticky bar booth at the Elk Bugle, empty shot glasses lined up in front of her like pawns in a very ugly chess game. She was talking on someone's cell phone—God only knew whose. She hadn't had hers when she left, that was for damn sure. Cell phones had permeated most areas of the public sector, true enough, but it was still taboo—and tacky—for a bride to clip one onto her gown. As she talked on the borrowed phone, she sniffed periodically into a tattered paper towel.

The bar patrons were all giving her an extra wide berth, although they did eye her curiously each time they passed. Still, any sane person knew a crying bride doing shots spelled dangerous territory. The bartender, indeed many of the bar patrons looked overtly relieved to see three women enter the place wearing wedding garb, too. Annette and Cris started right over to the booth, but Mercedes grabbed their arms gently. "Misery loves company, gals. You go to Lucy, I'll get drinks. Cristina, I'm assuming you'll want tequila?"

"Yes."

"Me, too," said Annette.

"Excellent, I'll make it three. And here"—she fished her cell phone out of her purse—"give Lucy mine. I don't know whose phone that is, but I'm sure she's put them over their monthly limit already."

Cristina took the phone, and Mercy headed to the bar. She leaned in and made eye contact with the long-haired, extremely buff and hot bartender. "Hi."

"Hey." He wiped his hands on a thick white bar towel and came toward her. "You with the bride?"

"We are. Thanks for watching out for her until we could figure out where the hell she'd run off to."

"Hey, man. No need. We watch out for all our patrons, but a flipped-out bride gets special treatment. She had no money with her. Didn't even pay the cab driver, but he didn't seem to mind. All her shots have been on the house."

Mercedes winced. "How many has she had?"

"Just the four." He leaned in and lowered his voice. "I watered them down a bit. It's not our usual practice, but I didn't want to make the problem, whatever it is, worse."

"Thank you. I'll repay you for them, of course. Is that your cell phone she's using, too?"

He nodded. "She started to wig when she realized she didn't have change for the pay phone, so I tossed her mine. Dude, I just couldn't stand by and watch a bride lose it in my bar. I'll take the hit with Verizon. It's all good."

She fished out a fifty-dollar bill and handed it over. "This is for the air time. And, hey, can you bring us a round of good tequila, salt, and lime. Definitely water down the bride's, but the rest of us could actually use it straight."

"You got it." He flicked a worried glance over toward Lucy, lifting his chin as he pulled four shots. "She get left at the altar or what?"

"No. She actually got married. She bolted from the reception when she realized what she'd done."

The bartender whistled through his teeth. "So I guess it's the high-speed train toward Divorce City then?"

Mercedes cringed. "Actually, it's a horribly long and unbelievable story, but it would be really good if you refrained from using the word 'divorce' at all."

"Got it. No D word. No variations thereof. Check."

His words made her smile. "My name is Mercedes, by the way." She stuck out her hand.

He wiped his again on the apron he wore, then shook hers. "Mercedes. Always wanted to drive one of those." He winked.

Heat flared in Mercedes's tummy.

"I'm Zeb. If there's anything else I can do, let me know."

"Just keep the shots coming." She tossed down another fifty for good measure. "But not too frequently."

He nodded once. "I'm on it." He cocked his head, studying her as he arranged the shots on a brown plastic-and-corkboard tray. "This is going to sound like a huge pick-up line, which it isn't, but you look really familiar to me. Have we met? I know I've seen your face somewhere recently."

Mercedes's stomach plunged. God, she couldn't even hide out in Lucy's preferred hideout joint. The tabloid smear pieces must've hit. Or *Hard Copy* ran their story. That figured. She averted her gaze. "N-no. I'm from out of town, actually."

"Hmmm." He looked unconvinced. "Well, you head on over to the table and I'll get these shots right to you. I'll be sure to give the diluted one to the bride—"

"Lucy."

"To Lucy. Don't worry. She'll be fine."

Mercedes smiled, but inside she felt sick. About Lucy, about the tabloids, about the whole damned mess. "That's what we keep trying to tell her. Believe me." She crossed over to the table and slid in next to Cristina. Annette was seated next to Lucy, patting her arm.

"She's talking to Ruben," Cristina whispered, out of the corner of her mouth.

"Oh, good. That's a positive step."

"She's also spazzing the hell out."

Mercedes snorted. "Clearly." She covered the side of her mouth and whispered, "The bartender's been watering down her shots, thank God."

"I hope he's not watering down ours."

"No. I made sure of that."

All of a sudden, Lucy blinked up and around at them through red, watery eyes. "Yes, they're right here. Really? Okay, hang on." She held out Mercy's cell phone to her. "Ruben. He wants to talk to you."

Mercedes popped off one earring, then took the phone and lifted it to her ear. "Hey."

"Thank God you all found her. How hammered is she?"

Mercy turned slightly away and schooled her tone. "Not so much. Do you want us to just . . . bring her back, or—"

"No."

A beat passed. "No?"

His sigh carried over the phone. "Look, God knows I love that woman, but she's not ready to come back, Mercy, and forcing her isn't going to do any good. She's stubborn."

"You've got a point."

"I know it's unorthodox as hell for a groom to pass off his bride for the wedding night, but will you guys just . . . stay with her? Whatever she needs? It won't help for me to be in her face right now, but I've told her I'll be right here when she's ready to come home."

"Ruben—" Mercedes was so astounded, she wasn't sure how to handle this. He really was the perfect guy. "Are you sure?"

"Absolutely. I said I'd do anything to make this marriage work, and if that means spending my wedding night alone while she hangs with her posse, it's all good."

Mercedes laughed softly. "I haven't thought of myself as part of a posse in twenty years."

"And I can't think of you women as anything but. Just get her home to me, yeah? However you can. But, Mercedes? No more Vicodin, babe. Please."

"Cross my heart," she said. "And, I'm sorry about that."

"De nada. We're married. That's what counts."

"I'll make sure she checks in."

"Stay out of trouble, yeah?"

"Us? Trouble?"

"Don't even get me started," Ruben said with a groan.

Chapter Twelve

everal hours later, Lucy was feeling slightly better—or at least well-anesthetized from all the tequila—when the nice bartender who'd loaned her his phone approached the table, wiping his hands on a thick white bar towel. "Ladies, I'm afraid it's last call. Can I bring you each another shot?"

"None for me," Annette said, her tongue loose and smile wide. "I'm the designated driver, you know."

"Oh, trust me. You're not driving anywhere," Zeb said, laughing. "I couldn't let you do that." He held out his palm. "In fact, why don't you give up your keys right now so I don't have to flatten your tires or something. I can't let four beautiful women do something crazy."

"Oh, no. I won't drive if you think I shouldn't."

"You shouldn't," Mercy said, sounding none too happy about it. "None of us should."

"But . . . how will we get back to Denver?" Annette asked, blinking, as if the notion had just struck.

Her friends grew solemn with realization, and Lucy glanced around at them. They'd been so intent on coddling her, none of them had considered the long, twisty drive back down the mountain into Denver. Now they were screwed.

"Zeb, I don't suppose you'd know of any hotels or cabins to rent for the night. I know it's really late," Mercedes said, in that husky-sexy voice that everyone except her adored. "But I guess none of us thought—"

Lucy appraised Mercy. Interesting. She'd love to see Mercy with a real man like this Zeb guy rather than those rich dipshits who kept breaking her heart. But did high-powered editors go for regular guys? Mercy certainly didn't seem to. Zeb rubbed the strong line of his jaw with his knuckles, considering the question.

"Preferably within staggering distance," Mercedes added as a wry afterthought.

"Well, now, I don't know of anyplace that close. But my buddy owns some rental cabins. It's a long shot, what with it being prime vacation season and all. Let me just give him a call." He pointed a finger at the other women. "How about the rest of you? Another shot? Nightcap?"

"Give us all a nightcap if I'm not driving," Annette said, with flourish. "Why not? Let's live a little."

Lucy smiled at Annette. How was it that women she'd known all her life could startle and amaze her on a regular basis?

"You got it."

After the bartender had left, Lucy looked beseechingly around at her friends. "I'm so sorry about this. I never meant to trap you guys up here without any of your stuff."

"Don't apologize," Cristina said. "We all do impulsive things. We're here for you. Ruben is understanding. We'll get you through this, Lucy, and who needs stuff anyway?"

Lucy sighed, resting her elbows on the table and her chin in her hands. "What did I ever do to deserve you guys?"

"Who said you deserve us?" Mercy arched a brow.

They were laughing when the bartender reapproached with a tray of tequila shots. "This one's on me." He looked toward Mercedes. "My friend has one cabin left, and he's leaving a key under the mat for you.

You can settle up with him in the morning. Anyway, it's not too far. I can drive you all over there if you'd like."

"That would be great," Mercedes said, then after a pause she added, "You're not one of those tweaked-out mountain man serial killers are you?"

"That's what I was going to ask," Lucy said.

Mercedes aimed her thumb at the bride. "She's a cop."

"Ah." He grinned. "Well, not to worry. I'm nothing that exciting. Plus, my house is walking distance and I can mountain bike it back for my shift tomorrow. It's not a problem." He looked at Lucy. "I can show you ID if you'd like."

She flicked her hand. "Nah, screw it. Life on the edge feels good right now." She appraised him, confident. "Besides, don't let the dress fool you. I could seriously kick your ass if I needed to."

"Duly noted," Zeb said, with an appreciative chuckle.

Mercedes nodded at him. "Okay, then. Thank you so much. I don't suppose you know of a store that's open on the way?" She glanced down at her gown. "I can tell you these dresses aren't meant to be slept in."

Zeb grinned. "Of course. There's a convenience store up the road. I think they even sell Broncos jerseys. You know, souvenir stuff. You ladies can sleep in true Denver style."

"God bless the Broncos," Lucy said.

After Zeb had set down their shots, salt shakers, and lime, including one for himself, he licked salt off his hand, lifted his glass, and said, tentatively, "Cheers?"

The women followed suit, glasses were tapped, and the booze was downed. Lucy noticed Zeb watching Mercedes again as he wiped off his mouth with the back of his hand. "I swear," he told her, wagging his finger, "I know you from somewhere."

Lucy smiled. "Oh, well she's—"

"Pretty easy to confuse with other people," Mercedes rushed to say, giving Lucy a quelling glance. Her face had gone slightly pale and pinched. Whoa. Okay, so she clearly didn't want the man to know who she was, but why not? She should be proud. Mercy could seriously *do* this guy if she wanted to, and as long as Damian was being an asswipe, why not? "I just have that look. But I'm not from around here. You don't know me."

He shrugged. "Okay, then. Whatever you say. Let me know when you're ready to leave and I'll drive you over." He winced. "Oh yeah. One downside: the place only has one king-size bed."

"Sharing a bed's no problem," Annette said. "We've been having slumber parties since junior high." The others nodded.

Zeb winked with the practiced flirtatiousness of a career bartender, giving them a slow smile as he backed away. "Sounds like a party I'd love to be invited to."

The small, rustic cabin was so far removed from any accommodations Cristina had stayed in recently, she felt like she'd landed on a different planet. The Plaza it wasn't, but she loved it. There was a huge moss rock fireplace, and even though it was early June, they built a fire. How could they not? She was both mesmerized and cheered by the crackle and flicker, the smell of woodsmoke soothing her soul like a salve. The nights were cool at 8,500 feet of elevation, and with the windows open, the temperature was just right.

The cabin also boasted a small galley kitchen complete with a tiny table and two chairs, a minuscule bathroom, and the lodgepole-frame bed, which was separated from the rest of the cabin by a tall folding screen.

They'd taken turns in the bathroom, removing makeup that should've been removed long ago, and changing into the Broncos jerseys Mercedes had bought for them all, along with a slew of other supplies, when they'd stopped at an all-night convenience store en route to the cabin. Now they sat cross-legged in a circle on the bed, drinking coffee and passing around a bag of cookies. Even though Lucy's wedding had gone terribly wrong, Cristina felt enveloped in safety, in friendship. It was odd to be spending Lucy's wedding night *with* her, but at least Lucy seemed to have chilled. In fact, she'd gone from manic to melancholy, which, ironically felt like progress. They'd spent their time in the bar talking about anything and everything except the fact that Lucy had walked out on Ruben, preferring to let her take the lead into that particular minefield. But she'd grown pensive since their arrival at the cabin, and Cristina had the sense that she was nearly ready to unburden herself if they just gave her enough love and room to collect her thoughts. If they just encouraged her. She glanced up at Annette, who nodded ever so slightly. She watched Annette glance at Mercedes next.

Mercedes, as always the leader, gave the prompt. She cleared her throat, straightened her back, and in a gentle tone, said, "You wanna talk about it, Lucy? We're your friends. Nothing you could say would change the way we feel about you."

Lucy didn't look up, but she started to cry silently, head bowed over the white plastic cover on her coffee cup. She ran her finger absentmindedly around the rim. "I can't believe I bolted," she whispered, "and yet I'm not ready to go back and face the mess I've made."

"You don't have to go back until you're ready," Cristina said, leaning forward to lay a hand on Lucy's bare knee. "Ruben is on your side."

"And it's not like you're missing your honeymoon, since that's taking place later," Annette added.

"Yeah." Cris gave Lucy's knee a squeeze and pulled away. "We're here for you, too."

"But I'm so ashamed." Lucy flicked a quick glance up at them before looking down again. "I'm thirty-eight years old, and I can't even handle getting married. You all have your lives so together. I just feel like an emotionally stunted imbecile in the presence of the three wise women."

For a moment, the room lapsed into stunned silence.

Holy shit, if Lucy only knew. Cris couldn't look at any of them, afraid she'd give herself away. Annette and Mercedes might have it all together, but her life was a sad, sorry jumble.

Annette started laughing first. Really belly-laughing. Surprised, Cristina's gaze cut to her face. She couldn't keep from joining in, and even Mercy's lips quivered up.

Lucy blinked at them, baffled. "What's so funny?"

Annette took a sip of her coffee and looked at Lucy straight on. "You think I have my life together?"

"Of course you do. You're one of the most together women I have ever known."

Annette huffed, shaking her head. "Let me tell you something. A few days before I came out here, I seriously contemplated running away, going somewhere so remote that no one would ever know I was a wife or a mother or anything other than what I told them. And all I would tell them is, 'My name's Annette. Leave me the F alone.'"

Shock zinged through Cristina, and she looked at Annette with fresh insight. Okay, so she'd known she and Mercy had issues, but she'd truly believed at least Annette had her shit together. And she'd used the F word! Or at least the F letter.

Lucy shook her head. "Annie, come on—"

"No, Luce. It's true. I spend my days alternately wondering if anyone in my family really appreciates all I do for them and fantasizing about having a different life. Or a life, period. Everyone in my family has a life except me."

"But they are your life," Lucy whispered.

"True, but sometimes I want more." She shrugged, color rising to her cheeks. "Sometimes I want to be just Annette."

"What are you saying, Annie?" Lucy's eyes had widened. "As long as I've known you, you've wanted marriage and family."

Annette nodded. "Yes, I do. I still want them, don't get me wrong. And they love me, too, almost to death." She blew out an impatient breath, seeming to search her mind for the right words. "I've lost myself. Lost myself to karate and teenage hormones and making dinner and everyone's schedules but my own. They love me, yes. But, they suck me dry. Some days I wake up and don't even know who Annette is anymore." Her chin quivered, and she bit her bottom lip to stop it. "It's not a good feeling to resent your loved ones, no matter how much you love them." Annette paused, shaking her head. "My dirty little secret? I've been having nightmares about going back. That makes me feel like the worst wife and mother ever."

Cristina felt a pang of true connection. All mothers felt this way sometimes. Didn't Annette know that? "Oh, honey. Why didn't you say something earlier?"

Annette hiked a thumb toward Lucy. "Because I was trying to get this one to the altar. This week wasn't about me."

Cristina smiled. They'd both been protecting Lucy.

"God, Annette. I had no idea you were feeling this way," Lucy said, her focus truly off herself for the moment.

Cristina cast a sidelong glance at Mercedes, who hadn't said much. She was, however, watching Annette intently. Clearly she cared, but she probably couldn't relate. Who knew?

"Want to hear my latest family crisis?" Annette asked.

"Of course," the three of them said simultaneously.

"Deborah has fallen in love."

"Oh, that's lovely, Annie," Lucy said.

"Isn't she, like, four years old?" Mercedes asked.

Annette smiled. "She's twenty. It's been a long time, Mercy, don't forget."

"Falling in love isn't a crisis," Cris said.

"I know. But wait, I'm not done. Deborah has fallen in love with another woman. A lovely, lovely young woman." Annette glanced around at them. "She came out to us a few weeks ago."

For a moment, they were all silent. "How do you feel about that?" Lucy asked softly. "I mean, I think it's fine. I work with a lot of gay women who are wonderful."

"I've *been* with women," Mercedes stated matter-of-factly.

"What?" Cristina shrieked.

Mercedes actually gave a small laugh. "Look, I live in New York City, I work in publishing. I'm liberal to the extreme. It's not that unusual. Don't knock it till you've tried it."

"I'm not knocking it, I'm just—" Cristina stared at Mercy mutely for a few moments. "God, I think I'm actually envious." She glanced from Lucy to Annette. "That's nuts, right?"

"Did you like it?" Lucy asked, intrigued.

Mercedes shrugged. "What's not to like? But that's a topic for a whole different night. Let's get back to Deborah." They all looked at Annette. "How'd she tell you? What happened?"

Annette bit into a cookie and chewed thoughtfully. "I have to say, I was surprised, but not shocked. And not disappointed. And"—she glanced at Mercedes—"on some level, I can understand her falling for Alex. For another woman, that is. I've never done it, but it makes sense to me on a visceral female level, and I applaud her ability to go after exactly what she wants. That had to be hard for her, coming out to us. As for me, I just want my baby to be happy."

"Is she?" Lucy asked.

"Radiantly so. It's painful for me to look at them together, but in a good way." Annette sighed. "The problem is the way Randy reacted to the news."

"Uh-oh," Cristina said.

Annette grimaced. "Yeah. It's not that he was cruel. You guys know my Randy. But he's a traditional guy, and he just couldn't bring himself to give Alex and Deborah his blessing. The girls left with Deborah in tears, and Randy has been prowling around, steeped in remorse ever since. He loves his children. He'll come around eventually. I think he already has."

"So why doesn't he call Deborah and work it out?" Lucy asked. "She'll understand the initial shock."

Annette gave a droll glance at Lucy. "Because, you see, it is apparently my job to make everything better in every way for my family. To bridge the gap, repair the rift." She threaded her fingers into the front of her hair, looking worn down. "I'm just not up to the challenge this time. I've accepted Deborah and Alex, and I don't want to be the go-between for Randy. He needs to deal with this himself."

"Have you told him that?" Cristina asked.

"Not in so many words." Annette paused, toying with a yarn tie on the quilt that covered the bed. "But, anyway, Miss Lucy, if you think I have my whole life together, you're absolutely wrong. Maybe these two do, but—"

"These two don't," Cristina said. Her heart pounded, and her throat went immediately dry, but she knew it was the perfect time to come clean. She flicked an apologetic glance toward Mercedes. "Or at least I don't."

All of them had been wondering about her for so long, and she could see the eagerness in their expressions. She moistened her lips with a quick flick of her tongue, trying to figure out how in the hell to blurt this out. She took a sip of coffee, swallowed, cleared her throat. Stalling, stalling, stalling. "You see, the thing is, I know all of you think Zach has been beating me"—she held up her cleansed wrists, bruises clearly visible—"but you're way off base on this one."

"Then what is going on?" Annette asked. "We're just worried about you, Cris, not passing judgment against Zach."

"But you have to admit, the evidence . . ." Lucy added.

Cristina nodded, but the motion felt jerky. She cast a sidelong glance at Lucy. "I'm most ashamed to say this in front of you, Lucy. I'm so sorry."

Lucy frowned. "Don't be ridiculous. There is nothing you could tell me that would change my feelings for you."

"Don't be so sure." A strained moment passed, and finally Cris said, "The bruises . . . are from handcuffs. I almost wish I could say we were into the kinky stuff, but no. Truth is, the day before I came here . . . I got arrested." The world-class expression of shock on Mercedes's face was almost worth the shame of the confession. "You see, I seem to have a little problem with"—she cringed—"shoplifting."

"Oh, Cris," Annette said on an exhale.

Cristina covered her face with both hands. It was out there now and she couldn't pull it back. It hung in the room like an odor. Should she have kept her mouth closed? Kept up the image? Wasn't that the sum total of her life? She felt like she'd just taken the biggest risk of her life. "God, I'm so ashamed."

"Don't be," Lucy said, although she did sound a little bowled over. "No one's perfect. Tell us what happened."

Cristina dragged her palms off her face and rolled the tension out of her tight shoulders. She studiously avoided looking at Mercy's face because, even though she was well aware there was no love lost between them, she'd be crushed if she saw even a hint of satisfaction there. "I don't know. I started about a year ago, on a whim. That sounds so horrid, but—"

"Stop passing judgment on yourself," Annette said. "Just tell us. We're not judging you."

Cristina took a deep breath in and blew it out. "Okay. I was shopping one day and the thought popped into my head, 'steal it.' Just like that. So I did," she said with a tired matter-of-factness. "And I had the money to pay, too. It's horrid, but I felt such a sense of exhilaration when I left, felt so much more alive than I had in years, it quickly became this sick, irrational addiction." She held up a hand toward Lucy. "Let me just say, I have managed to pay back every single shop owner after the deed. And I always try to atone by giving money to homeless people around San Antonio. A hundred bucks at a time. I swear, they cheer when they see me coming. I know, though. It doesn't make it better."

"This is a common problem with wealthy women, Cristina," Mercedes said, startling her. "We did an article about it in the magazine earlier this year."

"I know. I read it." She eyed Mercedes with gentle reproach. "I wasn't just blowing sunshine when I said I read your magazine faithfully."

Color rose to Mercedes's cheeks. Her throat moved with a tight swallow. "The point is, you can get help."

"Well, it looks like I'm going to have to now. My court date is coming up."

"Does Zach know?" Lucy asked.

"I didn't tell him. I just packed my stuff and split, like the coward I am. But I'm sure by now the news has slipped out into our social circle." She covered her face again and groaned, hardly able to bear the thought. "God, I don't know how I'm going to face it. That's the worst part. Zach's a public figure. A damned prime-time newscaster, of all things, in millions of living rooms every single night. His face is plastered all over buses and billboards. He's a key figure in San Antonio society, not just because of his job, but because of his time with the Astros and because of the family he came from. Like it or not, this will reflect on him. How is this going to affect his career? His family? The kids? God, the kids."

"He's a high-profile public figure who happens to love you," Annette said.

"He might, but . . . his mother despises me. This is going to validate every single evil thought she's ever had about me."

"What?" Annette said, clearly disbelieving.

"It's true. She has always despised me and never misses an opportunity to get her digs in. I'm just not good enough for her precious son. I do everything to keep that woman happy, and nothing is ever enough." She huffed, not humored at all. "Why in the fuck do Latina mamas raise their sons to believe they're gods? Don't they remember what it felt like for them to go through the turmoil of being married to a man who thinks he's entitled to fawning and worship?"

"That's probably why. They went through it, so, by God, their daughters-in-law will suffer through it, too," said Lucy.

Annette chuckled. "I'm glad I have girls. All I have to do is raise them to be self-sufficient and take no guff from anyone and I'll be successful."

"Sounds like you're doing a fantastic job," Mercedes said.

Annette patted her leg in thanks.

"From the time he could talk, I've raised Manuel to be a self-sufficient male. I've hammered it into his head that no woman worth having in this day and age is going to sign on to be his personal slave." Cristina shrugged. "I think it's working. He does his own laundry, helps with the chores. His grandmother thinks it's a travesty, my not treating him like a pampered little prince—just another area where I'm failing as a wife and mother, but screw her."

"Yes, screw her," Mercedes said. "Seriously."

Cristina sighed, absentmindedly touching the handcuff bruises on her wrists. "I have a good life. I do. A privileged life. But sometimes I feel like I've been cast in a role that is so far above who I really am. I mean, I'm from Denver's northwest side, not San Antonio's upper crust. Who do I think I'm fooling? Zach's mother is right—I don't belong. And sometimes it just gets too hard to keep trying."

"That's not true," Lucy said. "You belong as much as she does because Zach loves you and married you."

She shrugged, noncommittal. "Anyway, I guess the stealing was an outlet for me. A release that is going to come back and bite me in the ass big time now that I've been busted."

"Is that why you've been avoiding talking to Zach?" Mercedes asked. Her tone seemed soft and nonaccusatory.

Cristina paused, appraising Mercedes. When she felt satisfied that her question was just that—a question—she answered. "Yes. I'm just not strong like you guys. I'm scared shitless of the confrontation."

Lucy snorted. "Oooh, yeah, I'm so strong. I ran out on my wedding. On a man I love. Woman of the year, Lucy Olivera."

"You are strong," Cristina said, her tone firm. "You—all of you— have such substance to your lives." She paused, her eyes stinging with tears she did not want to shed. "I don't."

Annette leaned forward. "Yes, you do," she said sharply. "I don't ever want to hear any mother saying her life doesn't have substance, because I know how hard and draining raising kids can be. Remember Cassandra and Manuel. And you have the added burden of being obligated to society. Don't sell yourself short, Cristina. You're doing the best you can, hon."

Cristina juggled her nearly empty coffee cup in order to lean across the bed and embrace Annette. "I love you, Annie. I'd forgotten how much, and I'm sorry about that."

"Don't apologize. We have busy lives."

"So I guess it's only Mercedes who has a perfectly pulled-together life. Successful career in a tough industry, beauty, your pick of men," Lucy prompted.

"Damian dumped me," Mercedes said matter-of-factly.

Lucy cocked her head. "I thought you said you two were just going through a rough patch."

"I lied." She tossed her hair. "He dumped me for the day care director at the magazine. Sunshine Sanderson."

"Is that a real name?" Cristina scoffed.

Mercy gave a brief, bitter smile. "Yeah, puffy little slut. And here's the rub. Sunshine came up to my office to tell me how to run the magazine and I fired her. That pissed Damian off, and he had the balls to come to my condo and accuse me of . . . all kinds of terrible things." She shuddered. "The cops came."

"Oh no," Annette said.

Cristina hated to admit she felt almost hopeful for a comrade. "Did you get arrested, too?"

"No. No punches had been thrown yet." She quirked her mouth to the side. "I actually wish I'd gotten one or two in. And maybe one solid kick to the grapes."

"I'm so sorry, Mercedes," Lucy said, definitely sympathetic. "But really, your life is still pretty together. I mean, you can't help that your ex-boyfriend is a dickhead. In fact, I was thinking earlier that you should've hooked up with that cute bartender, Zeb. He had it bad for you, girl."

"Nice thought, but no, he didn't. He just recognized me."

"From the magazine?" Lucy asked.

Mercy hesitated. "Something like that."

Cristina watched Mercedes really struggle, and immediately knew there was more to the story. The question was, would she give it up? The rest of them gave it up.

"Is there more?" Cristina asked, feeling bold.

Mercedes drained her paper coffee cup, then crushed it in her hand and chucked it over her shoulder. "You want the entire ugly tale? Is that it?"

"Only if you want to share," Annette said, always deferential to other people's feelings. Cristina vowed to take a lesson from her, from all of them, actually. But not yet.

"I want the rest of the story," Cristina said.

"I do, too," Lucy added.

Mercedes unfolded her legs and crossed the room to pick up her tote bag. She pulled three newspapers—no, tabloids actually—from it and tossed them on the bed, front pages up. "Well, there you have it," she said in a hard tone. "The unvarnished truth. I picked these up with all the other supplies. Aren't they just pleasant?"

Cristina read the first headline, shock zinging through her. Mercedes was getting bashed in the tabloids almost as badly as Martha Stewart and Rosie O'Donnell had gotten hammered a while back. What a nightmare.

EDITOR OF <u>WHAT'S IMPORTANT</u> A FRAUD

Lucy lifted the top tabloid and they all leaned in and read the second headline:

MERCEDES FÉLAN, WHAT'S IMPORTANT? MONEY, MONEY, MONEY.

Annette blinked up at Mercedes first. "Oh, goodness, Mercy. Why didn't you tell us? I'm so sorry."

"I didn't tell you for the same reason you didn't tell us about your life. This week was about Lucy, not me." She stared down at the ugly headlines and unflattering pictures. "And besides, I was hoping Damian would come to his senses and abandon this smear campaign. Plus . . . I'm sort of hiding out."

"Damian did this? He lied about you to the tabloids?" Lucy demanded, her eyes flashing with anger.

"He and Sister Mary Sunshine went to the tabloids after I booted her." She grimaced. "Problem is, they're not all lies."

"Meaning?" Lucy prompted.

Mercy sighed. "In a nutshell, I'm not known as the easiest CEO in the world to work for."

Lucy crumpled a tabloid and threw it across the room. "God, who cares? If you were a man, it wouldn't matter. They'd applaud you for it. I want to hunt him down and kill him."

"There's no use." Mercedes climbed back on the bed and picked up one of the two remaining rags, studying the front cover. "The damage has been done. My career is probably over. All because I shitcanned the little slut who was fucking my supposedly monogamous boyfriend. And I'm in the wrong."

"It seems so unfair," Annette said.

"It is unfair. That part at least. But I'll be the first to admit that I'm not easy to work for, that I'm all about the bottom line. I was just trying to make the magazine a success. Now *it's* a success, but *I'm* one colossal failure." Mercedes shrugged. "And there is not a damned thing I can do about it."

"I don't know about that," Cristina said. "You know what they say, no publicity is bad publicity."

Mercedes turned the tabloid to face Cristina. "Get real. I'm the editor in chief of a magazine whose editorial slant is keeping one's life focused on what is truly important in order to live a simplified, fulfilled existence, and these articles accuse me of dictator-like behavior toward my employees, creating a hostile working environment, promiscuity, and a myriad of other ills. The readership will lose complete faith in me, mark my words. Our demographic will not tolerate this kind of behavior, whether they love the magazine or not. Whether it's true or not." She tossed the tabloid down angrily. "And believe me, they'll have enough people to corroborate the accusations. Like I said, I'm no Mother Teresa. My entire magazine staff, from the top editors to the lowliest mail sorter, despises me."

"That can't be true," Lucy said.

"Oh, it's true. Know what they call me?"

"What?" Annette said, visibly bracing herself.

"Merciless Félan. Shows-No-Mercy Félan. The Mercenary Félan." She barked out a humorless laugh. "Very descriptive, wouldn't you say?"

"Isn't there anyone on your side?" Lucy asked, sadly.

Mercedes hung her head back, staring at the beamed ceiling. "I suppose the publisher likes me well enough. I make the man a shitload of money, after all. People will put up with anything if you're making bank for them." She briefly thought of Alma. "My secretary . . . well, she's not necessarily on my side, but we had a conversation. Look, I don't want to talk about this anymore. Frankly, I'm enjoying being in denial for the time being." She glanced pointedly at Lucy. "But you see? No semblance of a perfect life here, babe. You're sadly mistaken. I've been divorced three times, dumped and slandered once, and my entire staff thinks I'm the Antichrist."

They all sat in morose silence for a few moments, then Lucy shook her head slowly. "How'd we all get so fucked up?"

The question was so simple, yet so profound. After a pause, they all burst into roll-on-the-bed, uncontrollable laughter. They'd all come clean. None of them was perfect. They all had problems. Somehow that provided Cristina with untold amounts of comfort. She felt safe within the confines of their strange and yet enduring friendship . . . even with Mercedes.

Exhausted from the day, and from their revelations, they all began to fade. One by one they climbed under the covers. Cristina turned off one bedside lamp and on the far side of the bed, Mercedes clicked off the other one. For a moment they lay side by side, staring at the fading glow of embers in the fireplace, each lost in their private thoughts. Annette, the closest to Cristina, began to sing that silly children's song, "There were four in the bed and the little one said, 'roll over, roll over.' " Mercedes countered with ninety-nine bottles of beer on the wall. When they'd stopped laughing like a bunch of pot-smoking high school sophomores, Cristina suddenly recalled an article she'd read on the plane. "You know those in-flight magazines?"

"Yeah," Lucy said, drowsily.

"I read an article on the way here about a reclusive Mexican medicine woman, a *curandera,* living somewhere in the mountains of New Mexico. It was really interesting. She's reputed to be able to change or repair people's lives. I mean, the article was part documentary and part legend. It talked about how many people in the area claim to have been saved or helped by her wisdom and magic, but not one single person was willing to admit ever having met her. I guess this woman is sort of like Big Foot."

"Wow," Mercedes said.

"Yeah. No one ever sees her, at least not anymore. No one even knows where she lives."

"That's really cool," Annette murmured.

Cristina sighed. "I remember thinking, as I was reading it, God, I wish I possessed that skill. Just think how I could change my life . . . if only . . ."

"I can think of a million things I'd do if I could change my life," Mercedes said.

"Me, too. That would be amazing," Annette said.

Lucy said nothing, and they all figured she'd fallen asleep. She needed to sleep; the day had been stressful, to say the least. Not wanting to wake her, the other three women whispered good night and drifted off in the big bed, in the little cabin, on Lucy's would-be wedding night. Cristina's final thought before falling into oblivion was, strangely enough, about the legendary medicine woman. What if she really did exist, and if she did possess the power to mend lives? What if she could mend *their* monumentally screwed-up lives? She felt a split second of hope before it dissipated.

Be real, Cris.

No one even knew where the *curandera* lived, or if she even truly existed. It was a nice fantasy, though, and Cristina fell asleep with a smile on her face.

Part Two

Chapter Thirteen

Annette should've known something was up the moment she got a look at Lucy the next morning. It was the day after The Ultimate Wedding Nightmare, after all. She should've been morose . . . or at least pensive. Instead, she jumped on the end of the bed, waking the three of them up with a jolt.

"Get up, slackers." Her smile absolutely sparkled. "I have breakfast ready and I've figured everything out."

Mercedes rolled over slowly and pushed herself up to sit against the headboard, her eyes bleary. "Please tell me you're talking about omelets, fried potatoes, and world peace."

"Pop-Tarts, instant coffee, and a plan of action, but then again, you did the shopping."

"True." Mercedes yawned and rubbed her eyes. "And world peace really is a pipe dream, at least as long as men and Republicans are in charge."

Lucy gave a little snort of laughter.

Annette glanced over at Cristina, still asleep on her stomach with her arms thrown above her head. She nudged her.

Cristina groaned. "So it is real, then?" she mumbled into her pillow. "Someone actually wants me awake at the crack of dawn? Haven't you psychos ever heard of beauty sleep?"

"It's almost noon," Lucy informed them. "And you're all beautiful enough. Now, wake up. I'm serious. I have a proposition you're going to love."

Annette sat up next to Mercedes. Slowly, and with much grumbling, Cristina finally joined the other two. "This better be good, Lucy. I swear to God. Chirpiness in the morning is a crime against nature."

Lucy grinned, holding up both hands. "It's good. It's absolutely perfect. Wait right here." She disappeared around the edge of the screen and returned, walking carefully, her eyes fixed on the three mugs of steaming instant coffee she carried. After she'd doled those out, she returned again with a mug for herself and a plate full of freshly toasted strawberry Pop-Tarts. She chucked a pile of sugar packets, stir sticks, and little creamer cups into the center of the bed, and everyone reached for their favorites. While they doctored their java, Lucy climbed onto the end of the bed, then sat expectantly on her knees facing her friends.

"What's this about?" Mercedes asked.

"It's about Cristina." She flipped her hand. "Or, actually, the story Cristina told us last night."

Cristina stopped blowing on her coffee and looked perplexed. "What are you talking about?"

"The *curandera.*"

"The—from the flight magazine?" Her brow furrowed.

"Yes. We have to go find her." Lucy held up a hand, warding off anticipated objections. "Before you say anything, just list—"

"*Find* her? Lucky girl, for Christ's sake, are you having another mental break? Haven't you reached your quota for the week?" Mercedes asked. "You're a newlywed. You can't run off with your friends on some wacky search for a reclusive medicine woman no one can even confirm exists."

"*Listen* for a moment." She glared playfully at Mercedes. "I borrowed your cell phone and I've already talked to Ruben. He's one hundred percent supportive. He'll be working anyway."

"Sheesh. You two are perfect for each other." Mercedes shook her head, sipped, then swallowed. "You're both criminally insane workaholics with severely questionable logic."

Lucy sighed with impatience. "Let me ask you this, Mercy. Do you really want to head back to New York City right now?"

A beat passed. "Well . . . no."

"Cris?" Lucy cocked one eyebrow. "Ready to face the music in San Antone? Or do you need more time with your friends?"

Cristina huffed. "Like you have to ask."

"Annette, I know you're busy, but—"

"Just tell us what exactly you're talking about, Lucy." The apprehension had already begun to spread inside Annette. Maybe the others could run away from their lives until the chaos settled, but her life *was* chaos. Didn't they get that? Running wouldn't help a thing.

"I think we should find her. Pack up our stuff, take a road trip, and look for her. I mean, come on. None of us are in the best of places right now, and if this lady can change lives—"

"Allegedly. Besides, how do you know we *can* find her?" Cristina asked. "I told you, the article made it almost seem like she was just an urban myth."

"But it had facts, too, right?"

"Sure, but—"

"How will we know if we don't try?" Silence. Lucy spread her arms. "Haven't you ever wanted to just take a wild leap of faith? Do something crazy and risky and filled with untold possibilities?"

"Oh, what—like spend your best friend's wedding night *with* her in some musty one room cabin?" Mercy asked in a wry tone. "Yeah, that was always up there on my list."

Lucy balanced her mug precariously on the bed, braced between her knees, and clasped her hands together, imploring her friends. "Please, I'm begging you guys. When will we ever have this chance again? Mercy and Cris, you two were planning on staying for a few days longer anyway. And your kids aren't even home waiting for you, Cris."

Cris tilted her head back and forth, lips pursed, thinking. "Well, that's true enough."

"What exactly do you plan to do when—if—we do find this woman? Long shot that it is." Mercy studied Lucy over the rim of her mug as she tipped it to her lips. She was trying to look skeptical, but Annette could see her interest was piqued.

"I don't exactly know," Lucy answered.

Apparently this part of her grand scheme remained as yet unplanned. That was Lucy for you, Annette thought.

"Why overthink the thing? Talk to her, I guess. Ask her stuff. Find out if there is a remedy for my jacked-up brain."

"And my jacked-up life," Cris said, softly.

"And my jacked-up career?" Mercy asked.

"Exactly." Lucy shrugged, her tone softening. "It could turn out to be nothing but a wild road trip, which would be fun in and of itself, but how will we ever know if we don't try? Please? It's been twenty years since we were all together. I just know this is right. I feel it, all the way down to my soul."

Annette could see that Mercy and Cris were intrigued, and why not? Annette herself was intrigued, but she also had obligations at home that simply couldn't be ignored. These three might be able to gallivant off on some great adventure, but it was impossible for her. Utterly, no-questions-asked impossible. She could hardly bear to hear the rest of Lucy's un-plan, because she wanted to go along so badly . . . but, God, she just couldn't swing it and she darn well knew it.

Feeling fifty kinds of left out and not proud of the enviousness welling up inside her, she threw back the covers, set her mug on the nightstand, and stood. Everyone looked at her expectantly, and she managed a smile. "Be right back," she said. "Nature calls." She didn't really have to go to the bathroom that badly, but it was a good excuse to get away for a few minutes and get her head together.

In the bathroom, Annette did her business, then braced her hands on the edge of the ancient pedestal sink and stared at her reflection in the cracked mirror above it. She wouldn't sulk. What was the use? She needed to accept the fact that her life wasn't like Mercy's or Cristina's or Lucy's. It never would be. She was obligated to other people, and that wasn't anything new to her. She was used to sacrificing her own desires for the needs of her children.

But is that all there is?

Shouldn't it be enough?

It's not enough.

"It's not enough," she whispered. Guiltily she looked away from her reflection and covered her face with her hands. How dare she indulge in these thoughts. It wasn't right. Still, she felt more distanced from her friends right then than she ever had, and she hated the bitter taste in her mouth, the resentment, the awful yearning.

She didn't know how long she'd been in the bathroom, but pretty soon a tentative knock sounded on the door. She jumped, spinning toward the intrusion. Her lower back rested against the cold porcelain of the sink edge, and she could feel a drop of water soaking into the back of her jersey. Her heart rattled; she laid a hand against her chest to slow it down. "Yes?"

"Annie?" came Lucy's muffled voice through the rustic pine door with the charming skeleton key lock. "You okay?"

Annette smoothed her unruly hair back from her face with shaky hands and took a deep, steadying breath. "Fine. Just a little hung over," she lied in a falsely cheerful voice. "I'll be right out."

"Okay, hurry. We've got Pepto and Alka-Seltzer and aspirin out here. We want to make some plans, too."

Plans. Plans that wouldn't include her, unfortunately, no matter how much she ached for them to. A lump rose in her throat and she swallowed it away. "'Kay. I'll be right there."

When she finally returned to the bed powwow, all three friends were watching her eagerly. She flashed a quick smile, focusing more on her coffee cup as she retrieved it from the nightstand than on them. "Sorry."

"So what do you think, Annette?" Mercedes asked, handing her a sizzling glass of Alka-Seltzer.

Come to think of it, she didn't feel so great. Tequila shots didn't generally play a part in her real life. She set her coffee mug back on the nightstand and started to drink from the rather vile-tasting glass of Alka-Seltzer.

"This ridiculous wild-goose chase of Lucy's might actually turn out to be fun," Mercy added, shrinking away when Lucy smacked her in the upper arm.

Annette looked at all three of them, one by one. "So, it's a go? This trip? Cris?"

Cristina nodded. "The more I think about it, the more fun it sounds. When will I ever have another chance at adventure in my lifetime? Never."

"Mercy?"

"Yeah, I'm in. What the hell, you know?"

"What's the verdict, Annie?" Lucy asked, offering a please-please-please-say-yes smile.

Annette sighed, then sat on the edge of the bed. "Look." She exhaled at length, then struggled with her words—and her emotions—for a moment. "As much as I'd love to go with you, I can't." The three began to protest, but she held up a hand. "I'm not trying to be a party pooper. But look at my life. Realistically. I have five kids. My husband is the sole breadwinner. I cannot expect him to take off more time to watch the kids just so I can run off with my girlfriends, as much as I'd want to. And I desperately want to, you have to know that." She searched their faces with her eyes, looking for acceptance. "We can't afford for him to take time off anyway, frankly."

After a moment, Lucy crawled across the bed and embraced her, and Annette held on tightly. "God, I'm so sorry I didn't even take into consideration your circumstances," Lucy said.

Annette rubbed her friend's back and shook her head against Lucy's neck. "Don't apologize." She pulled away, really trying to look excited and happy for them. "It's not like we're doing badly, but supporting seven people on one salary." She shrugged. "It's an amazingly enticing offer. I just can't. You all go and have a magical time. I expect regular updates."

Cristina hugged Annette next. "It won't be the same without you, Annie. You'll be so missed."

"Really," Mercy said, with a snort. "You truly are the only sane one in the bunch of us." She cast apologetic glances toward Lucy and Cristina. "No offense."

Lucy smiled. "None taken."

"None that weren't expected," Cristina added, her tone snarky-sweet.

Annette picked up another Pop-Tart and nibbled at one corner. "I actually don't like being known as the sane one. But whatever. I guess we are what we are. I can go with you partway, though," she offered, like an olive branch. "I have to drive back to New Mexico anyway, so I'll drive you to Las Vegas, then you can rent a car from there."

Lucy brightened immediately. "That's a fantastic idea."

"We can take turns driving," Cristina said. "Except Mercedes. She lives in New York City, so I'm sure her driving skills are rusty. I sure don't want her behind the wheel."

"Oh, shut your hole," Mercy said, her tone grumbly. "I can drive as well as any New York cabbie."

"Yeah, that's what I'm afraid of," Cristina said.

"I seem to recall you backing into a fucking Pepsi machine back in high school, Cris. It's not like you have room to talk."

"Stop bickering, you two, Jesus!" Lucy shook her head. "I swear, you sound like a married couple." She stood, fists on her hips. "Now that it's settled, what do you say we check out, drive into town to get our stuff, and hit the road? It's late, but we'll stop in Trinidad for the night if we get tired. That's a short first leg, and frankly I want to get this show on the road. ASAP."

"Let's do it," Cristina said, getting up herself and stretching her arms up toward the ceiling.

"I just want to make one thing perfectly clear," Mercedes told them, holding up a finger. "There will be no crime spree, and I'm not driving off a cliff for any of you women. Screw romanticism. Thelma and Louise can bite my ass."

Everyone laughed, the mood sufficiently lightened. Even Annette tried to be happy with what little time she'd have with her friends. It was, after all, better than nothing, and she'd always been a glass-half-full kind of person. She'd take complete advantage of the road trip time with her friends before delving back into real life.

Real life.

Shuddering, she pushed it out of her mind for the time being. Real life was too overwhelming, burdensome, and confusing . . . and she was still way too resentful of that fact to dwell on it.

By the time they'd all checked out of the Brown Palace and stopped by Lucy's empty house so she could pack a bag, Mercedes's enthusiasm for the trip had grown. Just to piss Cristina off, she insisted on driving for the first leg of their journey, and Annette had agreed, taking the front passenger seat. Problem was, the woman looked like someone had drop-kicked her puppy. Oh, she was putting up a valiant front for the rest of them, but clearly Annete was really disappointed about having to bow out of the big *Escape to Witch Mountain* gig.

Mercedes couldn't blame her. It was like not getting picked for a sports team in gym. Mercedes remembered that feeling all too well. She knew there was no swaying Annette from her decision—couldn't even blame her—but she'd been thinking about something that might bring a smile to her face in the meantime. Mercedes swiveled in the driver's seat and faced Cristina and Lucy as they buckled in for the journey. "First of all, do we all have our cell phones and chargers?"

"I do," Lucy said.

"Me, too," Cristina and Annette chimed in stereo.

She hesitated, studying the faces of these women. "You know, I had a thought," she said.

"Was it lonely?" Cristina asked, clearly still pissed about the driving thing.

"Yeah, very funny." Mercedes tossed her a fake, bitchy smile. "But, no. I've been thinking we should head to Annette's house in Las Vegas by way of Albuquerque."

Lucy looked around, as if for a hidden camera. "Yeeeeeah," she drew out, "I know geography wasn't your strong point in school, Mercy, but it's not exactly on the way from here."

"I know that, smart ass, but it's not so out of the way, either." Mercy remained focused on Lucy and Cristina. "And wouldn't it be nice if we could stop by and visit Deborah? Let her know we're on her side and meet this Alex who stole her heart?" She glanced over at Annette, whose face had already begun to shimmer with excitement. "You have time, right, Annette? Otherwise you'll get home a day early, and you deserve to enjoy all the time away that you'd planned."

"Oh," Annette said, on a sigh. "I would love that." She turned toward the back of the van, unabashed hope in her expression. "Lucy? Cris? Would you guys mind? It would mean so much to the girls, I know."

"Mind?" Lucy scoffed. "I think it's a great idea."

"I'd love to meet them, Annie," Cris added. "In fact, why don't you call them right now and let them know when we'll get there. Give them time to prepare for the onslaught."

Annette's eyes welled with tears, and she reached across and squeezed Mercy's hand. "And they call you Merciless. Idiots."

"Yeah, yeah. Just call Deborah, okay?" Mercy brushed off the compliment as if it bored her, but she felt it like a ray of sunshine warming all the dark, cold parts of her soul.

Annette dug her cell phone out of her purse and dialed. Mercy found she was holding her breath, and she glanced back to see Lucy and Cris doing the same.

"Debby?" A pause, then a laugh. "Oh, Alex. Hi, sweetheart. This is Debby's mom. You two sound so much alike. Is she there? Okay, thanks." Annette glanced toward her friends and whispered, "She's getting her," unnecessarily.

A few moments later, Annette's smile widened. "Hi, baby. Yes, I'm still in Denver, but guess what? How'd you like a visit from us?" She paused to listen. "No, from me and my friends. Yes, all of us." Another pause. "No, no. She got married, but . . . well, it's a long story, and we're all heading to New Mexico anyway. There's a *curandera* we want to find who . . . look, I'll explain all that in a minute. We need to get on the road. But if you'll have us, we can be there tomorrow morning, and if it's okay, we'll stay the night. Your Tías Cristina, Mercedes, and Lucy want to see you and"—she stopped, gulping back deep wells of emotion that reddened her face—"and they want to meet Alex and welcome her to the family."

After a moment, Annette laughed, and a tear ran down her face. She turned to the rest of them. "Deborah and Alex say they would love to have all of us. And they love you all for . . . for . . . just for—"

"We know," Mercy said, quietly.

"Kisses to them both," Lucy said, laying a smooch on her palm and blowing it toward Annette.

Annette nodded, then tucked a lock of hair behind her ear and went back to her conversation, giving Deborah the *Reader's Digest* version of what inspired the road trip, and the details, what few they had, about the *curandera.* Just hearing Annette's side of the discussion, Mercedes could tell Deborah and Alex were intrigued by and excited about the whole thing.

With an enigmatic smile on her face, Mercy fired up the engine and pulled into traffic. Yes. Visiting Deborah and Alex was the right thing to do. For the girls themselves, but also for Annette. Hell, maybe for all of them. She's always believed women needed to stick together more than they generally did.

And then women like Sunshine Sanderson entered the picture.

She wouldn't think about her. Hell, she deserved Damian. *Have at it, bitch.* Let Sunshine come to the awful realization that Damian wouldn't know what to do with his tongue even if she had explicit instructions tattooed on her fucking stomach. Ha! Mercy was done with that mess.

She grinned, feeling better than she had in weeks, thanks to the utter unexpectedness of old friends and all the amazing surprises they brought out in her.

Huh. Who woulda thunk it?

In their excitement, they'd decided to drive in shifts straight through to Albuquerque, even though they'd gotten an afternoon start. The girls were now expecting them to arrive very late that evening, and they'd assured them they were welcome to stay at the house, even though it wasn't a five-star joint.

Cristina, via the concierge at the Brown Palace, obtained a copy of the flight magazine with the *curandera* story in it before they left Denver. During Lucy's stint at the wheel, Mercedes fired up her computer and, using her spiffy cellular modem, accessed the Internet. Try as they might, though, they didn't find any further information about the *curandera*. They knew her name—Matilda "Tilly" Tafoya. Fat lot of good that did them, though. Cristina spent time on her cell phone calling various Chambers of Commerce in New Mexico, to no avail. This woman *was* like Big Foot. If she even existed.

As the twinkling evening lights signaled their approach into the outskirts of Albuquerque, Lucy's excitement about the trip had tempered to deflated desperation. She'd reached the sobering realization that she'd dragged her friends along on what really might turn out to be nothing more than a wild-goose chase, and that sucked. But even more, she was really disappointed about the idea of not finding the Tilly, as they'd begun to refer to her. Tilly felt like her last great hope—her only hope—for getting her shit together. If they didn't find her, what would happen with her life? With her marriage? Her stomach tightened. She couldn't even bear to contemplate it. The elusive Tilly felt like her only chance to break the Olivera curse.

Instead, she leaned her head up and looked at Annette in the rearview mirror. "Okay, Annie, lead me in from here. We should almost be there."

Annette gave her directions into a quaint but shabby neighborhood down Buena Vista, off Central Avenue fronting UNM. The aging enclave was comprised mostly of rental houses for students. Mature cottonwood trees soared above the street, their leaves—black at night—flitting in the slight breeze. In short order, the four friends pulled into the cracked concrete driveway of the crumbling 1920s adobe-style rental house Alex and Deborah shared. Objectively, it was a sad affair, but clearly the girls had tried to spruce it up, and that made it seem special. A Snoopy banner hung from a pole by the door, and two pots of red geraniums brightened the austere concrete stoop. Lights still blazed from inside. Lucy glanced at the dashboard clock—almost midnight.

"Gosh, we should've told them they didn't need to wait up. It's so late."

Mercy laughed. "They're college students, Lucky girl, and they're on summer break. Of course they'll still be up."

"Good point." She switched off the ignition, and for a moment they all just sat there, listening to the tick of the hot engine. "God, it feels good to finally be here."

"My legs have been cramped for hours," Annette said.

"My ass is asleep," added Mercy.

"Isn't it disheartening when your mind feels twenty but your body insists on reminding you that you're almost forty?" Cristina asked. "It's so unfair."

"My mind feels fourteen. It's not fun." Lucy swiveled around in her seat. "Shall we go on in then, ladies?"

"Absolutely. Let's go," Annette said. "I can't wait to see my baby." She twisted the handle of the side door and slid it open, then jumped out onto the driveway and stretched.

Just then, the front door opened, spilling light onto the tiny stoop. Deborah's face broke into a beatific smile, and she ran down the two steps, across the yard, and threw herself into her mother's arms. As the two held on, Lucy's heart clenched. Deborah looked so much like

Annette at that age. She was slim and vibrant and utterly adorable. Her black hair was bobbed at shoulder length and waved naturally.

As Cristina followed Annette out of the van and took her turn greeting and hugging Deborah, Lucy glanced up at the doorway and saw another slim, vibrant, and very attractive young woman standing there. Alex. She had a sheath of shiny straight black hair halfway down her back and wore UNM shorts and a plain black T-shirt. Stooped over, she had her finger hooked in the collar of a gorgeous little beagle who was going joy-bonkers over the arrival of new people, and she was watching Deborah hug Annette, a sweet smile on her face. Glancing over, she noticed Lucy watching her and raised a hand in greeting. Lucy raised a hand back. Already she could sense that Alex was good people. A smart choice for Deborah. She just *looked . . .* genuine.

"Let's get our stuff and get out," Mercy said. She'd been seated in the front passenger seat for this last leg. "It's so weird, but I can't wait to meet these girls. Don't they look so young?" she added wistfully. "They have their whole lives ahead of them and they probably haven't fucked too much up yet. God, I envy them that."

"Yeah." Lucy glanced over at Mercedes gathering up her purse and computer case. She reached over and touched her arm. "Mercy, can I ask you something that's none of my business?"

Mercy paused and turned to glance at Lucy. One side of her face was illuminated by the porch light, outlining the contours of her high cheekbones and strong, feminine chin, the other side dark. Her brow furrowed. "Sure. What are friends for?"

A beat passed, during which Lucy wondered why she was so damn curious. But she was. Maybe because she and Mercy were so close, and yet she hadn't known. It just seemed strange. Distancing. "When were you with women?"

"Oh, that." Mercy's face relaxed and she flicked a hand. "I don't know. A few times in the past twenty years. It was never anything serious. Just spur-of-the-moment fun times."

"So, you don't consider yourself—"

"I hate labels," Mercy said, holding up her index finger, "first of all.

And no. I don't consider myself—let's leave it at, I'm open-minded. Okay? It's really no big deal."

"Oh, I didn't think it was a big deal. I just think it's sort of . . . cool." She watched Mercy's profile. "You have so many layers to your personality."

"We all have layers." Mercy glanced over and winked. "It's called being human, babe."

"Does it bug you if I ask you questions?"

"No. If it did, I wouldn't have even told you guys. I'm not ashamed. Men, women, whatever. It's all about the person, not the gender, if you ask me." She glanced up at Alex, still hovering in the front door of the house. Lucy followed her line of vision. "That's what I hope to show these two. Celebrate who you are, whoever you are. They have nothing to be ashamed of. Love is always a beautiful thing."

Lucy warred with her next thought and then decided, what the hell? "Why didn't you tell me?" she asked, softly.

Mercy shrugged. "It never came up. And, like I said, these weren't love matches. Just silly flings." She studied Lucy for a moment, then squeezed her hand. Her tone dropped to a soothing level. "I promise you, Lucy, I have shared every significant event in my life with you. These weren't significant. Not to say I didn't enjoy them. Not to say that I wouldn't go there again if the situation was conducive. But if I'd ever fallen in love, you would've been the first to know, that I promise."

Lucy smiled, feeling better. "You're a good friend, Mercy. And a good person."

Mercy hefted a bag strap onto her shoulder and rolled her eyes. "Yeah, right." She pulled open her door and stepped down onto the driveway. "Tell that to *Hard Copy.*"

"Maybe you should," Lucy said quietly as Mercy shut the door. "Maybe we all should." She wasn't even sure Mercy had heard her, and it didn't matter anyway. With a contented sigh, Lucy exited the van and joined the others.

Chapter Fourteen

Considering the late hour, Annette made quick introductions, then Alex and Deborah set about showing the women their various sleeping choices in the tiny two-bedroom home. The boxy floor plan included their minuscule bedroom, plus a second cramped room with a frameless futon in the center of the *saltillo* tile floor, living room, kitchen, and bathroom. They'd borrowed an inflatable bed from a friend, and that was set up in the living room, next to a wheezy, tired-looking, hand-me-down couch. A strange nervous energy emanated from the two of them, which Mercedes found curious. She chalked it up to the fact that four women had descended upon them like locusts, without much warning.

Deborah tucked her wavy hair behind her ears—a mannerism she unwittingly shared with her mother—and avoided eye contact with any of them. "So, anyway, Mom, I thought you could sleep in . . . my bedroom with me. Alex will . . . take the couch, and then one of you can have the futon and the other two can share the blow-up bed. I-if that's okay."

Ah. She should've figured. The sleeping arrangements had the girls agitated, poor things. Mercedes imagined they'd fretted about it all day long. It was one thing telling your parents you were in love with a member of the same sex. Quite another to sleep together basically in front of one of them.

Mercedes glanced at Annette, watched her mouth open helplessly. Hoping to say what Annette couldn't find words for, Mercedes jumped in. "Deborah, don't be silly."

Deborah glanced up, startled. Annette looked grateful.

"You and Alex share a bedroom, right?"

She watched Annette's beautiful daughter's face redden, and her gaze dart Annette's way. "Well . . . um, yeah. We do."

Mercedes reached out and squeezed her shoulder. "We are guests in your home. You and Alex will sleep in your bedroom as usual, and the four of us will double up on the other two beds. It's not a problem. Right?" She looked around at the others, and they silently nodded their support.

Deborah's face turned a mottled almost-purple that telegraphed imminent tears. Odd, but Mercedes remembered that mannerism from when Deborah was a preschooler, which was basically the last time she'd seen her. Decades ago. Strange how such a thing had carried over into adulthood. Extra strange how Mercedes recalled it.

Deborah turned toward her mother, and the dam gave way. "Is that okay with you, Mom?" she asked, in a tone high and squeaky from her tears.

With a sympathetic click of her tongue, Annette pulled her vulnerable daughter into her arms. "Oh, baby." She kissed her hair, rocking her gently. "Of course it's okay. It's the way it should be. We didn't come here to judge you." She smiled at Alex over Deborah's head. "We came here to celebrate you. And to tell you we're proud of both of you for . . . for—"

"For being proud of loving each other," Mercedes said, firmly. *"Always* be proud of that. Don't let *anyone* dampen that feeling for either of you. I mean it."

Annette flashed her a quick, grateful glance. "Yes. Listen to your Aunt Mercedes. She's wise."

"Okay. Thank you. I love you, Mom," Deborah sobbed.

"I love you, too. And you, Alex. Come here." She extended one arm, and Alex moved into the embrace.

"Thank you, Mrs. Martinez," Alex said.

"You're a part of the family now and I don't ever want you to feel otherwise. Deborah's dad will come around, I promise."

That just made Deborah cry harder, lapsing into hiccups.

Alex started crying, too.

"Hey now, waterworks. We love you guys, too, and we support you," Lucy told them, joining in. One by one, the other women layered on to the embrace until they were one big, swaying group hug. They stayed that way for a few moments, before pulling apart one by one. Deborah and Annette were the last to break away. Deborah's eyes shone with happiness, and she brushed her tears away with the backs of her hands and then smeared them on the sides of her shorts. Alex moved up next to her and shyly took her hand. The girls shared a look of pure love that made Mercedes's heart clench. Looking around at her friends, she could tell they shared the reaction. Pure love was always difficult to witness. Why was that, she wondered? Because it was so rare? So beautiful? So damned unattainable for most of the poor saps muddling through this life?

"Okay, then. We'll sleep in our room." Deborah shrugged. "I guess you guys can do rock-scissors-paper to decide who gets the futon and who gets the blow-up thingie. Keep in mind, Bailey sleeps on the futon and you can't get him off it with a crowbar."

Cristina raised her hand. "I'll take the futon, then. I miss my little dog."

"I'll take the inflatable," Mercedes quickly said.

Annette and Lucy smirked at each other. God forbid Cristina and Mercy end up bunking down together. Even in the cabin, they'd had the buffer of Annette and Lucy between them in that lodgepole king-size bed.

Lucy spoke up. "I'll take the futon, too. I miss Rebel and Rookie. Cristina and I will take advantage of the doggy time while we have it." She inclined her head toward Annette. "That okay with you?"

"Of course." She grinned mischievously at Mercedes. "Then I can say I slept with a famous magazine editor. Twice."

"Mom!" Deborah exclaimed.

Mercy groaned. "Great. Just what I need."

"I'm only kidding, you two. Sheesh, lighten up." She rolled her eyes. "You're like a couple of puritanical church ladies. It was a joke."

Deborah and Alex laughed, then Alex spoke up, clearly more relaxed. "We're going to make you a big welcome breakfast tomorrow, so come to the kitchen hungry. We can get to know each other better then, after you've had some rest."

"Considering we had Pop-Tarts and instant coffee this morning— God, was that just this morning? It seems so long ago. Anyway, there are no worries about us coming hungry, hon, believe me," Lucy said.

The six women took turns in the tiny bathroom off the hall, and soon enough, they were snuggled down in their various beds. Annette and Mercedes made a little small talk, and then Annette rolled on her side, her back to Mercy. "I sure hope you all can find Tilly," she said, drowsily.

Mercedes sighed, grateful that she was bunking down with Annette. It was odd. Their lives were so vastly different, but she'd started to feel closer to her despite that. She felt safe around her. Real. She wanted to be a safe person for Annette, too, but she wasn't even sure if that was possible . . . or if Annette wanted it. "Doesn't seem likely, does it?"

"Nope. But for Lucy's sake . . ."

"Yeah, I know." Mercedes was silent for a moment, wondering about the wisdom of baring her soul at this juncture. Eh, why not? If she could bare it to anyone, Annette was a good choice. Besides, considering their current situation, perhaps it was something Annette needed to hear. She cleared her throat "Annette? Can I tell you something?"

"Yes, of course."

Mercy chewed on the insides of her cheeks, wadding the edge of the blanket in her hands. "I just want you to know . . . your life might be hard, and I don't doubt that at all. In fact, I wonder how you do it all sometimes without going insane. But it's something to be envied, too."

Annette turned back, making out Mercedes's profile in the bluish moonlight streaming in through the living room windows. Mercy couldn't bear to look over, but she felt the glance, felt Annette's unspoken gratitude. "Thank you, Mercy. What a sweet thing to say."

"I'm not trying to be sweet. I mean it. The love of a child"—she sighed—"I know they can be a handful, but that's a magnified love, Annie. And you've got it magnified times five. You live in a small, warm town, in a gorgeous state. Randy loves you. Sometimes . . . I just envy you your world is all. It seems carefree. I know it's not, but—"

"Oh, Mercy," Annette said, clearly touched. "I can't imagine anyone envying my life, but thank you. It does help me look at things with a lot more objectivity." She was quiet a moment. "I've thought the same thing about you and your life, you know."

"My life would kill you, Annie. It's not so great."

"You have a glamorous job—"

"For which everyone despises me."

"I can't believe that."

She sighed, not proud of the fact. "It's true. Besides, although I love it, it's just a job. It's not as glamorous as you might imagine. I don't have anyone to come home to at night and share my successes with, so what's the point?"

"I'm sorry, hon."

"Don't be. It's just the way it is." She paused, thinking. Always thinking these days. "I've always wanted kids," Mercy said wistfully. She turned to face Annette, her pillow crinkling beneath her head. "Did you know that?"

Annette ached for Mercy's vulnerable yearning. "No, I didn't know. You're not exactly an open book."

Mercy suffered a little stab of guilt. "I know. I'm sorry. I . . . guess it's my defense mechanism."

"For sure. But, Mercy, there's still plenty of time for children if you want them. You're only thirty-eight years old."

Mercy shook her head. "There's no time. My lifestyle isn't conducive to giving birth. Or raising children. Not to mention, there isn't a prospective father in the picture. I'd probably be the world's worst mother anyway."

"You would not." Annette searched her mind. "And you know . . . there are donors. Or you can adopt. You're a wealthy, successful woman. They'd let you adopt, no questions."

"Maybe before. Not since these tabloid stories hit," she said, softly. "I'm single, and I've been vilified in the press. That's two strikes against me, Annie, and I'm out."

"Doesn't it take three strikes for an out?"

Mercy smiled sadly through the darkness. "You don't have to try and fix my life. I just wanted you to know . . . sometimes I'd love to have *your* life. So maybe, when things get hard, you can remember that and feel better."

Annette swallowed hard. "Thank you. For telling me."

"And I wish you could come with us on the wild-goose chase. So much."

"Me, too."

They both lay silent for a few moments, then Mercy said, "Okay, well. Good night, Annette."

"Night, Mercy. I love you."

Mercy sighed, feeling so adrift, so undone by the simply stated, clearly genuine endearment. She wasn't sure if she could speak around the lump that had grown in her throat, but she finally managed to swallow past it and whisper, "Ditto."

In the other room, Lucy and Cristina lay side by side on the frameless futon, with a snoring beagle in between them. Both of them were absentmindedly petting Bailey's soft fur, and the dog was belly up, the epitome of utter canine contentment. "Thanks for coming with me on this crazy trip, Cris. I know it's not the easiest time for you."

"Give me a break, Luce. It's not the easiest time for any of us, especially you."

Lucy sighed, her heart heavy with disappointment and a strong sense of responsibility. Plus, she didn't want to think about running out on her wedding reception. Or Ruben. It was easier to focus on this trip, on the here and now. "I have a feeling the trip's going to be a bust. I was totally grasping at straws on this one. I admit it. I'm sorry."

"It could never be a bust with all of us together. Well, except Annette." A pause. "That's such a bummer."

"It really is." They remained silent for a few minutes, each lost in her own thoughts. "Okay, less depressing topic. Aren't Alex and Deborah adorable together?"

"Painfully so. God, the love is so evident on their faces. I wonder if I've ever been that open." She sighed. "I'm pretty sure I haven't, at least not since I met my monster-in-law and realized she hated my guts. It's all been plasticky since then. But Deborah and Alex . . . I'm glad Annette is okay with it, because they really seem happy. That's what counts in life."

"You know she would be. Annette is the least judgmental person I've ever met."

"So true. But things can change when you're talking about your kids, trust me. You want them to have carefree lives. Deborah hasn't chosen the easiest path."

"No. But she'll have lots of support."

"I wish Randy would come around."

"He will." Lucy imagined he already had but just didn't know how to go about fixing things. God knew, men weren't the best communicators in the world. Ruben was pretty amazing at it, though. Her heart clenched, and she pushed thoughts of her once-in-a-lifetime love, her— holy shit—*husband* away. "Would you be okay with it? I mean, if Cassandra or Manuel chose the same difficult path?"

She could tell Cristina was mulling it over. "I think I would. I'm not saying there wouldn't be some disappointment. Especially if Cassandra were . . . I want grandchildren."

"Nothing says two women can't give you a grandbaby."

"Well . . . true. You know, yeah." Another pause. "I think I'd be scared for Manuel if he was, just because of the health danger issues."

"Those aren't limited to the gay community, babe."

"Yeah, I know. I didn't say it was logical, it's just what pops into my mind as a mother. But I'd be okay with it. I want my kids to be happy. I don't want them to feel empty inside or try and live up to bullshit unrealistic expectations." She shook her head, groaning. "That way lies disaster, take it from me."

Lucy cleared her throat, knowing she needed to say more but unsure exactly how to broach it. She decided to just dive in. "Speaking of . . . that," she said, "I want you to know that I don't judge you at all for . . . the arrest."

"Really?" Cristina asked, her tone unabashedly vulnerable.

"Really and truly. You're my friend. I love you unconditionally. I'm sorry you're in this mess, and I'm sorry you felt so bad in your life that you had to do what you did, but I don't hold it against you."

"Thank you." Her voice shook. "You have no idea how much that means." Cristina sighed, absentmindedly toying with Bailey's sweet, floppy ear. "I am in a big mess, huh?"

Lucy turned on her side, propping herself up on one elbow, her head on her hand. "Nothing you can't resolve. And it's a misdemeanor, which is good. Not *good,* but it could be so much worse, Cristina."

"Yeah, that's what the cop told me."

"It's not going to be fun, though, I can tell you that much. And you'll have that on your record. You can't change the arrest. What's done is done. But how you handle it from here on out is what counts."

"The cop said that, too."

"It's sort of a cop spiel, I guess. But it's true." She nudged Cristina's shoulder with her fist. "Look at the bright side, we're all big messes right now, so you're in good company."

Cristina laughed, trying to keep her voice low. "Boy, that's the understatement of the century."

Lucy snickered, too, and after a few minutes, they settled down. Lucy flipped over on her back, staring at the ceiling. Her tummy growled. "I wonder what's for breakfast? When I was in college, my repertoire consisted of ramen noodles and leftover pizza. And orange pop. Always orange pop."

"Well, you've got to get that fruit group in for a well-rounded meal," Cristina joked. "But, Deborah and Alex seem a lot more mature than we did at twenty, don't they? Or is it just me?"

"No shit. It's not just you, believe me. They seem more mature than I do *now*."

Cristina clicked her tongue. "Don't be ridiculous. So you have a couple quirks. Don't beat yourself up about it."

"Quirks." Lucy snorted. "Way to minimize."

"I'm the queen of that." Cristina laughed softly again. "Hopefully they'll blow our minds and whip up some amazing breakfast concoction. I'm looking forward to just getting to know them better. Well, to that and coffee." Cristina adjusted, rustling the light covers. "Do you ever fall asleep at night anticipating that first cup of joe in the morning, Luce?"

"Yeah. I'm a caffeine addict as much as the next person." They lapsed into an easy silence again, listening to the beagle's happy snoring, petting his soft fur, thinking private thoughts.

"Do you think you and Mercedes will ever patch things up?" Lucy blurted out of the blue. She'd been thinking it, and it had just sort of . . . come out. But she wasn't sorry she'd asked.

Cristina remained silent for so long Lucy thought maybe she'd fallen asleep. But finally Cris took a deep breath and blew it out slowly. "I don't think so, Luce. Things are so far gone, I wouldn't even know where to start. I don't even know what needs to be repaired."

"That makes me sad, Cris. Truly."

"Yeah," Cristina whispered, after a few drawn-out moments of thoughtfulness. "Me, too."

L ucy had lain awake for about an hour the next morning, not wanting to wake Cristina or Bailey, both of whom were snoozing hard. She wasn't ready to face the day either, truth be told. In the sparsely decorated white-walled guest room, she interlocked her fingers behind her head and stared up at the ceiling. The enticing odors of coffee and cooking meat—chorizo?—wafted in from the kitchen making her stomach growl, and beyond the closed door, she could hear the muffled conversation and laughter of the others, though she couldn't make out their words. They'd have to get up eventually, but she chose to take advantage of this quiet time to get her thoughts straight, make some decisions.

Fact: they hadn't been able to glean any decent information about Tilly—not a bit—and she'd been wrestling with her next step ever since. Should she continue with the search? Write it off as desperation and go home to take her lumps?

By the time Cris started to stir, Lucy had decided the only logical plan was to abandon this ridiculous hunt before they spent precious time and money on nothing but pure disappointment. Thanks to her harebrained enthusiasm, though, Cristina and Mercy were all fired up. She didn't know how to break it to them that she'd lost her heart for it. But she needed to, and sooner rather than later. Avoidance was a beautiful thing, no arguments there, but they all needed to go home and deal with their problems. Chasing a pipe dream wasn't going to change a thing.

Cristina roused with a groan, rolled over, then raised herself to her elbows. She glanced around the little guest room, disoriented. "I think we're the last ones up," she said to Lucy around a yawn. "Why does it always seem so goddamn early?"

"Because we stay up too late."

"Yeah," Cristina said, running fingers through her hair. "And I'm way too old for this."

"Aren't we all? But we'd better join the others. They've been up for almost forty-five minutes."

"And you know this because . . ."

"I've been awake for an hour."

Cristina gave her a sharp look. "Why didn't you wake me?"

"And incur your wrath?" Lucy scoffed. "No thanks."

Cristina smacked her.

"Not really. You and Bailey were sleeping so soundly, I didn't want to wake you. Besides, I was enjoying just lying here thinking about stuff."

"Yeah?" Standing, Cristina dug through her bag for her China silk kimono. "What stuff?"

"Tilly. The whole trip. Ruben. Just stuff."

Cristina didn't speak until she'd slipped both arms into the sleeves of her kimono and tied the belt. Then she flipped her hair back and leveled a gaze at Lucy. "Losing your nerve?"

"It's not that," Lucy said, rising to rummage through her own bag. She slipped an oversize sweatshirt over her head. "Or maybe it is that, partly. But we haven't been able to find anything. I don't want to waste your time, or Mercy's."

"We're big girls, Luce. Let us decide what's a waste or not. Besides, we just got here." No comment from Lucy. "How about we make a pact not to give up until we do a little sleuthing in-state?"

"I don't know, Cris." Lucy sighed.

"Okay. Fine." She twisted her mouth to the side, thinking. "Then, how about we don't make any decisions until after we're properly caffeinated and our bellies are full of whatever they're making out there that smells so absolutely wonderful. Can you meet me halfway on that at least?"

Lucy smiled. "Well . . . okay."

By the time they joined the others, sunlight streamed through the window over the sink, bringing cheer into the otherwise dismal little kitchen. The girls had the back door open to draw in the cool breeze and morning birdsong.

"Well, if it isn't the two sleepyheads," Annette said, smiling happily as they entered the kitchen. She and Mercy sat at the little rickety dinette while Deborah and Alex bustled about the kitchen preparing breakfast together as if they'd done so for twenty years.

"Morning," Lucy and Cristina said in unison.

Alex set steaming mugs of coffee down in front of them. "Did you sleep okay on that futon from hell?"

"It was perfect," said Cristina, smiling up. "And that beagle of yours is an angel. Thank you." She lifted her mug in a small salute.

Lucy, meanwhile, watched the two girls move around the kitchen in perfect synchronization. They worked so well together, moved so well together, she found it poignantly sweet and yet painful to witness. How was it that two twenty-year-old young women could get it right, and a supposedly mature thirty-eight-year-old woman like herself couldn't? Was she just defective?

"What's that wonderful smell?" she asked Deborah, who was moving sizzling meat around in a skillet with a spatula.

"It's linguisa sausage. Have you ever had it? It's Portuguese." She smiled toward Alex. "Alex is Portuguese on her mother's side, and her grandma sends it to us in dry ice from San Francisco."

"Other side of the bay, actually." Alex winked at Deborah, softening the correction. "San Leandro."

"Whatever," Deborah said. "It's yummy, that's all I know."

"Well, it smells wonderful."

"You'll never guess what these two girls were doing during our drive here, Lucy," Annette said.

"Uh . . . let's see." Lucy tilted her head and shifted her eyes toward the ceiling. "What would I be doing if my mom and her crazy friends were descending upon me? Cleaning house?"

Alex and Deborah laughed.

"Nope, they were researching our very own Tilly."

Lucy blinked in surprise at the two girls, hope floating inside her.

That she hadn't expected. "Really?" She almost didn't dare ask. "Did
. . . did you find anything worthwhile?"

"Lots," Alex said.

"Alex is a whiz at research," added Deborah, proudly. "She has a
4.0 GPA, and she's studying a double major—Native American Studies
and Native American Linguistics."

"What do you plan to do when you graduate?" Mercy asked.

Alex laughed. "Who knows? I'll probably be a lawyer."

Lucy's heart started to pound inside her chest and she ignored the
banter. Could it be true? Could their formerly cold trail have grown
warm again, thanks to a couple of brainy college students? This detour
of Mercy's might have been more inspired than any of them realized.
"So, are you going to share what you found out?"

"Later," Deborah said, lifting the sauté pan off the burner, the mixture of linguisa and scrambled eggs still sizzling. "But first we're going
to eat while it's hot. We have to feed our brains before we use them. My
mom taught me that." She smiled at Annette, then began dishing up the
breakfast. There were only four chairs around the tiny table, so she and
Alex sat up on the countertop, side by side, legs dangling.

In between bites and yummy sounds, Lucy glanced around guiltily
at her friends. "I have to confess, I was ready to give up this chase
today."

Mercedes stared at Lucy with an incredulous expression, fork in
midair. "After all we've been through? Are you crazy?"

"Yeah, well-established fact. But we weren't getting anywhere, Mercedes. It all started to seem desperate and stupid. I didn't want to pull
you guys into my neuroses."

"I thought you had more tenacity than that," Mercy said, shaking
her head and going back to her breakfast.

That stung. "Well . . . thank God for college students who know
how to do research." She raised her coffee mug to Deborah and Alex,
who shared a satisfied grin. "If we have a trail, I'll gladly follow it."

"We definitely didn't find any concrete evidence of where she is
right now," Alex warned, "but we do have a trail. We know where she

lived at one point and approximately when she fled the town. Do you know, some overzealous religious group came after her claiming she was a witch?"

"That's really awful."

"Aren't my girls smart?" Annette asked.

"Yes, proud mama," Lucy joked. "They are." She glanced up at their hostesses. "All *six* of them," she said pointedly.

Alex grinned. She sipped her coffee, then addressed Lucy, Mercy, and Cristina. "I was thinking . . . after we finish breakfast and everyone gets ready, I could take you three around the town for a few. We can have lunch at the Frontier Restaurant on Central. It's a cool local hangout." She nudged Deborah playfully with her shoulder. "That way this one can have some private mommy time before you all have to leave."

"That's a great idea," Lucy said. Cristina and Mercedes murmured their agreement.

"Aunt Lucy?" Deborah asked. "I know my mom's probably going to lecture me about being rude later, but what happened at your wedding to make you run off?"

"Deborah!" Annette exclaimed.

Deborah rolled her eyes and tilted her head toward her mother. "Didn't I tell you?"

Lucy reached across the table and patted Annette's hand. "It's okay, Annie. They put us up on a moment's notice and did all that research. They deserve to know."

"Our lives are completely screwed, in a nutshell," Mercy cut in with a matter-of-fact tone. She lifted a finger. "Let this be a lesson to you. With age does not necessarily come wisdom."

The girls looked intrigued. "What do you mean, screwed?"

Mercedes glanced around at her friends. "Oh, long story. With me, it's my career and men." She made a withering face. "With Cristina—"

"It's my personal life," Cristina said.

"And your aunt Lucy's just been a whack job from day one." Mercy slipped an arm around Lucy's shoulders and pulled her closer. "No offense."

"Yeah, bite me."

Deborah laughed, then glanced at her mother. "What about you, Mom? Is your life screwed up, too?"

Annette straightened up. "Don't be ridiculous, baby. I'm perfectly fine. Eat your breakfast."

The three elders, minus Annette, exchanged not-so-subtle glances. Didn't Annette realize nothing would change if she didn't let people know how she was feeling? But this was her daughter and it wasn't their place to pry.

"Well, I think you're all totally awesome," Alex said. "No one ever promised life was going to be logical. I mean, take us for example." She smiled gently at Deborah. "Neither of us ever expected this . . . but she blindsided me. I wouldn't have it any other way, either."

Deborah leaned closer to Alex. "Now you guys see why I couldn't help but fall in love?"

"Of course," Mercedes said. "But we never doubted your judgment. We've known your mother for a long time. It comes as no surprise that she'd raise such a smart, savvy daughter."

Annette stood, crossed to the counter, and wrapped her arms around Deborah, her eyes shining with moisture. Come to think of it, Deborah's eyes were a little misty, too, as she returned the embrace. Like mother, like daughter, in a big way.

Which was good. All good. Lucy couldn't think of a better role model for Deborah to emulate.

Chapter Fifteen

After the others had left for their campus tour and lunch date, Annette and Deborah sat cross-legged on Deborah's living room floor, drinking coffee and chatting about school, recipes, flowers, clothes—just about everything. A gentle breeze sucked the gauzy white curtains out the open window, then blew them in again, along with the hot sage fragrance of a Southwest summer.

They hadn't had this kind of one-on-one time in forever, it seemed, and Annette wanted to flash-freeze the moment and store it away in her heart. She could look at Deborah's features and see her instantly as an infant, a toddler, a young girl, a teen. Deborah would be her baby forever, but she was a woman now, mature for her age and so engaging. Annette hadn't felt this relaxed in months. Maybe even years.

"I'm so glad you guys came, Mom," Deborah said, during a lull in what had thus far been a light conversation. Annette had known the topic would turn more serious eventually, and she was ready. Deborah quirked her mouth to the side sadly. "I really needed to see you. I've been so . . . I don't know, icky about stuff since . . . Dad."

Annette felt a stab of pain to her soul. "Your father will come around. I promise you that." She reached out and ran her hand down Deborah's cheek. "He's a good man."

"I know he is. That's what makes this so hard. I love him and, God"—Deborah rolled her eyes— "I want his approval. Is that babyish of me?" She crinkled her nose.

Annette laughed. "Of course not. I still want Grandma's and Grandpa's approval, you know."

"You do?" Deborah looked hopeful and vulnerable. Also a little surprised.

"Of course. We always want our parents' approval." She sipped. "But you have to temper that need with the knowledge that you're doing what you have to do—what you want to do—to live a happy life. It's your life, bottom line, and that's the most important thing. Be happy."

Deborah's shoulders lifted with a deep inhale, then dropped on a sigh. Her eyes took on a dreamy, far-off look of pure, unadulterated contentment. "I am happy."

"I know you are, baby. Anyone who looks at you can tell."

A pause stretched, and then Deborah looked squarely into her mother's eyes. "Are you happy?"

Annette's stomach jumped, and she glanced away, making busy work of picking a piece of lint off the area rug. "Of course I'm happy. Don't ask silly questions," she said way too fast. The question had caught her completely off guard.

Deborah uttered a sound of frustration. "God, don't lie to me, Mom. I bared my soul to you in the scariest way possible and you can't even look at me to answer that simple question. I'm not a child. Please, just . . . be honest with me."

Annette's eyes filled with tears, and she blinked up at her daughter, so grown-up. So insightful. She wanted to talk, but she wondered about the wisdom of being blatantly truthful. She gave a small shrug of one shoulder. "I'm a little stressed out. It's not the easiest thing in the world, raising five kids."

Deborah bit one corner of her mouth and ran her finger around the rim of her mug. "Do you regret having so many of us?" she asked in a soft, wary tone. "Or having any of us at all?"

"Oh, gosh," Annette whispered, horrified. She set her coffee aside, did the same with her daughter's, then took both of Deborah's hands in her own, caressing the smooth knuckles with her thumbs. "I have never regretted a single moment of life with you girls. You know that. But sometimes—" She cut herself off, pressing her mouth into a thin line, and shook her head.

"Tell me, Mom."

Annette wrestled with how much angst a parent should lay on a child. She'd read all the parenting books. But Deborah deserved to be treated like an adult. She had more than earned that right. Annette exhaled her tension slowly. "Sometimes I just think my life is . . . meaningless. Except for you girls, of course, and Daddy," she rushed to add. "But *my* life. What do I do with *my* life? Zip."

Deborah's eyes went round. "That's ridiculous. Don't you see, none of us could've turned out the way we have without you. You're our rock."

Annette's throat tightened. She couldn't speak for a moment. She reached over for her mug, buying time with a sip of coffee. "I know," she said when she'd regained her composure. "But look at my friends. They've all accomplished such amazing things. Even Cristina, outside raising her children, has done such . . . phenomenal things with her life. *Her* life. Do you understand what I'm saying?"

"Yes, but—"

"Other than raise you girls and take care of your father, what have I done? Nothing."

"What do you want to do, Mom? Go to college? Get a job?"

"I . . . I don't know. That's the problem."

A thick pause hung between them, but Deborah's searching gaze never left her face. "Mom, I think you should go on this road trip with your friends."

"No."

"Yes, Mom. *Yes.* You deserve it." Her voice grew impassioned and she squeezed her mom's fingers tighter. "You've more than earned it. Can't you see that? You never do anything just for you, and now you have the chance to do something so . . . once in a lifetime." Deborah sighed. "You need to go. I feel it. This is something you just shouldn't miss. Please, please, please go with Mercy, Cristina, and Lucy."

Annette shook her head, a melancholy smile lifting the corners of her mouth. "I can't, baby. Much as I would love to, and believe me, I would. I'm not trying to be a martyr here. But your little sisters are so whiny and needy without me there and your daddy can't take any more time off work."

"I know." Deborah moistened her lips nervously and slid her mother a sidelong glance. "But Alex and I have discussed it."

"Discussed what?"

"Listen." She held up a palm. "Just listen before you say no. We've researched Tilly, and we both think you can find her if you try hard enough. I really believe she's out there."

"Yes. I do, too."

"Ruthie and Mary worship us. And we love them." She shook her head with exasperation. "Plus, I'm never going to patch things up with Dad unless I make the first move. He's doing that silly stoic Latino male thing."

"Irritating, isn't it?"

They laughed, but for the first time, Annette felt the tug of anticipation, a frisson of possibility running down her spine.

"Both Alex and I are off for summer break and neither of us have jobs. We're doing some volunteer stuff with Habitat for Humanity, but we can take time off. How about if we go home and take care of my sisters?"

"Oh, Deborah, I can't let you—"

"We're not being completely selfless, I promise you. This way, Dad can see how well Alex and I are doing together. We love each other and we're not abnormal." She straightened her spine. "I won't hide from him, Mom. I love Alex and I'm proud of that. But he's my father. I love him, too, and I want him in my life."

"I don't want you to hide, either, baby."

"He won't have to miss any more days at work this way. Ruthie and Mary won't even miss you if they have us, no offense, and we can take Bailey. They love Bailey." She leaned in and spoke with passion. "I want to make up with Dad, and this way, he can't avoid us." She smiled shyly. "Plus, then you and your friends can go get your grooves back, so to speak, which Alex and I think is such a totally awesome thing. Just the thought makes me so proud of you. I hope I have the guts to do something so spontaneous when I'm your age."

Annette simply stared at her daughter for several long moments. She was so overwhelmed with love, she couldn't speak. If she did nothing else worthwhile in her life, she could die knowing she'd raised an amazing, mature, selfless, wise woman who could take on anything with strength and confidence and panache.

God, please let her sisters turn out so centered.

Finally she pulled Deborah into a fierce hug. They held on for several moments before Annette turned her face and kissed Deborah on the neck. "You're sure, baby?"

"I'm sure. We're both sure, Alex and I. I think it will be fun to hang out with my little sisters. We'll teach them how to swear in three languages."

"Don't you dare!"

"I'm kidding."

"Goodness, I love you so much, Debby." Tears pushed out of the corners of Annette's eyes, and she held on tighter. "How'd I ever get so lucky as to end up with a daughter like you?"

"It wasn't luck," Deborah said, softly, her breath warm against Annette's cheek. "It was you. You made me who I am today, and I just want to say . . . thank you." Deborah kissed her on the cheek. "I *want* you to go with your friends."

Annette pulled back and laughed through her tears, wiping them away with the backs of her hands. "Okay. I'll go."

"For real?" Deborah's eyes shone with excitement.

"For real."

Deborah clapped. "They're going to be so thrilled."

To say the others were thrilled was an understatement of epic proportions.

"Annette!" Lucy exclaimed, her eyes shining. "You're kidding? This is so wonderful." Everything was finally coming together.

"It wasn't my idea." She pointed at Deborah and Alex.

Lucy grabbed Deborah first, lifting her off the floor and swinging her around, then moved on to Alex. "You two have no idea how much this means to me. To all of us."

"Yeah," Alex said through her laughter. "We sort of have an idea. That's why we want to do it. Plus, we just think the prospect of finding Tilly rocks so much."

Lucy looked toward Mercedes and Cristina, both of whom were smiling. "Isn't it wonderful?"

"Perfect," they said in unison.

"Good then." Deborah clapped her small, shapely hands together once. "Alex and I are all packed. So is Bailey. As soon as you're all ready, we can hit the road. The sooner the better, I think."

"I'm packed, too," Annette said, to her friends. "I'll call Randy while you guys get ready."

"We can help you map out an initial search route, based on our Tilly research, on the drive to Vegas," Alex added. She had her hands tucked in the back pockets of her denim shorts, and she rocked back and forth on her feet. "You'll be on your own eventually, but we can get you started, at least."

"God, this is fantastic. I packed my stuff up this morning. How soon can you guys be ready?" Lucy asked Mercedes and Cristina. "Five minutes? Ten?"

"Eager, are we?" Mercy smirked.

"Ten minutes, it is," said Cristina, moving toward the guest bedroom to gather her stuff.

"I can do it in five," Mercedes said.

"Yeah? I'll race you," Cris said, in a deceptively friendly singsong tone.

Mercy scrambled toward her bag in the corner of the living room and began unceremoniously stuffing her belongings into it. "Like *you* could beat me at packing."

"Watch me."

Lucy shook her head, smiling. Competitive to the bitter end, those two. But looking on the bright side, she knew neither of them would come close to taking five full minutes, now that the gauntlet had been thrown, which meant they were that much closer to embarking on their search for enlightenment. For once, she didn't feel like telling Mercy and Cristina to give it a rest. This was one show she wanted to get on the road, and if their ongoing battle to one-up each other accelerated that, well, more power to them. *Have at it, girls.*

Annette had taken the wheel for the drive from Albuquerque to Las Vegas, and the other women were huddled around Alex and Deborah in the back. The girls were pointing out pertinent information on a big, cumbersome foldout map. As the miles passed beneath the car, the women tried valiantly to concoct some sort of plan that didn't make it seem like they were off on a hell-ride to nowhere.

"You're going to head toward the Jicarilla Apache Nation, which is headquartered in Dulce"—Alex pointed—"up here, see?"

"And, that's where Tilly last lived?" Lucy had a pen poised over a black-and-white composition tablet upon which she'd been taking copious notes.

"She didn't live on the reservation, no. But nearby."

"Okay, but what's the name of the town she lived in?"

Alex made a face. "That's the thing. Tilly always preferred to live rural. Very rural. So she wasn't really *in* a town, much less near a town, if that makes sense. She does the subsistence farming thing, as far as we know. But the nearest town we could find—"

"—is Dulce," finished Deborah. Her tone turned almost reproachful. "And, remember, if you're on Indian land, you're in a sovereign nation. There are rules and ways of showing respect you just have to follow."

Mercedes gaped in wonder at Lucy. "Aren't the adults supposed to be telling the college students to behave, Lucky girl? Sheesh."

One corner of Lucy's mouth quivered up. "Apparently, our reputations precede us."

Mercedes tilted her head, conceding the point.

"Like what, girls?" Cristina asked. "The last thing I want to be is disrespectful."

"No photos, no sketching, no videos," Deborah ticked off on her fingers. "Don't wander into any of the homes."

"Like we would," Mercedes said, scoffing.

"But, I'm just saying. I mean, people do that. Can you imagine?" Deborah shook her head. "Let's see, what else?" She looked to Alex for assistance.

"Remember that any dances or ceremonies you might come across aren't entertainment," Alex said. "You're allowed to watch. Just don't do anything tacky like clap or talk to the dancers or get in the way."

"We're really going there with a goal in mind," Lucy reminded them, gently. "This isn't a vacation."

"True. But still," Deborah said. "You don't know what you'll run into. Don't pick up pottery shards or walk on ruin walls. Oh, and don't approach *kivas*."

"All that sounds reasonable," Cristina said.

"Here's a biggie. Don't bring drugs or alcohol onto Indian land," Deborah said, and Alex nodded.

"*Great*." Mercedes said sarcastically. "Sounds like my kind of place. Not. Know of any convents we can visit on the way? Maybe I can join up. Surely I'm just what they're looking for."

Annette, from the driver's seat, just laughed.

Alex grinned at Mercedes. "It's really not that big of a deal. Just . . . be respectful. It's their land. And Dulce is really right on the edge. I'm sure you can find a place to get a drink outside of the town."

"We'll be respectful, girls, promise," Lucy said. "We do understand that. But getting back to our search, where exactly . . . ish was Tilly's last known place of residence?"

"Geez, you sound like a cop, Aunt Lucy," Deborah said. "Just the facts, ma'am, and all that."

"I am a cop, doll face." She tweaked Deborah's nose.

Alex was still in planning mode and pretty much ignoring all the banter and side comments. "As far as we can tell, she lived somewhere between Dulce and Chama. But it could've been in the area of . . . well, between there and Lindrith."

Mercedes leaned closer to the map, frowning, tracing town names with her fingers. "Okay, those are in two completely different directions from Dulce."

"Yes. But if you triangulate that area, you should be able to find someone, somewhere who can help you."

"We have to triangulate?" Lucy sat back, overwhelmed. Bailey was curled up and snoozing on the seat next to her, and she began stroking his fur absentmindedly. "I guess it was too much to ask to just find an address for the woman?"

Alex grinned. "Uh, yeah. If it were that easy, she wouldn't be sort of a legend. But the searching will be the best part. Wait and see."

"So you say. I wish you could come with us as a guide."

"Sorry," Deborah said, hooking her arm through Alex's. "She's on sister duty with me. You can't have her."

"But you can call us whenever you need direction or new ideas," Alex said, smiling toward Deborah. "I swear, we're almost as excited about this search as you four are."

"Just do us a favor," Mercedes said. "Don't let your lives wander so far off track that you have to go on some wacky, unplanned midlife quest to find a woman who can—hopefully—get your shit together for you."

"Stop swearing in front of my child, Mercy," Annette said.

"Sorry."

Deborah rolled her eyes at her mother's overprotectiveness. "No promises," she said. "Screwing up is part of life. You four are no different from anyone else muddling through."

Mercy blinked at Deborah a few times, then asked, "How'd you get so wise in twenty short years?"

Deborah smiled toward her mom, then reached up and squeezed Annette's shoulder. "I had a good teacher."

Within an hour or so, they were pulling into the driveway at Annette's house. Deborah and Alex had grown nervous and quiet over the past several miles. Annette felt for them; she knew they were scared. She glanced back in the rearview mirror at their matching deer-in-the-headlights expressions.

"This is going to be fine," she said, in a soothing tone. "Dad was glad to hear you were coming. He was."

Deborah said nothing, but took in a deep breath. She looked more apprehensive than Annette had ever seen her, more so than when she'd come out to them, and that was saying something. Alex squeezed Deborah's hand, then let go, rubbing her palms together.

Heck, Annette couldn't blame them for worrying, but she just had a feeling everything was going to be fine. Funny how a little time and perspective could really change a person's outlook. A week or so ago she'd thought the situation between Randy and Deborah was a major insurmountable crisis. Now it seemed a little bit more like just another speed bump on the crazy road called life.

Annette switched off the ignition, but before the group could alight from the van, Randy had opened the front door and stood on the stoop, smiling. Annette's heart clenched at the sight of him. Yeah, all doubts and worries aside, she loved this man with her whole heart and soul.

Ruthie and Mary squeezed past him on either side and ran to the driver's side of the van, bouncing up and down outside Annette's door, waving at her. Annette grinned, setting the emergency brake before opening the door. Mercedes had been right. The love of one's children was a magnified, pure, beautiful love, and she never wanted to take it for granted.

She opened the door and the twins attacked her with hugs and kisses and manic chatter. She half listened, giving noncommittal answers, all the while watching the scenario unfold between Deborah and Randy.

Deborah got out of the van and stood, hesitant and clearly not emotionally prepared for Dad's Censure, part two. But it wasn't to be. Randy stepped off the porch and crossed the yard to her in long, fast strides. He grabbed her in a bear hug, one hand on the back of her head, and he rocked her slightly.

"Debby, baby. I'm so sorry."

Deborah burst into tears. "Me, too, Daddy."

"No. No. You don't have to apologize."

"I love her," Deborah said, her voice wobbly.

Annette watched Randy look up at Alex, still perched on the running board of the van, her hand wrapped around the doorjamb, bottom lip caught up with worry between her teeth. He smiled, beckoning her down to join them. "I know. I understand love, because I love you and your sisters and mother so much. That part, I understand completely, okay?" Alex approached cautiously, and he pulled her into a hug, too. "I'm sorry, Alex. I never meant to hurt either of you."

"It's okay, Mr. Martinez."

Bailey barked sharply from the van, and the three of them pulled apart laughing. Alex turned and lifted the little guy down so he could run around the yard like a dog on crack. Ruthie and Mary abandoned their mother to happily chase Bailey, and Annette moved closer to her husband.

Randy leaned in and kissed her, a sound of satisfaction low in his throat. "God, babe. It's good to see you. Even for just a short time."

She crinkled her nose. "It's really okay if I go?"

"Of course. Who needs you?" He winked, then grabbed the back of Deborah's neck with one hand and the back of Alex's with the other. "The three of us have a lot of talking to do, and the twins are thrilled to have some sister time. Don't you worry about us."

Annette reached up and touched Randy's cheek. "You're a good man."

"A little slow sometimes"—he made a regretful face at Deborah, who laughed—"but I do my best." He looked from Deborah to Alex apologetically. "I can't say I completely understand your choice, girls—"

"Love isn't a choice, Daddy. The heart has a mind of its own. You should know that."

"You're probably right, and I'll try, okay? I love you." He looked at Alex and winked. "And anyone my Deborah loves is okay in my book. I know we raised you with good instincts."

The three of them hugged again, and Annette released a breath. Everything would be fine, just as her friends had assured her. Randy would spend time with the girls, and he would see. Love was love.

For the first time, she felt like she could truly run off with her friends, worry-free. She glanced around the yard, the same as when she'd left it. The house looked warm and welcoming, the grass had been mown. Ruthie and Mary rolled around with Bailey, shrieking with laughter as he bounced and twirled and kissed their faces. Randy held hands with Deborah and Alex, and Deborah looked radiant. Even Sarah and Priscilla looked happy, now that they'd wandered out onto the porch to somewhat join the fray, in that standoffish, teenage way. She blew them kisses. They blew them back. Life went on, even when she wasn't there. She felt one small pang of . . . something. Worry that they didn't need her? But she pushed it away. This was a good thing. A huge weight lifted from her shoulders, and she realized what Deborah had said was right. This trip was destiny.

Feeling fifteen years younger and buoyant with hope, Annette simply couldn't stop smiling. And she couldn't wait to get on the road! They had a map, a plan of action, and the full support of their families. What more could they ask?

Chapter Sixteen

"Excuse my French, but where in the fuck are we?" Mercy asked, with an edge of exasperation, glancing around at a whole lot of nothingness outside the van windows. Out here, one damn sagebrush or piñon tree looked like the next, and signs were few and far between. "Didn't we follow the map?"

"I'm not exactly sure where we made a wrong turn," murmured Lucy, her head bent over the map, bottom lip pinched between her fingers in concentration. "Of if we even *made* a wrong turn. I mean, according to these mile markers, we should be somewhere near . . . Cuba?"

"If we're near Cuba, we *really* made a wrong turn," Mercedes said, sitting back and crossing her arms.

Annette laughed. "Cuba, New Mexico, silly. It's pretty close to Lindrith. Wasn't that one of the towns the girls thought Tilly might have lived nearby?"

"It was," Lucy said.

"I say, we stop," Cristina offered. "I'm hungry."

"I agree," Mercedes said.

"Count me in," Lucy added, tossing the map aside.

"Okay, majority rules," Annette said, flicking on her blinker in preparation for the exit into Cuba proper. "I'm more than ready to be out of this van."

Cuba, New Mexico, occupied a choice spot at the edge of the Santa Fe National Forest along U.S. 44, which connected this part of the state with the popular Four Corners area. A bonus, because the well-traveled highway meant, for a town this tiny, Cuba had a lot to offer in the way of food and lodgings. If they had to blow off course, in other words, Cuba was a good place to get marooned.

Mercedes was harboring a huge sushi jones, but since that wasn't an option in this metropolis, she let the other women choose the dinner spot. They dithered over a pizza joint with a blue-accented adobe storefront, but it lost out to a small but quaint, new-looking diner on Main Street with neon beer lights glowing from the window. Shortly, they found themselves seated on a small, covered patio, listening to tinny light rock piped out from the jukebox inside the restaurant. The table was standard round redwood fare with wrought-iron chairs that didn't really match, but managed to be charming and eclectic anyway. Sizzling-meat smells from the grill mingled with that distinctive summery odor of sun-warmed vegetation from the surrounding area. All in all, the choice was pleasant.

Mercedes sat back against the ornate but not so comfortable back of her chair, alternately enjoying the famous red glow of the New Mexico setting sun, and watching the waiters and kitchen workers bustle around through a windowed door adjacent to her seat. Cristina, Lucy, and Annette were busily studying the maps and notes from Alex and Deborah, but for the time being, Mercy couldn't drum up any interest. Hadn't they had enough for one day? Besides, she wanted a Vicodin. Badly. In fact, she wanted one so much, she was distracted by the painful urge.

Their waitress approached on quiet mouse feet, and Mercy turned to look at her. Her name tag read "Senalda." She had to be all of five feet tall, sixteen years old, and about seven months pregnant. Her distended belly reached the table several seconds before the rest of her showed up. Her face was flushed from heat and exertion, damp tendrils of her long, black hair sticking to her high cheekbones. How she stood on her feet the full shift was a mystery, but women did what they had to do.

Always had.

"Evening. You like something to drink?" she asked sweetly in a heavily accented voice, her pen poised over a pad she'd pulled out of her apron pocket.

Mercedes remembered the neon signs in the front window, but asked anyway, "You serve beer, right?"

"Yes. Tap or bottle?"

Glancing around at her friends, she noticed none of them were even paying attention to the conversation. She rolled her eyes. "How about a pitcher of whatever you have on tap and four glasses. And water."

Senalda scribbled something onto her pad and nodded. "Coming up. Take your time with the menus."

"Thank you," Mercedes told her.

"De nada."

After Senalda had waddled away, Mercedes snapped her fingers several times. Her friends glanced up. "Earth to the rest of you, I just ordered us a pitcher of beer, so if that's not what you wanted, you're S.O.L.—sorry."

"Oh, good. That's perfect, Mercy." Lucy set aside the composition notebook and picked up the laminated two-sided menu. "Sorry, we were—"

"Yeah, I know."

"I guess we should decide what we want, though," Lucy said, surveying the menu and tapping at her bottom lip with her fingers.

"What are you having, Mercy?" Annette asked, after perusing hers for several minutes.

"Buffalo burger with cheddar cheese, side salad."

"That sounds good." Annette set her menu aside.

"Times three," Lucy added, following suit.

And hopefully a pill or two with a beer chaser, Mercedes thought, mentally amending her dinner selection to include what she really wanted at this point in the trip. God. Why couldn't she handle life without the goddamn things? It was such a weakness, and she loathed weaknesses. She crossed her arms over her torso, defensive for no apparent reason. It wasn't as if anyone could hear her thoughts. The rationalization was, nothing in her life was worth a damn, so why shouldn't she indulge in something that made her forget it all for a while? They couldn't be *all* bad for her.

"I think I'll go for the smothered bean burrito," Cristina murmured. "Although the chiles rellanos sound good, too."

"Have the burrito," suggested Lucy.

Cristina shrugged. "Okay."

The little waitress returned with their beer pitcher and expertly poured them each a glass with minimal head. She doled out tall tumblers of ice water, lemon wedges, and straws on the side, and little napkin-wrapped packs of silverware. Afterward, she retrieved her order pad from her apron pocket and smiled tiredly at them. "You ladies have decided yet?"

They rattled off their choices, but before she could leave, Mercedes reached out and touched her arm lightly. "Can I ask you a quick question?"

The waitress looked surprised, but nodded.

"Do you know about a *curandera* named Matilda Tafoya who may have lived in this area at some point?"

Senalda smiled shyly and shook her head. *"Pero,* there are many *curanderas* if you need someone. I can tell you names."

Mercedes smiled sadly. "No. Thanks anyway."

Senalda lifted one shoulder slightly. "Your dinners will be ready soon." She touched her name tag. "Please ask for Senalda if you need something else."

The waitress left, and Mercedes glanced at her friends and shrugged. "It was worth a try."

"Definitely," Lucy said, planting her elbows on the table and resting her chin in her hands. She frowned. "You feeling okay, Mercy? You look a little . . . pinched."

A thought popped into her head. Guilt stabbed her, but Mercedes grasped for an easy lie anyway. She grimaced and rubbed at her leg, hating the fact that she was so weak and deceptive, but there it was. "My hamstrings are really bothering me. Must be all that time in the car."

"So, take a pill," Lucy said, like it was nothing. If she only knew. "That's what you have them for." She winked. "Well, that and drugging your friend to get her to the altar."

Mercedes smirked, then played at tilting her head, like the thought had never crossed her mind. "You know, good idea. I guess I will take one." Hands shaky with relief at the "permission," she dug in her bag and tapped two pills into her palm, hiding one. She threw them into her mouth and washed them down with water, feeling instantly better. Not because the mellow had hit, but just because she knew it would soon. "So, what's the plan?"

"Sleep, tonight," Annette said. "We can stay at the Del Prado Motel right down the street if no one has any objections, then hit the road for Dulce tomorrow. It's not far from here, now that we've looked more closely. We're not so off-track. I think we were all just overtired on the road."

"Okay, that sounds good." Mercedes quirked her mouth to the side. "It's probably time I checked in with Alba and found out what kind of fallout we're looking at anyway from the tabloid stories and *Hard Copy.*"

"Yes, I'd like to talk to Ruben. Just to say hi." Lucy's expression glowed with yearning.

"I'm going to call Deborah, too, and see if they're ready to run screaming back to Albuquerque yet." Annette smiled.

They all looked at Cristina. She wrapped her hands around her upper arms, rubbing slightly, and looked out over the western horizon. "Pretty sunset, isn't it?"

No one said a word.

Their food came quickly, and they ate in near silence. Everything was surprisingly good, fresh, and perfectly prepared. Just as Mercedes was starting to feel the calming effects of the pills she'd taken, the sound of a tray dropping, followed by a hushed argument coming from just inside the door to the kitchen, startled her. Glancing over, she saw a red-faced Latino gripping Senalda's upper arm hard enough to leave welts. His face was a mask of anger, his body language projecting "threat," loud and clear. Her gut lurched, and she felt her insides going shaky and ice cold—a decades-old deadening reaction to witnessing physical violence. She'd go to her grave insisting that nothing was worse than watching your own mother get beaten. As a child, it had left her feeling powerless and terrified and angry.

The man leaned in to mutter something through his clenched teeth, and the poor girl flinched slightly, turning her head from him like a puppy who was used to getting smacked. With his other hand, he grabbed her chin and yanked her face back toward his. When she pulled away again, the man reared back and slapped her face hard enough to make her neck snap around.

Mercedes recoiled as though the slap had stung her own cheek. "Oh, *hell* no." Could that actually have happened? Was she hallucinating?

"What?" Lucy asked.

The man slapped Senalda again, this time a vicious backhand, and Mercedes felt a hot rush of anger bubble through the innate permafrost of her emotions. Her initial wave of helplessness being overtaken by blind rage. Things were different these days. She wasn't helpless or terrified. She was no longer a child at the mercy of a mother who couldn't—or wouldn't—take care of herself. She was still, however, blindingly angry about her mother, her stepfather, this asshole beating up on the waitress—all of it. She couldn't stand it.

The man slapped Senalda a third time, and she cowered against the wall protecting her distended belly. "Jesus, what's wrong with people?" Mercy searched frantically past Senalda and the man. Why in the hell weren't any of the other restaurant workers jumping in to help?

"What?" Lucy demanded again, straining to see what had prompted Mercy's outburst. "What's going on?"

Fueled by fury and emboldened by the beer, Mercy didn't even answer. She shoved her chair back and stalked to the kitchen door. Yanking it back, she grabbed the man's arm, making sure to dig her nails into his skin. He wore a white wife-beater T-shirt, the irony of which struck her as not so funny, and a pair of black jeans. His gaze shot to her face, his eyes narrowed and contemptuous.

"Let her go," she said, deadly calm now that she'd taken action.

The man, at least three inches shorter than she, puffed his chest out and looked Mercedes up and down with unveiled derision. "Who the fuck are you?"

Mercy stepped closer, using her height to her advantage, looking down on him, and hardened her voice to knife-blade sharp. "I'm your worst fucking nightmare if you don't let her go, asshole. Now."

By that time, Lucy had come up behind Mercedes to see for herself what the commotion was. She pushed past Mercy, who was in a stare-down with the brute, and grabbed his arm near the wrist. Mercedes wasn't sure what Lucy had done—some painful cop trick, no doubt—but the guy's arm went straight and back, bending him forward at the waist. "Ow. Jesus, let me go, you stupid bitch."

"Not happening," Lucy said, in her cop voice.

"You get a thrill over picking on pregnant women smaller than you?" Mercedes rasped through clenched teeth. She realized that her limbs had begun to shake from the adrenaline rush. "What kind of weak half-man are you?" She glanced over at Senalda, whose eyes had gone round with either fear or surprise. Her cheekbone had begun to swell and her face bore telltale red marks that would turn into bruises before morning. Her whole body tremored, too, and the red finger marks remained pressed in the tender skin of her upper arm. Mercedes, overcome by protectiveness, guided the young woman behind her.

"That's my girlfriend, man. I can do what the hell I want." He spit toward Mercy's foot, but she pulled back quickly enough to avoid it hitting her shoe. "Mind your own business, *puta.*"

Lucy shifted the position of his arm, and the man stood up straight, bowing back onto his toes. He winced in pain. She caught the eye of the cook who was watching slack jawed as the confrontation went down. Lifting her chin toward the cook, she ordered, "Call the cops. Now." Her stony tone left zero room for argument.

The cook swallowed, his Adam's apple bobbing as he looked from the man Lucy held to Lucy herself, then he nodded once and turned to rush away.

Behind Mercedes, Senalda had started to cry, a beat-down, pitiful sound that broke Mercedes's heart. Annette and Cris approached. Mercedes glanced at them over her shoulder and said softly, "Take her out to the table."

Annette slipped one arm around the young woman's shoulders and eased her away. Mercedes heard her say, "It's okay. You're safe now."

But was she? Mercedes thought, a lump of dread hardening to sick fear in her gut. They were here for one night and then gone. No doubt Senalda would have to stay here with this piece of shit, and the way the system worked, he'd be out of jail in a day, if he even went for that long. He'd vent his anger over the whole mess on the young woman just as soon as he could get his hands on her again. That's what they always did.

A shudder ran through Mercedes. God only knew why she was sticking her nose into a stranger's business, but she just couldn't stomach the thought of walking away. She felt like she'd snap. The last few weeks had been so stressful, and she was more than ready to unleash her frustration on someone who really deserved it. She looked into the guy's flat black eyes and saw every abusive asshole she'd ever come into contact with.

She got into his face again. "If you ever touch her again, you weak bastard, I'll make sure you'll regret it."

"Mercedes," Lucy warned, softly.

"No, Lucy. *No.*" Mercedes's face heated as she brushed away Lucy's admonition. She jammed a finger toward him. "I'm sick of fuckheads like this thinking they can push people around. For God's sake, she's *pregnant.* If he's acting that way now, what happens after she has the baby? He beats her? Breaks her bones? Puts her in the hospital? And what about the baby?"

"I know, babe," Lucy said. "I just meant, let the cops handle it."

"But will they?" Mercedes demanded, feeling pushed up against a brick wall and ready to fight. "You know as well as I do how the system works, Lucky girl. He'll get a slap on the wrist, nothing more. Meanwhile Senalda is trapped without any recourse. Where is her family? Her support system?"

Lucy sighed, looking down. She knew it was true. "I don't know. I don't know the woman. You can't save all of them."

"Someone has to save at least one of them."

She studied Mercy for a few moments, tweaking the idiot's arm every once in awhile to keep him in line. "So what are you suggesting?"

Mercy spun away, running fingers into her hair. "I don't know, I don't know, I don't know," she said on an exhale. Her heart thudded in her chest. She'd had enough of standing by and watching this shit to last a lifetime, though, that much she did know. This time, at this moment, she felt like she'd reached her limit. She was too emotional, too caught up in the anger and resentment from years of watching her mom just . . . take it.

In short order, the cops showed, and Lucy badged them and spoke to them briefly. They hooked the little man up, all of them ignoring him as he spat insults and threats at Mercedes, Lucy, and Senalda. After they'd stuffed him in the back of a patrol car and drove away, Mercedes took a deep breath, consciously dropping her shoulders. She asked the cook for a second pitcher of beer, then walked back out to their table on wobbly legs to join Annette, Cristina, and Senalda, who had calmed down but looked worried and subdued.

"It's no good," she said, rubbing her hands together. "It's a problem."

Mercedes sat down next to her and took her hand. "What's not good? Are you okay? My name is Mercedes, by the way."

"I'm okay," she said meekly. "But this happens before. He'll be back. It's a problem for me." She cringed in pain and laid a hand on her distended abdomen.

Mercedes knew just what she was saying, and guilt knocked the wind out of her. She should've considered the woman's situation before she rushed in like some fucking superhero. That's the last thing she was. Rubbing Senalda's free hand softly, she asked, "Where is your family?"

"In Mexico. Puebla." She tilted her head toward the door that led to the kitchen. "I came here with him . . . for the baby. My family . . . I'm not married, you know? He wasn't always this way. Only since we got here."

Mercedes nodded. "Can I ask you . . . how old are you?"

"Nineteen." She raised her liquid brown eyes briefly to meet Mercedes's, then looked down at her own lap.

Okay, so a little older than Mercedes had imagined. That was good, at least. "Do you want to go home?"

"*Sí, pero* all the money I make, he takes. I have no way."

An idea flashed into Mercedes's head. "You'll come with us, then," she said, in a rush. "I'll pay for you to get home, whatever you need. You have to get away from him."

Senalda blinked up at Mercedes, clearly disbelieving. "I don't understand. Why you do this for me?"

Mercedes sighed. Why, indeed? "Because . . . it's wrong, what he does. I don't know. Maybe because I'm sorry I interfered." But she wasn't. "I've made things worse and I want to make up for it. Please, let me do this. He's never going to change."

"*Sí,* I know." Senalda's lips shook. "I'm afraid of him." She winced again, rubbing her belly.

Mercedes's gaze dropped to watch Senalda's small hand, and an alarm bell went off inside her. "Are you feeling okay?"

"It's just the tension. Plus, he kicks me a lot."

"You don't have to be afraid. Come with us. We'll take care of you until we can get you home." She glanced down at Senalda's belly again. "Have you seen a doctor for the baby?"

Senalda shook her head. "Only *la partera*. The midwife. She comes to the house."

"That's good," Mercedes said. "Good enough. And everything is okay with the pregnancy? Is it your first?"

Smiling tentatively, Senalda nodded. "He's good."

Nodding, Mercy reached up to rub her brow while she perused logistics in her mind. A plan. That's what they needed. "Here's what we'll do. We can go to your house while he's with the police, and we'll just leave. Okay? Do you trust us?"

"Yes." Senalda looked around at all of them, her eyes filling with moisture. "I have pray for an angel, and I got four. God is good to me."

Mercedes looked up to find her three friends thoughtfully watching her interactions with the young woman. She hadn't even considered soliciting their opinions before inviting this pregnant teenager to join them. "Is this okay with you guys?" she implored, hoping they wouldn't protest. "I can't leave her to him. Please. I just—"

"No, of course you can't," Annette said, looking grave. "It's the only solution, and I'm all for it."

"Me, too," Lucy said, at the same time Cristina nodded.

"Good. Then let's get our check paid and get out of here," Mercedes said, strangely disinterested in drinking any of the beer from the new pitcher. Maybe it was sympathy sobriety for Senalda. Maybe it was just because it felt good to be focusing on someone with problems bigger than her own. Her career might be over, but so what? A job was a job. Senalda was living in a cesspool of physical danger with literally no way out. It made Mercy's problems seem petty and meaningless by comparison. Besides, Senalda wasn't looking at her like she was Merciless Félan, a woman to be scorned and loathed. She was looking at her with gratitude and respect. Sure, it wasn't the real world, but go figure, it felt good anyway.

They had driven out to a small, dilapidated house on the fringes of town so Senalda could gather her surprisingly few belongings, and then they'd piled back into the van, their home away from home. The overall tone during the drive had been subdued, serious. All of their planned phone calls to The Real World were postponed in the interest of the here and now.

Instead of staying right smack in the center of town, they'd decided, at Senalda's suggestion, to stay at the Circle A Ranch, situated about five miles north of Cuba, in the Santa Fe National Forest. Mercedes had called ahead. The Circle A offered hostel style accommodations, but that was okay with all of them. Should Senalda's estranged boyfriend be released, it was unlikely he'd find them there.

They would be sharing a bunkhouse, but it would just be the five of them, which worked out fine. All the rooms and the suite were booked, so it was the bunkhouse or nothing. Per instructions, they stopped to buy towels and a few other supplies, which weren't provided for travelers unless they were staying in the rooms or suite.

Lucy drove, and Annette was in the passenger seat navigating. Cristina sat in the back, trying not to look like she was scrutinizing Mercedes's interactions with Senalda, but she was. She'd never seen Mercy so nurturing, so soft. It was almost as if Senalda were her own blood relation, and in her deepest, most secret place, Cris hurt. She bit her bottom lip to hold back the clutch of pain in her throat. How could Mercedes be so kind and caring with a stranger and so cold with her, someone she'd once called her best friend? What had she done?

Cristina had been so impressed by Mercedes's courage confronting Senalda's abusive boyfriend back at the restaurant. God, he'd been a class-A creep; he'd have to be to brutalize a very pregnant, very tiny young woman right in the middle of a public place. But that hadn't stopped Mercy. Hell no. She'd marched into that kitchen without a moment's hesitation, which had been the absolute right thing to do. Too many woman died because people were afraid to get involved—Cristina knew that intellectually. But she couldn't help but wonder if she'd have done the same in Mercy's position. The truth? Probably not.

With a small sigh, Cristina turned to the blackness beyond the window and stared at her muted reflection in the glass. When had she become such a coward? She tried to think back to a time when she hadn't been afraid of her own shadow, and she couldn't. As a child, she'd feared her parents' reproach. She'd done everything she could to become the perfect obedient daughter just to avoid it. In high school, she'd been so fearful of not being accepted, of not being liked. She had gone to great lengths to make sure that didn't happen, but it happened anyway. Mercy despised her. Another stab of pain struck.

Now in her marriage, she was so goddamned afraid to stand up to her punitive monster-in-law, so afraid to confront Zach and ask him why he never stood up *for* her, so afraid of the members of society finding out she wasn't really part of their class and never would be. Fear. Her life was completely shaped and guided by fear, and that sickened her.

Mercy, on the other hand, could be a monumental, world-class bitch from hell, but she wasn't afraid of anything. She brashly went after what she wanted, boldly did what she felt was right, regardless of personal consequences.

God, Cris didn't want to be impressed with Mercy, didn't want to feel that tug of old friendship, love, and respect for the woman. Mercy had stomped her heart and continued to do so, twenty years later. Why should she care?

But she did. So much that it ripped her up inside.

She wanted to be as confident as Lucy, as nurturing as Annette, and primarily, as courageous as Mercedes. Especially now, with all she needed to face Zach, the Aragons, and everyone else in her gossipy inner circle in San Antonio. Right then, on the drive toward the Circle A, Cristina yearned so badly to be someone—anyone—other than who she was: Weak. Scared. A woman so deeply in denial about everything that was wrong with her shell of a life, she would insist it was anything but empty.

Lies. Cover-ups. Mirror tricks and illusions.

The realization of how little her life meant saddened her profoundly, and she just couldn't seem to shake her funk, especially on this particularly black, moonless night in the middle of nowhere, New Mexico.

"Are you on a holiday together?" Senalda asked them after they'd checked into their bunkhouse at the Circle A and settled in for the night. The sparsely decorated dorm sported pale walls and black metal-frame bunk beds topped by thin mattresses covered with deep blue bed-spreads. It was like being at summer camp again, Lucy thought. Rose-colored curtains twirled gently in the breeze from the open windows. The bunk facilities had been so inexpensive, Mercedes bought out one whole room, even though several open bunks remained. They really wanted to be alone, though, and this made it almost seem like a suite.

Senalda and Annette had claimed bottom bunks. Lucy sat cross-legged on her bunk above Annette's and Mercedes stretched out on her stomach in the bunk above Senalda's. Cristina had a bottom bunk all to herself, with no one above her, and she lay curled up on her side, look-ing distracted and a little sad, Lucy thought. She made a mental note to ask her later what was up, but she had a sense Cris was focused on her arrest.

Lucy glanced at Mercy before answering Senalda's question and took her shrug to mean they had nothing to hide. "We're actually searching for that *curandera* Mercedes asked you about at the restau-rant," Lucy told Senalda. "We have information that she used to live in this area, but we don't know where."

"And, this *curandera,*" Senalda asked, her interest clearly piqued. "Why her? There are so many?"

Lucy quirked her mouth to the side. "It's sort of a long story, but we've heard she has certain abilities, and we all have a few . . . issues." Senalda looked confused. "Problems. In our lives," Lucy clarified. "We want to consult her and see what she has to say."

Senalda nodded sagely. With her hair down from the braid she wore at the restaurant, she looked even younger. "Tell me again her name, please?"

"Matilda Tafoya," Mercedes said, from the upper bunk. "She's also known as Tilly. We call her Tilly." Mercedes scooted to the edge of her bunk and hung her head over. Senalda was staring off into the distance thoughtfully. "Do you think you might know her after all?"

Senalda shook her head. "But I know a man. He has live here his whole life and knows everyone. Maybe I can help you?" She seemed hopeful. "I can ask him for you."

"That's nice offer, but you have enough to worry about," Lucy said. "How about if you just give us his name and we can ask him ourselves."

Senalda smiled. "Some of the people will not trust four city strangers asking questions. This man, maybe he is this way. You help me, I want to help you, too. I live here now almost one year. They trust me. You speak Spanish?"

"Very little," Lucy said. "But I understand it. And I'm pretty good with Spanglish."

"Me, too." Mercedes said. "Mostly."

"I speak it," Annette said, "but not perfectly."

Cristina simply didn't answer.

"A lot of people here speak only Spanish."

Mercy and Lucy exchanged a glance. "I hadn't thought of that," Lucy said. "We do need people to be forthcoming with us. And we have to be able to communicate clearly. Does this man speak only Spanish?"

"He speaks English." Senalda gave an impish smile. "I think, maybe, he won't speak it to *you*."

Okay, that would be a problem, Lucy thought. She hadn't considered the possibility of people not wanting to help them.

"How long will you be able to help us? How far along is your pregnancy, I mean?" Mercedes quirked her mouth at Lucy. "I don't want her to stay so long that the airline won't let her fly home. What month do they stop letting pregnant women fly?"

"I think it's the eighth month," Annette said, "but I'm not one hundred percent sure. We can call and ask."

"How far along are you?" Mercy asked Senalda again.

"Only six and a half month." She touched her tummy. "It looks like more, *pero* I am small."

"Okay, so we have time," Lucy said. "Still, I'd like to get her on a plane within the next two weeks, just to be safe."

"If we don't find Tilly within the next two weeks, I'll need to go home anyway," Annette said regretfully.

"Yes, me, too," Cristina murmured. They all looked at her. She'd been so quiet, they'd almost forgotten she was there. "I do have that court date hanging over my head."

For a moment, they were silent. What could they say?

"Okay, so we have a deadline," Lucy said. "If we don't find Tilly within two weeks, we cut our losses and go home to try and figure things out for ourselves. Deal?"

"Sounds reasonable," Mercedes said. She hung her head over the bunk one more time and smiled at Senalda. "And we're grateful for your help, Senalda. *Gracias.*"

The young woman smiled shyly at Mercedes, but with great affection. *"De nada.* I will do anything to repay you for your kindness to me."

"Just have a healthy baby, honey," Mercedes said, in a gentle tone that seemed so out of character for her. "And be safe. Stay away from men who hurt you, okay?"

Senalda nodded, and Cristina rolled away from the rest of them, pulling the blankets up over her shoulders. She didn't even say good night.

Lucy frowned. The tectonic plates underpinning their four-way relationship had gone through a subtle shift with the addition of Senalda, and Cristina seemed the most affected. But she wasn't sure exactly how or why. All she knew was, Cristina seemed subdued, separated from the rest of them. Luckily they'd have two full weeks together. Lucy loved Cris, and she'd get to the bottom of it sooner or later, even if she had to corner her and force it out of her.

"Good night, Cristina," Lucy said, pointedly.

A tension-wrought beat passed. "Night," Cristina murmured, not turning back.

Lucy looked at Mercy, a question in her eyes. Mercedes just shrugged. She was as clueless about Cristina's melancholy as the rest of them. Annette shared a similarly baffled look. God, Cris really needed to talk to Zach. Lucy made another mental note: encourage Cristina to take the first steps in facing her problems. What was that old saying . . . those who can't, teach?

Chapter Seventeen

The ancient adobe home looked so weathered and intrinsic to the high desert landscape, it could have simply risen up out of the earth where it stood, Lucy thought. She and the others had decided to wait outside while Senalda went in to talk to the old man and his wife about Tilly. After Senalda and the man had exchanged a few words, he'd peered out the screen door looking, as Senalda had warned them, more than a little suspicious. The man was as weathered as his home, as indigenous to the rural vista, too. The brown skin on his face resembled wear-softened but deeply tooled leather. He wore a pale blue linen *guayabera,* dusty blue jeans, and cowboy boots that had seen their share of honest field work. Nothing was for show out here.

Lucy was petting a particularly cute and friendly goat that had been wandering about the yard when they'd arrived and had trotted over to say hello. As the man scrutinized them, she raised a hand in greeting. His expression unchanged, he lifted his chin just slightly before stepping back to allow Senalda inside his home. Before she entered, she turned back and gave them an encouraging smile and a thumbs-up.

The waiting began.

After checking out of the Circle A Ranch that morning, they'd driven deep into Rio Arriba County, somewhere between Lindrith and Dulce. They followed Senalda's directions, which brought them to this dirt road off of Highway 595—that they would've missed if not for her—and ultimately to the man who reputedly knew everyone.

"Don't you feel like we've stepped back a century?" Mercedes whispered.

"Yeah," Lucy said. "It's surreal."

Mercedes scuttled a few steps away as the goat reached out to take a nibble of her shirttail. "Hey, you little bastard. That shirt cost me three hundred bucks."

Lucy laughed, shoving her hands into her back pockets and rocking on her feet. "Only you would wear a three-hundred-dollar shirt in rural New Mexico."

Mercy made a face at her. "It's not like I packed with this adventure in mind, Nancy Drew."

"Good point. But I'm glad we're here, even in another century with people who are suspicious of us." She stopped rocking, suddenly nervous. "Maybe that's what it will take to find Tilly. God, I hope so. I'm desperate."

"Don't be desperate, Lucky girl." Mercy grabbed her long hair and shook her head gently. "Ruben loves you. Tilly or no Tilly, you two can work it out if you can avoid being a total dumbass about the whole thing."

Lucy wasn't so sure. Besides, she didn't have a very good track record of not being a total dumbass.

The little goat clomped away in search of something to eat since Mercy's shirt was a bust, and Lucy crossed her arms tightly over her torso, surveying the property. A slightly swaybacked barn lurked in a stand of oak trees toward the back of the yard, and a new-looking shed occupied a fresh cement pad a little closer. There was also a white-washed chicken coop and a vegetable garden with a high fence around it, no doubt to keep out the wild beasties. A rusted-out Ford step-side truck from the 1940s looked remarkably like expensive mixed-media yard art, with high grass growing up to brush against its perimeter.

Cristina and Annette were wandering among a few free-range chickens, dancing away and squealing like a couple of girlie-girls each time one of the cluckers came too close to their ankles. Chickens playing with chickens, Lucy thought.

After what seemed like forever, the screen door to the house squeaked open, and a smiling woman in a starched cotton housedress beckoned them forward with her brown loose-skinned arm. Nervous, Lucy exchanged a raised eyebrow glance with her friends before leading the way toward the house.

"Buenos días, Señora," Lucy said deferentially, offering her hand. "I'm Lucy Olivera."

"Welcome, welcome," the lady said, grasping Lucy's proffered hand in both of hers for a squeeze before standing aside to admit her into the inner sanctum, which smelled of cinnamon, melted candle wax, and that morning's chile.

Each of them repeated the hand-shaking ritual, and in short order, they were seated in a blue-walled living room decorated in an over-whelmingly religious motif. Catholicism was alive and well out here in the country, boy. No argument there. Lucy had almost genuflected before taking her seat on the sofa, by pure habit alone.

A gilt-framed portrait of the ubiquitous long-haired, white-skinned, blue-eyed Jesus dominated one end of the living room above a lace-covered half-round table pushed up against the wall. The table held a blue-robed statue of the Virgin, burning votive candles, a rosary, prayer cards from dog-eared to new, and various framed photographs, no doubt of family members who'd passed on.

The thick adobe walls kept the inside of the small home cool and comfortable, despite the radiating June heat baking the exterior of the property to a shimmery southwestern glow.

The woman—they still didn't know her name—had doled out cups of tea, which they all balanced nervously on their knees, sipping only occasionally. It was the man they really needed to win over, and they all knew it. He still looked expressionless and slightly suspicious, but they'd been welcomed into the house. That was something, at least.

"Why you wanna find Señora Tafoya?" he asked gruffly.

Lucy cleared her throat, taking the lead. "We read a magazine article about her, señor, and—"

"Here, I have it," Cristina interrupted, rifling through her bag. She produced the flight magazine and handed it across to the man with a Colgate smile. He gave her, then the magazine, a perfunctory glance, then set it aside and refocused on Lucy.

"See, we all have a few . . . problems in our lives, and we'd dearly love to meet Tilly—um, Señora Tafoya—and ask her advice. According to the article, she has some . . . specialties." He said nothing. Lucy cleared her throat nervously. "If you have any idea how we can find her, we'd be most grateful."

"Where you from?" he asked.

"Originally we're all from Denver." She glanced toward Annette. "She lives in Las Vegas now with her family. Five children, all girls. One of them in college already."

The man nodded respectfully at Annette, who smiled.

"Cristina here lives in San Antonio, Texas, with her husband and two children. Mercedes lives and works in New York City—"

His eyebrow hiked at that piece of news.

"—and I live in Denver still."

He nodded, pursing his lips, searching all their faces as if trying to unmask them and expose their motives. After a tense silence none of them wanted to break, he took in a decisive breath through his nose and blew it out. "I don't know where la Señora is."

He paused, and Lucy felt her stomach sink.

"But," he continued, "I know where she used to live before they ran her off."

Lucy expelled a breath. She swallowed convulsively, saying nothing. Afraid to disrupt the spell.

"I can draw a map," he said with very little enthusiasm.

Lucy placed one hand over her heart, balancing the teacup with the other. "That would be . . . so wonderful."

His glance dropped to their footwear, and one overgrown white eyebrow raised. He said a lot with those brows, Lucy realized, without uttering a single word. She and Annette both wore tennis shoes, but Cristina sported expensive-looking mules and Mercedes wore high, wedge sandals that probably cost as much as Lucy made from the police department in an entire pay period.

"It will be a four- or five-mile hike from here, this cabin."

"We're not afraid of hiking," Mercedes told him.

The man shook his head, as though washing his hands of the whole thing. Crazy women deserved to hike in high heels, his body language seemed to say. "Wait here, then. I'll make you a map." He looked at his wife, giving her a small jerk of his chin. "Lenora, make the ladies a meal to take."

"Oh, that's not necessary," Annette said. "Very kind of you, but don't go to any trouble."

The stoic man studied Annette for a few seconds, then dismissed her comment without addressing it and jerked his chin toward his wife a second time. "Lenora."

She immediately stood and bustled into the ancient but immaculately clean kitchen. The man crossed to a small dining nook off the living room. After gathering supplies, he bent over the dark wood table. One arm braced, he took to a large sheet of paper with a Sharpie marker he'd retrieved from a drawer in the buffet, carefully drawing them a map that would hopefully lead them to clue number one on their hunt for Tilly.

If only he knew how inept they'd proven themselves to be thus far at reading maps . . . but Lucy wasn't about to tell him. He might change his mind. She wasn't sure what they'd find in the cabin, but it was the only handhold on this downhill slide to failure, and she was more than happy to grab onto it.

Still tense and wanting desperately to show these kind people that they were respectful and so grateful for their help, Lucy sat stock-still and listened to the opening and closing sounds of cupboards and the refrigerator coming from the kitchen. She glanced toward Senalda, who smiled and gave her an encouraging nod. Somehow that calmed her.

This was good. They were getting somewhere. Finally.

Armed with water and food provided by Lenora and a crude but understandable map sketched by her enigmatic husband, the four of them stood on the far edge of the property exchanging temporary goodbyes with Senalda and the elderly couple. The old man, who'd never bothered to introduce himself, eyed Mercedes's and Cristina's shoes dubiously. Lucy caught his gaze and spoke the words he probably wanted to say but wouldn't. He was too formal to comment on strange women's clothing and footwear choices, no matter how wrong they were for the situation. "Mercy, Cris, are you guys sure you don't want to change into more appropriate footwear before we head out?"

They both glanced down.

"I didn't bring anything more appropriate," Cristina said, seeming surprised by the suggestion. "These are the most comfortable shoes I have."

"Don't worry about me," Mercy said, brushing away the concern with a flick of her hand. "I walk miles in the city every day. These shoes are fine."

"*Hijuela,*" the man said, under his breath.

"We're not exactly walking on paved sidewalks, babe," Lucy reminded Mercedes.

"We're not hiking the Himalayas, either."

Lucy shrugged. "Okay, if you think so."

"You have coats, *sí?*" Senalda asked. "With night comes the cold here. Even in June."

"We don't plan to be gone until nightfall." Lucy patted a tote bag she'd slung over her shoulder. "But I have sweatshirts for everyone. And a first-aid kit."

"I guess we're ready then," Annette said, sounding apprehensive. She scanned the horizon. "Are there wild animals around here?"

"Of course," the man said, bluntly. "It's the forest."

Lucy and Annette exchanged a worried glance, but Lucy patted a fanny pack she wore around her waist. "I'm packing heat. It's all good, Annie. Promise."

They took turns hugging Senalda, thanking Lenora and her husband for watching over her and the van while they hiked off. After a chorus of *"de nadas"* and "good lucks," the four women headed out. They'd decided that of all of them, Annette was the least bad at reading a map, so she was assigned navigation duties. They took off in a northwesterly direction, through a deceptively rugged landscape dotted with ocotillo and chollo bushes, sagebrush, juniper and piñon trees. The air smelled of summer heat, dry earth, and sunshine. Birds and flying insects provided a sweet kind of musical soundtrack as they walked. Off in the heat-hazed distance, a volcano-shaped mesa guided them; it had been prominently noted on the map.

The going was slow as both Mercedes and Cristina realized quickly that their footwear choices truly did leave a lot to be desired, despite their initial denials. Cris stopped every few feet to pick pebbles and stickers out of her mules, and each time Mercedes turned her ankle on the uneven ground, they stopped to fawn over her and check for sprains and swelling, which just resulted in her growing crankier by the minute.

An hour into their hike, they'd made meager progress. Lucy stopped to sit on a boulder and reassess their options. When Mercy and Cris finally caught up with them, looking flushed from the heat, annoyed, and in pain, Lucy said, "I don't know if this is going to work, babes. We're unprepared."

"We're fine," Mercy snapped, joining her on the boulder and crossing one leg over the other knee to rub her sore ankle. "Let's just keep going. We finally have a trail. Why stop now?"

"Because," Lucy said, as if talking to a dim-witted child. "Neither you nor Cristina are properly dressed. If either of you bust an ankle, or even sprain an ankle, we're screwed for the rest of the search. Do you realize how long it would take us to get you help? And you'd just be out here, incapacitated, with the rattlesnakes and other animals."

They were silent a moment, considering that.

"You're wearing a three-hundred-dollar designer shirt, for Christ's sake."

Mercy glanced away.

"If it rains, Cristina's going to get those heels stuck in the mud and we'll have to crowbar her ass out," Lucy added, in a disgusted tone. "We don't even have a crowbar. It's absurd."

"So, what do you suggest?" Cristina asked. She actually looked hopeful that the hellish hike might end.

"Let's cut our losses and go back. Maybe we can find a shop that will sell hiking gear, and we can get what we need and try again tomorrow."

"And waste a whole day?" Mercy balked.

Lucy spread her arms wide. "Do you honestly think we're accomplishing anything?"

Annette stood off in the shade of a piñon tree, studying their homemade map. From her sentry point, she glanced up and surveyed their surroundings, shading her eyes with one bladed hand. "Darnit, I think we're going in circles."

Lucy raised her eyebrows. "See?"

"We can't just go crawling back, though" Mercedes said, glumly. "Lenora's husband already thought we were the biggest pack of ill-prepared city dwellers to ever darken his doorstep. You could see it on his face."

"So what? We were. We *are*." Lucy stood and faced her and Cristina, her arms spread. "There is nothing wrong with admitting you're out of your element." She flipped a hand toward Annette, still poring over the map with a quizzical expression on her face that, frankly, didn't inspire a whole lot of confidence. "We should go back while we still know how to get there, unless you want to make the New Mexico papers . . . four stupid city women die in the wilderness wearing designer footwear and walking in fucking circles looking for an abandoned cabin."

"That *would* be awful," Cristina admitted.

"I bet we'd be spoofed on Leno and *SNL,* though," Mercedes said with a smirk. "That wouldn't be so bad."

Lucy gave Mercy a withering glance, then called over to Annette. "We *do* know the way to get back, right?"

"I think so."

" 'Think so' is not cutting it for me, Annie," Lucy said. "Do we or don't we?"

"We do, we do, stop pushing." Annette took a deep, cleansing breath, then joined them. "Look, we're tired. We're hot. We're cranky. I'm sure Mercedes's ankles are sore."

"They're fine," Mercy snapped.

Annette ignored her. "I think we should eat the meal Lenora was nice enough to make us, rest, gather our wits, and then head back. Lucy's right. We're improperly dressed." She chewed the inside of her cheek for a moment. "And"—a sigh—"we need to face the fact that none of us can read a damned backcountry map."

"I'm good with geography in Denver," Lucy said. "But having the mountains as a permanent directional reminder really helps."

"And what about the wild animals?" Annette asked.

"Lions and tigers and bears—oh no!" Mercy said.

Annette reached out to smack her.

Mercedes held up both palms. "Fine, fine. We'll turn tail and run back. But I swear to God, when we head out tomorrow it will be with a paid guide. I don't care how much it costs. I'm sick of getting lost."

"Deal," Lucy said.

"I'm in," Annette added.

"Me, too," said Cristina. She opened the backpack she'd been carrying that contained the food Lenora had prepared, then passed around bottles of water, foil-wrapped sandwiches, nectarines, and small bags of cookies. They settled in on the big, flat boulder and started to eat.

The meal was excellent. Of course, they could be eating uncooked ramen noodles at this point and they'd taste good. A hike into hell didn't need to be long to make a woman appreciate a hearty snack.

Mercedes swallowed a bite of her sandwich, took a drink of water, then cleared her throat. "What do you think Senalda told them to convince them to help us?"

Lucy laughed. "I don't even want to know. You have to admit we probably stick out like sore thumbs in these parts."

"I bet they felt sorry for us," Annette said, smiling before she popped a cookie in her mouth. "Sometimes you just have to be compassionate with inept people. I know that's not an image we want to claim, but look at it from their perspective."

"I thought they were very sweet," Cristina said. "Drawing us a map. Making us food. Even Mr. Grumpy, in his own way, was sweet." She chewed thoughtfully for a moment. "Does he remind any of you of your fathers?"

A round of "yeps" ensued.

"Shit, are they all the same?"

Lucy grinned. "You remember what Cristina's dad used to tell us when we'd drive into downtown Denver to watch the midnight showings of *Rocky Horror Picture Show*?"

Annette, Cristina, and Mercedes answered in tandem. "You watch where you're walking. Some day, a black van will pull up next to you girls, drag you inside, shoot you up with drugs, and they'll have you working the streets inside a week."

The four of them cracked up, especially Cristina, but the laughter was bittersweet. Cancer had claimed her father several years earlier. He'd always been *über*controlling and overly dramatic, but he'd also been a good man, and Lucy knew Cristina missed him something fierce. "Can you imagine what he'd do if he knew what was going on with us now?"

Cristina shuddered. "He'd kick my ass over this arrest thing. He'd probably disown me. And good old Catholic guilt would make me feel the need to confess, even knowing that."

"He wouldn't approve of what I do for a living, either," Lucy mused. Mr. Trevino had always treated her like a second daughter, had treated all of them that way. "He'd be in a blind panic. A pseudo-daughter of his, going in on dangerous drug transactions without a vest, a weapon, a wire, or anything but her wits."

Cristina stopped chewing. "That *is* kind of scary, Luce."

"No kidding," the other two chimed.

"I wish you hadn't said anything," Annette added.

Lucy shrugged. "It's all good," she said dismissively. "I'm well-trained. I do it all the time. It's my J-O-B, you realize."

"Well, maybe you shouldn't tell us about it then, because it's going to give me nightmares," Annette said.

Lucy rolled her eyes. "Fine."

"He'd freak out about Mercedes living in the big, dangerous city, too," Cristina said, still thinking about her father. She tilted her head to the side. "In fact, the only one of us he'd approve of is Annette."

"Great. Of course," Annette moaned. "Predictable Annette, doing what everyone expects of her, no questions asked." She wagged a finger. "Someday I'm going to surprise all of you."

"Bring it on, babe," Lucy said. She finished her sandwich and balled the aluminum foil it had been wrapped in. She took in a breath and released it on a sigh. "I miss your dad, Cris."

"Yeah." She twisted her mouth to the side. "I do, too, the ornery old dictator."

"We all do," Mercedes said, in a rare moment of honesty.

Cristina blinked over at her in surprise.

"I always used to wish I belonged to each of your families. Especially yours, Lucky girl."

Lucy's jaw dropped. "Are you high?"

Mercy shook her head. "Don't knock them. I know they're overwhelming, but the way you all love one another. It's really something to be envied. You should try being a little more grateful for what you have."

"Mercy's right," Annette said. "I bet if you went home right now, the Oliveras would gather the forces and support you through this trying time, no questions asked."

"Yeah right." Lucy bit out a monosyllabic laugh. "Dudes, I ditched my husband at the reception, need I remind you. And never went back." Lucy's droll tone matched the expression on her face. "I'm not thinking there'd be much support."

"Don't be so sure. They're weird," Cris said, "no argument there. But you can't deny the ferocity of their love for one another. And they're always willing to draw a new person into the fold. That's something."

"Yeah, it's called necessity. With our astronomical divorce rate, what choice do we have?"

Cris shook her head, refusing to acknowledge Lucy's self-deprecating comment. "You really do have something rare in your family, Lucy. Someday you should step back from everything about them that annoys you and take a good long look at how cool they are. How tight-knit. How vigorous in their sense of love and connection."

Lucy glanced down, toying with the ball of foil in her hands and avoiding the guilt she felt. "Maybe you're right. I mean, I love them. I just don't want to end up like all of them."

"Nothing says you have to, except your addled brain," Mercy said firmly. "Ruben loves you, you love him. If you want it to last, it'll last."

"I want it to last," she said softly. Painfully.

"Then it will," Mercy said, as if it were just that easy.

"Ruben is the best thing that ever happened to me."

"No shit, Sherlock."

"Well, she admitted it. That's the first step." Annette reached across and patted Lucy's leg.

Lucy sighed. If love were enough, her family wouldn't have the notorious history they did. "You just don't understand."

"Don't fucking insult us," Mercy said, indignant. "We're your oldest and best friends. We understand a hell of a lot more than you give us credit for."

Lucy peered up at her, duly chastised. "I'm sorry."

Mercy jabbed a finger toward her. "Sometimes, Lucky girl, when you think the whole world doesn't understand something, it's really *you* who desperately needs insight into the situation."

One side of Lucy's mouth lifted on a weak smile. "I agree, Mercy. I do need insight. Definitely. And that's why we're going on the hunt for Tilly. She's going to give me the insight I need. I just feel it."

The three of them stared at her for a few moments, saying nothing. Finally Cristina stood up, brushing crumbs off slacks that were never meant to be worn hiking or picnicking on a boulder. "On that note, let's get the hell out of here and back to the house. Call me crazy, but I don't imagine the stores around here stay open until nine o'clock at night. And if we want to head out tomorrow—"

"We do," Mercy said. "We have a deadline. Believe me, I know from deadlines. We need to avoid any more false starts or . . . we may never find her in time."

The reminder of their limited time sobered them all, and they hiked back in thoughtful silence.

Chapter Eighteen

The old man actually laughed when he saw them hobbling back into the yard, a bedraggled, sweaty quartet of defeated women. He didn't look quite so formidable: the laughter transformed his entire face. In fact, his whole demeanor had changed. Gone was the gruff, stoic figure who reminded them all of their fathers on their very worst days. This man had an easy manner and a twinkle in his deep brown eyes—at their expense, naturally. But they were ready to take the ridicule. God knew, they'd earned it.

The man propped his rake up on its forked edge and leaned on the handle. "That was faster than I expected."

Lucy smiled wearily. So he'd been testing them. Funny. "I hope you didn't place any bets."

"I'm not a gambling man," he said.

"We really weren't dressed properly," she said, a completely unnecessary admission. "Plus . . . we got lost."

He shook his head, set the rake aside, and crossed the yard to face them. "I am Esteban. You can call me that."

Lucy tucked her chin. "Thank you."

Esteban propped his fists on his hips and blew air out through his nostrils as he studied Mercedes's and Cristina's dust-covered, beat-to-shit feet. Finally he angled his head toward the door to his home. "You two go inside. Lenora will tend to your feet with a soaking and some salve."

"Oh, that's not—"

"Thank you," Mercedes said, interrupting Cristina. She reached over to squeeze her arm just below the elbow. They didn't want to start insulting their unwitting host now that he finally seemed welcoming, did they? "We appreciate it. Don't we, Cristina?"

Cris pulled her arm away, slanting Mercy a slightly reproachful glance. "Of course we do."

Esteban nodded, then addressed Lucy and Annette. "And for you two, I made a list. There is a shop not too far. If you're serious about searching for la Señora, you need the proper gear. Many parts of New Mexico remain wild. It's not a city park."

"Our thoughts exactly," Lucy said.

"Senalda will drive with you so you don't get lost," he said, one corner of his mouth showing the smallest of quivers.

Annette and Lucy smirked at each other. "Thank you."

Mercedes cleared her throat, assuming her businesslike persona. "After we're properly outfitted, we'd like to go look for the cabin again. Tomorrow. Perhaps I could pay you to guide us there this time?"

He shook his head. "I won't take your money, but I will guide you. I have to work in the morning, but we can leave tomorrow in the late afternoon. It will be cooler then." He shook his head. "It's good you had the sense to come back."

"Why didn't you stop us before we left if you knew we were going to fail?" Annette asked.

Esteban gave a small, noncommittal shrug. "The four of you didn't seem ready to listen. I decided to let the land and the failure teach you the lesson. I knew you'd return."

Lucy grinned. "I guess we're pretty transparent."

"City folks," he said with a shrug, as if that were explanation enough. His expression turned more serious. "Senalda told a lot of things to Lenora and me. *Muchas gracias* for helping her at the restaurant." He expelled a troubled breath. "We didn't know . . ."

"No thanks necessary," Mercedes said. "I couldn't stand by and watch that happen. None of us could. It was the only thing to do."

"She's a good girl, Senalda."

"She is," Lucy said. "She exudes it."

Esteban nodded, lips pursed, and eyed Mercedes with a mixture of wariness and respect. "She calls you her angel, New York. You know that? I didn't know there were angels in New York City."

Mercy laughed at his nickname for her, and at the assumption. "I'm no angel, believe me. But thank you. Anything I can do to help her is my pleasure."

He didn't exactly smile at Mercedes, but his eyes glowed with a sort of reserved deference. Soon enough, he reached into his back pocket and removed a sheet of paper, folded into quarters. Opening it, he smoothed it out and studied it for a moment before handing it over to Lucy. Clearly, he'd deemed her leader of the pack. He lifted his chin toward Mercedes and Cristina. "Take these two inside for Lenora, then find Senalda. Go soon, before the store closes. I've called ahead. Most items will be waiting for you, but they'll need your sizes for the shoes and clothes."

"Okay." She bestowed a sincere look of humble gratitude. "Esteban, you've gone to so much trouble—"

"De nada." He flicked that away with a work-worn hand, not even letting her finish the compliment. "Lenora will have dinner ready when you return, so don't take long." He gave them a playful look of warning. "You don't want to miss Lenora's chile. Hottest chile you'll ever eat . . . if you can survive it." He glanced one more time at Mercy's and Cristina's feet, shaking his head. "Somehow, I think you can."

Hours later supplies had been purchased, Lenora's fiery-hot chile had been enjoyed (survived?), and the four friends felt more at home and comfortable than they had for a long time. As late afternoon mellowed to gold, then to mango, and finally to the world-famous crimson New Mexico was known for, Lucy could understand why Georgia O'Keeffe had retreated to this land of light. It had a healing effect that would be difficult to explain to someone who wasn't right there, basking in the soul-soothing Technicolor glow.

They helped Lenora tidy up the kitchen, then Lucy grabbed her cell phone and wandered off toward the barn for some privacy so she could call Ruben. She hadn't talked to him in several days, and she missed him like an amputee misses a limb.

The setting sun had streaked the red sky with dusky purple as she took a seat on a small bench outside the barn. The goat, whose name was Rudy, she'd learned, trotted up for a pet. She absentmindedly stroked the stiff hair on his head as the phone rang once, twice, three times.

"Hey, baby girl."

Lucy felt immediately better, a smile lifting her mouth and settling her shoulders into relaxation. He sounded like the same old Ruben, despite the fact she'd ditched him on what should've been the most important day of their lives. Ugh. "Hi," she said, softly. "Are you busy?"

"Never too busy for you. Where are you?"

"The middle of nowhere. Somewhere outside of Cuba, New Mexico. I'm petting a goat."

After a startled moment of silence, Ruben laughed. "You're the strangest woman I've ever met, Lucy del Fierro."

The mention of her new married name—even though she planned to hyphenate—made her tummy flop anyway. Or it could've been his rough purr of a voice reaching down inside her. "Gee, thanks. I think."

"So what's with this goat, *querida?*"

She filled him in on their current lodgings and the failed attempts to find the *curandera.* He laughed out loud when she regaled him with the tale of the inappropriate shoes, asked concerned and thought-provoking questions about Senalda. Ruben was perfect for her. He didn't tell her to be careful, and she appreciated his trust more than she could say. "We're heading back out tomorrow, this time with Esteban as a guide."

Ruben whistled low and long. "That's a brave man, hiking off into the middle of nowhere with you four. Go easy on the old guy, yeah?"

"You know we will." Small talk, updates, blather. Lucy had had enough of it. She sighed. They had so much to talk about, and she needed reassurance. Surely he needed a bit of it himself. "Are we still okay, babe?"

His tone softened. "Of course we're okay."

"I ditched you on our wedding night, Ruben."

"I know. Just think of the stories we'll be able to tell our grand-children."

Her heart jumped. "I'm too old to have kids and I'm not taking ma-ternity leave from the job. Remember?"

"Okay, our granddogs," he amended, easily.

Lucy laughed, the end of it snagging on a tender emotion. She bit her lip against the unexpected, choking wave. "Is my family going apeshit?"

"Pretty much."

"Great." She slumped back against the warm barn wall.

"Don't worry about them, Lucy. You never did before. Just focus on you. Then, when you're ready, on you and me. Do what you have to do, then come home to me, baby girl."

"I'm trying, Ruben." She closed her eyes.

"I know. And that's all I ask. I love you, Lucy. I love you so much. This time apart? Ain't nothin' but a thang, babe. I'm swamped at work anyway. Don't even miss you."

"That sucks."

"Yeah, it's a lie, too." He chuckled. "We're gonna make it through, you and me, because we're meant to."

Annette carried her cell phone out to the front porch and settled into one of the woven strap-and-metal chairs she remembered from her childhood. She dialed her number. The phone rang once, and Randy picked up. "Hello?"

"Hi, honey," Annette said.

"Hey, stranger." Again, she could hear the smile in his voice. Come to think of it, she'd always been able to hear the smile in his voice. It was one of the things that attracted her to him. No matter what was going on in their lives, he always sounded happy to hear from her. What an amazing gift. "How's the big hunt going?"

"We have some leads," she said, not wanting to talk about their quest. "How are things with the girls?"

"Couldn't be better, actually," he said, sounding slightly chagrined. "Alex and Deborah have the energy of a couple of camp counselors in dealing with the twins. They're amazing, and the twins are in heaven. Never a dull moment."

"So they're not ready to run screaming back to Albuquerque, thankful they only have a dog?"

"Nope. Not even close."

Annette paused. She didn't want to push him, but she wanted to know. "And how are the three of you doing?"

He sighed. "It's hard for me, Annie. I won't lie to you. I just never pictured—"

"I know."

"But she's the same old Deborah." He sounded surprised.

"Of course she is, silly."

"Except she seems . . . happier." Annette could hear in his voice that the admission had been a difficult one for him.

"Much. See? And very settled. We couldn't ask for more with a twenty-year-old college student, Randy. Things could be so much worse. With all the partying out there, the Ecstasy, the STDs—"

"Uh, I'm a strong man, but I don't want to think of my daughters and sex in the same sentence."

"Sorry." She grinned. "I'm just saying, we did good."

"Yeah." He paused. "We did. All I ever wanted was for my girls to be happy." He paused. "All of them, Annie," he said, with emphasis. "Even you. You realize that, right?"

Her torso tightened, and she recognized the kick of emotion as raw fear. As a child, she'd love sticking the tips of her fingers into melted candle wax, but she always avoided the flames. Too close. Too scary. Too painful.

She *so* didn't want to talk about her own issues.

Couldn't bear to.

"I am happy, Randy," she said, in as light a tone as she could muster.

"Well . . . good." He didn't sound convinced. "But if you're ever *not* happy, you know you have my total support in doing what it takes to change that, as long as it doesn't involve kicking me to the curb. Whatever you need . . . time alone, a job, going back to school."

Annie shook her head. "Did Deborah talk to you?"

"Just a little."

"That darn girl," she said, affection masked in annoyance.

"It's all good, honey. She just cares about you, and she knows I do, too. Take your time with your friends and focus on Annette, okay? I may not have ever told you, but I never expected you to sacrifice you . . . for us."

"I didn't."

Randy sighed. Clearly he wasn't going to argue. "We're going to be here waiting when you get back. Loving you. Always loving you, no matter what you need."

Tears sprung to Annette's eyes. "How'd I get so lucky?"

"It wasn't luck. You deserved it, Annie baby, always. You still deserve it. All of it. To be happy, to be loved, to be appreciated. You are the best woman I know." He blew out a breath of regret. "Maybe I haven't told you that enough. That's my failing. I'm sorry."

Annette swiped away an errant tear with the back of her hand. "Maybe. But I always knew, Randy. And you're the best man I know. Keep that in mind when you're working through this stuff with Deborah and Alex. We gave Deborah—all our girls—an example of true, abiding love that stuck with them. We've lived it." She pictured Alex and Debby together, making breakfast, holding hands. "Look past the gender issue, Randy, because they're so right for each other."

"I know," he said softly. "I'm trying to see it that way, too. It's getting easier, if that helps."

"It does."

"Have fun with your girls, honey. Don't worry about anything here, okay? We miss you like crazy, but we're doing just fine."

"No more canned Hormel chili?" she teased.

"You heard about that, huh?" He laughed softly. "Nope. That Alex is one heck of a cook. The twins are in hog heaven. I must admit, I'm right there with them on that."

"See?" she said simply.

"I see," he said. "More and more every day, thanks to you. As always, Annie, thanks to you."

Mercedes took her cell phone out and sat in the backseat of Annie's minivan. She'd never called Alba at home, but she needed to face up to the ugly reality that she was the current media whipping post and plan a strategy to change that. The phone rang twice, then a tiny voice picked it up.

"Hello?"

Thrown by the fact that a child had answered, by this little unexpectedly human glimpse into her secretary's private life, she stammered her answer. "Uh, hi. Is your mom home?" Odd that she'd never thought of Alba as a real person, with a life outside the workplace. What did that say about her?

"May I ask who's calling, please?"

Mercedes smiled. A little executive secretary in the making, this one. "Sure. Let her know it's her boss, calling from New Mexico."

"'Kay, hang on."

The phone clonked down unceremoniously, and Mercedes listened to tiny running footsteps as the child dashed off to retrieve her mother. While Mercedes waited, she focused on the rich, breathtaking sunset. She could seriously get used to sunsets like this, to the curative powers of this rugged, unruined land. There was no concrete jungle to be found here, and surprisingly, considering how much she adored city life, she loved it.

Moments later, a flustered-sounding Alba picked up the phone. "Ms.—Mercedes? Is that you? Are you really in Mexico?"

"It's me. In the flesh. But I'm in New Mexico, not south of the border." She scrunched up her face. "I hope it's okay that I called you at home."

"O-of course. You just surprised me."

"Are you busy?"

"Nope. Running the kids through bath time, but I'm on the older ones, so they're fine alone."

"Okay, so tell me. How bad are things?"

Alba sighed. "Well, could be better. The publisher has been doing a pretty good job of warding off the worst of the paparazzi assault, but we've had to hire an intern to deal with all the reader mail."

Mercedes let her eyes flutter closed, and her stomach plunged. "Bad?"

"Not all of it. About fifty-fifty. You have a lot of fans out there."

She huffed. "Yeah, out there. Not in-house." Alba didn't deny it. "Have subscriptions dropped off? Ad sales?"

"Slightly, but nothing to worry about. Surprisingly, our stock is holding steady, so that's positive." Alba hesitated, as if weighing the wisdom of continuing. Finally she asked, "How was the wedding?"

Wow. They were talking about non-work-related issues. And it didn't bother Mercy at all, she realized. "Beautiful, actually. Stressful, as weddings are, but still beautiful. This whole New Mexico thing is a long story for another time, but I might not be home for another two weeks."

"That's probably best, actually. Until things die down."

"Sure. But I'm going to have to address the issue head-on sooner or later, Alba. I can't just hide forever and hope it will go away, as much as I want to."

"This is true. We can figure it out when the time comes."

We. Mercedes warmed, the simple two-letter word leaving her completely flummoxed. Perhaps she did have *one* ally in-house after all. Swallowing back emotion that, for once, she didn't berate herself for, she forged ahead. In earlier days, she never would've considered asking this question, but right then it seemed the thing to do. "How are you doing, Alba? Everything okay with you? I know you're right there in the line of fire, and I'm sorry about that."

A beat passed. When Alba did speak, she sounded stunned. "Me? I'm doing fine. Like I said, the publisher is screening the worst of it out."

"That's good to hear."

Alba cleared her throat. "A-and, I meant to tell you—again—thank you for the raise. It's made a world of difference in my household, I can't even express—"

"I'm glad," Mercy rushed to say. She didn't want Alba to feel beholden. "You earned it. You work hard, you put up with a lot of shit." She let that hang there for a minute while she weighed every one of her next words. "Don't think I just gave it to you. I appreciate you, Alba, and the work you do."

"Wow." Alba huffed a little surprised laugh. "Thanks. I don't know what you're doing over there, Mercedes, but this trip has done you a world of good already."

Cristina carried her bag into the bathroom, allegedly to get ready for bed. Instead, she sat down on the closed toilet seat and retrieved her cell phone from her purse. Her hands shook and her mouth went Sahara dry. Switching the little thing on, she did a quick check. Voice mail messages: 34.

Thirty-goddamned-four messages.

She clicked buttons until she got to the list of missed call phone numbers, so she could check who the incoming calls had come from. Zach. Zach. Zach. Zach. Zach.

All Zach. Zach times thirty-four equaled Major Problems.

She squeezed her eyes shut and prayed, really begged God for the strength to just call her husband and come clean. Face up to what she'd done. Clearly he already knew, so what was the point of avoiding him?

There wouldn't be thirty-four voice mail messages stored on her phone if he hadn't gotten wind of the arrest. She should just . . . do it.

Come on, Cris. Have a little courage.

Her heart started to thud as she waited for that courage to show up and mobilize her. Sweat slicked her palms, and her breathing felt shallow, insufficient.

She waited.

And waited.

But the courage never did quite materialize.

With a stab of anguish, Cristina hit a few buttons and deleted all thirty-four of those messages without listening to a single one. She simply couldn't. Nausea roiled in her stomach. Yes, she was a horrible wuss—the worst of the worst—but bottom line, she wasn't ready to face it all yet.

Would she ever be ready? Would she *ever* be as strong as her friends, as able to catch life's inevitable curve balls without flinching from the sting against her palm? Would she ever be anything other than a world-class coward who didn't even get the chance to drop the ball, because she shied away from it time after time?

Feeling defeated and ashamed, Cristina tucked the phone away, stood up, and began to go through her intricate skin care regimen by rote, drawing comfort from the routine. She might not be able to handle the more difficult aspects of her life, but by damn, she had the mundane rituals down to a fucking art form. That had to count for something.

Keep telling yourself that, Cris. Loser.

It seemed like they'd been hiking for hours the next afternoon, and also strangely like they'd been going in circles. But hey, Esteban knew the area, and they basically didn't know their asses from a set of holes in the ground, so who were they to question? Lucy thought. Finally they rounded a copse of oak and piñon trees and came upon a sun-weathered cabin sitting all by its lonesome in the middle of an expanse of native grasses, scrub oak, and sage abutting the butte. They should've found this the day before. Esteban's map had been more than clear, Lucy realized, with disgust.

"Is this it?" Lucy asked, her heart quickening.

"*Sí.* Let me go in and have a quick check first."

"Oh, you don't have to do that for us," Annette said.

Lucy glanced at Annette and smiled. Her friends brown eyes shone with barely reined anticipation. Clearly Annie was as excited as she was about finding the cabin, about the infinite possibilities the discovery offered.

"For wild animals," Esteban told Annette. "They like abandoned shelters. Unless you'd rather—"

"Enough said." Annette held up her palms. "Have at it."

Wired with expectation, the four women huddled outside together, pulling off their packs and stretching, letting the hot sun dry the sweat on their backs. The heat and fatigue from the hike was all but forgotten as they awaited Esteban's all clear with a sense of hope and promise. Lucy felt utterly effervescent with triumph. They had found the cabin—a clear indication that Tilly did, indeed, exist. She might seem like a legend, but she was a real flesh-and-blood woman after all. Just the idea that they might be able to find their way to her, with the help of whatever clues the cabin might hold, was enough to make her bust with joy.

"What do you think is in there?" she asked the others.

"Spiders," Mercedes said deadpan. She crossed her arms. "Rats maybe, or a snake here and there."

"*Cállate.*" Annette chastised, rubbing her upper arms. "Do you want me to have nightmares forever?"

Mercedes smiled at her. "I was only kidding. Just trying to get to Lucy."

"Thanks a lot," Lucy said. "I meant, what about Tilly?"

"I knew what you meant, and I guess that remains to be seen," Mercy answered. "Patience is a virtue, Lucky girl."

"Like you've ever been virtuous."

Mercy smirked. "True enough."

By the time Esteban returned, the sun had settled comfortably on the horizon, rich and orange-gold and ready to tuck itself behind the hills for the night. He nodded to the women. "It's all clear. Too clear," he said ruefully. "Nothing left but bare floors and bare walls, I'm afraid."

Lucy's heart dipped a notch and she fought to maintain her optimism. "But . . . that's okay, right? Maybe we can just have a look around."

"Of course." Esteban shrugged off his backpack and began pulling out the components of a one-person tent. "And the outhouse is a short walk out the back door. I checked it, too. All clear."

"*Out*house?" Mercedes asked, incredulously.

Cristina raised a brow.

"What, you want a full marble bath ensemble with a bidet?" Lucy asked, in a sarcastic tone.

"No, but a flush toilet might be nice."

"God, you're so pampered," Lucy said, shaking her head.

"Bite me," Mercy whispered, so as not to be overheard by their host and guide.

Lucy turned her attention to Esteban's activities. He'd removed all the necessary parts from his pack and had begun to set up the tent in the shade of an ancient oak. "What's with the camping gear?"

He lifted his chin toward the rapidly setting sun. "We can't make it back tonight. The hike is too long. You four bed down inside the cabin. It's comfortable and safe enough. I'll be out here in the tent."

"Oh," Annette exclaimed. "You don't have to stay outside. You're more than welcome to stay inside with us."

Esteban inclined his head. "No. It's not proper. I don't mind the tent. Now, go on in. You have matches for your candle lanterns? It's going to be dark soon."

Lucy patted her pack, which she'd also slung off her shoulders. "Got them right here."

"Then go get settled while you still have the light." He indicated a fire pit several feet removed from the cabin. "I'll start a fire and we can heat the dinner Lenora sent before we part for the evening." He pointed over to a metal pump in the ground. "There is water if you want to wash up. Do it soon, after the cabin is set up. It won't be so easy in the dark."

The four women glanced toward the pump. "Okay," Annette said, then focused on her friends. "We can take quick turns."

The other three nodded.

"We'll start back tomorrow morning when you're ready," Esteban told them. "After you've seen your fill of the cabin, of course, though I'm not sure how it will help you find la Señora."

Lucy shrugged. "Yeah, well, you never know what's going to happen," which seemed like the understatement of the century. Her optimism renewed, Lucy led the way into Tilly's abandoned cabin, praying they'd learn something, anything about the woman whose existence she had come to rely on so heavily in the last few days.

Chapter Nineteen

The cabin was, no lie, bare-ass empty.

Rough-hewn wood beam walls; plank floor; one small, rectangular window of wavy glass on each of the four walls. Period. An old-fashioned wood cookstove sat abandoned and forlorn in one corner next to a long countertop with some empty shelving above it and empty cabinets below. No bathroom, no bedroom, not even running water. Empty.

Dismayed, Mercedes stood just inside the door and watched her friends trooping excitedly through the hollow box of a house like it was the damned Taj Mahal. What the hell were they smoking? Did they honestly think they were going to gain any insights about Tilly from this completely-stripped-of-everything hovel in the middle of no-where?

Disgusted, she let her pack slide to the floor, then ran her hands through her sweaty hair. She felt gritty and sticky, her legs ached, and a blister had popped on her left heel, making the last half hour of the hike feel like ten years in a fucking foreign prison, replete with daily burn torture. And for what? The pleasure of sleeping in a—rustic was too mild a term—cabin that it had taken them hours of hiking to reach? For the joy of pissing in a smelly-ass hole in the ground out back?

Fuck. This sucked. Another day wasted.

Supremely annoyed, she consoled herself with the knowledge that she had wine in her pack. Two bottles, at that. She couldn't wait to get to it, because they sure as hell weren't going to be spending the evening gleaning useful tidbits about Tilly's whereabouts from this nasty little saltbox of a cabin. Mercedes had never been claustrophobic, but right then she needed to get the hell away from everyone before she exploded.

"I'm going out to the pump to clean up," she told the others in a defeated tone she didn't even try to hide.

They didn't catch it anyway, so consumed were they with their misplaced glee over the so-called "find." Annette turned to her with a smile on her face. "Okay, hon. I'll roll out your bed. Where do you want to sleep?"

"Wherever, Annie. I don't care." Mercy bent over her pack to rifle through for some soap, a towel, and, of course, her trusty vitamin V. A couple of those would, at least, make this train wreck of a day more tolerable.

"Let's all sleep right in the middle of the room," Lucy suggested, like it was one big party. Whoopee!

Mercedes didn't look up, but she rolled her eyes. The whole damn cabin was "the middle of the room," couldn't Lucy see that? Mercedes flipped a towel over her shoulder and pocketed her soap and pill case. Bending down again, she extracted the wine bottles, gripping the necks between the fingers of one hand as she ferreted out the corkscrew. She held them out to the room at large. "Someone open these so they can breathe. If I have to use an outhouse, I'm damn well going to be drunk when I do it."

Lucy laughed.

"What?" Mercy snapped, *so* not in the mood for happy people.

"Jesus, bite my head off. You're just so . . . you." Lucy took the bottles and corkscrew, walking across the room to set them on the counter.

"Yeah, really amusing," Mercedes said, totally unamused, as she yanked open the cabin door and tromped out, limping slightly from the stabbing pain in her heel, and feeling only a tiny bit guilty for having gone for the throat with her best friend. But, shit. Why were they all so bluebird-on-my-shoulder excited?

Another sharp pain stabbed her in the heel and she cringed, walking a bit more gingerly. Moleskin, her ass. Her new hiking boots had rubbed right through the worthless stuff. She couldn't wait for some running water. Maybe she'd find this whole bullshit trek more amusing when she no longer felt like she'd been rolled in sand and Crisco for the past three hours, but as she walked out into the evening, she seriously doubted it.

To her surprise, however, she found that Esteban had set up a makeshift screen around the pump for privacy, using long sticks and some lightweight tarps he must've packed. The simple, unexpected gesture knocked the edge off her anger just like that. Tension seeped from shoulders, and her frown eased.

She glanced toward Esteban, who had his little camp all set up in the shade of the great oak. He was squatting at the edge of the fire pit, a small but homey blaze, already crackling and whipping orange flames and light gray smoke into the air. He fed the fire with deft, economical movements. She had noticed earlier that day, he went about all his work in the same manner, calmly and with great control.

As if sensing her, he glanced up. She pointed toward the pump and raised her hand in thanks. He nodded once, then turned his back, either to afford her more privacy or to snub her. Oddly cheered by this, a smile lifted her lips. It wasn't a secret that he harbored a bit of prejudice against her for living in New York City, but she liked the crusty, old guy anyway. Maybe more so because of his suspicious attitude, who knew?

Feeling better, she stripped down behind the screen and took a quick, bracing sponge bath beneath the ice cold stream of the pump. She gasped every time the water hit her skin, but by the end, she felt clean and alive, infinitely more enthused about the evening that stretched ahead. She realized that she hadn't been annoyed with her friends over the cabin, or with Esteban over the blister-popping hike. Those were just a smoke screen. The truth was, when they'd entered the cabin, she had been choked by a wave of profound disappointment that they hadn't found evidence of Tilly. That's all. She wasn't sure how much Cristina or Annette yearned to find Tilly, but Lucy, at least, was fully invested in locating the *curandera*. Although Mercy kept her feelings to herself as a general rule in life, she was with Lucy on this one. Her yearning to find Tilly, to have the reports of the woman's reputation be true, was blinding in its intensity. In fact, Mercedes wasn't sure what would happen in her bleak future if they didn't find the woman. She'd become *that* dependent on the thought of someone being able to fix her life.

Sad, but true.

But now, clean and feeling more philosophical about the whole thing, she could accept that searches like these were often one step forward, two steps back. She could deal.

Minus underwear, she dressed quickly in her hiking clothes and headed back to the cabin whistling. When she reached the cabin door, she suddenly realized she hadn't taken a Vicodin. Hadn't needed to, strange as that seemed. The craving simply hadn't overtaken her like it usually did. With her hand resting on the doorknob, she hesitated. Should she take one now while she had the chance. She pulled her bottom lip in between her teeth as a short internal debate raged, but she decided, finally, to forego the pill. She didn't need it.

"What can you tell us about her?" Lucy asked Esteban as they sat on logs situated a safe distance from, but still near, the fire pit, relaxing after dinner. The smell of wood smoke surrounded them. "I mean, whatever you're willing to share. There isn't much information out there."

Esteban nodded. "It's best that way. What *do* you know?"

"We know they ran her out of this place because they thought she was a witch," Annette offered.

Esteban inclined his head.

"We read that she's supposed to have powers to change people's lives," Cristina added. "Which is what drew us here in the first place, as you probably know."

"Ah, yes. The magazine." Esteban glanced skyward, as though asking for patience.

"So is it false, what they wrote in the article?" Cristina asked, dismay wrapped like a tangled rope around her words.

"I'm not saying it's false."

"It's true, then?" Lucy asked.

"I'm not saying that, either."

"What are you saying?" Mercedes asked, trying not to sound as direct as she felt. Why did men always beat around the bush in conversations? *Just spit it out.*

Esteban sighed. "La Señora is a very learned and respected *curandera.* We were so fortunate to have her in this area, even for a short while. Her skills with the herbs." He squeezed his fingers together and kissed the tips. "And, *sí,* she was part counselor, like you have heard. Helping people with their problems." He paused, making pointed eye contact with each of them in turn. "But she's no magician. She's not going to cast a spell and make your lives perfect, if that's what you expect."

"We don't necessarily expect anything. We just want to meet her and . . . see what she has to say," Lucy told him. It wasn't one hundred percent true. They did sort of wish Tilly had magical powers. It would make things so much easier.

Esteban studied her for a moment. "I wish I could tell you where she has gone. I'm sorry. La Señora was always private, to herself, you understand?" They all nodded. "She could make you feel like she'd known you forever, but you didn't feel the same about her. She is . . . an enigma."

"What does she look like?"

Esteban leaned his head to the side, mouth tilting down. "This is not a question for a man. I didn't take note of her appearance. She looks like an old woman, I guess."

Annette laughed, and Esteban smiled. Of the four of them, he seemed to like Annette the most. Perhaps because she was a New Mexican herself. Perhaps because she was a mother. It didn't really matter. She was one of them, and his affinity for her gave them a leg up.

"Was she married? Did she have children, grandchildren, any family at all?" Lucy asked, single-minded.

Esteban's eyes twinkled as he said, "I'm sure she had a mother and father at one point. It's the way of things."

"You know what I mean," Lucy said.

"*Sí,* but I don't know of any family. Like I said—"

"She was very private. An enigma." Lucy sighed.

"*Sí.*"

"God, I hope we can find her," Mercedes said, staring off into the distance.

"Keep trying," Esteban suggested. "What other choice do you have but to give up? And is that really ever a choice?"

Silence fell over them as they considered the profundity of his question. He boiled it down to something so simple, Lucy thought. Then again, maybe it *was* as simple as that. Perseverance paved the way to most amazing things life had to offer, didn't it?

After they'd cleaned up the campsite, and bid their good nights to Esteban, they made their way to the cabin and settled onto their bedrolls for an evening of wine sharing and "whine" sharing. The six candle lanterns they'd carried along were tiny, but they emitted a good amount of soft, flickering light. The corners of the cabin remained shrouded in shadow, but that just made their little illuminated circle of sleeping bags seem that much cozier, that much more intimate.

Mercedes still hadn't felt the need to pop a Vicodin, but she kept them in her pocket just in case.

A woman could never be too cautious.

Lucy seemed particularly melancholy, staring into her plastic wine-cup-slash-coffee-mug as though the reflection of candlelight on the wine's surface might provide her with insight, like a crystal ball.

Mercy cocked her head. "What's up, Lucky girl?"

Lucy's shoulders raised and dropped. "Just missing Ruben. Wondering if our marriage is going to last. You know, light, happy thoughts. Ha."

"Have you talked to him recently?" Annette asked, leaning forward to snag a wine bottle and top off her cup. She aimed the bottle out, offering with her eyes, and Cristina held her cup out for a refill, too.

"Yeah, we talked yesterday."

"How did he sound?" Mercedes asked.

"Just like he always sounds. He's busy with work, a little distracted there, I guess, but that's nothing new." She crinkled her nose. "Apparently the Oliveras are in an uproar. But to quote Ruben, 'don't worry about them. You never did before.' "

"Man's got a point." Mercedes drained her mug of wine and refilled it.

"You know," Lucy said, hesitantly, weighing each word before she uttered it, "the whole Olivera curse thing is . . . only part of my problem. I guess I haven't mentioned that before."

"What are you talking about?" Cristina asked, baffled.

Mercedes looked around. All three of them seemed as confused as she felt. Thank God it wasn't only her.

Lucy twisted her mouth to the side. "The thing is, I don't have a good track record of longevity with men. My past is littered with guys I dated and discarded along the way. I've been thinking that maybe I'm just meant to be a rolling stone. Maybe marriage is a mistake for me, even if I do love Ruben with my whole heart. It takes more than love to make a marriage last—case in point, my whole family."

"Oh, Luce," Annette said, her big, compassionate eyes troubled. "What part of marriage scares you the most?"

Lucy laughed. "All of it. Being committed. The whole legally binding decision part." She pushed her hair back, then bent her knees up against her torso and wrapped her arms around her legs. "The thing is, I tend to get restless in relationships. I always have. And I don't like to be held back, forced to fill expectations that don't fit who I am."

"Has Ruben held you back? Forced you to fulfill expectations that don't fit for you?" Mercedes asked.

"Well . . . no," she hedged. "But we've never been married before. We only lived together."

"And you think the plain fact of being married makes a difference?" Mercedes leaned in, her tone sharpening. "A little fucking piece of paper? Get real."

Lucy pinned Mercy with a stare. "Didn't it for you?"

"No. It didn't. The commitment comes way before the paper, Lucky girl, and you should know that. And no piece of paper is going to keep you married, either. That's up to you two."

Silence settled over them, and Lucy looked dubious. Finally she rested her chin on her knees.

When Annette spoke, her voice was soft and understanding. "Luce, honey, it's normal to get restless in a marriage. I do." That brought Lucy's head up. "I'm sure Cris does, too."

"And I did," Mercy added. "Although my three husbands were dickheads, so don't listen to me. Sorry. Don't mind me, I'll just drink and be quiet."

Annette flashed a quick, sympathetic smile toward Mercy, then continued. "It's not the crime of the century to wonder, to feel restless. It's the way of things. The whole point is making the commitment to stick it out through the hard parts, to remember why you fell in love and know it's worth it. No one ever promised the fireworks would last forever."

"I want them to last forever, though."

Annette shrugged. "Well, it happens for some people. But it ebbs and flows, too. Maybe you and Ruben will have more flows than ebbs. But the point is"—she paused for emphasis until Lucy looked up at her, waiting—"you'll never know if you throw in the towel before you give it the chance."

"Plus," Cristina added, "you can't gauge your marriage based on previous relationships." She flipped her hand. "Most of the relationships I had before I met Zach meant nothing to me."

Mercedes's stomach clenched violently. Just when she'd begun to feel more Zen about the whole thing, Cristina had to stick a knife in the wound.

Obtuse as always, Cristina went on. "But that's okay. Live and learn. They were fun times, albeit temporary, and no one got hurt in the process."

Mercedes's mind immediately flew back to Johnny Romero. The old, familiar anger began to seep into her bloodstream, tensing her jaw and making her heart pound with a toxic mixture of shame and bitterness. She reached out and grabbed a wine bottle, refilling her mug almost to the rim.

Of course, none of Cristina's guys meant shit to her.

Of course, she didn't seem to care.

Of course, she'd crushed her best friend in the meantime, whiling away the hours with guys she didn't give a damn about, oblivious to the collateral damage, because that was Cristina's M.O. back then.

But no one got hurt in the process, right Cristina?

Mercedes's yearning for a Vicodin returned full force. Cristina could flippantly talk about past loves like they were so much detritus left on the hurricane-tossed beach of her life. She had no fucking clue that any of it meant anything to Mercedes, and even if she did, would it matter?

Goddamn, Mercedes cursed herself. Why were her emotions so mercurial? One minute, she was coexisting in mutual, sort of comfortable wariness with Cristina, the next minute, she wanted to kick her ass.

Mercedes stumbled to her feet, red-hot angry and needing distance from all that she was feeling.

"What's up, Mercy?" Lucy asked.

"Just stretching the hamstrings," she said too sharply.

"They bothering you?"

No, I'm stretching them because they feel just fine, she thought snidely. "Yeah," she muttered. "I'm feeling a little tight." As the others talked, Mercedes prowled the deep shadows of the cabin, fighting to fend off the pent-up rage cresting inside her, the urge to lash out at Cristina, to hurt her. It made no sense. Johnny Romero was a long-ass time ago. He was just a high-school romance, anyway. She needed to let it go.

She couldn't.

It wasn't just Johnny. He was merely a symptom of a larger underlying disease that had festered within her and Cristina's friendship, eventually suffocating it.

In the darkest corner, she fished two Vicodin pills out of her pocket and, with her back to her friends, quickly washed them down with her wine. Yeah, really safe and healthy, mixing narcotics with alcohol. But who the fuck cared? All she knew was she needed a barrier, physical or pharmaceutical, from all she wanted to tell Cristina. Tell her? She wanted to unleash on the pampered little princess. Now wasn't the time or the place, though. In fact, there wouldn't ever be a time or place, because Cristina didn't matter to her anymore. She didn't need a woman like Cristina Trevino Aragon as a part of her life.

Mercedes drained her glass and set it on the countertop adjacent to the cookstove. She tuned out their conversation and just paced, fighting to focus on all that was good in her life, to reach that centered place that always seemed so far out of her grasp.

Fact: she'd built an amazing career.

Which might now be destroyed . . .

Fact: she was the CEO and editor in chief of a major magazine, her baby, her entire creation.

But she might get shitcanned over the controversy . . .

Fact: she had an amazing apartment on Sutton Place in the most invigorating city in the country.

With no one to come home to . . .

She stopped pacing, jammed her fingers into the front of her hair. Fuck, this wasn't working at all. Nothing was good in her life. Nothing, nothing, nothing. She might as well join the others; nothing was ever going to change. Turning, she took a step toward the sleeping bag circle, but her foot hit a plank that sounded different from all the others. She stopped, stepped back, and clomped down on it a couple of times. Sure enough, it sounded hollow.

Squatting down, Mercedes knocked on the plank with her fist. Definitely hollow. Feeling a sudden surge of excitement, she wiggled the edges of the plank and found them loose. Pulling more vigorously, she finally managed to work the piece of floorboard off. She set it aside and peered into the crevice, not able to see much for the darkness.

"Give me one of those candle lanterns," she said, to the room at large. She reached her hand in, wondering if she'd regret that decision, and started when it connected with what felt like a cigar box. "Oh, my God."

Her exclamation drew the attention of the others, and Lucy pulled down one of the candle lanterns and stood up. "What are you doing over there, Mercy?"

Without answering, Mercedes reached into the hollow and felt around the edges of the box. Definitely a box. Lucy's candlelight swayed over the hole, and Mercy's pulse thrummed harder. She extracted the fragile, faded Cremo brand cigar box. The label advertised cigars for five cents, The Cream of the Tobacco, "certified" for your protection. She was almost afraid to lift the hinged cover. With her luck, it was the coffin for a long-dead pet rat. She took a deep breath and opened it anyway.

The first thing she saw was a handwritten note lying atop a stack of memorabilia:

Property of Matilda Tafoya

Thrilled, astounded, her heart in her throat, Mercedes bestowed a stunned look on her friends, all of whom were watching her with unveiled curiosity. "You're never going to believe this. I just found a box of Tilly's stuff."

Chapter Twenty

They'd sat and sifted through Tilly's box of treasures until the wine was but a memory, and the fat white candles in their lanterns had guttered to smoky darkness, one by one. By then, they'd learned enough to refuel their excitement for the search ahead, a search that had begun to look less and less like an desperate exercise in futility, and more like something that might actually come to fruition.

So much for an empty cabin not being able to cough up any clues. The box must've just been a convenient place for Tilly to store her notes and papers, which she'd clearly forgotten in her haste to flee the cabin. It wasn't the kind of thing a person would miss for long, but it offered up a wealth of information that could lead them to her. After setting aside some meaningless lists, photographs, and a couple of notecards in a language none of them recognized, they had cheered when they found a birthday card to Tía Matilda from a niece—with a return address label on the envelope.

Tilly, apparently, had family near the southern New Mexico town of Truth or Consequences—which was ironic on a variety of levels. Either way, the next day, when they hiked back, it seemed much shorter and more direct. They showered, collected Senalda and offered profuse gratitude to Lenora and Esteban for the invaluable help and hospitality. By early afternoon, they were on the road again heading directly toward truth . . . or consequences? That remained to be seen.

Annette relayed the information they'd gleaned to Alex and Deborah who immediately jumped on the research trail and promised to call back if they learned anything. Granted, Tilly'd had family in T or C at one point, if the card and notes they'd found in the box were any indication, but that didn't mean they were still there. Or that the family would be forthcoming about her whereabouts—that was a biggie. All clues pointed to the fact that Tilly didn't want to be found, which could pose a problem no matter how promising the evidence. All they could do was drive and hope. As Esteban had told them, it was that or give up.

About an hour into the trip Cristina's cell phone rang unexpectedly. Just like that, the car filled with tension. Cris looked around at her friends, all of whom were studiously ignoring her and the ringing phone. They were all well aware that she was avoiding Zach. She'd meant to turn the damn phone off . . . in fact she *had* turned it off. Hadn't she? She glanced around suspiciously at her friends, lingering on Lucy's slightly guilty profile, before extracting the dratted thing from her handbag. She read the caller ID screen, knowing before the number came up what it would show.

Zach. Call number thirty-five.

"Answer it, Cris," Lucy urged.

Cristina began to shake, and her stomach churned with acid. The phone rang again, vibrating slightly against her palm. "I . . . I can't," she said. "I'm sorry. I know you think I'm being weak and stupid but I just can't. Not yet."

"When?" Lucy asked, but her tone was compassionate and supportive, not demanding. "You're not being weak and stupid, but this thing isn't going to disappear, and the dread is only going to grow bigger and more unmanageable the more you avoid it. You need to talk to your husband. He loves you."

"Jesus, Lucky girl, if that's not a textbook case of the pot calling the kettle black, I don't know what it is."

"Shut up, Mercy," Lucy snapped. "This is about Cristina, not about me."

"Oh," Mercy murmured sarcastically. "But, of course."

Lucy flipped her off behind her back.

"Maybe I could just disappear and never return to Texas," Cristina said, ignoring them both.

"And never see your children again? Live as a fugitive from the law?" Lucy asked. "Great plan."

Cris switched the phone off on the fifth ring. Despite Lucy's logical arguments to the contrary, silencing the ring that nagged like a past-due notice from the collections department of her conscience was her only choice. She avoided Lucy's eyes, feeling ashamed and scared. "I'm not going to run. I promise. I was just being flippant. But please . . . let it go. I can't face Zach. I can't face his demonic mother," she amended, stating the last word as if it were a particularly nasty curse. "And don't turn my phone on again. Please."

Lucy didn't deny having done it. Instead, she just sighed. "I'll say this and nothing more. The longer you wait, the harder it will be. Just remember, Zach loves you. Shut up, Mercy," she added, to curtail any further side commentary.

Mercy cleared her throat but didn't say a word.

"Perhaps he does." Cris offered a humorless slash of a smile that wasn't really a smile at all. "But Zach also loves his image, his status, and his family reputation, and I have most assuredly fucked those up beyond repair." She glanced at Senalda. "I'm sorry about my language."

"De nada," Senalda told her.

"That depends," Mercedes said.

"What depends?"

"Zach's image. Or whether you've irreparably damaged it. It all depends."

"How do you figure? Depends on what?"

"On the spin you put on the whole thing." Mercy shifted in the front passenger seat to look back. "I've been contemplating my whole mess, which"—she held up a palm—"granted, is a little bit different. But similar in a lot of ways, too. I think I might be able to salvage some of my reputation, such as it is, if I can only find a positive spin for what has happened."

Cris huffed, crossing her arms over the seat belt and her torso. "Yeah, well as soon as you spin yours, you're more than welcome to try and spin mine. But right now, I'd rather just live in denial. So if you all don't mind, please focus on your own problems and leave me to mine. No offense. Good luck, though," she said to Mercedes, and meant it, "with the whole spinning thing."

Cris tightened her arms and focused her attention pointedly out the window. She was *so* done talking about this, done thinking about it. Luckily, her friends seemed to take the hint, and the car lapsed back into silence.

About a half hour outside T or C, on a desolate stretch of highway that looked like every other desolate stretch of highway in the Southwest, Annette pulled the van into a dusty gas station parking lot and parked it in front of one of the two ancient flip-number pumps. "If we don't get gas, we won't make it," she told the others. "Sorry, I know we're almost there, but—"

"If we need gas, we need gas," Lucy said. "What's to be sorry for? You're doing that indoctrinated female thing, Annie, and apologizing for your actions. Don't do that."

"Sorry, Luce. Oops, there I go again." Annette met Cristina's eyes in the rearview mirror. "Do you mind doing the pumping? I really need to stretch my legs for a few."

"Of course not. It's my turn to pay for gas anyway." Cristina removed her seat belt. "Anyone need anything from inside while I'm there?"

"Water for me," Lucy said.

"I'll take a Diet Pepsi," added Mercedes.

"Same here. Thanks, Cris," said Annette, before peering nonchalantly at Mercedes. "Care to take a quick walk with me, Mercy? I'd like the company, and you have been having trouble with your hamstrings cramping."

"Absolutely." The two women alighted from the van and headed off down the shoulder of the road.

"Anything for you, Senalda?" Cristina asked.

"I just need the bathroom," said Senalda, her voice slightly pained. Cristina felt a pang of sympathy for the young woman. A road trip could be trying in any circumstance. But at seven months pregnant, with your organs shoved around and your bladder squashed into oblivion, it ratcheted up to the excruciating level. Cristina knew. She'd traveled with Zach and the team as much as possible when she'd been pregnant with the kids, and it had been hellish more often than not.

"Oh, hon, let me see." Cristina scanned the property—two nondescript, flat-roofed buildings with little style and zip in the way of inviting facades. But they sold gas and snacks. In this part of the country, that's all they needed in order to thrive. Only one other vehicle occupied the lot, a yellow Toyota pickup with a mismatched camper shell, idling unoccupied near the front doors. Cris finally spied his and hers bathroom doors in the smaller of the two structures, which sat behind the actual gas station. She pointed it out to Senalda. "I think it's back there. You run on back. I'll buy you some milk and juice and water."

"Just what I need," Senalda joked, as she waddled out of the van, holding on to her torso protectively. "More to drink."

Lucy and Cristina laughed. Just before Cristina got out of the van to pump gas, Lucy touched her arm. "Do you mind if I stay in here and call Ruben? I could go pay if you like."

"Absolutely not. Call that honey of yours." She smiled. "I'm perfectly capable of pumping and paying for gas."

"Thanks, Cris."

"Missing him?"

Lucy rolled her eyes. "Like you wouldn't believe."

"Well, hey, at least one of us wants to call her husband." Cristina jumped out of the side van door before Lucy could launch into her you-must-call-Zach diatribe.

Annette had been searching for ways to get Mercedes alone ever since the night they'd spent in Tilly's cabin. She didn't know what had triggered it, but one minute they'd all been talking casually as a group, and the next Mercedes's entire demeanor had changed, darkened into something remote and unreachable. She'd distanced herself from all of them, and yet her anger radiated through the room. Her mood had been unmistakable. If she thought no one noticed or cared, she was wrong.

Annette would never forget how sweet Mercy had been the night they shared the inflatable bed at Alex and Deborah's house, how vulnerable and forthcoming. She wanted to repay the favor. She cared about Mercedes, more than she'd expected to after all these years of silence. She had a mother's instinct, and something told her Mercy needed to know she was loved.

They'd walked for several yards before Annette released a breath. Mercedes had waited in silence, or maybe she was just enjoying the dusty, hot walk—Annette couldn't be sure. But if she was going to launch the discussion, she needed to go for it.

"Mercy . . ." Annette hesitated. "I have to say something to you and I want you just to listen."

Mercedes blinked, looking confused. "Okay . . . sure."

"Last night . . . in Tilly's cabin . . . I know something was bothering you when we started talking to Lucy about marriage." She raised a finger when Mercedes opened her mouth to speak. "Just let me finish," she said in her best mother-of-five voice. "Let me get through it."

With a slightly amused smile, Mercedes closed her mouth and made a zipping motion over her lips with her hand.

"Look," Annette said, placated, "I know you're a private person, and you don't open up to just anyone. I'm not prying into your business. You might be surprised to know that I'm the same way." She gave Mercy a sidelong glance, and Mercy conceded the point with a nod. "But something triggered your mood last night, and I want you to know . . . you can talk to me about it, if you ever get the urge to talk to anyone."

Mercy stopped walking and faced Annette.

Annette, fearing a shut down, held up her palms. "I know you're much better friends with Lucy than with me, and I understand. You'd probably much rather talk to her."

"Annie, that's not—"

"On the surface, it would appear we have nothing in common in our lives. I'm just a mom and you're . . . this amazing, famous icon in the publishing world."

"Oh, Annie. You're my friend, too."

Annette rolled her eyes, but with a good-natured smile. "How many other friends do you have who are stay-at-home mothers of five?"

"That's *so* not the point. I don't care what you do for a living, and if raising kids is what you do, I respect you for it. You know that." Her tone lowered and went slightly soft. "We talked about the kid thing."

Annette nodded, digging the toe of her tennis shoe into the soft dirt of the shoulder rhythmically. "You're right. We did. And that's partly why I'm talking to you now." She peered up at Mercedes, squinting in the sun. "I just want you to know . . . that *I* know something is bothering you. I know you're in pain"—she clenched a fist to her chest—"inside. Don't bother denying it. I've known it for a long time, and I hurt for you."

"Don't waste your worry on me."

"Too late. But it's okay. I don't expect you to spill your guts about it, but I care about you. Remember that." Annette peered up at her beautiful, fierce, self-protective friend and watched a swirl of emotions cross Mercy's face.

Her eyes grew moist, too, and she bit her lip. "Thank you," she whispered, sounding choked.

"That's all I had to say."

Mercedes pulled Annette into a hug. "God, you're such a good friend, and after I've been no kind of friend at all for way too many years," Mercedes said. "It's no wonder your family adores you."

"Ha."

"They do. Don't play dumb." Mercy studied her for a moment, too. "I'm glad we've found common ground, too, Annette. And if I ever want to talk . . . you'll be the first to know."

"I'd be honored."

As Cris waited for the large gas tank to fill, she glanced wistfully down the road after Annette and Mercedes. Heat waves shimmered up from the cracked black pavement, blurring the outlines of the two women. But she didn't miss the intimate way they talked, didn't miss the hand-holding or the hug they shared.

Cristina turned away, her eyes stinging. She wrapped her arms around her torso to fend off the hollow sense of loss. Mercedes, it seemed, could love everyone except her. It shouldn't hurt this much, but God.

One tear escaped and ran down her face. She flicked it away, then tilted her head back to ward off any followers, careful to keep her back to Lucy, who still sat in the van huddled up with her cell phone. Hopefully she was too caught up in Ruben to even notice Cristina's stupid swell of emotion.

How could she despise Mercedes one moment and miss her friendship so intensely the next? The van finished filling, and Cristina replaced the pump nozzle, recapped the tank, and closed the fuel door. As she crossed the pavement, she rifled through her bag for her credit card, but her mind remained on Mercedes and Annette . . . and Mercedes and Senalda . . . and Mercedes and everyone else who wasn't her.

Call her pessimistic, but the whole bleak situation and all the far-reaching emotional fallout the rift had scattered through her world indicated one thing: an insurmountable personality flaw in her own character. She closed her eyes against an acrid pain churning in her stomach.

Cristina approached the gas station, looking forward to air-conditioning, and pulled open the door. The front display of tabloids drew her gaze immediately. All of them featured full-page headshots of Mercedes. From there, she sought and located the cash register, and it struck her as odd to notice the clerk behind the counter standing with his hands in the air. It took a full several seconds of confusion, denial, then realization before her mind grasped that she'd walked into the middle of a robbery.

By then, the gun was pointed at her.

"Don't even think of moving, lady."

Adrenaline flooded Cristina's system. She flicked a quick glance through the door toward the van. Lucy was out there. Instinctively she took one small step back toward the door.

"Stop right there," said the armed man, stepping a foot closer to her. "I'm not joking." He looked nervous and threatening—always a bad combination when a gun was involved.

Cristina froze. She couldn't see anything but the round black barrel of that gun. Fleetingly, she thought about telling the guy she was a criminal, too. Common ground and all that. The absurdity of it all struck a solid blow, and she began to laugh out loud. In fact, she couldn't stop laughing. A second later, she was full-on howling out of control, holding her torso. Her maniacal laughter seemed to confuse the man. He shifted from one foot to the other just long enough for her to catch a glimpse of the clerk behind him. Initially the robber had been blocking the clerk, but as she looked at the frightened young man now, he seemed to be signaling her to keep the guy's attention. Maybe he had a panic button, she thought. Or a shotgun.

Her mind lurched back to an article she'd read in Mercy's magazine several months ago . . . all about surviving dangerous situations. What had it said about robberies again?

Most robberies that evolved into homicides happened because something startled the robber. You were supposed to give them what they wanted, not startle them, keep them calm.

"I'm going to lift my hands slowly, okay?" she told him, through her giggles. "I'm not here to stand in your way and I won't cause you any problems." The article also said she should warn the robber of any possible surprises. "I have four friends with me. All women. I don't think any of them are coming in, but if I see them headed this way, I'll tell you. Okay?"

Whether with her uncontrollable laughter or her honesty, she seemed to have thrown him off. He hesitated, then flicked the gun barrel to the side. "Just get over there by the stack of Coke cans and shut your mouth. And set your fucking purse on the ground slowly."

She squatted down at the knees, ever so slowly, and set her Kate Spade bag on the dusty white industrial linoleum. "There it is. I'm going, okay? I'm not going to get in your way," she said, finally regaining some composure.

Careful not to let her gaze give her away, she used her peripheral vision to see that the clerk had gotten out a baseball bat. He signaled Cristina with a determined but cautious nod. When she was almost at the hand-stacked pyramid of Coca-Cola cans near the robber, she feigned twisting her ankle and fell forward, knocking the pyramid over, causing a thunderous crash as the cans hit the linoleum. Two of them burst open, spraying sticky Coke toward the robber's legs. Cristina followed them down, rolling to safety as best she could behind a metal display of Twinkies.

All at once, the power in the store had shifted. The clerk took his chance and swung hard at the robber's head, connecting with a solid blow. The sound made Cristina's stomach lurch.

The robber's knees crumpled, and as he fell to the ground, the gun went off. Cris wrapped her arms around her head and cringed at an incredibly loud explosion, which was immediately followed by the sound of shattering glass. "Fuck!" Had she yelled that? All she could think about was her kids.

"Are you okay?" she heard the clerk call out.

Cristina chanced a quick peek at the robber and saw he was out cold, the gun still in his hand. She scrambled up and sort of crab walked toward him, kicking the gun out of his grasp first, and then all the way across the store. "I'm fine."

Just then, the front door flew open with a violent jangle of the bell, and Lucy barged in, gun drawn. "Freeze! Police! Nobody move."

"It's okay, Lucy," Cristina said, breathing in gasps like she'd run a marathon. "He's knocked out. We're fine."

Lucy eyed Cristina on the ground, took in the clerk. "You're okay?"

The clerk nodded, then answered in a shaky voice. "Yeah."

Lucy tucked her gun in the waistband of her pants, right at the small of her back, then crossed to the knocked-out robber, restraining him quickly with a pair of cuffs she pulled from her back pocket. After double-locking them, she glanced up at the clerk. "You call the cops?"

"I hit the panic button."

"Okay, that means they're on the way but they probably think the robbery is still in progress. Call 9-1-1 and let them know the suspect is in custody. Tell them who's on scene, too, so they don't think we're suspects." She flashed her badge. "I'm a narcotics officer from Denver PD in Colorado, if they ask."

"Right," he said, then he glanced at Cristina with a glow of admiration. "God, lady, you were awesome. You came in at the right time. Shit. I saw my life flash before my eyes."

Pride bloomed in Cristina's chest. "You did great, too."

Lucy crossed quickly to Cristina and squatted down, offering her a hand and studying her face with a mixture of horror and concern. "You okay, babe? Really?"

"Yeah," Cristina said with wonder, surprised to realize it was true. She'd just foiled a goddamned robbery using nothing but quick thinking and guts. She grinned at her friend. "I'm great. I really am."

"Holy shit, when that front window blew out, I thought the worst, Cris. It was—" Her voice caught. Lucy suddenly pulled her friend into a fierce hug. "I'm so sorry I wasn't there when you needed me."

"But you were," Cris said. "You brought the handcuffs."

The bell to the front door jangled again, and Annette and Mercedes ran in, both breathing heavily. They took in the destruction, the cuffed robber, Lucy, and Cristina on the floor. "What in God's name is going on?" Mercy asked.

Lucy glanced over her shoulder. "Cristina just walked in on a robbery. Stopped it, too."

The clerk came back. "Cops are on their way."

"Good job. Go ahead and lock the front door until they get here." She turned to her astounded friends. "Mercy, Annette, you two wait outside in the van with Senalda."

Annette studied Cristina. "Are you okay?"

"I'm fine, Annette. Really. I knocked the cans over on purpose to cause a distraction so the clerk could hit a home run on the guy's head," she said. "It was a technique I remember reading about in Mercy's magazine. The distraction part, I mean. All of it. It really worked, too."

Mercy actually smiled. "I remember that article."

Cristina laughed. "Well, I'm sure as hell glad I'd read it. I don't know what I would've done otherwise."

Mercy crossed her arms and shook her head, admiration in her gaze. "We'll have to do a follow-up for a future issue. Care to be interviewed later?"

"Are you kidding? I'd love it."

"Go on, you two," Lucy urged. "Before Senalda gets out of the bathroom and gets in the middle of all the police swarming in. Trust me, they'll draw down on her. The last thing she needs is that kind of stress with the baby."

"Okay," Mercy said. She glanced at Cristina one last time. "Good job, Cris. But don't ever scare us like that again."

Cristina sank back to the floor and leaned against a candy display. She took a deep breath in, blowing it out slowly and realizing she hadn't felt this fantastic in a long time. Fighting crime even beat *committing* it, for the high it gave her. Maybe she'd become a cop. A cop with a theft record. Again she laughed out loud.

Yeah. Maybe not.

Chapter Twenty-one

The tail end of their trip to T or C was delayed by the robbery investigation, of course, during which Cristina was touted as a quick-thinking hero. It turned out this particular felon had been robbing outlying gas stations all over three counties, and the police hadn't had any good leads on the guy. She was referred to as brave so many times by the officers who responded to the gas station, and by her friends, she actually began to feel like the designation fit. The crisis and her reaction to it so bolstered Cristina's confidence, she felt the sudden urge to call Zach. How scary could a difficult conversation be when she'd survived—indeed thwarted—a damned armed robbery?

When they finally arrived in Truth or Consequences, and had checked into their motel, they all went their separate ways for a few private minutes to regroup. Senalda immediately claimed one of the beds for a nap. Lucy headed off to the store to pick up snacks. Mercedes jumped into the shower, and Annette and Cristina settled onto the second king-size bed to sift through Tilly's cigar box of treasures again, hoping, *praying,* they'd come across something they'd missed.

Cards, notes, recipes, lists, and inexplicably, a photo of a good-looking young man with a bunch of donkeys. The back of the photo said merely "Yiska." Most of the written items were in English, some were in Spanish, yet others in a language they figured to be a Native American dialect. They set aside those they couldn't understand, or that clearly had no deeper meaning. The rest, they scrutinized. They were seeking anything at all that might lead them to Tilly.

On the one hand, all four of them felt twinges of guilt for digging through Tilly's private property, but their motives were pure. When they found her, they planned to return the box. Surely Tilly hadn't meant to leave it when she fled the little cabin, and maybe the box held some memento for which she'd been searching. They'd be heroes, and she'd repair all their lives out of sheer gratitude. Wouldn't *that* be nice and tidy?

They'd all become convinced that the magical little box held the key to finding Tilly, but try as they might, Cristina and Annette couldn't find any overt clues in the thing.

Disheartened, Cris stood, stretched, then shrugged her handbag over her shoulder. She wanted to call Zach while her confidence was still high from the robbery. "Look, Annie, we're getting nowhere and my eyes are starting to cross. I'm going to go stretch my legs. Get my head straight."

"Want company?"

"Actually, I have some thinking to do."

"Of course," Annie said. "You go on."

Cristina slipped from the room without telling any of them about her true intentions. She didn't think she could stand to see the encouraging, hopeful looks on their faces. This phone call was something she needed to do alone. Now that her courage had received a much-needed booster shot, she was as ready as she'd ever be. She chose one of the blue lounger chairs that surrounded the small fenced-in pool, and sat on the edge of it. The southern New Mexico sun sizzled above, heating the top of her dark hair and causing perspiration to pop up on the back of her neck. Many of the hotel patrons were taking advantage of the clear blue pool water to cool off, and Cristina breathed the clean, wet smell of

256 / Lynda Sandoval

it in, feeling cloaked in anonimity. She was alone in a crowd here—her favorite state of being.

Regardless of her pumped-up bravado, as she dialed Zach's number, her heart began to thud against her rib cage. Her friends had been right—she'd compounded the problem by ignoring his phone calls for more than a week. He wasn't going to be happy, but she could handle it.

The phone rang twice before Zach picked up. "Cristina? Is that you?"

"It's me." A sun-soaked breeze twirled her hair around her face, tickling her cheekbone. She pushed a lock behind her ear.

"My God, what in the hell is going on?" He sounded exasperated and relieved all at once. "Where are you? I've been leaving you messages for days."

"I-I know. I'm in New Mexico with my friends."

"New Mexico? But I thought Lucy and Ruben were getting married in Denver?"

"Yeah, they did. But . . . well, I'll explain all that later. It's a long story." She bit her lip for a moment, overcome by a wash of remorse. "But . . . as for the rest, I'm sorry. Zach. I was . . . scared to call. I'm just . . . so sorry."

His long pause said more than any words ever could. "So it's true then?"

She sighed, tuning out the pool merriment around her. "Yes, it's true."

"God, Cris. Why?" His voice went husky. "We have enough money for you to buy whatever you want, whenever you want."

She closed her eyes, stung by the profound disappointment in his tone. He'd never understand that her shoplifting compulsion wasn't a money thing, so why even bother with the inane explanations. She wasn't sure if she could make him understand, because it didn't make sense, even to her. Some masochistic part of her wanted to ask what their social circle knew, what his mother knew, but her courage ducked into hiding for the time being. She could only face censure from one person at a time, and today belonged solely to Zach.

"I don't even know what to say. And I won't make excuses. I did it. I got caught." She took a deep breath and blew it out. "I'm ready to face up to the consequences."

"Just tell me what happened? How could something like this have—was it a mistake?"

"No, it wasn't a mistake."

"So you did it on purpose?"

She debated hedging, glossing over the ugliest parts of her little compulsion, then decided she might as well get it all out. "Yes. On purpose."

"Cris." A long pause ensued. "I don't get it."

She hung her head, threading the fingers of her free hand into the front of her hair. She couldn't blame him for being disappointed in her, but she decided, as long as she had his attention, she might as well bare all. "The thing is, I'm unhappy, Zach. I have been for so long."

"Unhappy how? We have a wonderful life."

"We do. In many ways, yes. I love you and the kids so much, but . . . your mother hates me and never misses an opportunity to bash me. It's damaged my self-esteem more than you know."

"Come on, Cris." Zach sounded skeptical. "You're the most poised, in-control woman I know. You always have been. It's one of the qualities I love most about you."

She shook her head, even though he couldn't see her. "No. It's just a facade, a way for me to get through each day. Truthfully? I'm scared all the time. Your mother—God, Zach. She makes me doubt myself, doubt our marriage. I just—"

"You have to understand—"

"No. Let me finish. And I *don't* have to understand," she said, with uncharacteristic firmness. The man needed to cut the apron strings once and for all if their marriage was going to last. She felt suddenly desperate to make him hear her. "I'm your wife. You chose to spend your life with me, and yet you have never once stood up for me when your mother starts in. It makes me feel so . . . out of place. Like her negative opinion has been validated by the one person I want to believe in me."

258 / Lynda Sandoval

"I do believe in you."

Cris ignored him. Words were just that, and in the scheme of things, they didn't mean shit. "I try so hard with her and nothing ever works. She's determined to find me lacking."

"She's a difficult woman," he conceded.

"So why don't you defend me? Do you agree with her?"

"Of course not. It's just—" He released an impatient sound, as though unable to find the appropriate words. "She's my mother. I don't want to fight with her. She and Dad have done so much for me."

"I've done a lot for you, too, Zach," she reminded him in gentle, chiding tones. "I bore your children, I've followed you everywhere for your career, I try to be a good wife to you."

"You are a good wife."

"Then make me feel like it," she told him, emphatically, clutching a fist to her chest. "Tell your mother I'm a good wife, don't just tell me. Show her where you stand. Make it clear she needs to accept me or stay out of our lives. She's destroying us, Zach. She's destroying me."

"God, I'm sorry," he said, after a long, stunned pause. "I didn't know. I was trying to keep you both happy and you got the short end of the stick. I never intended for it to be that way."

She softened slightly. "Yeah. Zach, I never meant to start . . . stealing, either." Ugh, the word tasted ugly on her tongue. "I guess"—she sighed—"this won't make sense probably, but it was an outlet for all the pain I was feeling in my life. In *our* life. I don't know. An adrenaline jolt to make me forget. All I know is . . . I can't go on this way."

"What does that mean, 'you can't go on this way,' Cristina? Are you asking me for a divorce?"

Cristina actually laughed at that notion. "Of course not. I love you and I'll love you forever. I want to spend my life with you and the kids."

"Good. Shit, you scared me."

"But . . . I'm not finished." She paused to let that register. "You're going to have to choose between placating your mother and being a good husband to me. I can't take any more of her abuse. And it *is* abuse, no matter how subtle. Next time it happens, I expect you to defend me. To nip it in the bud. Next time and every time."

"I hear you."

"Do you? Do you really hear what I'm saying?"

"Yes. We can work on this. I promise things will change." A beat passed. "But can we please discuss the arrest for a few minutes? So much has happened. We need to—"

"Of course." She gulped. *Oh. That.*

"It's been hellish here, babe. I've had to address the issue on the show after it was all over the papers, and I didn't even know what to say because my own wife left me totally out of the loop. Do you have any idea how much that hurt?"

Regret kicked her in the gut. She couldn't imagine how hard that had been for Zach to face that kind of scrutiny on the evening news. He'd never been in the limelight in a negative way. "My turn. *I'm* sorry."

Zach blew out a long, weary breath. "It's over and done. Apology accepted." His tone took on a subtle reproach. "But you should've called me. You should've trusted me that much."

Three rambunctious boys ran screaming across the deck and jumped, pulling their knees up and bombing into the pool. They sent up huge sprays of chlorine-scented water. Cristina ducked from it. "You're right."

"I don't want you to ever doubt yourself or my love, ever again, okay? What my mother thinks is wrong, and I don't agree with her. I never have."

"I wish I'd known that." So much wasted time.

"I should've told you. I should've told *her.*"

She sighed. Shoulda, woulda, coulda. The whole world knew that problems arose in a marriage when the communication died, but still people couldn't avoid it. Why was that? Were humans that slow on the uptake? "We've got a lot to work on. But I want to."

"Me, too, babe. Me, too." His tone changed, became a little softer. "Look, about the arrest . . . I've pulled some strings with the judge here. He's an old friend of the family."

Cristina laughed wryly. "Of course."

"Hey, don't knock it," Zach said. "He's willing to consider dismissing charges or a few other options. You need to call him, though." He rattled off a phone number, which she hastily scrawled on a receipt from her purse.

She had to call a judge. Ugh. On the other hand, though, relief riddled through her. Not because of the judge's consideration, but rather because of the whole incident and what it had brought about. Considering her repayment of the store owners, she hadn't *truly* hurt anyone but herself with what she'd done. She'd set a poor example, sure. But in the grand scheme of things, her problem had led her to the present, to Truth or Consequences, New Mexico, of all places. Her friends, her experiences, even find the courage to stand up to Zach—none of it would've happened had she not been caught. "Thank you for listening . . . and for talking to the judge," she added reluctantly.

"I'd do anything for you, honey," he said, in a deep purr. "I guess you didn't know that."

"I guess not. But I know now."

"Are you going to call the judge?"

"I'm going to handle it, Zach. I promise. Listen, though. This is my problem, and from here on out, I'm going to handle it on my own, despite your family connections. I don't need you to run interference anymore."

"Well, if that's how you want it." He sounded dubious. "Let me know how it goes."

"I will. Promise." She hung up realizing she hadn't told him anything about Lucy's botched wedding, about Tilly, about the foiled robbery—all that had happened since she'd arrived in Denver. One traumatic admission at a time, she supposed, but the omissions made her feel distant. There would be opportunities to regale him with everything after she returned to San Antonio.

Before heading back to the room, Cristina dialed the number she'd written on the receipt, ignoring the fear in her throat. She focused on the children playing next to the pool while the line rang, and held her head higher than she had in a very long time. Maybe forever. She would speak with the judge, but she'd also handle things her way—and that didn't include worming her way out of consequences she deserved. Smiling to herself, Cristina suddenly felt like everything would be all right.

L ucy glanced up when Cristina entered the motel room and thought, immediately, that her friend looked different. Calmer, more serene. More confident. "Where have you been?"

"Out by the pool. Calling Zach," she added, in a proud tone.

"You called Zach?" Annette asked, excitedly.

Even Mercedes turned her attention from Tilly's cigar box of treasures to listen.

Cristina nodded. "And then"—she glanced from one friend to the next, clearly enjoying their suspense—"I called the judge dealing with my shoplifting case."

"You're kidding?" Lucy said, bouncing onto her knees as best she could without waking the still sleeping Senalda. "Tell us everything."

Cris filled them in on her and Zach's conversation, and his "family connections" with the judge.

"So did he dismiss charges?" Lucy asked.

"He was willing to. I told him no."

"Huh?"

Cris dropped onto the edge of the bed tucking one foot beneath her, then grabbed for the bag of potato chips Lucy held and began eating them. "I told him I had no interest in weaseling out of my punishment. I mean, what kind of example would that set for Cassandra and Manuel? Hasn't the shoplifting and arrest been enough of a bad example already?"

"I'm so proud of you," Annette said, looking misty-eyed.

Cristina beamed. "Thank you. I'm proud of myself, too."

"So what are they going to do to you?" Mercedes asked.

"I have a private sentencing meeting with the judge in three weeks.

He *did* save me the embarrassment of a trial, since I pretty much admitted everything to him."

"That's good. Zach ought to appreciate that."

"Well, it's something, at least. I told Judge Cartwright I wanted probation and community service, because it's what I deserve. I'll pay a fine, too, if he thinks I should. Whatever. I'm not going to do jail time, I know that."

"No, you wouldn't for this," Lucy said.

"Anyway, we're going to figure everything out then. He told me to be thinking of what type of community service would be best, in light of my crime."

"Wow." Lucy crossed her arms, her eyes shining with respect. Cris might not be able to see it, but she'd grown so much already on this trip. "So did Zach blow a gasket over that? I mean, did you call him and give him the scoop?"

"I did, and nope. No gasket-blowing. I told him it was my crime and I would handle the repercussions my way. I didn't want to use the family name." She shrugged. "He was . . . a little annoyed that I didn't just go for dismissal after all the trouble he went through to speak with the judge. But Judge Cartwright was impressed that I took responsibility, I'm comfortable with how it worked out, and Zach will just have to get over it."

"Nice," Mercy said, sounding like she meant it.

"Yes, good job," echoed Annette.

"How do you feel?" Lucy asked.

Cristina laughed. "Only about a million times better than when I got here." She scrunched her nose. "I *do* feel bad about putting Zach in an awkward position on the news show. I guess he had to address the situation live, and he had no clue what was going on. That must have just really sucked."

"He'll get over it," the three friends chimed in unison.

"He's Zach Aragon," Lucy added, with a smirk. "He's invincible, remember? I'm sure he finessed his way out of it and earned more admirers in the process."

"True. How could I forget, I'm married to Superman." Cris grinned. "Enough about me. What's the Tilly plan?"

Mercy held up Lucy's notebook, waggling it.

"We've written down every address in that cigar box," Lucy said. "Whenever you're ready, we'll just get in the van and go from one to the next."

"I'm ready now." She glanced at Senalda. "What about our little mommy?"

"Let her sleep," Mercy said, gazing upon the young woman as if she were a cherubic child. "We can leave her a note and bring back dinner later. Poor doll, we've been running her ragged."

A couple hours of absolutely fruitless door-knocking later, the four of them returned to the motel room, frustrated but at least bearing pizza and copious amounts of red wine. They'd driven back in almost mournful silence—especially after someone called the cops on them. Okay, so it was strange, four women knocking on doors cold, asking probing questions, but none of them looked threatening. Facts were facts: they'd exhausted every lead in that cigar box, to no avail. No one in this damn, dusty town knew Tilly. At least, no one was willing to give her up. None of her relatives lived at the addresses they'd gathered anymore, and the four of them didn't have anywhere else to turn. They didn't want to admit defeat, but Mercy knew they were all reaching the end of their enthusiasm for this fruitless search.

They pulled into a parking spot outside the motel room and Annette turned off the van. For a moment, they all just sat there. "What now?" Annette said.

"Let's just eat," Lucy suggested, in a downtrodden voice.

"Screw food. Let's get hammered," Mercy countered. "Pizza has never made me forget my woes, but wine often does."

"At least temporarily," Cris said.

Mercy shouldered the front door open. "Good enough for me."

As they alighted from the van, Senalda waddled out onto the sidewalk smiling like she'd won the Lotto. Mercy's heart lifted. The young woman looked so excited, surely it couldn't just be due to their return. Mercy's throat tightened, but she tried not to get her hopes up.

"You're back," Senalda said. "Is *muy bueno.*"

"How did everything go, honey?" Mercedes asked, crossing over to embrace Senalda. She pulled away and looked down toward Senalda's middle. "And how's our little one doing?"

Senalda laid a palm protectively over her tummy. "We're fine. I feel much rested and I have great news."

Eyes fixed on the younger woman's face, one hand gripping her arm, Mercy waited breathlessly to hear what Senalda would say next. She prayed it was something along the lines of Tilly lives down the street and she's meeting us for dinner.

"I was hours on the phone with Deborah and Alex, also reading the cards in Tilly's cigar box." Mercy's whole body tensed as she waited for more. "We believe *la curandera* lives close to here. In the Caballa Mountains. We think you can find her here."

Lucy whooped and cheered while Mercedes stood dumbstruck. How could they have missed something in that damned keepsake box?

Lucy pushed past Mercedes and hugged Senalda. "That's fantastic! But how? We read those cards over and over, and we visited all the addresses."

The others gathered around, their excitement crackling.

Senalda laughed, a happy wind-chime sound. "It was the donkeys. With the man."

"That weird photograph?" Annette exchanged a baffled glance with Cristina. "How could that possibly lead you to Tilly?"

"That, and the cards."

"But we read all the cards. To death," Mercy said.

"The cards you could not read. In Navajo."

"That Sanskrit-looking stuff was Navajo? Do you read Navajo?" Annette asked, marveling.

"No. But Alex—"

"Go figure," Mercedes said, smirking. "Whiz kid strikes again."

Senalda nodded. "She studies the Indian dialects in university. I faxed her the card from the hotel office, and she was able to . . . what's the word?" She twirled her hand.

"Translate?"

"Yes. *Sí*. Translate."

"So what does it say?" Lucy pressed.

"It's a card to thank *la curandera* for the birth of a baby. The donkey man's baby. I have look, and I find him here in town. He is called Yiska. He knows where *la curandera* lives."

Lucy grasped Senalda's wrists, lowering herself to the younger woman's height. "Senalda, you're an angel! Did you talk to this Yiska guy?"

"*Sí*. His people come from the Alamo Band Reservation near Socorro, but he lives here now, with his wife and daughter. He will take you to *la curandera* tomorrow."

Tomorrow? Just like that? Lucy couldn't believe it. She couldn't even speak. A lead on Tilly's whereabouts *and* a guide to keep them on track? It was almost too good to be true.

"We're sure it was Tilly who delivered his baby?" Mercy asked, hand resting on her throat. "He's not confusing her with another *curandera* is he?"

"For sure, I cannot say." Senalda gave them a smug smile. *"Pero,* his daughter's name is Matilda, named for *la curandera* who helped with the birth. They call *la niña* . . . Tilly."

Lucy exchanged wordless, electrified glances with her three friends. Her brain could scarcely wrap around the idea that they were this close. What had started as a whim had turned into something real, something that could actually happen. Something that could change the course of Olivera history. She hated to admit to herself that she truly hadn't expected this. She'd been fully prepared for a wild-goose chase followed by the four of them slinking home, all stupid and apologetic.

"He wants to leave at noon tomorrow, if that's okay."

"It's perfect," Cristina said. "No more time to waste."

"Yiska says the way is long, but is okay. He will meet you at Caballo Lake and bring the donkeys for you to ride."

Annette laughed, a shocked, monosyllabic sound. "We're riding the man's donkeys?"

"Oh my God!" Cristina added.

Lucy glanced over at Mercedes, who crossed her arms and smirked. She propped one foot on the curb. "Well," she said with feigned seriousness, "I've never ridden a donkey before, but considering the quality of my ex-husbands and boyfriends, I guess you could say I've straddled an ass or two in my day."

"Mercy!" Lucy shrieked, covering her mouth to laugh.

Mercy winked. "I'm just sayin'."

Lucy released a long, relieved sigh. Senalda and—once again—Deborah and Alex had come through for them in a big way. Tilly was no longer a myth, but a woman within reach. Best of all, Mercy was joking around again, which meant she would likely bounce back from the tabloid calamity, especially now that they had a lead on the woman who just might be able to help them all.

Lucy felt certain Mercedes would emerge from the ashes unscathed, and most likely in a better position than she'd been in before. That was Mercy—she always landed on her feet. If she felt she needed Tilly's help to stick that landing, well, luckily, it didn't seem like a matter of *if* they'd find Tilly anymore, but *when.*

Thank God for young people, Lucy thought, sending up a quick prayer for Deborah, Alex, and Senalda. Without them, she and the others might still be lost on the highway in the middle of nowhere, fighting over the goddamned map.

After a celebratory dinner of pizza, and a long soak in one of T or C's hot springs, the four of them decided not to risk pushing Senalda too close to her due date before flying back to Mexico. This was a first pregnancy, and Senalda was only nineteen years old; the baby could easily come early. As much as they would miss her, they knew it was time to do the unselfish thing and send her home to her family as promised.

Mercedes bought her a business class ticket to Mexico City on American Airlines for the following morning. Senalda called her father, who enthusiastically agreed to make the sixty-odd mile drive from Puebla to pick her up. Contrary to her fears, her family didn't care that she was unmarried and pregnant. They just wanted her home with them.

In their typical act first/think later fashion, they now had to rise before dawn and make the two-hour drive to El Paso to drop Senalda off at 6:30 A.M., so she could make her flight. The plan was to see her off, and then drive back in time to meet Yiska at Caballo Lake a little after noon. They'd have plenty of time, but they'd also undoubtedly be exhausted by the end of the first day on donkeys.

Annette watched Mercedes carefully. She was subdued all evening as she helped Senalda pack. She presented her with an extra suitcase stuffed with gifts, clothing, and supplies for the baby she'd bought the evening before. She also gave Senalda money, prepaid calling cards, healthy food for the flight—you name it. Mercy looked so conflicted to be sending the pregnant teen off on her own.

Annette ached with empathy for Mercy's impending loss. She knew Mercy and Senalda had bonded like mother and daughter, and how hard Mercy would take it when Senalda said her final good-byes. They had all done a lot of growing on this trip, and Mercedes seemed particularly fragile lately. Or maybe Annette was just seeing her more clearly after all the bonding they'd done. Mercy pretended to be impervious to the emotions of mere mortals, but Annette knew better. Mercedes felt deeply, which was why she protected herself so ferociously. Sensitive people who had been hurt built stone walls around their hearts.

The whole thing saddened Annette.

How much could Mercedes handle before she cracked? Then again, if she did crack, she might let off enough pressure to help her see there was a light at the end of the dark tunnel she'd been stumbling through. She might see that there were people out here who loved her and forgave her weaknesses, who thought she was perfect as is, sharp edges and all.

Annette addressed Lucy and Cristina. "Why don't the three of us go for a walk? Work off some of this pizza and—" She made exaggerated eye motions toward Mercy and Senalda, who were too caught up in their organizing to even notice.

"Great plan." Lucy stood. "Mercy, do you mind if the three of us go off for a bit?"

Mercy glanced up, distracted. "No, go on."

Without ceremony, the three of them hustled from the room.

"Are you excited to see your family?" Mercedes asked, her voice shaking only a tiny bit. How had she become so attached to this young woman so quickly? She absolutely *hated* to see her leave, even knowing it was the right thing.

"*Si*. It has been many months." She touched her distended tummy, her tone lowering sadly. "Many long months."

"Tell me about them."

Senalda sat on the edge of the bed, sighing gratefully for the respite. "My father, he is a kind man. He works in the art gallery. He puts the . . . how you say—" She drew a rectangular motion in the air in front of her.

"The frames?"

"*Si*. He puts frames on the pictures." She twisted her mouth to the side. "I believe he wanted to be the artist, but with all of us—"

"How many brothers and sisters do you have?"

"Two older brothers. Three sisters. Two younger, and one is my twin."

"You're a twin!" Mercy exclaimed. "That's wonderful."

Senalda nodded. "Sophia. I miss her. She's in university now. I wish—"

"What do you wish?" Mercy settled onto the bed next to Senalda and took one of her hands.

"I wish I think more. About life. My future. I wish I go to university with Sophia. But now"—she glanced down at her belly—"now my life is being mama."

"Honey, mothers can go to college."

Senalda shrugged, then dipped her head and remained silent with her thoughts for a few moments.

"What about your mother?"

"She died," Senalda said. "Long time ago, when she have my youngest sister, Juanita."

"Oh, God. Senalda, I'm so sorry."

"*Gracias. Pero,* papa has taken good care of us. I feel sorry when I see the . . . hunger in his eyes at the gallery. I know he wants to do more than frame, but—" Hand flipped up, she rubbed the tips of her fingers together.

"It's always money that holds us back," Mercy said. "But I'm willing to bet he's a happy man. He has a wonderful family, you." She smiled, shocked to feel tears stinging her eyes.

"Do you have family, Mercy?"

Mercedes bit her quivering bottom lip, then shook her head regretfully. She reflected on Annette, the life she lived, on all she herself had set aside in order to make it in the magazine business. "No. It's just me. My life is so . . . complicated. All I have is my job." And a load of regrets.

Senalda grabbed both of Mercy's hands in her own, squeezing them tightly. "You are a mother. To me. I have not had someone in so long. You make me feel like I have a mama again, looking out for me, loving me."

Mercedes smiled at the young woman through watery eyes, then pulled her into a gentle hug. Senalda's words, her sincerity, meant more to Mercedes than any stupid tabloid smear fest. If she got nothing else out of this trip, she'd always carry Senalda's words in her heart. "Thank you," she whispered. "You make me feel like I have a daughter, too."

God, how was she going to let this young woman get on that plane and leave her life forever?

Four A.M. was a disgustingly early hour, but they all roused with minimal groaning and piled, bleary-eyed, into the van. The two-hour drive was long and quiet and coffee-scented, thank God.

At the airport, Annette, Cris, and Lucy stood back and allowed a very subdued Mercedes to check Senalda in before the four of them walked with her to the security checkpoint. They could go no further, so they stepped aside to say their farewells. Lucy, Cris, and Annette hugged her good-bye, wishing her and the baby well and thanking her for all her invaluable help. When the hugging and cheek kissing ceased, they stepped aside to allow Mercedes a private moment with her. Annette kept an ear on the conversation, however, out of concern for Mercedes. She could almost feel the splits in Mercy's emotional armor.

Mercy took in a deep breath and blew it out. She offered Senalda a bright smile. "Well. Do you have everything?"

"*Si.* I can't—" Senalda's words broke on a sob, and Mercedes pulled her into a hug, rocking her and stroking the back of her head. "I don't want to go."

"Shh, it's okay. You do want to go. You belong with your family and they love you."

"You're my family, too," Senalda said.

Mercy swallowed, squeezing her eyes shut. "Forever."

"Thank you," Senalda whispered, crying against Mercy's shoulder. "I will never forget you. Someday, I'll repay you."

"*De nada,* sweetie. It was my pleasure. And you'd better not forget me." Mercy pulled back, but held on to Senalda's forearms. She sniffed and lifted her chin, but still hadn't shed a tear. "And you know you can call me anytime, for anything, right? I mean it, okay?"

"I know. I have your phone numbers."

"You go home and have a healthy baby. I bought you disposable cameras. I expect rolls and rolls of photographs when he or she is born, okay?"

"I love you, Mercy," Senalda said.

Annette's throat clogged with tears; she could only imagine what kind of punch the statement had landed on Mercedes's heart. Mercy rolled her lips inward and held her breath for the longest time. Annette was just about to step forward and offer her support, when Mercy regained her composure. She pulled Senalda into one more gentle hug, then kissed her on the cheek. "Ditto," she whispered.

"Excuse me?" Senalda asked, confused.

Annette watched over Senalda's slight shoulder as Mercy grappled with her emotions. "That means . . . I love you, too." She schooled her features into a signature Mercedes placid smile and pulled away. "Now, go. Go, go, go. I don't want you to be late for your flight."

Senalda nodded, tears running down her face. She looked every bit the teenager she was as she blew them all kisses, which they returned. Then hefting her small tote bag carry-on to one shoulder, she lumbered toward the X-ray machines.

Lucy and Annette moved to stand on either side of Mercedes immediately. Lucy wrapped an arm around Mercy's waist and laid her head on Mercy's shoulder. Annette grabbed Mercy's hand and squeezed, pleased when Mercy held on. Cris moved up next to Annette, standing close. They watched until Senalda had made it through the checkpoint and turned to wave one last time. When she'd disappeared from view, Mercedes released a breath.

"You okay, Mercy?" Lucy asked.

"Yep. Fine. Let's go."

Spoken a bit too quickly, Annette thought. The veneer had to crack sometime. When they got out to the parking lot, sure enough, Mercedes started sniffling, then progressed to little sucking sobs, and on to full, wrenching tears. She cried so hard, she couldn't catch her breath. They stopped at the back of the van and guided her to sit on the rear bumper so she could let it all out. The three of them gathered around her.

"What the hell is wrong with me?" she wailed, when she could finally suck in enough air to facilitate speech.

Annette smiled, squatting before her and resting her palms on Mercy's knees. "Nothing is wrong with you, Mercy. You love her like a daughter. You protected her. It's understandable. You should have seen me when Deborah left for college, and she lives within easy driving distance."

Mercy blinked up, the tears still coming full force. "Really?"

Annette nodded. "And truly." She looked up at Cris, hoping to draw her into the conversation, yearning to be some sort of a bridge from one strong, stubborn friend to the other. "You cried when Cassandra and Manuel left for Europe, right, Cris?"

"Like a baby. And I was PMSing, too. It was ugly."

Annette raised her eyebrows at Mercy. "See?"

"I miss her so much already." Mercedes cried harder, doing very un-Mercy things like wiping her nose on the backs of her hands and snorting. "I'm a horrible person. Everything in the tabloids is true," she said, switching course without warning.

"Don't be ridiculous," Lucy told her. "If everything they published were true, you never would've helped Senalda."

"I'm p-p-promiscuous," Mercy said, on a shuddering inhale.

Annette almost laughed. "So what, Mercy? You're single. You can do what you want."

"I'm adi-di-dicted to Vicodin," she wailed.

Now that came as a surprise. Annette shared a worried glance with Lucy, who sat down next to Mercy on the bumper.

"What do you mean, babe?" Lucy asked, cautiously. "I thought you took that for your hamstrings?"

Cristina rifled through her purse and handed Mercedes a pocket pack of Kleenex.

"N-no, I take it because I can't handle my f-fucked up"—she paused to blow her nose with a giant honk—"life, and I have a doctor who doesn't mind pushing drugs."

Everyone remained silent for a moment.

"No one likes me. I don't even like myself. I'm a bitch and a slut and a dictator and an . . . an addict," she finished on a shame-filled rasp.

"So?" Cris asked, surprising them all into looking up at her. "I'm a criminal. And I don't do drugs, but I'm addicted to Botox. See?" She made some facial expressions, and nothing above her eyes moved. "Without it, my forehead looks like an accordion. Trust me. No one's perfect," Cristina said. "Cut yourself some slack. And forget the stupid tabloids."

The Botox admission distracted Mercedes enough that her crying slowed to sniffles. She blew her nose once more, then asked Cris, "Did it hurt?" while scrutinizing her forehead.

"What? Oh, the Botox?" Mercy nodded. "Not much. The shots sting a little, and sometimes you get this weird crunchy feeling as the stuff goes in, but it's over"—she snapped her fingers—"just like that. And a few days later, no wrinkles. It's a damned miracle, if you want to know the truth."

Mercedes assessed Cris's face. "It looks good."

"Thank you." Cris smiled gently. "Now, what do you say we wipe away our tears and head back to ride some donkeys?"

"Wow," Lucy said, dryly. "An offer we can't refuse."

Mercedes sniffled a couple of times, then got to her feet. "I'm sorry, you guys. I didn't mean to melt down."

"Melting down is what toddlers do," Annette said, rising to give Mercy a hug. "What you did was simply . . . human. It's okay to release emotions, you know."

"Releasing emotions sucks ass," Mercedes said. "Although I do feel a little bit better," she admitted grudgingly.

Lucy laughed. "See?" A beat passed, and she added softly, "If you want to give me the Vicodin, Mercy, I'll keep it for you. If it will help."

Mercedes flashed a fear-laden glance through her lashes. "Not today, okay, Lucky girl? Not yet."

Lucy nodded. "When you're ready."

"If I'm ever ready."

"You'll be ready sometime. No pressure."

They got in the van, with Annette driving, Mercy in the passenger seat, and Cris and Lucy behind them. Mercy flipped down the mirror to wipe her eyes, then touched her forehead with the pads of her fingers. Her gaze met Cristina's briefly in the mirror, then she smacked the visor away. "You know what? Maybe we should all get Botox," she suggested.

"Ride donkeys, rescue abused teenagers, spill guts, get Botox. It sounds reasonable to me. It really does. We might never find Tilly, and our thighs might be sore from the donkey riding, but at least we'd look good at the end of it."

Cristina started laughing, and she and Mercedes shared a smile reminiscent of their former closeness.

Annette said a silent prayer that this moment was the first step toward Cristina and Mercedes repairing their relationship. She really believed that needed to happen if Mercedes was ever going to be able to move on. Maybe Cristina, too.

As she pulled onto the highway, Annette came to another realization brought on by the morning's activities. Mercedes didn't need Tilly to make her problems disappear, and she didn't need some guy to love *her* in order to soften her or turn her life around. What she needed was someone to nurture and love unconditionally. Someone to care for, someone who needed *her,* who could see through her toughness to all the sweetness inside. Mercedes needed a family of her own, be it traditional or newfangled. She'd be such a good mother. It didn't even matter if there was a father in sight. Mercedes was the strongest woman Annette had ever known, and she could raise a family alone without batting an eye or breaking a nail.

If only Mercy would realize this.

Chapter Twenty-two

Fueled by excitement and adrenaline alone, the four of them had gotten a much-needed second wind by the time they arrived at the specified parking area by Caballo Lake to meet Yiska later that day. Even Mercy had perked up, although it was clear she was still feeling the loss of Senalda like a knife gouge to her soul. Lucy could sense a certain . . . hollowness that she'd never seen in Mercy before.

They parked the van, got out, then stood looking out over the clear blue water toward the dry brown rise of the mountain range beyond. Tilly was somewhere out there, Lucy thought, almost close enough to feel. She knew the others were experiencing the same thrill of anticipation, the same hope that, finally, their goal was within reach.

"We'd better look for Yiska," Cristina said finally, consulting her watch. She scanned the parking lot. "We're right on time, but since we've never met the guy . . ."

They might've had a difficult time finding Yiska alone, even with the complete description provided by Senalda before she'd left and the single photograph in Tilly's cigar box, but there was no missing a man leading five docile donkeys. Annette erupted in delighted laughter when she saw the animals clip-clopping toward them across the parking lot, dutifully following a youngish, very good-looking man in camping garb. "Oh, look at them. They're cute. This will be fun."

Mercedes snorted. "Yeah, if you're into straddling farm animals. I'll remind you of how cute you thought they were after two days in the saddle, okay, Annie?"

"Do you think it's going to take two days?" Lucy asked, dismayed. She wanted to find Tilly now. Right now, like at the other end of the parking lot, preferably. Let the pain end, for God's sake.

Mercy shrugged. "Just speculating. Senalda"—her voice broke for a split second, but she pulled it together like a pro—"said it was a long way."

"Let's hope it's not that long. Long is a relative term, you know?" She smiled at Yiska, who was coming toward them, as if they wore signs that read, "We're the fools who can't follow a map!" He waved. They waved back.

When he reached them, he broke into a smile, too. "I guess I found the right four women, huh?"

He looked like the character Johnny Depp played in the movie *Chocolat.* A little rugged, a little wild. Very bad boy hot, but with a core of sweetness. Lucy figured if they had to spend two days on donkey back in the untamed mountains of New Mexico, it couldn't hurt to have a hottie for a guide. Even a married hottie with a wife and new baby. She stepped forward and extended her hand. "You must be Yiska. I'm Lucy."

"Ah, the police officer," he said, with a grin. It wasn't a question. He shook her hand warmly. "Nice to meet you. And let me guess." He looked over the other women, then pointed at Annette, "You're the mama with five kids, yes?"

She nodded, looking proud. "That's me."

He peered from Mercedes to Cristina and back again, stroking his chin thoughtfully. "This one's harder."

Mercedes and Cristina blinked at each other in surprise. Lucy knew neither of them would think they were at all like the other. Amusing, since they were so much alike in a lot of ways.

Finally he pointed at Mercedes. "This one's just a guess, but New York City?"

She smirked. "Yes. Mercedes. Nice to meet you. What gave me away?"

"The edge."

"I have an edge?"

"You have an edge," all three of her friends answered together, and Yiska confirmed it with a nod.

"Huh. Who knew?"

"Only the whole universe," Lucy said, wryly.

"And Cristina," Yiska said finally. "From San Antonio."

"That's me." Cristina dipped her chin.

"Great, I think I'll be able to keep you straight. Now, let me introduce you to my group." Yiska's donkeys were oddly named Bach, Mozart, Chopin, Beethoven, and Bob Dylan—Bob for short. Bob was Yiska's personal donkey, but he let the others pick their own. Cristina immediately went for Chopin, because their names started with the same letter. Lucy chose Bach because of his one syllable name and mellow attitude. Annette snapped up Mozart because he had "cute ears," and Mercedes didn't really care. She wasn't too amped about the idea of riding one anyway. By default, she ended up with Beethoven, which was fine with her.

"So where exactly are we headed?" Annette asked, once they were all mounted up, per Yiska's instructions, and their packs had been securely fastened to the donkey's sturdy backs. The donkeys stood in a circle, waiting patiently.

Yiska pointed toward the mountain range. "Up," he said.

They all looked, with more than a little trepidation. They'd read up on the mountain range after Senalda told them where the *curandera* might live. The Caballo Mountains were flanked on the west side by Caballo reservoir, and on the east side by the Jornado del Muerto. Journey of the Dead—that didn't bode well.

"How far up?" Lucy asked, cautiously.

"It's about a three thousand foot elevation gain from here, but we don't have to go all the way to the top."

"Thank God for small freakin' favors," Mercedes mumbled.

One corner of Yiska's mouth lifted, but he clapped his hands together once, then smoothed the palms against each other rapidly, trying to fire up their excitement. "Okay, let's get this show on the road, yeah? Do you have enough water? I have a backcountry water purifier if we need it, but it's best to be as prepared as possible in case we're not near a water source."

"We have it all," Lucy assured him.

"Tents and sleeping bags?" he double-checked, looking dubious. Apparently their reputations for ineptitude had grown so large they'd been eclipsed by them. "I guarantee you, we'll be camping at least one night."

"She lives that far out?" Lucy asked.

"Yep," Yiska said.

Mercedes groaned, glancing skyward. "Somebody kill me and send me to hell immediately, instead of making me ride a donkey there. Please, for the love of God."

Lucy grinned at Mercy's exaggeration. She was as eager as anyone, if not more, to find Tilly. Hell, Lucy knew Mercy would walk over broken glass to find the woman if she had to; a couple days on a donkey were nothing. But she just had to be Mercedes. Lucy felt warm and fuzzy. She wouldn't want Mercy any other way.

"We're set," Lucy told Yiska. "We have everything. For once in our lives, we're well-prepared and ready to go."

He took her at her word. "Let's hit it, then. I'll lead the way. Just fall in behind me, single file until we're off-path. After that, you can pair up if you want. Whatever works."

Yiska took off, and Mercedes fell in behind him. Cristina followed her. Lucy looked over at Annette and hiked her shoulders. "I'm really looking forward to this, Annie."

"Ask me how excited I am after our first day's ride." She leaned forward and patted Mozart's neck. "My new pal and I should get along fine, but I'm iffy on sitting in this position for hours on end."

"You'll do great," Lucy assured her, indicating that Annette should precede her. "You've had five kids."

Annette barked a laugh. "Yeah, and none of them were donkey-size when I popped them out, trust me."

"But just think, you can go home with awesome toned inner thighs." Lucy shrugged. "Okay, so they might be raw . . ."

"Every woman's dream," Annette said, rolling her eyes. "Voluntary chafing. Yippee."

Hours later, Mercy groaned. "I'm never riding a farm animal again. My salient parts have been numb for two hours."

"Mine, too." Lucy gazed with painful yearning toward their guide. "I wonder how much longer we have to put up with this?"

As though psychic, Yiska brought Bob around and stopped, waiting for the women to reach him. He still looked fresh and serene, completely pain and cramp free. How did he do that? When they'd circled up, he studied their weary grimaces. "I'm getting the feeling you're all done for the day."

Cristina raised a hand. "I'm *so* done."

"Me, too," Annette chimed, with a stretch and groan. "Stick a fork in me, I'm fall-off-the-bone done."

Mercy nodded, and Lucy didn't say anything, but she didn't need to.

"Okay, then." Yiska studied their surroundings, a little shadow of reluctance in his eyes. "We can set up camp here then, but I need to tell you, we're in prime rattlesnake country. The up side of that is the snakes sometimes keep the bears at bay, and it's prime bear country, too."

"You're kidding, right?" Annette asked.

Yiska shook his head. "You probably missed the bear scat back there, but did you see the overturned boulder? Or the torn-up logs?"

"Yes," Lucy said. "I saw them."

He pursed his lips and nodded sagely. "Bears."

Annette groaned, bending over to hug Mozart around his sturdy neck. "Why can't all animals be as sweet as this guy?"

"Nothing will hurt you," Yiska assured her. "I'm good with backcountry safety, and I can teach you. First things first, don't wander off alone. And don't step or stick your hands anywhere you can't see clearly."

"Yeah," Annette said, wryly, "because there's a risk of that happening. I guess no one warned you I'm a world-class wimp about creepy wild animals?"

Yiska laughed. "Seriously, I want you all to be extra careful when gathering firewood. Step *on* the logs or rocks, not *over* them, okay? And stay out of the brush. I have antivenin"—he patted his pack—"but I'd rather not have to use it."

"I wholeheartedly second that emotion," Cristina said.

"What else should we do?" Mercy asked.

"Sing loudly when you're walking into new areas. Clap, cheer, anything. Let those bears know you're coming. Baby bears are cute, however their protective mamas are anything but. If you see a cub, talk in a calm, low voice and back away in exactly the direction you approached. Chances are, you won't get between the mama and the cub that way."

Annette paled and sort of . . . swayed atop her donkey. She gripped her saddle horn tightly. "You are really scaring me. If I see a bear, I think I might just pass out."

Yiska tilted his head and looked sympathetic. "Don't be scared, be smart. We'll evict that city slicker attitude out of all of you before the week is out."

Lucy didn't want to think about the "week" comment. If it took a week to find Tilly, she'd lose what was left of her mind. "Okay, where should we tie the donkeys?" She whimpered as she swung her leg off the saddle. "I am more than ready to bid Bach good night." She patted his neck and let him nuzzle her hand. "No offense, little buddy."

Yiska pointed to a copse of small piñon trees. "Tie them there, then we'll do a snake check and set up camp. My wife, Elaya, sent up a meal for all of us. Dried corn stew and fry bread. Fruit, too, and wine."

"Wine," said Mercedes, with celebratory flair. "Finally the man's speaking my language."

Yiska grinned. "I'll cook and you all can relax."

"Can we also grill you for info about the *curandera*?" Mercedes said, easing her leg over Beethoven, then grimacing as her foot hit the ground. "Oh my God, I'll never do another lunge." She rubbed her sore inner thighs.

"We'll talk about her."

"Good food, discussion about Tilly, copious amounts of alcohol," Lucy said. "Sounds like a perfect evening to me." Well, almost, she amended in her mind. Perfection would include Tilly walking into their camp with a magic life-repairing potion, a cache of bear and snake repellant, and Ruben. Barring that, the wine would have to do.

Shortly thereafter, the donkeys had been fed and watered, and camp was set up. The five of them encircled the campfire to eat the fabulous beef and corn stew and fry bread, each piece complete with a hole in the middle, which had spiritual significance for members of his tribe, Yiska had explained. Now they were getting serious with the wine and relaxing into the sunset-drenched evening, enjoying the wood smoke crackle of the fire and the company and conversation.

"Tell us about the *curandera*," Annette suggested, after they'd exhausted the subjects of weather, food, bears, snakes, family, police work, New York City, and the Houston Astros.

Yiska eyed her for a minute. "You know most of what's important." They started to protest, but he lifted his chin toward Mercy. "No, really. You do. Instead, tell me about the box you found."

"Tilly's cigar box?" Mercy asked. "Oh, we call her Tilly."

He smiled. "She calls herself Tilly, too."

"See?" Lucy said, excitedly. "It's fate."

Yiska nodded, conceding the point. "Tell me about Tilly's cigar box, or whatever it was that brought you to T or C in search of her. Senalda told me some, but I want to hear it from the four of you."

Lucy took charge, quickly explaining about the magazine article, their quest and how Mercedes had found the cigar box beneath the floor of the abandoned cabin. She felt like she'd told this tale a thousand times. "We're going to return the box when we find her," she assured him. "But the simple fact that we did find it, when it had obviously been hidden . . . well, we feel like that was a sign we were meant to find her, too."

"I believe in signs." Yiska leaned forward to top off all their plastic mugs with wine, eyeing them as he poured. "Can I tell you a legend?"

"A Navajo legend?" Annette asked, intrigued.

"Zuni, actually." Yiska rubbed his jawline with the back of his hand. "But I grew up with the story. A lot of the local tribes share at least some history."

"Please do tell us," Annette said. The other three nodded, then waited attentively.

Yiska cleared his throat. "A long time ago, it was always dark, but it was also always summertime." His voice took on a soothing storytelling cadence that left them all mesmerized. "Coyote had trouble hunting because of the dark, but nevertheless, he went off hunting with Eagle. They came upon a powerful people, the Kachinas, and learned that they had the sun and the moon in a box. When the Kachina people went to sleep, Coyote and Eagle stole the box."

"Why, that little thief," Annette teased.

Cristina dropped her gaze, Lucy noticed. Despite handling her arrest so admirably, she was still pretty ashamed of the theft thing, and who could blame her?

"Eagle carried the box at first," Yiska continued, "but pretty soon the manipulative Coyote convinced his friend to let him carry it."

"Uh-oh," Lucy said. "I've watched the Road Runner cartoons. This can't be good."

Yiska laughed softly. "Yeah, you guessed it. The curious Coyote couldn't keep himself from opening that box. The sun and moon escaped and flew up to the sky. This provided light to the land, of course." He paused, looking from one woman to the other, his expression inscrutable. "But it also took away most of the summer heat, and that's why we now have winter."

Everyone was quiet for a moment. Finally Mercedes cleared her throat. "I don't belong to Mensa or anything, but is that an interesting way of telling us to be careful what we wish for?"

Yiska shrugged one shoulder, then raised his cup to his lips. After he'd drunk from it, he said, "It's just a legend. We learn from legends what we need to learn."

"What do we need to learn?" Mercy persisted.

"Only you know that."

"Are you saying we shouldn't have opened Tilly's cigar box?" Lucy asked. "Was that a mistake?"

"I'm saying everything has two sides."

"Meaning what?" Cristina asked.

Yiska shook his head, amused by their relentlessness. "Meaning, you have to take both sides of every decision, every choice, every gift, no matter what those sides are. Good with bad. Happy with sad. Sorrow with joy. Anger with happiness. Insight with confusion. All of it."

Annette smiled. "Thank you, Yiska," she said, releasing him from the hook the other three had him on. "That's a good lesson to remember. And a great story, too. It'll sure give us all something to think about as we fall asleep, won't it, ladies?"

Chapter Twenty-three

Later that night, they bagged up all their food and the clothing they'd worn while they were cooking and eating, then suspended the bags from high tree branches, far away from their tents, as Yiska had instructed. That way, if bears did venture in for the goods, they wouldn't have to actually enter the camp to get anything. Cold comfort. None of them was thrilled by the prospect of bears anywhere in the vicinity, and in the scheme of things, the suspended bags were pretty damn close. But it was better than nothing.

While Yiska worked on safely extinguishing the fire, the four friends, each wearing a battery-operated headlamp, walked a short way from the camp to a small stream to wash their faces and prepare for a night in the snake-infested, bear-infested wilds. They gripped hands and sang "It's a Small World After All" loudly while they walked, praying any lurking bears would give them a wide berth. Annette figured Lucy's off-key bellowing would scare any beast to within an inch of its fuzzy life, which gave her a measure of relief. The woman was successful and multi-talented, but, Lord, singing was not one of the skills on her résumé.

When they were done, they scuttled quickly back to camp to find

Yiska piling small stones and sticks outside their two tents. Annette and Mercedes were sharing one, Lucy and Cristina the other. Yiska had his own small cocoon of a tent, which he'd set up on the opposite side of the fire pit from theirs, and Annette noticed a similar pile of sticks and stones outside his tent flaps, too.

"What are you doing?" Cristina asked him.

"Risk management." He looked up from the pile outside her tent, then cast an apologetic glance at Annette. He now knew just how squeamish she was about wild animals, and he didn't want to scare her. "I'm not saying we have to worry, but if a black bear comes in the camp and tries to mess with your tent tonight, you fight back hard with sticks and stones. Yell at him, too, and don't let up. They hate that. They're really very wimpy."

"I thought sticks and stones would break your bones but words could never hurt you?" Mercy joked.

"Doesn't apply to bears." Yiska grinned. "They hate loud noises, and they're not too keen on getting pelted with sticks and stones, either."

Mercy scoffed. "You're right. They are wimps."

"Aren't you supposed to play dead if a bear attacks you?" Lucy asked. "I think I saw that on the Discovery channel."

"With grizzly bears, yes. And during the day. I don't think we need to worry about grizzlies." He flipped his hand. "We've mostly got black bears in this area."

"You say that like it's a good thing," Cris said.

"I can't believe we even have to think about this!" Annette threw her hands up in disgust. "Why didn't I stay home with my kids? Their bears are stuffed with polyester foam and completely harmless, right down to their button eyes."

Mercedes smacked her lightly on the upper arm. "Stop being a baby, Annie. They're just bears, for Christ's sake."

"Can I shoot them?" Lucy asked.

Yiska grimaced. "I'm not a big fan of shooting them. This is their land, after all. We're the invaders."

"How very Zen of you, Yiska." Lucy rolled her eyes playfully. "But the question remains, can I shoot them?"

He nodded. "If one is actually attacking"—he held up a hand—"which is rare. And even then—what do you carry?"

Her hand went automatically to her fanny pack. "A forty-five."

He twisted his mouth to the side. "Probably won't do much. The loud sound might scare them, though, so you could set a couple shots off in the air. But you'll have a hell of a time killing a bear easily with a forty-five."

"Do you really think we have to worry?" Annette asked, looking dismal and pale. "I don't want Lucy to shoot a bear."

"You can't be a wuss *and* a bleeding heart, Annie."

"Be quiet, Mercy." Annette scowled, crossing her arms. "I can't help it if I'm afraid. It doesn't mean I want the entire bear population wiped out."

"It's probably not a big worry," Yiska said to Annette. "Believe it or not, bears *do* try to avoid humans, at least until they've gotten a taste of human food. But it's better to be prepared than not."

"Yeah," Mercedes said, with a smirk. "That's a premise we always live by, right gals? We're always prepared. Those cookie-schlepping little Girl Scouts have got nothing on us."

Yiska and the others laughed, then he turned serious again. "One other thing before you all hit the sack. Pull your hiking boots inside the tent and keep your doors zipped."

"What do bears do with boots?" Annette asked.

He shook his head. "This is about the snakes, actually. They like to curl up inside them."

"Oh, my Lord," she said, shaking her head and fanning her face. "Quick, Mercy, let's get in the tent. I can't hear any more of this. I'm going to pass out." She flipped a hand in a quick wave as an afterthought as she fled toward the questionable safety of the Gore-Tex tent. "Good night all."

A round of G'night-John-Boy-type farewells ensued, and everyone retreated into their tents for a well-earned rest.

It wasn't until almost dawn that the bears came.

Mercy's eyes snapped open, adjusting to the burgeoning first light as her mind raced to replay and then classify the sound she'd just heard. Her heart hammered in her chest as her mind raced and the grunting and snuffing grew closer. She listened to the sound of things being up-turned in their camp and clutched the light sleeping bag to her chest, feeling frozen and horribly exposed. For all intents and purposes, they were in a little fabric doggy bag.

Scarcely drawing breath, she listened more intently. Maybe she was just imagining the sound, after all of Yiska's talk and Annette's fear. It probably wasn't a bear at all. It was probably Lucy. Hadn't she always snored like a trucker?

Suddenly the looming, unmistakable silhouette of a big-ass fucking bear cast a shadow on her side of their tent. A twang of fear seized her middle so violently, she lost her breath. The sniffing came so close, Mercedes felt dizzy. She reached over and clutched Annette's arm, rasping. "Annie. Don't freak out."

"What?" Annie lifted her head, bleary-eyed and still half asleep. Just then, the bear lifted its paw and ran it down the side of the tent, rip-ping a clean gouge in the fabric about a foot long.

Mercedes screamed, squeezing her eyes shut. She almost pissed her-self, swear to God, and the worst part was, she couldn't move.

Annette, on the other hand, Ms. Terrified of Scary Animals, scram-bled out of her bag without a moment's hesitation and began yelling at the top of her lungs. Anything and everything that came to her mind streamed out of her mouth in as threatening a tone as Mercy had ever heard.

Annie grabbed for the small pile of sticks and stones that she'd car-ried inside the tent, unzipped the door quickly, then faced the bear head-on and began pelting him with her arsenal. She threw like a girl, but so what? At least she was doing something. Mercedes, on the other hand, lay paralyzed by fear, watching the whole unbelievable scene go down through the open tent flap. She didn't help at all.

Thankfully, Yiska heard the ruckus and flew bare chested out of his tent as well, joining Annette in the attack. The brown bear was just a teenager, small in the scheme of things. But his claws were long, his teeth were sharp, and he looked about double Annette's size. Mercedes closed her eyes and willed him gone.

Annette and Yiska pelted the animal with two full piles of stones and branches until he finally trundled off into the woods at a loping self-protective clip.

When he was well and truly gone, Annette sank to the ground, shaking from head to toe. "Holy, holy, holy shit," she said.

Lucy and Cristina emerged from their tent and ran over. "Are you okay, Annie?" Lucy asked, her voice filled with horror. "God, I think you scared five years off my life."

Annette laughed, sounding a little manic and not at all amused. She reached up and grabbed Lucy's shirt, pulling her off balance until their faces nearly touched. "Let me tell you something, Luce. This visit with Tilly had better be worth it, because if I ever have to face a bear again, I'm holding you personally responsible. And I won't scare five years off your life, I'll kick five years off your butt."

Lucy went down on her knees, hugging Annette and laughing. "Okay, I promise. No more bears. But, God, you did great."

"I listened to Yiska. And yes, I'm the type who reads the safety information card on every flight, too." Annette pulled out of Lucy's embrace and wiped a bead of sweat off her forehead, then dried her hand on her shirt. Her voice still shook. "Call me anal, but I like to be prepared."

Yiska squatted down in front of Annette and smiled broadly. "See there? You did exactly what you were supposed to do and it worked like a charm. You'll be fine out here."

"I'm sorry I wigged, Annie," Mercedes said, finally crawling out of their tent. "I just froze."

"Don't worry about it," Annette said. "The claw came through your side of the tent. I'd have panicked, too. I think I did panic, actually, but all I could think about was sticks and stones and yelling."

"You reacted immediately and without fear," Yiska said.

"Oh, there was fear," Annette said, laughing. "I was one big ball of panic and fear. I just didn't want him to hurt any of us, that's all."

Mercedes groaned. "God, Annie, I so suck."

Yiska winked at Mercedes. "Just stick with this one. She'll keep you safe." He patted Annette's knee. "Those mama bears got nothing on this mama bear."

Annette grinned, feeling proud of herself, exhilarated, and hungry as a . . . well, she hated to say it but hungry as a bear. Near-death experiences did that to a person.

After the excitement of their morning wake-up call from Yogi, the women were more pumped for the second day's ride. Soreness and chafing aside, they spent their time singing popular camping songs—"99 Bottles of Beer on the Wall," "Ate a Peanut," and the ever popular and singularly brilliant, "We're Here Because We're Here Because We're Here Because We're Here."

The ride took them into hilly country, dense with trees and brush and smelling of sage and wildflowers. Every so often, they would lapse into silence, just to appreciate the landscape, the proliferation of butterflies and birdsong. Quest aside, this time together had been a soothing balm to all of their souls. Reconnecting with one another, focusing on issues and situations outside their normal realm and larger than themselves had proven to be a much-needed activity.

A few minutes into their afternoon ride after lunch, Yiska guided them around a huge jutting wall of granite and schist, and to their utter surprise, up to the front of a stone cabin that looked like it had been carved out of the stones it abutted. They would've missed the damn thing had Yiska not been with them. The four of them fell immediately silent, gaping at the tableau before them, afraid to hope.

"Is this it?" Lucy asked, in a reverent whisper, scarcely able to believe it could be true.

"It is," Yiska said, dismounting easily. "Wait here for a moment. Let me just see if Tilly is around." He headed off toward the side of the cabin.

When he was no longer in sight, the four of them eased off the donkeys as well, and gathered into a tight circle, crackling with anticipation. Mercy grabbed Lucy's hand and held it tightly. "God, what if she wants nothing to do with us?"

"I can't even think about it," Lucy said, shaking her head.

"That won't happen." Cristina looked from one friend to the other. "Finding Tilly was fate. None of us can deny that. Even if she only has a few minutes for us, she'll have time. We rode all this way, Annette scared off a bear. Everything that's happened to us up to this point . . . Senalda and Esteban. Lenora, too. And Yiska. None of it would've happened if we weren't meant to find this woman, if she wasn't meant to help us." She paused, grimacing. "Plus, I've been riding a donkey for a day and a half. My ass is chapped."

Lucy smirked. "I'm sure it's the ass argument that will sway her, Cris."

"Cristina is right, though," Annette said. "From all accounts, Tilly's a kind, caring woman. She won't turn us away."

On cue, Yiska rounded the corner of the house in the company of a tiny white-haired woman wearing blue jeans, a crisp white blouse tucked in, and a potting apron. A wide, welcoming grin tooled lines into her sun-browned face.

Oh my God, it was her. No one moved.

Tilly came to face them, planting fists on her trim but soft hips. "So. You finally made it."

Mercedes gasped.

"You . . . you expected us?" Lucy asked, mesmerized.

"I did. I just didn't know how long it would take you to get here. You actually did a bang-up job."

Cristina gulped, audibly. "Did you have some sort of . . . premonition about us?"

Tilly laughed, a rich, solid sound. "No, *m'ija*. Nothing so exciting. Much as I'd like to perpetuate that myth about myself, it was a little more direct."

"What do you mean?" Annette asked. "Like, a vision?"

"No visions." Tilly fished in the deep pocket of her denim apron and retrieved a small state-of-the-art cell phone. "I had phone calls from all over the state. Friends and acquaintances telling me that four city women with more heart than sense were on the hunt for me. I knew it was just a matter of time. Heart always wins out over sense." She winked.

After a moment of stunned silence, the whole group burst into laughter, charmed by the little dose of reality. This might look like an enchanted forest, and Tilly's house might look like a cabin right out of a fairy tale. Tilly might be revered and respected, she might be a legend to some. But she was also a flesh and blood woman reminiscent of their own sweet *abuelitas,* and she was infinitely more connected to the real world than they'd expected. She had a cell phone, for God's sake.

Sure, a bit of the mystery surrounding her had fizzled with this new insight, but it also made her slightly more accessible, less intimidating, which was nice.

"It's so . . . incredible to finally meet you." Lucy stepped forward and offered her hand. "I'm Lucy Olivera. I hope you don't mind us invading your privacy. We just need—"

"I know," Tilly said. "And it's no trouble." She looked at Yiska. "In fact, we've discussed arrangements. I'm going to need time with you all . . . that is, if you're willing."

"We're willing," the four of them said together.

Tilly nodded, as if she'd expected them to say this. "Yiska has agreed to return in five days to retrieve you. The cabin is small, and I don't have electricity or running water," she warned. "All you've got is a well with a pump, a solar shower, and a composting toilet out back."

"We don't care," Mercy said, her voice firm and impassioned. "We don't need luxuries. We're just so grateful to be here with you finally."

The other three friends gaped at Mercy, who was probably the most grumpy and high-maintenance of them all. If she was ready to rough it with Tilly, they were, too. More than ready. They'd been working toward this moment for . . . God, it seemed like forever. It seemed unbelievable that they stood before her now.

"Bueno," Tilly said. "The four donkeys will stay, to make the ride back for Yiska easier."

"And, I'm going to take off," Yiska told them, raising a hand. "Not that it hasn't been a pleasure, but I miss my wife and baby girl."

"Of course you do," Annette said, moving forward to embrace him. "Thank you for helping me with the bear."

Yiska laughed. "Like you needed help."

The other three took turns hugging Yiska good-bye and thanking him for everything. They never would've found Tilly without his help. Or without Senalda's help. Or Esteban's, Lenora's, Alex's, Deborah's. They had a whole lot of people to thank when this journey was over.

But they'd found Tilly. Their Holy Grail.

Whether or not she could help them remained to be seen.

Tilly walked Yiska back to Bob for a final farewell, and the four of them huddled close.

"You know," Mercy mused, "from a city dweller's perspective, a person would never agree to stay in a remote area with a total stranger and no means of escape for five days, unless they harbored some sort of death wish."

"Yes," Lucy said, "but it's Tilly. Did you see her? She's tiny and . . . as old as my grandma."

"Oh, I know. I'm not worried," Mercy said. "I'm relieved. I'm just saying, it seems so strange that it feels this right."

"What do you think it's going to be like?" Cris asked.

Annette scratched her cheek, thoughtfully. "I'm sure we'll talk about our problems and Tilly will help us work through them. Esteban said she was like a counselor. Isn't that what counselors do?"

Lucy grinned. "It'll be like an encounter week. Cool. I've always wanted to do something so New Age."

"You know, I actually think I'll be able to talk about my problems with her," Mercy said. "As a rule, I hold most of my emotions inside—"

"Gee, really?" Lucy said.

Mercy smacked her and went on. "But something about Tilly, about everything we went through to find her. My life is so fucked up, I'm not going to squander this chance."

"Nor am I," Lucy said. "If anyone can break the Olivera curse, it's got to be Tilly."

"I won't lose out, either," Cris agreed.

"I feel pretty happy with the way things are going in my life these days," Annette said, "but I'm open to new ideas."

They all exchanged glances, eager for the "encounter week" to commence. They would spend the next five days soaking in the sage advice doled out by the all-powerful *curandera* and at the end of it, they'd be better, more enlightened women. Right?

They couldn't wait to see what happened next.

Okay, so the encounter week concept was a pipe dream. After seeing Yiska off, Tilly had fed them a high energy snack and some sort of vile-tasting herbal beverage and then put them directly to work. A subsistence farm, she explained, did not run itself. She'd have more time to talk to all of them if the work got done quicker, and ten hands were better than two.

The woman had a point, and she was putting them up for free for five days. But this farming shit wasn't all it was cracked up to be. Mercedes's back ached, she had blisters on her palms, and she couldn't feel the soles of her feet. Sweat ran down her spine and pooled at the waistband of her pants. A necklace of dirt was her only accessory. She hadn't done this kind of physical work since she was a kid, and God willing, she'd never do it again. She would grudgingly admit that the hard physical labor filled her with a sick sort of satisfaction, but she'd never admit it aloud.

Her biggest unvoiced complaint was that Tilly had paired her up with none other than Cristina the Perfect and Annoying. She had balked—inside—but something about Tilly made her reluctant to complain. She and Cris had been assigned to gardening duty, of all things. They'd weeded, watered, harvested, debugged (the least pleasant part;

tomato bugs were vile, vomitous creatures), and replanted until Mercedes ached for the gray concrete comfort of New York City.

She and Cris had gotten off to an awkward start, but by day three, they'd fallen into a pattern of working without speaking, backs to each other, which suited both of them perfectly.

Enter Tilly.

If Mercedes didn't know better, she'd think that Tilly had an agenda. Cheerfully, as always, she moved them to a smaller garden that didn't allow for much personal space. Within minutes, the tasks had them tripping over, rather than studiously ignoring, each other. The forced proximity prompted them to revert to their nitpicking, competitive ways.

You're stepping on a plant.

Excuse me, but you just threw a dirt clod on my foot.

Do you mind moving out of the way of my basket?

Mercedes found herself clenching her jaws and pulling weeds with a little more vehemence than necessary. Frankly, if Cristina gave her one more "helpful hint" about the way she chose to complete her assigned chores, she was going to deck the woman right in her wrinkle-free face. God, this wasn't progressing like she'd expected. If she had to be stuck working alongside someone for the next five days, why in God's name did it have to be her biggest nemesis in the entire universe?

Mercy might have admired the way Cris handled her whole shoplifting thing, but that didn't mean she liked her, and it certainly didn't mean she wanted to spend time with her. Mercedes wanted Cristina, and all reminders of her, out of her life. If things kept up, though, she would have to discuss the situation with Tilly. She might alienate the *curandera,* but at least she wouldn't get arrested for murder and spend the rest of her life in prison as Big Bertha's bitch.

By the fourth day, Lucy had grown a little worried about the progress, or lack thereof, being made by her friends. This time with Tilly wasn't turning out at all like they'd expected. Mercedes and Cris had regressed into their snitty, bickering ways, and after the whole Vicodin/ Botox admissions, Lucy had truly hoped they might mend the rift in their friendship. For God's sake, it had been two decades. Holding anger inside like that was not only stressful, but unhealthy.

None of them wanted to question Tilly's decision to have the two enemies work together, though. But she and Annette couldn't help but harbor visions of imminent disaster. Tilly just didn't understand the complicated history.

On the flip side, she and Annette were having a grand old time working with Tilly inside the house, helping her package and label dry herbs and mix up tinctures and remedies to be grabbed and adminis- tered at a moment's notice. Lucy almost felt guilty for the piece-of-cake assignment. Every time she glanced out the window at Mercy and Cris, their faces seemed a bit more grim, their motions slightly jerkier and im- bued with annoyance. It couldn't be fun for them hearing laughter and conversation wafting out from inside the little stone house. Neither she nor Annette wanted to offend their lovely hostess, though, so they con- centrated on the job at hand and prayed for the best.

The question came when Lucy was bundling dried sage into sticks to be used for purification purposes, tying them with lengths of red cot- ton string.

"So, tell me about this marriage of yours," Tilly asked casually, never stopping her constant, efficient motion.

Lucy's stomach plunged. Her hands stilled for a second, but she re- covered quickly. "What do you want to know?"

"Do you love him?"

Okay, that was an easy one to answer. "More than life itself. And he loves me the same."

"Hmm." A long pause ensued. "And so the problem is simply that you believe in this family curse, yes?"

"Well, it's real," Lucy said, feeling a bit defensive. "It's not like I'm making it up. No first marriage has ever lasted in my family. Ever."

"No first marriage. That does seem to be a problem."

Lucy sighed. Just what she wanted to hear. She gave the *curandera* a beseeching look. "What can I do? I don't want to lose him or our marriage just because my name is Olivera."

"I can't tell you what to do, *m'ija*. But I can tell you that the power, the answer to all your questions, lies within both you and Ruben. You need to stop focusing on the curse and try to focus on finding a solution."

I went through weeks of turmoil to find you for that *advice?*

It sounded like Tilly was saying she should solve her own problem, but that couldn't possibly be right. Lucy tried to hold it back, but she felt a full-on pout emerging. If she could solve her own goddamn problem, she wouldn't have needed to suffer wedding humiliation, donkey blisters, and bear attacks to find Tilly in the first place. Wasn't that much obvious? Her hope deflated like a punctured lung.

"What are you thinking?" Tilly asked. "And don't lie."

Heat rose to Lucy's face. "I won't lie."

"Just checking."

Lucy cleared her throat. "I was thinking, if I knew how to solve this, I would've already done it."

"You don't know how because you aren't focusing on saving the marriage, you're focusing on fear that it will end." Tilly moved over to her apothecary cabinet and pulled out a couple of drawers and pushed them back in before finding what she sought. She scooped three spoonfuls of weedy powder into a tall glass of water, stirring the concoction to a murky gray before handing it to Lucy. "Bottoms up."

Lucy eyed it warily. "What is it?"

"Just drink it. It'll give you clarity."

One corner of Lucy's mouth lifted. "You know, if you were anyone other than *you,* I'd never drink this."

"Of course. That's what makes you good at your job. But this is your *life,* Lucy. Drink it. I'd never do harm. I think you know that, or you never would've sought me out."

Lucy nodded, sniffed the glass, then grimaced.

Tilly grinned, shaking her head. "Things that are good for us aren't always pleasant, Lucy. Sometimes you need to just hold your nose and go for it."

Lucy did so, gulping the vile lumpy stuff down until it was gone. She didn't want to prolong the agony. She waited for something miraculous to happen, which of course, never did. Instead, her stomach growled, she felt as defeated as ever. Soon they were back at the herb table doing their work.

Depressing, Lucy thought. Maybe the big fucking joke was on them. They were free labor for five days, after which they'd be sent away to figure out their own damn lives—something they probably should've done in the first place. Maybe *that* was the lesson. She sincerely hoped she was wrong.

"You know," Tilly told Annette a little while later, "you have a knack with this. I'm impressed."

Annette blinked up at her, startled. She'd simply been lost in the rhythm of the work, contemplating what she wanted to be when she grew up, so to speak. Deborah had asked her what she wanted to do . . . go back to school, get a job, whatever. The sad truth was, she didn't know. "Really?"

Tilly nodded. "You aren't even measuring the herbs anymore. You're doing it by feel." She held up a hand just as Annette had been about to apologize. "That's not a problem. I've been watching you and you're getting it right. But not many people have a sense of what feels right and what doesn't. *Curanderismo* is a science, but it's an art, too, and you have to have the feel for it. You do. That's something special, Annette."

Annette smiled shyly. "Thank you. I gotta tell you, I'm really enjoying this. Can I ask, how did you come to do this kind of work, Tilly?"

The old woman shrugged, never stopping her efficient motions. "When I was a little girl, I got into a tangle with a rattlesnake. My parents took me to the local *curandera,* and she cured me. We had no money to pay, but my parents were so grateful. They offered to have me work with *la curandera* in order to repay the debt, and she agreed." Tilly flashed a smile. "She became my mentor. Taught me everything I know. As I got older, I even lived at her home. My parents saw that I had a gift, that the woman was fostering the gift. It was meant to be."

"That's a great story," Annette said.

"What did you want to be when you were a child?"

Annette tipped her head to the side. "I don't know. I guess a wife and mother."

"You say that like you're not happy."

"Oh, I'm happy. I love my family. But sometimes . . ."

"You want more?"

Annette sighed, feeling guilty. "Yes. Isn't that terrible? I have a perfect family and I want more, more, more. It's such an American attitude."

"It's a human attitude," Tilly corrected. "Just open your mind, Annette. You'll find what you seek."

If only it were that easy, Annette thought, disillusioned. She turned for a moment and glanced wistfully out the window. Catching sight of Mercedes and Cristina, simmering in the heat of the New Mexico sun and the firestorm of their own restrained anger, made her forget her own problems. "Forgive me for saying this, Tilly, but I do sort of feel sorry for those two."

"Sorry?" Tilly raised her eyebrows. "Trust me, Mercedes and Cristina will do just fine out there." The room fell into dubious silence for several moments; Lucy, Annette, and Tilly worked in harmony. When Tilly cleared her throat, she and Lucy glanced up.

"We might need a third person in here, though, for tomorrow," Tilly said. "I want it to be fair, so I think I'm going to make it a contest. Whoever gets the most work done between the two of them wins."

Annette's heart clenched, and her gaze cut sharply to Lucy's face, which had blanched. She could tell they were thinking the same thing. Things were about to get ugly.

"Yes. That's what I need to do. Give them a little incentive, a little contest. I'll be right back," Tilly said, wiping her hands on her apron.

After Tilly left, Lucy and Annette shared a grave stare. "Holy fuck," Lucy whispered. "What a nightmare."

"Well, it ought to bring out their competitive spirits," Annette said in a falsely hopeful tone. "Right?"

"Competitive spirit, my ass." Lucy shook her head and went back to her work, but Annette could feel the tension radiating from her. "They're going to kill each other, Annie, and you damn well know it."

Lucy was right. "What should we do?" Annette rasped, feeling as though the situation was spiraling dangerously out of control. Her stomach was upset, and she couldn't concentrate on the work. She worried her bottom lip between her teeth.

Lucy spread her arms. "What *can* we do? Tilly's running the show here and she just doesn't know their history."

"Should we tell her?"

Lucy twisted her mouth to the side. "I don't think so. I don't feel right telling her how to handle things. We sought her out for her wisdom and assistance. Maybe things should just play out the way she wants."

"I agree. But Mercy and Cris. What should we do?"

Lucy lifted one shoulder tentatively. "Pray for the best, I guess, and avoid the shrapnel when the bomb drops."

Chapter Twenty-four

"I swear to God, Cris, if you kick the side of my shoe one more time I'm going to brain you with this fucking hoe."

Everything inside Cris instantly flamed with anger. Mercedes had grown bitchier and bitchier as the day progressed from hot to hotter to miserably sweltering, and she was sick to death of it. It wasn't like they had room to spread out in this godforsaken little potato patch Tilly'd assigned them to hoe. Boiling blood pounded through her veins and she wanted to tell Mercy to go screw herself, but why get things started?

She took a deep breath and clenched everything she had. "Look," she said, as controlled as humanly possible considering she wanted the woman dead, "if I kicked the side of your shoe, I assure you it was unintentional."

Mercy barked a laugh, then impaled the garden bed with her hoe up to the handle. "Oh, sure," she said, in a tone soaked in sarcasm and innuendo. "Everything with you is always unintentional, isn't it, Cristina?"

Cris tossed off her flowered gardening gloves and whirled to face Mercedes. "What the hell is that supposed to mean?"

Mercedes, bent at the waist with her ass in the air, continued to work without acknowledging Cristina. She even had the audacity to hum. She hummed!

"I asked you a question," Cristina said, her jaw tight.

Mercedes ignored her. Infuriated her, too.

Anger pulsed through Cristina until her temples throbbed and she couldn't feel her extremities. It wasn't a premeditated act, but before she knew it she'd shoved her foot full force against Mercedes's ass, knocking her flat on her face in the dirt. God, it felt good.

Mercedes scrambled over into a crab position, then sat on the edge of the garden wiping dirt off her cheeks. "I'm so going to kick your ass for that."

"Yeah?" Cristina widened her stance. "Bring it on, you passive-aggressive bitch. I'm tired of your veiled barbs. I'm tired of you ignoring me. If you've got something to say, nut up and *say it*. For once in your life, cut the poor-me act and speak up." Cris dipped down to her bucket, picked up one of the dirt-covered new potatoes they'd been digging up and chucked it. It bounced off Mercedes's head with a sick, satisfying thunk.

Mercy let out a squawk of surprise, then leaped to her feet. She held a palm over the dirt-smudged knot growing on her forehead, her eyes blazing with rage. "What the fuck's the matter with you?" She demanded. "You could've knocked me out!"

"I wish I had," Cris yelled, reaching for more potatoes. That first toss had felt so good, she wanted to pelt Mercedes until her basket was empty. "Then I wouldn't have to listen to your snide ass anymore." She reeled back and threw one like she meant business. Take that. She hadn't married a Houston Astro for nothing. "And I wouldn't have to put up with your ice-cold attitude anymore." She pitched another, kicking up her leg in the back as she threw.

Mercy dodged the first missile, took the second one in the hip, then lunged for her basket and armed herself with potatoes of her own. " You just don't want to listen to anyone, do you, Cris? It's all about you, you, you." Mercy landed a spud right in Cristina's solar plexus, bending her over.

When she'd caught her breath, Cris said, "You are the most self-serving, grudge-holding bitch I've ever met, you know that, Mercy? You throw out snotty comments, but you aren't woman enough to tell me why, or what they mean." A potato went sailing, but Mercy ducked. She countered with a lob of her own. Cris turned, but it caught her in the shoulder. Rubbing the sting away, she yelled, "It's no wonder they call you Merciless! You fucking are. And it's no wonder why everyone despises you, either, because you're an evil, vindictive slut. I used to love you, Mercy, but I wouldn't piss down your throat if your gut was on fire, do you know that?"

"That's such a cliché!" Fresh out of potatoes, Mercy yanked up a dirt clod and wailed it at Cristina. It hit her in the chest, breaking up and raining dirt all over her shirt. Some of it went down her V-neck and settled in a gritty mess inside her bra band.

"A cliché that fits, because I wouldn't."

"I hate you, Cristina Trevino," Mercy screamed, arms rigid by her sides. "I *never* loved you."

"Liar! Goddamned liar! You were my best friend."

"You don't know how to be a friend," Mercedes growled.

Unexpectedly, Mercy's words brought a sting of tears to Cris's eyes. It only pissed her off more. She would not cry over Mercedes. "You don't even know how to be a human being! Just ask your entire staff."

Mercy's scowl deepened. "I'm glad you got arrested," she spat. "I hope your life is ruined and your mother-in-law disowns you. I hope Zach kicks your ass to the curb. You deserve every sorry thing that ever happens to you!"

"Fuck you!

"No, fuck you!"

"You wish!" Cris yelled, rolling her eyes.

"Don't flatter yourself, you homophobic, Republican WASP-fucking-wannabe," Mercy yelled back. "Even if I were into women like you apparently *think* I am, you'd turn me straight in a red-hot second." She waved an arm at the donkeys. "I'd sleep with Beethoven before I'd touch your skinny, shoplifting, society-poseur ass."

Cris's jaw dropped. Low fucking blow. Throwing things was no longer satisfying enough. Forearms raised like a linebacker, Cristina rushed Mercedes and shoved her full-force in the chest, gripping onto her shirt. She heard a satisfying rip as they toppled to the ground together, rolling over until she straddled Mercedes's hips. "I'm so sick of your shit! I never did anything to deserve the evil way you treat me," Cristina yelled, reeling back and smacking Mercedes square across the cheek.

Mercy's head snapped around, but she recovered quickly and bucked Cristina off her. "My ass. And like I give a damn anyway. Your opinion means shit to me." She reached over and grabbed Cristina's hair, wrenching her head back.

Cristina gave a demonic laugh, breathing heavily. "You act tough, Mercy, but you fight like a fucking girl."

"Oh yeah?" Mercedes yanked Cris over on her back, then landed a fist right in her breadbasket.

"Oof!" Cristina coughed and curled into a fetal position for a second before straightening out again.

"I'll show you how a girl fights, Cris." She landed another gut punch, but Cristina tightened against it.

In the aftermath of the punch, Cris brought her knee up and nailed Mercedes in the chest, knocking her back on her butt. She hadn't taken six years of Kenpo Karate lessons for nothing. "You're a tough girl now?" Cris sneered.

"Tough enough to kick your lame ass." Mercy lunged.

Cris rolled out of the way. "Give it your best shot, Mercy. I'd love to send you back to New York City with that fucking chip knocked off your shoulder."

"You put it there. You might as well try to knock it off."

Cristina's jaw slackened. "What's that supposed to mean?"

"It means fuck you. Want me to spell it?"

"You're not even woman enough to be honest with me," Cris yelled. "No wonder all your husbands dumped you! You have the communication skills of an immature seventh-grader."

"And you have the shopping habits of a"—Mercy shrugged— "wow, of a two-bit North Side criminal. Just what you are."

Cris slapped Mercy's face.

Mercy slapped back, and Cris took advantage of the post-slap moment to knock Mercy to the ground again. The two of them scrambled and rolled, throwing punches and insults . . . and dodging what they could without a whole lot of precision. They'd each scored points and committed egregious errors, but whose fight it would ultimately be was anyone's guess.

Annette's head shot up when she heard the yelling. "Uh-oh." She abandoned the herbs and moved to the window, resting her fingertips on the sill. "Oh no. Oh!" She flinched when Cristina bounced a potato off Mercy's forehead, then whipped around. "Lucy!"

Lucy dropped the knife she'd been using to chop herbs with a clatter and rushed over just in time to witness Mercedes and Cristina yelling at the top of their lungs and scrapping like a couple of street kids. Adrenaline surged through her system. She wheeled around to face Tilly, who was calmly mixing herbs at the table. Her words came in a rushed, urgent jumble. "Tilly, I'm sorry. We should've told you. There's a lot of bad blood between Cris and Mercy. They never should've worked together."

"Mm-hmm," Tilly said, glancing up to offer a placid smile. "But they're working together now."

"No," Lucy said with gravity. Her cop instincts were screaming at her to break up the brawl. "They're kicking each other's as—I mean, they're fighting. Like, physically fighting. In the yard. Right now."

Annette gasped, covering her mouth, and Lucy turned back to the window only to see Mercy land a punch in Cristina's gut.

"Lucy, my God, go stop them!" Annette cried, flapping her hands helplessly.

"She'll do no such thing," Tilly said, her tone level.

Annette and Lucy both whirled to face her. "B-but, they're going to kill each other," Annette said.

Tilly laughed. "No, they aren't. Don't you see?"

"No. What? What don't we see?" Lucy pushed, her frustration mounting. Tilly's sedate conversation wasn't working for her.

"That this was the point," Tilly said, her voice calm and softly modulated. Listening to her, you'd never know that two grown women were engaged in a knock-down-drag-out fight in her yard. "They'll never restore their friendship if they don't get the pent-up anger out, and Mercedes would never have gotten it out without the proper . . . shall we say, provocation?"

Annette blinked in surprise, sharing a quick glance with Lucy before turning back to Tilly. "You set them up?"

"No, *m'ija.*" Tilly grinned, her eyes crinkling with kindness and wisdom. "I just made it impossible for them to continue avoiding each other. Destiny did the rest. You see? Destiny always does the rest."

C ristina and Mercedes were both breathing so heavily, their punches—and insults—grew weaker and weaker. Finally Cristina sank to her knees, then sat with them folded under her and started to cry. "What did I do to you?" She spread her arms and implored Mercy, looking at her directly for the first time in decades. "Why do you find it so impossible to talk to me?"

Mercy lost her fight, too. She sank down on her butt and gingerly touched the goose egg on her forehead, wincing from the tenderness. It was strange. She felt like she'd barfed out a torrent of anger toward Cristina, anger that had festered inside her since high school like an untreated infection.

Since high school.

Suddenly, in light of everything she'd gone through in her life, in light of everything they had been through recently, that concept seemed utterly ridiculous. She pressed her lips together in an attempt to hold it in, but the laughter found its way out in spite of her efforts. The first few gales squeezed through her mouth in snorts until she relaxed her jaw and just let them flow freely.

"What's so funny?" Cristina cried harder, her nose running and turning almost purple-red.

It had always done that, Mercy thought, feeling a rush of acknowledgment and silly affection. Rudolph the grape-nosed whiner—that's what she had always called Cris when she cried like this. Mercedes flopped onto her back on the ground and laughed so hard and so long her ribs ached and her throat burned. She laughed until she couldn't take a breath, and then her tears came, too. Suddenly, like a flash flood through a narrow canyon. She couldn't control them, not one bit.

"Why are you crying?" Cris asked, in a watery tone.

"Shut up. *You're* crying, too."

"So?"

"So?"

Cris stopped crying, shook her head, and started laughing, while Mercy continued to cry, sniffling and snorting like she'd done when Senalda left for Mexico. Cristina finally pulled herself together. She crawled over and sat on top of Mercy's stomach, pinning her shoulders down and looming over her.

"Stop it. Get off me," Mercy cried, her throat gurgly.

"No. Not until you tell me what in God's name I did to make you hate me. Will you please tell me? You were my best friend, goddamnit. I loved you." She softened her tone. "I still love you, and I can't stand this. Not anymore. Will you please, please, please just talk to me? How can we—"

"If you'd shut the hell up, Cris, maybe I could get a word in edgewise." Mercy's tears had finally dwindled.

Cris blinked in surprise, then sat upright, releasing Mercy's shoulders. "Okay. Fine. Talk."

"No. Not until you get off me." She bucked weakly. "I hate to break the news, sister, but you don't weigh half an ounce anymore, like you did in high school."

"Gee, thanks a lot." Cristina crawled off Mercedes, stood up, dusted off her hands and then offered one to Mercy. They clasped palms, and Cristina yanked Mercedes to her feet. She studied the purple hematoma on Mercy's forehead, feeling a stab of guilt. "Sorry about that."

Mercedes rolled her eyes. "For Christ's sake, don't go all church lady on me now, Cris. It was a hell of a shot. You own bragging rights."

Cristina smiled. Shoulder to shoulder, they wandered over to a bench situated beneath a row of piñon trees and sank onto it. Cristina grimaced, laying a palm on her stomach. God, she was going to be sore.

"Does it hurt?" Mercedes asked.

"Yep."

"Good."

"Shut up."

"You shut up."

A pause. "So . . . what did I do?" Cristina asked.

"I don't know." Mercedes blew out a breath. "It suddenly seems so ridiculous."

Cris huffed. "Wow, I'm glad that only took you twenty years to fig-ure out, you total dumbass."

"Shut up."

"*You* shut up."

Mercedes flashed her a brief, sad smile. She struggled with her words, chewing on the inside of her cheek. "The thing is, you were bet-ter than me. Always. You had a mom and a dad who loved you. I had a mom who—" She pressed her lips together.

"I know."

"I know you know. You're the only one who really knew all of it. I lived in your shadow, Cris, and it got fucking tiring."

Cristina laughed, but the sound was more regretful than amused. "No, you didn't. That's the shame of this whole thing. The only thing I had going for me was my looks, Mercy. You had—still have—so much more."

Mercy shook her head. "Who's the dumbass now, Cris? You always sell yourself short. Always have."

Cris pulled her chin back and stared at Mercedes incredulously. "Oh, and you don't?"

"Shut up."

"You shut up." Cris spread her arms wide and raised her voice. *"Stop* telling me to shut up!"

"I would, if you'd ever shut the hell up," Mercy said, in an exasperated tone.

Cristina sighed.

Mercy was quiet a moment, and when she spoke, the four simple words released the grudge she'd been holding for more than half her life. "You stole Johnny Romero."

"What?" Cris shrieked, whipping around to face her.

"At the prom." Her chin quivered. "You were supposed to go with what's his ass, and Johnny was supposed to go with me. But then what's his ass fell through, and you . . . stole Johnny."

"You and Johnny were supposed to—Jesus, why didn't you tell me? Why didn't *he* tell me?"

Mercedes realized Cris had a point. She wasn't a mind reader. Mercy should've confronted her twenty years ago. She started laughing and reached for Cris's hand. "You know what? Fuck Johnny Romero."

"I never did."

"And I always wanted to."

Cris groaned, resting her head on Mercy's shoulder. "God, we're a pair."

"It's your fault."

"My ass."

"Shut up, Cris."

"No. You shut up."

They both shut up finally, and Mercy listened to the bugs and birds, the life in the forest. She listened to Cristina's breathing and remembered just how close they used to be. Closer, even, than she and Lucy had remained. As close as sisters. Of course, Cris had always played the role of the annoying younger sister. "So do you think we can be friends again?" Mercy asked. "After all this time?"

Cris didn't lift her head. She was quiet for a long time. "Do you want to be, Merce?"

"Yeah." A beat passed. "I do."

"God," Cristina whispered. "Me, too."

They looked at each other, then hugged for what seemed like forever. They had twenty years of hugging to make up for, after all.

L ucy and Annette were still standing at the window spying on Cris and Mercy when Tilly's cell phone rang. "There we go," Tilly said.

They turned toward her. "What's going on?" Annette said, as Tilly bustled across the room to grab the phone from its charger, which was plugged into a generator used specifically for the phone.

"If I'm guessing correctly, there is about to be a brand-new baby in the world." She held up a finger and snapped the face of her phone open. "Hello?"

Annette and Lucy turned back to the window and saw Cris and Mercy embrace, "It's about time," Annette whispered.

Lucy nodded. "And to think, all these years we ran interference between them. If we'd just let them duke it out, it could've ended a long time ago."

Annette hiked one shoulder, then crossed her arms beneath her bosom. "Things happen when they're supposed to, Lucy. And exactly as they're supposed to."

Lucy bumped Annette playfully with her hip. "You sound a whole lot like Tilly."

"That's good, because Tilly's a whole lotta wise."

"Annette," Tilly said, and they both turned toward her again. "I have to go deliver this baby. I'd like you to come with me."

"Really?" She tossed a glance at Lucy, then looked back toward Tilly. "I'd love to go with you."

Tilly nodded once, all business as she gathered up what looked like an old-fashioned medical bag. "Lucy, you'll continue chopping the herbs?"

"Of course."

"Don't bother mixing them. Annette and I will do that when we get back." She glanced toward the window. "And don't interfere with destiny. Leave those two to themselves, okay? They have two decades of hurt to work out."

"Whatever you say, Tilly."

The old woman stopped before Lucy and patted her cheek with a veiny hand. "You're such good girls." She turned heel and headed out of the house at a speedy clip. Annette gave Lucy an excited, eyebrow-raised grin, then trailed out the door of the cabin behind her.

Just like that, Lucy was alone.

And all she could think about was Ruben.

"Are we going to ride the donkeys?" Annette asked, hustling to keep up with the agile *curandera*. She remembered the two-day ride to reach the cabin. She couldn't imagine them making it to civilization in time for a birth—not even of a first baby.

Tilly gave her a sidelong glance and an enigmatic little smile. "We're actually going to hike."

"The mother lives that close?"

"Closer than you think," Tilly replied.

"I thought you lived out here in the middle of nowhere all by your lonesome? We didn't see any other houses."

Tilly didn't answer.

They started up over a hill, and dismay suddenly struck Annette. She'd been flattered when Tilly asked her to go along on the birth, but she didn't think she could keep up this hiking pace for long, especially up and over a series of hills. But, to her surprise, on the back side of the hill sat an old but clean Jeep Wrangler . . . parked next to a rough but passable road.

Annette stopped short, and her face broke into a wide grin. "You tricked us."

The old woman laughed as she fished a ring of keys out of her medical bag. "I didn't trick anyone. You four tricked yourselves. I just didn't correct the assumptions you made about me." Tilly opened the driver's side door and hauled herself in. Annette got in the other side.

"So, how close are we to T or C?"

Tilly fired up the engine, then winked. "About half an hour on the road. Probably two hours on donkey."

"Two *hours?* Don't you mean two days?"

Tilly laughed as she backed out of the pull-out and bounced onto the road. "Two days, sure, but only if you're going in circles. A lot of circles."

Annette laughed. "Yiska tricked us, too!"

"An old woman's got to have a bit of mystery, don't you think, *m'ija?* How fulfilling would your quest have been without it?" She waved her hand vaguely at Annette. "Seat belt on."

Annette did as she was told; she'd learned that it didn't pay to question Tilly. She had also learned in the past couple minutes that hope and magic and dreams and wishes could drive people to reach amazing goals. She settled back for the thirty-minute ride into T or C feeling charmed, and more at peace than she'd been in a good, long while. Tilly might not be as magical as they'd imagined, but she'd managed to get Mercedes and Cristina talking in a matter of days. Maybe she was a saint, instead, because that had been a true miracle.

Lucy finished chopping all the herbs, flowers, and roots, leaving them in little volcano-cone piles all over the thick wooden worktable. Mercy and Cris were still embroiled in conversation, so she prowled the cabin restlessly, studying all the jars and bottles and boxes that Tilly had made up and labeled—mostly in Spanish. She didn't know what any of it was used for, but she found herself amazed by the wealth of knowledge stored inside these stone walls. The house might not have modern conveniences, but it felt warm and inviting anyway. She let her eyes travel around the room, taking it all in.

Her gaze moved over the generator, then jerked back of its own volition. With a zing, she realized she and Tilly had the same type of cell phone . . . hence, the same kind of cell phone *charger*. She could plug in her own charger or use Tilly's even. She could call Ruben.

She smoothed her palms down the sides of her hiking pants, then glanced at her pack in the corner of the living room, feeling a twinge of guilt. She was supposed to be here communing with a wise woman. But why shouldn't she plug her phone into the charger and give Ruben a quick call? It wasn't like Tilly had told her not to, and her chores were done. In fact, her only instruction had been to leave Mercy and Cris alone, and what better way to do so than calling her honey? When she talked to Ruben the whole world disappeared. She wouldn't even remember Cris and Mercy were on the property.

Feeling ever so slightly like she was breaking a rule, Lucy dug out her cell phone and plugged it into the charger. She held her breath until she got the dial tone, then relaxed into a smile. She dialed Ruben's number, but got a busy signal. Busy? The man had call waiting and voice mail.

She tried again. Busy.

With a sigh of frustration, she dialed her voice mail instead. Surely there'd be a message from Ruben. Her call connected on the first try. After punching in her password, she held her breath. One message. Smiling, scarcely able to wait until she heard Ruben's rough silk voice, she punched the number one with a shaky finger. And then she heard him.

"Hey, baby girl." Her stomach contracted. "I've been giving this thing a lot of thought, and I finally realized there's only one solution to the marriage problem for both of us. We need to get a divorce."

Chapter Twenty-five

Annette had attended five births prior to this one, but she'd always been the one on the table with her feet in stirrups. This experience had been completely different. The woman, Leticia Mondragon, had delivered a healthy six-pound, nine-ounce, bald-as-a-bowling-ball boy, and Annette had never felt more exhilarated. She'd begun to contemplate the idea of going back to college to become a nurse, specializing in obstetrics. The thought of four years in college, after twenty years away from high school, scared the bejeebers out of her, though.

Annette cleared her throat. "Tilly, can I ask you a question?"

"Of course, *m'ija.*"

"Do you think it's selfish for a mother of five, who has one in college and two more due to enroll in the next couple years, to contemplate entering college herself?"

"You want to go to college?" Tilly asked.

"Sort of." Annette wrapped her hand around the shoulder strap of her seat belt. "Although the thought terrifies me."

"What would you study?"

"Nursing, I think. Obstetrics." She flashed Tilly a shy look. "To be honest, I really loved helping deliver that little life into the world. I've never given it much thought, but this experience opened my eyes. I'd love to do it again."

"I didn't go to college, you know."

"Yes, but you're a *curandera*," Annette said.

"Only because someone a long time ago saw that I had a knack for it, and she taught me everything she knew."

Annette's throat constricted, and she glanced over at Tilly without speaking. Was she saying . . . ?

"You see, the four of you came to me on a quest, but I've been on a bit of a quest myself. To find someone with the skills, with the desire . . . so I can pass on what I know." She reached over and patted Annette's knee. "Destiny may have led you four to me, *m'ija,* but destiny also brought me to you. I'm not going to be around forever, you know."

"Don't say that."

"Why not? It's true. I'm not afraid of death."

Unexpectedly, tears rose to Annette's eyes.

"But I do want to pass on my knowledge to someone who will make good use of it." A beat passed. "I think that person is you, Annette Martinez. If you're interested."

Annette laughed and cried at the same time. "Are you kidding? Of course I'm interested." She leaned over and tried to hug Tilly, but doing so caused the Jeep to bounce over the ruts in the road and Tilly scolded her.

When she'd righted the vehicle, Tilly flashed Annette a smile. "*Bueno.* Knowing this gives me peace."

"It gives me peace, too. I've been searching for something I can do, something to fulfill my life." Annette clutched her fist to her chest. "I love what I know of *curanderismo.*"

"You have a lot to learn," Tilly warned.

"Oh, I know. And I can't wait. I can only hope to be half as good as you are, Tilly."

"You'll be better than I am, Annie. I'll make sure of it."

By the time they parked the Jeep behind the deceptive little hill and hiked over, Annette was ready to break into a flat out sprint to reach her friends. She couldn't wait to let them know she was going to be a *curandera,* trained by one of the finest *curanderas* in the country! She caught sight of Lucy sitting between Cristina and Mercedes on the bench beneath the piñon trees, and hoped that she'd finished up with the herbs. Tilly had specifically told her not to bother Mercedes and Cristina, and she'd hate for them to offend the lady now.

When she got closer, she could see that Lucy was crying. Alarmed, she stopped briefly, then broke into a jog. She reached them quickly, out of breath. "What's wrong? What happened?"

Lucy cried harder, but both Mercedes and Cristina glanced up, their expressions grave.

"It's Ruben."

Annette's heart clenched with terror.

"He left a message on her voice mail," Mercedes said, softly.

"He wants a divorce," Cristina finished, her voice a near-whisper, her hands cradling Lucy's elbow as she wept.

Annette sank to the ground in front of Lucy and laid her cheek on Lucy's knee. Lord, have mercy. Just when it seemed like everything was falling into place, and then this. Perhaps the Oliveras truly *were* cursed and Lucy had been right all along. She squeezed her eyes shut. What a horribly depressing thought. For once, Annette didn't have a single word of encouragement that could make this better.

Everyone was so worried about Lucy, they didn't even bother to show their surprise when Tilly led them to the Jeep parked by the hidden road. The drive back to Caballo Lake, where they'd left the van, was grave and silent, except for Lucy's soft, heartbroken crying. Tilly pulled the Jeep up behind Annette's van, then Mercy and Cris loaded up all their luggage. They helped Lucy into the van, kissed Tilly good-bye, and got in themselves.

Annette and Tilly embraced outside the driver's door. "You okay to drive?" Tilly asked.

"I'm fine. I just want to get her home."

Tilly nodded. "Please tell her to keep the faith. Things will work out as they're meant to work out."

Annette bit her bottom lip, tears stinging her eyes. "I know. It's just . . . if you knew Ruben." She sighed. "They're absolutely perfect for each other. It's such a waste."

"Trust destiny, *m'ija.*"

Annette wicked away a tear with the back of her hand. "I'm trying. We're all trying."

"And call me the moment you have news."

"I will."

Tilly patted her hands and dipped her chin. "When this is all worked out, you and I will make some plans, okay?"

Annette nodded, embracing Tilly one last time. "Thank you for everything. I'll call you."

It was early morning when they pulled up in front of Lucy and Ruben's house in West Highlands. Lucy glanced at the house, her expression lanced with pain.

"Do you want us to go in with you?" Annette asked.

"No," Lucy replied, in a toneless voice. "I have to do this alone." She hiked her bag over her shoulder, then looked at each of her friends in turn. They were going to get a motel room nearby and wait. "I'll call you . . . when I'm done."

Mercedes reached over and squeezed her hand. "We'll come and get you. Anytime, day or night. Okay?"

Lucy's chin began to wobble. She bit her bottom lip and nodded firmly. "Wish me luck." She huffed. "I guess my Tía Manda's double toaster idea will come in handy after all—" Her voice broke, and her eyes filled with tears.

"Don't start," Cristina demanded. "Just go talk to him. He loves you, Lucy. I know you can work this out." She reached over and grasped Mercy's hand. "Believe me, even when you think things are completely impossible, you can work them out if you try hard enough."

Lucy's heart felt like splintered glass in her chest as she fitted her key in the lock and opened the front door to her house. To *their* house—hers and Ruben's and the dogs'. But not anymore. God, how would they split things up? Their lives were so intertwined, so enmeshed. She hadn't thought beyond anything other than the fact that Ruben wanted a divorce. It was so so so much worse than that, she suddenly realized, soaking in the little house she loved so much.

Rebel and Rookie, having heard the telltale sound of the key in the door, came at her in a barrage of yips and barks and dog toenails on the hardwood. She squatted down and consoled herself in their soft fur, their unconditional love. When she looked up, Ruben stood in the archway from the living room to the dining room, filling the space and looking at her—oddly enough—with love radiating from his eyes. He took one step forward and opened his mouth as if to speak.

"No, wait." The tears came in an uncontrollable rush, and she stood quickly, holding out a hand. "Ruben, please, let me say what I need to say before you say a word. Please. Just this once." She sucked in a huge lungful of air and waited.

He stopped where he was, looking baffled, and nodded once.

Lucy smeared away her tears and sniffed, then picked up Rookie and cuddled him to her chest. "I . . . I want to tell you that I understand. Everything. I'm heartbroken, and I will always love you and only you, but I wouldn't want to be married to an Olivera, either. I don't blame you."

"Lucy—"

"No! Let me finish," she implored.

He hesitated, emitting a frustrated sound before nodding.

"I'm not going to stand in your way at all. In fact, we haven't con- summated the marriage." Her face flamed, and she slid her gaze toward her feet. Would she really never make love to Ruben again? She couldn't bear the thought. "Well," she amended, "not *since* the marriage, that is. I think, in light of that, we should be able to annul."

"I'm not annulling this marriage, Lucy. We need to get a divorce."

Lucy cried harder. "Fine. Fine. I was just trying to make things eas- ier for you. For . . . us. But if you want all the legal schmeagal stuff—" She stopped to sniffle loudly. "I'll do whatever you want, Ruben. Just let me pack a bag and I'll go stay with . . . my mother. Ugh. Scratch that, I'll stay with Annette or—"

"Baby girl, it's my turn to talk. Okay?" He crossed the room in two strides, took Rookie from her arms and set him on the floor, then pulled her toward him. "You misunderstood me, baby. Completely, totally, one hundred percent misunderstood."

Lucy gaped at him. "How could I possibly have misconstrued the statement 'I want a divorce,' Ruben?"

He laughed softly, rocking her in his arms and stroking her hair. "You goof, I told you I'd do anything to make our marriage work. Don't you remember that?"

"Yeah, but—"

"I want to divorce you so I can marry you *again*," he whispered against her temple. "So I can be your second husband. Your forever husband. It's the perfect solution. I can't believe no other Olivera hus- band or wife has thought of it."

Stunned, Lucy pulled back and stared into his face, afraid to hope but equally afraid not to. "You don't want a divorce?"

"I want a divorce, but not a real divorce in true Olivera style. I want a divorce, then I want to marry you again."

Suddenly it all became crystal clear to her. Lucy laughed, then jumped into his arms and wrapped her legs around his waist. They rained kisses over each other's faces, and Lucy continued to cry. This time, however, her tears came from joy. Why in the hell hadn't she thought of this herself? "God, Ruben, it's perfect. You're perfect. Why didn't we think of it sooner?"

"Because you split."

"I know. I'm sorry. God, I love you so much."

"I love you, too, baby. And I'm never letting you get away." He kissed her long and deeply, and she kissed him back with just as much banked passion.

Ruben pulled away, his eyes at half-mast with desire. Still supporting Lucy beneath her thighs, which were wrapped around him, his face broke into a slow, sexy smile. He carried her toward the staircase and headed up. "Yeah, that annulment idea?"

"It is better. Do you think it could work?" she asked.

"Not a chance."

"But it would be cheaper."

"Doesn't matter, babe, and we won't be eligible anyway, because I plan to consummate our first marriage right now, right here, all night long."

Lucy moaned, nestling her face in his neck, inhaling his spicy scent. "Oh, God. Only you would spend thousands of extra dollars for a divorce just to get jiggy sooner."

"You complaining?"

She grinned up at him. "Nope."

He laughed softly, deep in this throat. "Believe me, the added expense of a divorce rather than an annulment will be well worth it." He reached the top of the staircase and moved quickly to the bedroom, where he deposited Lucy gently on the bed and followed her down. "Well, well, worth it."

And it was.

Epilogue

From: OfficerO@CopWeb.com
To: MomOf5@MartinezFamily.com;
           ZachAragonFan@texasnet.org;
           Editor_in_Chief@WhatsImportantMagazine.com
Time: 07:21:30 AM Mountain Daylight Time
Subject: SAVE ME FROM MY FAMILY!!!!!!!

Annie, Mercy, Cristina:

Somebody kill me!!! In a complete turnaround, my friggin' family is nagging me to have the new wedding (1) in Denver at the Cathedral, and (2) replete with a full Catholic Mass. A full fucking Mass—can you even imagine the torture? (Sorry for using the words "fucking" and "Mass" in the same sentence, Annie, but you're just going to have to forgive me, because these Oliveras—UGH!!!). We NEVER get married in churches because of the whole curse thing. But now they BELIEVE in the validity of the marriage because I've been divorced once. Never mind that I'm marrying the same man. My family—crack smokers, I swear.

Anyway, can you say, LEAVE ME ALONE?!?!?!? I've told them until I'm hoarse, this time I'm doing it MY way. If they want to participate as guests, they're more than welcome, but this ceremony is about ME. About US—me and Ruben. Did I tell you guys my stepfather is renting two school buses to drive family out to Tilly's place for the big day? It's like a Dysfunctional Family

Road Trip From Hell. :-D I can't wait to see you all. I've missed you so much over the past three months (I know, I know—we talk on e-mail every few days, but still), and heading back to New Mexico with you guys brings back all kinds of great memories. I've heard September in New Mexico is just beautiful. Perfect for an outdoor wedding, in any case.

Fill me in on whazzup in the worlds of Cris, Mercy, and Annette. Can't wait to see you! Love to my girls, Lucy

From: Editor_in_Chief@WhatsImportantMagazine.com
To: OfficerO@CopWeb.com;
            MomOf5@MartinezFamily.com;
            ZachAragonFan@texasnet.org
Time: 09:19:24 AM Mountain Daylight Time
Subject: RE: SAVE ME FROM MY FAMILY!!!!!!!

<<<Fill me in on whazzup in the worlds of Cris, Mercy, and Annette. Can't wait to see you!>>>

Lucky Girl,

Your family cracks my ass up. I can't wait to see those big school buses. I hope they remember to bring the Red Vines.

As you know, Senalda and little Angelo took me up on my offer to move to New York until Senalda finishes school. I feel like I'm a second mother and a grandma in one fell swoop, and I feel better about life than I have in years. I've cut down to four days a week at the magazine so I can watch Angelo one of the days Senalda is in school, and it's always my favorite day of the week. For the other days, we've hired a nanny who treats him like her little grandson. Senalda is an amazing mother, and her family has accepted her and the baby one hundred percent. I'm so happy. Hey, unmarried people get pregnant. It's the new millennium—get over it.

My circuit on the talk shows is winding down, and things at the magazine are picking up speed. My little "spin" on the whole thing seems to have worked. Being humble and honest—I learned that from you, Annie. Having a thick skin—got that part from you, Lucy. Facing up to what I've done—that's purely Cristina. Thank you all. Anyway, nothing could be tougher than riding those damn donkeys.

I'm also happy to say I have been Vicodin free, other than two lapses (cut me slack, I'm human, and I've been addicted for years), for five weeks. I tell you, being around that precious baby Angelo is a big enough high. I can't wait for you guys to meet him.

I've already told Cris this, but the follow-up article we ran on surviving armed robbery has been a huge reader favorite. We're planning on running the article about recovering from compulsive shoplifting in the next issue. Cris is big, big, big! Crime pays, eh, Cris? (Just kidding, shut up.)

I can't wait to see you guys, either. I love you all.

Cheers,

Mercy

P.S. Sunshine dumped Damian after charging almost sixty thousand bucks on his various credit cards. THERE IS A GOD!!! Karmic justice in action. I hope his dick rots and falls off, but that's just me wanting to add insult to Mother Nature's injury.

From: **MomOf5@MartinezFamily.com**
To: **OfficerO@CopWeb.com;**
      ZachAragonFan@texasnet.org;
      Editor_in_Chief@WhatsImportantMagazine.com
Time: **07:40:32 PM Mountain Daylight Time**
Subject: **RE: SAVE ME FROM MY FAMILY!!!!!!!!**

<<<<I've already told Cris this, but the follow-up article we ran on surviving armed robbery has been a huge reader favorite.>>>>

I'm one of those readers, Mercy!! The article was fantastic, and how cool of the police to let you run some crime scene photos in the magazine! It made the whole article that much more real. (Even sitting on the floor of that place, with all the toppled Coke cans, you looked beautiful, Cristina! Beautiful and brave.) I hate to rejoice in other people's misfortunes, Mercy, but Damian got exactly what he deserved. I'll pray for him.

Lucy, I'm not sure New Mexico will ever recover from the influx of Oliveras, but it's going to be so much fun. :-) Hang in there. You're so right—this time, the wedding is all for you and all about you. It'll be beautiful.

As for me, I'm busy in midwifery school and training on top of that with *las parteras.* I have to say, I enjoy learning the old ways best. Those *curanderas* are amazing, and they all think I have a gift for it. <blushing> Of course, the recommendation from Tilly helped immensely. I love it so much. I spend a full week of each month with Tilly, and I tell you, I learn more in seven days than I learn the whole rest of the month. I haven't felt this alive and engaged with my family and myself in decades.

The girls and Randy have adapted to the idea of me working as a midwife. Deborah and Alex think it's "übercool," that I'm "getting back to my roots," whatever that means. Those girls. Ha ha! Speaking of them, they're exceedingly happy, and both of them are getting straight A grades this semester. I'm so proud.

Mercy, you and Senalda bring that precious baby boy straight to his Tía Annette when you arrive. I never got the chance to raise a baby boy, but I'm going to hog him as much as I can.

That's all for now. Ruthie and Mary are about to kill each other. Some things never change, but I like it that way!!!!

XOXOXOXOXO—

Annette

From: ZachAragonFan@texasnet.org
To: OfficerO@CopWeb.com;
MomOf5@MartinezFamily.com;
Editor_in_Chief@WhatsImportantMagazine.com
Time: 12:27:08 AM Mountain Daylight Time
Subject: RE: SAVE ME FROM MY FAMILY!!!!!!!

<<<<Some things never change, but I like it that way!!!!>>>>

SO true, Annie. ;-) Hello, all! Things here are great and getting better, but I'm still overbooked on the charity circuit. That's okay, though, because I'm picking and choosing my own charities these days, and that bullshit image stuff is out the door.

I finished my community service, but I'm continuing to volunteer with the women's transitional house until I can get my own place up and running. So much red tape—permits are a bitch, I tell ya. Anyway, I'm thinking of calling it Tilly's Magic—what do you think? It doesn't really sound like a transitional facility, but we're going to do a ton of promotion, so hopefully the name will become well-known. We're going to serve women coming out of rehab, jail, abusive situations, and also those getting off welfare, or recovering from divorce after not having worked for decades, helping them with the transition back into the workplace.

In addition to giving classes on filling out applications, writing résumés, interviewing skills, and job etiquette, I'm also going to have a business clothes exchange of donated items—like, a full store!—and teach classes on hair, makeup, dressing for success on a budget, and assertiveness. We plan to hold AA and NA classes at night in the meeting room, and I'm even going to have a day care and a job placement service. It'll be a one-stop transition shop! Hey, Mercy, how about profiling Tilly's Magic in the magazine when we're up and running? It was your idea, after all. ;-) Hint, hint—yes, I'm a free-publicity whore. So sue me.

Mercedes, you were right about another thing, too. Being on probation and speaking openly about my crimes and the arrest has really bridged a gap between me and the clients I hope to serve. I'm working with a lot of them now as a volunteer in the county transition home. They're able to see we're more alike than different, and I like that. I'm able to see it, too.

Let's see . . . what else? I've weaned myself off Botox a bit, which is good. I was starting to look a bit too "Hollywood Wife" for my liking. But the best news is, after their big talk, Zach's mom sent me an apology letter. It was a little stiff, but I have to forgive some things. I truly think the woman was born with that stick up her ass, poor thing. I called, and we got together for lunch. It SUCKED at first, but then I started telling her all about Tilly's Magic. She loved the idea and invested an ungodly amount of money to help me get it off the ground. She even hosted a fund-raiser, which was a smashing success and raised oodles. I still mourn all the years lost when she treated me like shit, but I guess better late than never. As long as we can have some kind of positive relationship from here on out, I'm happy enough.

Anyway, that's it on my end. Lucy, I can't WAIT for this wedding. And just think, no one will have to drug you to get your ass to the altar this time. Will wonders never cease? (I hope not!)

Abrazos, Cristina

From: OfficerO@CopWeb.com
To: ILoveLucy@CopWeb.com
Time: 06:15:15 AM Mountain Daylight Time
Subject: I Do

My Ruben—

I can't wait to marry you. Again. This time is forever, and with no angst. I promise.

Love you always,

Your Lucy

From: ILoveLucy@CopWeb.com
To: OfficerO@CopWeb.com
Time: 07:56:00 AM Mountain Daylight Time
Subject: RE: I Do

I told you we'd work it out, baby girl, and I also told you I'd do anything to keep you. Oh ye of little faith. You might be a little high maintenance (kidding . . . sort of), but you're worth it to me, Lucy. You always have been, you just couldn't see it. This time IS for real, and forever. Last time was, too, but hey, I can dig your Olivera stuff, and I'm actually pretty cocky about the fact that you'd marry me not once, but twice. I'm a legend at the department, but of course, you know that.

I love you, and I can't wait to re-consummate. (What can I say?)

Your ex-husband/soon-to-be husband forever, Ruben

Wedding morning in the Caballo Mountains dawned bright and blue-skied and perfect in a way that doesn't happen without a little divine intervention. Lucy was sure Tilly had something to do with it, although the *curandera* had denied it, brushing off the compliment and blaming the picture-perfect day on New Mexico.

They held the wedding outside, and Lucy wore a flowing white ankle-length dress—cool and casual. Ruben looked jaw-droppingly sexy in all white himself. They were surrounded by a Technicolor crush of family and friends who loved and supported them. Mercedes, her surrogate daughter, Senalda, and Senalda's adorable son, Angelo, Cristina, Zach, and the kids were happily in attendance, as were Annette, Randy, and her brood. Guests of honor included Yiska, Bob, Beethoven, Bach, Chopin, and Mozart; Lenora and Esteban; Rebel and Rookie; and the original wedding attendants, most of them friends of Ruben's.

It went without saying that the Oliveras, including all the steps, rounded out the crowd.

Lucy felt no stress whatsoever as she and Ruben held hands and faced each other. They stood atop a bed of honeysuckle blossoms they'd had flown in, and just like always when she was with Ruben, she felt completely alone in a crowd.

Yiska started off the ceremony reading the Navajo wedding prayer, then turned the show over to Tilly, who was an ordained minister in addition to all her other incredible talents. When it came to Tilly, wonders never did cease.

Tilly brought the crowd to laughter and then to tears with her tale of Lucy, Cristina, Mercedes, and Annette searching for and eventually finding her. She talked about taking control of one's path, of not settling for what life hands you. She talked about fate, destiny, and most of all, love. At last, she led Ruben and Lucy through their heartfelt vows, and when she pronounced them man and wife and they kissed, no one doubted for a moment that it would last forever.

Not even Lucy.